I0642548

AVELER FOR

Qty _____ Date _____

Qty _____ Date _____

Cut By: _____

Scanned By: _____

Scanned B _____

Praise for David Saul Bergman's *Prodigal Sons*

"Even better than *Unpardonable Sins*, *Prodigal Sons* takes readers on a twisting journey through some of the darker recesses of Mennonite community. David Saul Bergman's hero, minister John Reimer, is a compelling protagonist—a good man struggling to move beyond the sorrows of his past and to make sense of a world where the claims of faith do battle with, and sometimes conceal, crude desires and bitter resentments. Full of vivid characters, insidious plots, and witty dialogue, *Prodigal Sons* is a briskly entertaining story and a rich exploration of the trials of family, community, and spiritual belief. A terrific spin on the noir tradition!"

> —SEAN McCANN, professor of English, Wesleyan University, and author of *Gumshoe America: Hard-Boiled Crime Fiction and the Rise and Fall of New Deal Liberalism* (Duke University Press) and *A Pinnacle of Feeling: American Literature and Presidential Government* (Princeton University Press)

"At the outset, *Prodigal Sons* is a deceptively gentle, lightly satirical narrative, but one that steadily burrows into the seamy noir detail of small-town Mennonite life in Kansas. It also gives us the shadow side of Chicago preacher and sleuth, John Reimer. Something of a wayward son himself, Reimer is forced to confront his own unpredictable inclinations. In this gripping sequel to *Unpardonable Sins*, he solves a crime by using, and living, an inside-out prodigal son myth."

> —ARMIN WIEBE, author of *Murder in Gutenthal* and *The Salvation of Yasch Siemens* (Turnstone Press)

"*Prodigal Sons* finds Mennonite preacher John Reimer back home in Kansas, sent there on sabbatical both to fill a pulpit vacancy and find his balance after the violence he recently encountered in Chicago. And here the complicated Mennonite community at the edge of the Flint Hills opens its arms: As he enters into his pastoral duties, Reimer's parishioners lavish him with casseroles, trust his guidance, offer up stories, and drag him right back into danger. This second novel resonates like a bell: with deep and thoughtful theological notes as well as higher reverberations that hint at secrets yet to be told. The writing is confident, detailed, and compelling, and the reader begins to know John Reimer not only as a man who can unravel a mystery, but as someone who has negotiated church politics, faced down his fears, endured unspeakable personal pain—and remained somehow true. Read this book not only for the crime-solving, but also for the rich descriptions of the tallgrass prairie, complex family dynamics, and astounding meals."

—PATTI WHITE, author of *Particularly Dangerous Situation* (Arc Pair Press) and *Pink Motel* (Anhinga Press), professor emerita, University of Alabama

"John Reimer, Renaissance pastor and sleuth, returns to his Kansas Mennonite roots during a 'sabbatical exile' from his Chicago church. No surprise that his first official visit is the sheriff's office in this absorbing depiction of what most seminaries don't teach. You'll want a front-row seat to this compelling crime novel that straddles the realms of faith and felony."

—WALLY KROEKER, Canadian journalist and former editor of *The Marketplace*

Also by David Saul Bergman
Unpardonable Sins
Praise for *Unpardonable Sins:*

"A gripping narrative that intertwines Chicago history and weather, politics and police, with Mennonite potlucks, church politics, and Karl Barth. *Unpardonable Sins* . . . undercuts simplistic explanations of why and how human beings live and find meaning. This mystery novel by an astute observer of Chicago street life and a master wordsmith will introduce you to a Mennonite pastor you will not soon forget."

—JOHN KAMPEN, Dead Sea Scrolls scholar and author of *Matthew Within Sectarian Judaism*, and distinguished research professor, Methodist Theological School in Ohio

"The history of detective mystery novels is littered with tough cops and boozed-out private sleuths who track down bad guys and bring them to justice. But until I picked up *Unpardonable Sins*, I never came across anything like the exploits of a Mennonite minister in pursuit of a ruthless killer on the North Side of Chicago. John Reimer is a middle-aged, semi-burned-out pastor of a dwindling congregation who finds himself trying to solve a young man's murder . . . *Unpardonable Sins* crackles with fascinating characters, clever dialogue, and surprising twists and turns."

—AL GINI, former professor of business ethics at Loyola University Chicago and author of *The Importance of Being Funny* and *Why We Need More Jokes in Our Lives*

"A rousing murder mystery that's also an absorbing inquiry into sin, guilt, sexuality, violence, and responsibility, *Unpardonable Sins* features a host of memorable characters, most notably John Reimer, the earnestly, vulnerably inquisitive Mennonite preacher-turned-sleuth. This entertaining, provocative novel immerses us in the streets and politics of Chicago, and the mysteries of family, faith, and action in this lovely, brutal world."

—JEFF GUNDY, author of *Without a Plea* and *Somewhere Near Defiance*

"Mennonite pastor John Reimer is the gritty protagonist I've been waiting for—secure in the soil of deep roots, resolute about justice and truth, unafraid to confront his flaws and theological vagaries, and confident that holiness has no coin if not fleshed out in action."

—WALLY KROEKER, former editor of *The Marketplace* magazine

"'The hand of a farmer crushing the hand of a lawyer'! Perfect! I loved *Unpardonable Sins*! It is a classic form now, and David Saul Bergman pulled it off beautifully and brought it some new life, too."

—SEAN MCCANN, author of *Gumshoe America: Hard-Boiled Crime Fiction and the Fall of New Deal Liberalism* and professor of English at Wesleyan University

"Two of my favorite types of novels in one—a clergy sleuth and a Chicago murder mystery. It is reminiscent of a Sara Paretsky novel because of the rich landscape of the city of Chicago a few decades ago . . . a delicious read. I look forward to a sequel, please."

—PEG FRENCH, retired Methodist minister, Port Crane, New York

Unpardonable Sins is one of those books that's hard to put down . . . The book really satisfies that contemporary detective noir feel. Reimer is a fearless introspective Mennonite preacher with odd friends and he loves a big breakfast. He makes me want to go back to Chicago and Ann Sather and have something besides the cinnamon buns which I love . . . Some of the best dialogues are over loads of food. The story is well-paced, like that *chug-chug* sound of cars on an amusement park ride . . . paced and regulated pulsating tension moving up and up until boom. Little booms . . . and then the big boom. Wild!"

—MITCH LEVENBERG, author of *Principles of Uncertainty and Other Constants: Stories* and *The Dementia Diaries*

"*Unpardonable Sins* is a novel thick with grit, characterization, and more than a nod to Anabaptist identity, recognizing that most Mennonites are both in and out of the world, for better or for worse. This is, without a doubt, the first book to span the sacrament of ham gravy, hate crimes, the Kansas Mennonite Men's Chorus, Chicago-style political intrigue, and a Mennonite Central Committee relief sale quilt."

—TIM HUBER, *Anabaptist World*

"It's a lurid plot, as crime fiction tends to be. Strong language and sleazy scenes are part of the hardcore charm. Yet *Unpardonable Sins* is a book with a conscience. Reimer's world is terminally messy. 'The problem was that getting to the truth so often clashed with making people feel better,' he thinks. 'It was the conundrum of his gospel calling: the sword that divides; the balm that heals.'"

—ROBERT MARTENS, associate editor, *Roots and Branches*

"In this suspenseful urban murder mystery, the dirt of western Kansas meets the grit of the north end of Chicago's lakefront. John Reimer, a crumpled Mennonite minister who finds himself rummaging around the underbelly of The Machine, is a refreshing change from the usual hard-bitten sleuth of the more traditional American detective novel. The good reverend has an annoying habit of ruminating on scriptural passages and other theological references that may, or may not, be clues for the reader in solving a couple of particularly gruesome murders. And while Reimer tries to give as good as he gets, he's clearly more suited to philosophical rumination than to Chicago-style street violence. Reimer may be something of a unique character in the Chicago crime business and the identity of the murderer a surprise to the reader, but the explosive violence of the novel's climax quite took this reader's breath away. Perhaps in the sequel Reverend Reimer might be tempted to stay on more familiar turf and tackle *Unpardonable Sins* within the Mennonite community, assuming such sins exist there. I can't wait to find out what he decides to do next time."

—JUDITH S. McCUE, retired Great Books Foundation Socratic instructor, Chicago

"This novel is a solid entry into the field of urban mystery: fast-paced, vivid, and violent. I could easily have spent more time with this intriguing cast of characters, especially of course the Mennonite preacher who finds himself dragged into the investigation of a brutal murder. I'm hoping that future novels in this series will provide more backstory—and more theology and church politics—as well as more of Chicago with all its grit and weather and neighborhood restaurants. Me, I love the details. A good read, this one."

—PATTI WHITE, author of *Particularly Dangerous Situation* and *Pink Motel*, and professor emerita of English, University of Alabama

"The first Mennonite hard-boiled fiction!"

—ALLAN KROEKER, filmmaker and director of 38 *Star Trek* episodes, including the finales of *Star Trek: Deep Space Nine*, *Star Trek: Voyager*, and *Star Trek: Enterprise*

Prodigal Sons

Prodigal Sons

A Novel

~⧸

David Saul Bergman

RESOURCE *Publications* · Eugene, Oregon

PRODIGAL SONS
A Novel

Copyright © 2025 David Saul Bergman. All rights reserved. Except for brief quotations in critical publications or reviews, no part of this book may be reproduced in any manner without prior written permission from the publisher. Write: Permissions, Wipf and Stock Publishers, 199 W. 8th Ave., Suite 3, Eugene, OR 97401.

Resource Publications
An Imprint of Wipf and Stock Publishers
199 W. 8th Ave., Suite 3
Eugene, OR 97401

www.wipfandstock.com

PAPERBACK ISBN: 979-8-3852-6156-7
HARDCOVER ISBN: 979-8-3852-6157-4
EBOOK ISBN: 979-8-3852-6158-1

This is a work of fiction. Names, characters, businesses, events, and incidents are the products of the author's imagination. Any resemblance to actual persons or places, living or dead, or actual events is purely coincidental.

Scripture quotations are from New Revised Standard Version Bible, copyright © 1989 National Council of the Churches of Christ in the United States of America. Used by permission. All rights reserved worldwide.

for Traci Dziatkowicz
and Elizabeth Classen Born

But when he came to himself he said, "How many of my father's hired hands have bread enough and to spare, but here I am dying of hunger! I will get up and go to my father, and I will say to him, 'Father, I have sinned against heaven and before you; I am no longer worthy to be called your son; treat me like one of your hired hands.'"

—Luke 15:17–19

The invidious comparison now becomes primarily a comparison of the owner with the other members of the group. Property is still of the nature of trophy, but, with the cultural advance, it becomes more and more a trophy of successes scored in the game of ownership carried on between the members of the group under the quasi-peaceable methods of nomadic life.

—Thorstein Veblen, *The Theory of the Leisure Class* (1899)

You don't seem quite to have made up your mind whether it's a case for a policeman or a clergyman.

—Sir Henry Baskerville, in *The Hound of the Baskervilles* by Arthur Conan Doyle (1902)

Exit Chicago

Chapter 1

An enforced sabbatical. So that's what it was going to be.

Only one week earlier, Reverend John Reimer had scattered his wife Viola's ashes in a copse of trees at Montrose Beach, near the bird sanctuary. And now here he was, sitting with head bowed at the old jury table in Lakeview Mennonite Church's boardroom, listening as Waldo Wedel, District Minister, read what sounded like a verdict. Wedel, known simply as W.W., or by his detractors as W. W. III, was flanked by two of the North Central District's Faith and Life committee members: Hofer of South Dakota and Grunau from the Minneapolis congregation. Joining the group were two more individuals of striking appearance: the congregational moderator, Nancy Huefflinger, who sat ramrod straight and at attention (all lawyerly professional polish and looking slightly more pale than usual), and the congregation's ministerial committee chair, Alan "Ranter" Wiebe, a nephew of W.W. and a man not afraid to let his acerbic flag fly. He was a seminary academic with a post at the Divinity School in Hyde Park, and he had recently cut off his ponytail. John watched him and wondered what he was trying to prove. The facial contortions at least provided distraction from the drone of W.W.'s voice.

"We have decided your summer sabbatical from Lakeview is an excellent idea, and we recommend that you lengthen it. The facts are not in dispute. After two, maybe three, attempts on your life in the spring of this year—an attempted shooting that shattered your office window, a car bombing that you narrowly escaped, and a scuffle in a lakefront park that imprinted you with serious contusions although not serious injury—the five voting members of this committee unanimously agree: It is prudent that you take this extended leave away from Chicago, both for your safety and the safety of the congregation. We recommend a six-month leave,

3

extending through Thanksgiving and possibly the end of the calendar year."

Hofer and Grunau nodded meekly, like Rosencrantz and Guildenstern. John tried to get a read on Nancy and Alan. Nancy shifted in her chair and looked directly at John. He could see the pain in her eyes. Alan slouched a little lower in his chair. W.W., sitting there at the head of the table in all his rotund, self-satisfied glory, had ensured in advance that his will would be carried out at least by a 3–2 vote, but he was more than happy to ride the wave of unanimity. That was how Waldo liked things to work. The beauty of magical "consensus" that could always be further buffed by pious declarations. Nancy and Alan wouldn't have any choice but to go along. John fought down a smoldering ember of rage.

Waldo looked around the table at his unsmiling colleagues and continued. "There is one particular congregation looking for interim leadership over the summer and fall as they begin a pastoral search process. They were enthusiastic when I mentioned you, John. They want you. And in my opinion—and it's just my humble opinion—you'd be perfect."

"Yes?"

"They want you in Kansas," Waldo said.

"Kansas?" John said dully.

"You are familiar with the church. Many people in the area know you. And many of them knew and loved Viola."

"Not Ebenholzer."

"No, but close. Marion Hills. I will follow up by phone when I receive more details from the congregation's committee this weekend. And I hope you give it serious consideration."

Waldo looked at his watch. "I think some of us have to get to O'Hare." Hofer and Grunau were already putting on their coats. Waldo seemed in a rush to leave, packing up his briefcase and heading out to the foyer for his parka.

John was not entirely sorry. He had dreaded the prospect of a ministerial lunch and the interminable small talk, the potential of Waldo asking further granular questions about the "scuffle" certain to provoke discomfort. Ten minutes later, after group hugs and handshakes, the members of the Faith and Life Commission were in a cab on their way to the airport.

John listened to the click of Nancy's heels on the hallway floor echo as she walked to the foyer to get her coat. She returned, buttoning up, and put her hand on John's forearm. Her steely composure was unyielding.

"I know you're unhappy, John. I'm so sorry."

Alan joined them in the hallway. The three of them stood in a huddle. The lights were off and John suddenly felt like a special conspirator with his closest associates. John noted a slight tremble in Nancy's lower lip.

"Look, nobody is happy about this," Alan said, "but it is happening for the best reasons. You have to get out of town for your own safety."

"Are you serious?" John asked.

"Why would I not be? Listen to me. I know my uncle well enough. He sees you as a little gnarly. A softhearted do-gooder who asks questions about the wrong people and invites trouble now and then. Throughout that meeting, I watched him pat himself on the back for being the Great Protector. He thought of himself as solving your problems. He sees himself as the wise elder, saving you from your foolishness. You have to let it go. Uncle Waldo's always been a blame-the-victim kind of guy. You know, if you get beat up, it's because you made a bad choice and were asking for it. Not really sticking to your job and getting involved in nasty bullshit you should have left to the cops in the first place. Plug in the cornpone cliché of your choice. He thinks you brought it on yourself, you know what I mean? So he's telling you, the sheriff, to get the fuck out of Dodge."

"Yeah, get out of Dodge and go to Kansas. That makes sense. A kind of rehabilitation in store for me?"

"Something like that. And once again, in my life, I find myself on the same page as Waldo. Please note that this almost never happens. Once upon a time we both actually agreed Nixon was bad news. I thought he was a rotten scoundrel because he bombed Vietnam during Christmas, and Waldo believed he was the literal Antichrist for making nice with communist China. It's too tedious to explain. Right now, we agree your safety means leaving Chicago, and soon. That's what I thought during that meeting. And now I'm contemplating a little road trip to Kansas myself."

Alan ran his hand through his spartan hair. He looked down at the floor and then met John's gaze directly. "My spring semester is almost over. Why don't we do the road trip together? Let me be your personal driver to Marion Hills. Consider it my gift. We can air out all our grievances on the way. Besides, you don't have a decent car yet for such a voyage. We'll take mine."

"Hey, Alan," Nancy said, now smiling. "I like it that you lost the ponytail. You no longer look like a sad old rich man who longs to drive a yellow Corvette."

"Thanks," Alan said. "Okay, I have to admit. A student told me I was starting to look like a roadie for Fleetwood Mac. I took the hint." He looked at John. "I'm serious. Let me drive. I insist. We're doing this."

⁓⁂

John was on his way out the front door of the church when Nancy ambushed him. Where had she been lurking to pounce?

She grasped his elbow. "Wait." She was biting her lower lip.

"Yes?"

"There's a lot I want to say right now," she said. "I want to have a conversation."

"Do we start with your unanimous collusion with Waldo or what?"

"You're right. It was unanimous. We didn't disagree. And we avoided tangling you up in ward politics, the corrupt alderman, or awkward details about your superior police work. We helped Waldo keep his nose clean. It was a pretty harmonious meeting."

"Yeah, nice going. You delivered it just the way he likes it."

"John, I know Waldo is not fond of all your ideas. He's afraid of them. He's a traditional clergyman, a wannabe bishop, as far as I can tell, but he genuinely cares about your well-being. And I do, too. Look, you can't deny the threats to your life. That is real. I just don't believe Waldo is trying to engineer a ministerial replacement for you, as you seem to think. He's not *that* malevolent."

"Don't be too sure," John said.

"Don't be bitter. Mind you, he did say something during our deliberations about you being a little reckless at times. But I heard him say that with a touch of envy."

"I'm not bitter. What else did the man say about me that you're not telling? I was just thinking about a run along the lake. Maybe you should join me. I could show you my old-man stamina."

"I would, and as a matter of fact, I have a proposition for you and I'm not quite sure how to present it."

"I'm all ears."

"It's your last full week in Chicago before you leave for Kansas."

"Yes . . . and?"

6

"Here's my proposition. I rent a property every year and have been thinking about buying it. It's in Gills Rock. The farthest point of the Door Peninsula mainland, not far from the ferry departure. Just across the water from Washington Island. I'm going out there tomorrow, or maybe even later this afternoon if I can get a few things off my desk at the office. I'm inviting you out. Could you possibly drive tomorrow?"

"Is this a spur-of-the moment thing?"

"I've been thinking about it for a while. I wondered if you could come up and take a look at the cabin and give me advice."

"Should I bring my overalls? Carpentry and plumbing tools? Will I be mucking around on the roof or in a crawlspace? Are you thinking a day trip?"

"I was thinking several days."

John was silent. "You're serious."

"How can I show you how serious I am?" She leaned in and murmured in his ear. She put her hand on the side of his head. "I'll leave you a detailed message on your answering machine. That's one of the other things we need to talk about. It's time we replace it, and get you a Hotmail account and a desktop computer. I mean, the millennium is not that far off."

"Is this a business trip, then?"

"Oh, I think so."

Chapter 2

So Waldo had described him as reckless. Well, well. On certain points there was probably no denying it. He would have to go up to Gills Rock and see the cabin for himself, John thought.

He drove the freeway from Chicago through Milwaukee. Farther north, at Sturgeon Bay, he crossed the high, arcing bridge over the channel and picked up Route 42. Engineers had knifed through the base of the Door in the early twentieth century to allow Great Lakes shipping a shortcut passage, and since then, the captains no longer had to navigate the treacherous waters, known as Death's Door, at the northern tip of the peninsula. Funny that Nancy was contemplating a purchase up there with a view of all that. That would be like her, all right. Always facing things head on.

He looked again at the printout of his directions, unfolded on the passenger seat beside him. The house was near Porte des Morts. The French had named it after hearing stories from Winnebago and Potawatomi natives who carefully considered their chances before stepping into a birch canoe.

Crossing the bridge, John saw the pleasure boats on the water. It was still early in the season, and they were sparse. He turned up the heat in the car a notch. The sun was bright but the wind buffeted his car. He headed north on the narrow tongue of land sandwiched between the waters of Lake Michigan to the east and Green Bay to the west.

On either side of the two-lane highway, fields were adorned with round, tractor-sized bales of hay and neatly painted red and white dairy barns. A few roadside stands were already open, with a smattering of cars parked in their lots. They sold firewood, apples, cherries, homemade pies, preserves in Ball jars, smoked fish and deer jerky, the ubiquitous fudge—all the bounty of the Door. This initial stretch within the county line always altered his sense of time, and he remembered when he had first crossed into this space with Vi many years before. As the car decelerated, his mind achieved clearer vision. He looked again at the printed-out directions beside him. It was the last local stretch that would require concentration. She—Nancy—was bringing him closer.

He continued north. Egg Harbor, Fish Creek, and Ephraim, the original port on the peninsula, settled by the Moravians, prized for its deepwater harbor. Through Sister Bay and past the Piggly Wiggly supermarket. The long open stretch of road before Ellison Bay, the peninsula scant of people, rolling acres of cherry and apple orchards. The last gas station, a general store, a nineteenth-century frame house with a sign in the window that said Pots by Thor. He continued through on the hilly road that twisted and turned toward Gills Rock. The signs announced Ferry Ahead. He followed them until he could see a line of five cars driving onto one of the boats.

He took the last available exit before the boat ramp, a left turn. Porte des Morts Drive. Here the tall trees moved and creaked in the wind slicing up from the channel.

He found the numbered mailbox and glided through the woods toward the split log cabin. It was situated on a generous lawn with a flagstone patio wrapped around the southern exposure and entrance. Perched on a bluff, the house's northern face overlooked the foaming water of Death's Door. John looked through the scrim of trees that thinned out here. The water churned with whitecaps, and the green line of Washington Island in the distance was barely visible.

He asked himself where the sun had gone and when the weather had changed. He spotted an unused stone barbecue pit in the yard that was sprouting flowers and tall weeds, whipping in the wind. A massive granite picnic table close by looked fashioned by Fred Flintstone, awaiting a platter of smoked brontosaurus. He parked his car on the driveway beside the detached garage, fifty yards from the house. He got out and stretched.

A woman came out of the house, and from a distance, John had no idea who she was. He wondered if this was the right address. She wore knee-high black leather boots and black tights. She moved with sturdy, deliberate athleticism. She had on a short, checkered wool skirt and a bulky sweater and red knit cap that came down tightly around her ears. John thought this might be the realtor Nancy had spoken of. Then the woman called his name, and he tried to rearrange what he saw with the data in his head. How could this be?

"Could you help me move some of this firewood inside?" She pointed at the sky. "I'm afraid we're in for it."

He waited to say her name. He had to get closer for confirmation. The voice was hers, but as he came forward, he searched her face one more time, scrutinizing it for familiar details to swim into view. He wouldn't say her name until he was sure. He wondered if his mind wasn't working right. He came closer and she looked at him.

She walked toward him.

"Nancy," he said.

She said, "Is everything all right?" She took him by the shoulders and appraised him. His hands were around her waist.

"I had the strangest experience just now," John said. "I didn't recognize you."

"What?"

"I didn't know who you were. Uncanny sensation. I thought for a moment I was in the wrong place. Then I thought you were the realtor."

"You crazy old man. Too many hours on the road?"

He held her away from him and looked at her from head to toe and blushed. "So many things," he said. His uncontrollable shock of white hair was standing straight up. His lined face was ruddy with the wind, his glance slightly askew. The wind gusted through the trees overhead, and he felt a first heavy drop of rain hit his forehead.

She considered him and the dimple in her cheek deepened. "Look at me again. It's okay to look. I give you permission."

He looked.

She took the cap off her head and he admired the contours of her skull under the closely cropped hair. "Do you recognize me now?"

"Yes."

She looked down and said, "You've never seen me in a skirt. That's why you were confused."

"I had an epiphany, it seems."

"I hope it is the first of many."

"I operate on a shallow level."

"Yes, because you're a man. You had never seen my legs before."

She ordered him to carry the firewood into the house before he retrieved his suitcase from his car. He stacked the wood carefully by the fireplace, which dominated the center of the cabin's main living space, then she showed him his bedroom and bathroom suite. He readied himself for dinner. He knotted a green striped tie. Maybe too formal for a weeknight, but he liked being the best-dressed man in a dining room. Better that than the opposite. She looked at him and nodded her approval. They briefly stood, side by side, looking out the north window of the house at Death's Door, miles of foaming water separating their habitat from the island. The water hurled itself in crashing waves against the wooden dock at the base of the rocky bluff.

"I'd show you the staircase down to the water's edge, but we can save that for later, if the storm hasn't torn it off the cliff." She buttoned up her coat. "Did you bring an umbrella? We'll take my Blazer."

They raced like two kids across the yard to the garage. She drove them to Fish Creek with her usual reckless abandon.

Chapter 3

"Gudmundur Gudmundsson," Nancy said to John.

"Too many syllables," John protested.

Their waiter, who doubled as the Whistling Swan's sommelier, reappeared by the table. He was a young man with a trace of acne, and he could have just as easily been sitting in front of a game console playing Mario Brothers. With practiced hands, he uncorked a bottle and poured their red wine, portioning carefully into their glasses, his left hand held with bent wrist behind his blazer. Nancy sampled her wine and winced. "A tad too brown," she said to the sommelier. She requested the wine menu for further consultation, and he went to fetch.

"Anyway, this Gudmundsson chap was the economist Thorstein Veblen's best friend on Washington Island, where he spent summers starting in 1896. Three years later he published his first book, *The Theory of the Leisure Class*. The one he's famous for. Galbraith called it one of two books by American economists of the nineteenth century that is still read."

John said, "I'll have to read it. And what was the other one?"

"I have no idea. Some guy named George. Anyway, Veblen was already teaching at the University of Chicago, after hopping through graduate programs and collecting degrees at Hopkins, Yale, and Cornell. I wish I knew how much influence Gudmundsson had on Veblen's book."

"Where did Gunner go to school?" John asked.

"Gudmundur. He was self-educated. The locals held him in awe because he subscribed to five different newspapers. He and Veblen liked to sit on the porch of the boardinghouse and, as my generation would say, shoot the shit. Maybe during one of those conversations Veblen came up with his immortal phrase, 'conspicuous consumption.' Or maybe

Gudmundsson did. Those two words sum up the whole foundation of the American economy. Maybe the whole American worldview."

John looked at Nancy with respect. "You know, I like a woman who doesn't wear her learning lightly."

"I take that as a compliment, although I think you are fucking with me."

"Where did you pick up all this lore?"

"My senior thesis at William and Mary. When I learned that he spent his summers on Washington Island over a period of thirty years, I made my first visit. Just before law school. You and I could do a pilgrimage day after tomorrow to the cabin he built. There's a ferry to the island."

"Tell me more about law school," John said.

The sommelier returned. Nancy asked about a vintage toward the top of the list that sounded Italian and expensive. John thought it had the word "Agricola" in the title. The sommelier brightened and straightened his skinny, slightly soiled tie. John noticed he wore scuffed black penny loafers and needed a haircut. He radiated attitude. He looked like a dissolute frat boy from Dartmouth, and the shiny circles under his eyes indicated bad sleep habits. But he spoke with a global, encyclopedic grasp of vineyards.

"Soft mouth feel, almost pillowy, fruit notes of blackberry and apple with chalky undertones. A hint of chocolate and leather toward the end, but it closes very clean. To drink it, one feels the sinuous journey to Le Mans, with a finish that is pure straightaway. One of my favorite reds on our list. A very good choice indeed."

<hr />

The gristled remains of John's New York strip steak lay before him. He tore off a piece of baguette and spread butter on it and used the crust to mop up the last polenta streaking his plate. He savored the mouthful of bread with polenta and sauce, then quaffed some wine. Nancy toyed with her arugula.

"Speaking of conspicuous consumption," John said, "I don't feel we've done too badly ourselves in that regard." He looked around the paneled dining room where the clientele sat at tables, each neatly squared away under white linen. The wait staff hustled in and out of the double doors to the kitchen, and from the bar area outside the dining room, a low roar emitted and the occasional eruption of laughter.

"Wait till you taste their crème brûlée. Their flan isn't bad, either. Look, I'm a worldly Mennonite, John. My daddy had expensive tastes. He started to develop a habit for seafood restaurants in Civilian Public Service in North Carolina in the early fifties. And he and Mom raised me in the Tidewater, where she is from and where he decided to practice law. It's full of all kinds of jagged history and decadence. Not exactly a bastion of racial justice. When we visited Dad's relatives in Lancaster County we felt out of place. They were worrying about all kinds of other things. I always had that feeling of an expat Mennonite, even within the Virginia conference. We got treated as if we were a little further away from the Kingdom of God, know what I mean?"

"But Chicago seems familiar to you. It suits you."

"Yes. Home sweet home. You talk about Waldo and how he sees you as a dangerous liberal. Guys like him are familiar to me. My dad told me we were considered a little bit on the edge. He didn't mind that."

"It's going to be an interesting reentry in Kansas," John said. "I know all the people but the passage of time and where I've been means I've changed. I know this, but do they? It might not be a seamless transition."

"Just be glad it's only an interim thing. Interim assignments can be liberating, you know. You'll be back, at the very latest, in November. I'll see to that."

"You'd better. I have mixed feelings about playing the return of the native. You ever read Hardy?"

"No. But lots of Dickens. *Bleak House* was practically the Bible for one of my favorite professors in law school. He taught law and economics at Columbia, but his true passion was Dickens. *Bleak House* topped his list. That slow, grinding case in Chancery. You asked me before about law school. New York changed me. *Bleak House* probably played an over-sized role. Of course, the main thing is I came to the city with my stately Southern drawl and quickly adjusted, and now I talk twice as fast. Maybe sometimes to my detriment. But tell me about Hardy."

"In *The Return of the Native*, Hardy's hero Clym goes back to his rural birthplace, a place called Egdon Heath, located in a vast expanse of grassland. It's in Hardy's larger imaginary realm called Wessex. The descriptions at times sound like parts of Kansas. Few trees, mostly grass, good for growing grain and cutting sod.

"So Clym goes back home. He has several reasons. The main one is to take care of his mother, a widow. Dad is dead. Clym has spent a lot of time away, living in the city. He's an idealist who wants to start a school back home for poor benighted yokels that remind him of himself. Naturally he falls for a voluptuous brunette named Eustacia Vye. Clym's mother hates Eustacia and some of the locals believe she's a witch."

Nancy poured more of the sinuous wine with the straightaway finish into John's glass. John's eyes traveled over her fine features. "Continue," she said. "I like the part about the brunette." She batted her eyelashes. "How does it end?"

"Eustacia wants to get away from the prairie and dreams of going to Paris. I suppose Veblen would call it consumer desire. She wants to move there. Because this is Hardy, the ending cannot be a happy one. Clym permanently damages his eyesight because he reads too much, usually late at night by candlelight. That's what book learning will do for you, Hardy says. It will wreck your health. Eustacia thinks of her new husband as a pedantic ass with insufficient ambition, so she develops other romantic interests."

"Do go on," Nancy said.

"By the end of the book Hardy has blitzed the reader with his usual megadose of despair and death. Following Shakespeare's example, he litters the stage with bodies. Clym is a solitary figure who becomes a preacher—how does Hardy put it?—let me see if I can remember: 'some said that his words were commonplace, others complained of his want of theological doctrine; while others again remarked that it was well enough for a man to take to preaching who could not see to do anything else.'"

"Brutal," Nancy said. "Actually, I've heard that said about preachers on more than one occasion. What else *can* they do?"

"Wait a minute, I'm playing property inspector for you tomorrow, right? I even brought my toolbox. You're about to discover if I can actually 'do anything else.' But back to Hardy. Hear me out. You want a happy ending? Here's Hardy's version, and I quote: 'But everywhere he was kindly received, for the story of his life had become generally known.' He's almost the ideal candidate for an interim minister. A kind of harmless, benign fool."

"All right, Mr. Hardy, you are much too hard on yourself. He speaks to you, though, doesn't he?"

"Yes. The most a man of Clym Yeobright's persuasion can hope for is to be kindly received. I hope for that in Kansas."

"Waldo doesn't have any doubt. And neither do I. They know you. They know your story."

"Well, up to a point. Of course, in small towns I'm familiar with, the natives usually think they know everything about you. Maybe I'll surprise them."

"Shall we order dessert?" Nancy said. "I feel we need a satisfactory conclusion to this meal. We can drive back to the cabin and continue the lesson in front of a toasty fire."

The sommelier came by their table and pointed at the bottle. "Did that please you?"

"Wonderful," Nancy said. "Now, if we could have two crèmes brûlées, please, and espresso for two."

John interjected and held up one finger. "This man knows his limitations. Make that one crème brûlée. With two spoons. Thanks."

"At your service," the young man answered.

—✦—

"Good planning to bring the firewood inside," John said. The grass in the yard was spongy underfoot and the world thoroughly drenched. At the door of the cabin, Nancy put a hand on John's shoulder and with the other unzipped one of her boots. She repeated the motion for the other foot and stepped inside.

"Can you check on the fireplace? Make sure the flue is open. It was quirky last time I used it."

John went into his bedroom and took off his tie and jacket and threw them on the chair. He came back out and knelt by the fireplace. He located the flue lever and pushed it open. He held his hand out in the interior of the chimney and felt for the draft. After he found a box of matches in a kitchen drawer and crumpled up some newspaper, he went looking for kindling. He asked Nancy if she had a hatchet handy.

"Yes, and I am a huge fan of *Little House on the Prairie*."

"Well, in the dark woods of Wisconsin, I expect a cabin to be fully equipped."

"Try the utility closet by the fridge."

He found a hatchet on the pegboard inside and carried it and a couple of pieces of firewood out to the patio. He turned on the yard light and split the lengths of pine into a dozen pieces. He returned and balled up four sheets of newspaper that he grouped together under the grate. Then he lit a match underneath and held it until the flame caught the newspaper and sent up a wisp of smoke. The column rose inside the flue.

When it didn't back up, he arranged kindling in a crisscross on the grate with a couple of larger pieces of wood on top. The fire started to crackle. Satisfied, he stood up and turned toward the couch.

Nancy sat with legs folded under her wool skirt. "Come here and sit with me."

He came toward her. He wondered at his sense of expectancy. She pulled him down gently by the lapels of his shirt, open at his neck, and put her lips on his mouth. Her fingers were lightly brushing the back of his neck and his hands went to her waist. He felt the wool of her skirt stretched across her thighs. She said, "I have been waiting for you to give me an honest kiss for such a long time now, Reverend Reimer. I don't even know—"

His lips stopped her speech. After a time, he felt her tentative searching tongue, and he opened his mouth for hers. She smelled pleasantly of wine and perfume. A few heavy drops of rain hit the north-facing window and a bolt of lightning lit up the interior of the cabin. A crunching crack of thunder started across the channel and rolled across the water of Death's Door.

Later she said, "Please, yes." He cupped the fullness of her breast beneath her sweater. Her skin was smooth and marvelously warm. Then he brought both hands into play. Now it was his turn to stop, and looking at her in the flickering light of the fire after the more complete illumination of the lightning, he said, "Nancy. I'm a little out of practice at this, you know."

"John, trust me. We have all the time."

She knelt on the couch to face him and arched her back. She pulled off her sweater in one easy motion. "Can you undo this?" She lifted her arms and invited his hands around her back to find the clasps and unhook her. Her eyes danced. She took off her earrings, tilting her head one way and then the other. Her warm garment fell away. He let his fingers trace down the sides of her body. His earlobe brushed her nipple and she pulled his head against her chest until he heard her heartbeat. She turned the full power of her splendid body on him then. She took both his hands and placed them on her chest and he felt her nipples stiffen beneath his thumbs. He felt like a rough beast walking out of a strange swamp anointed by a fully fleshed spiritual being. She put both her hands on the back of his head as she drew him toward her and he felt her fingers play in his hair.

"You are lovely," he said.

"Am I?" she answered.

Later, she took him to bed. "You have good hands, John. Give me more."

"What have I been doing during the last hour?"

"You know what I mean."

"Do you mean like this?"

"Yes. Yes. Mmmm. Go slow. Right there. Yes."

"Like this? You have to direct me."

"Oh, I will, don't worry."

She taught him all the places and ways; she made straight the path, though not without a few detours and pleasant excursions. She guided his hand with intent. And he wondered at her completeness when she sent a mounting series of arias to the rafters of the cabin.

She rested then said, "Now let me take care of you, John." When she put her other hand on his face, she felt the tears there. "What is this?" she said.

He moved his head from side to side. Then she lowered herself down on him slowly, sitting just so, where she could ride him carefully, gently and more tightly, and eventually she found a slow gallop and when she felt his pace start to build, she tightened down more with her thighs and her knees. He opened his eyes wide and drank her in. He was laughing, too, in spite of himself, and she began to urge him on until he could not turn back even if he had wanted to. He felt the bottom half of his body bursting, disintegrating, falling away, until he cried out and shouted someone's name. His throat was hoarse.

She put her hands on his face and felt more of his tears. "You said her name."

"I know."

"It's okay. It's okay." She used her thumbs to dry the flesh beside his eyes. She kissed his lips and lay on top of him with her breasts pressed against his chest, her body extended the full length against his. He could feel her breathing and her heartbeat. Afterward she stretched alongside him and put one of her legs over his, and after her breathing had become regular, he lay awake, inhaling her, his hand resting on the lovely curve of her waist, and he wondered what else lay in store for this castaway itinerant preacher on his way to Kansas.

He arose from the bed. His eyes had fully adjusted to the dark, and he walked the hall to check the fireplace. He pushed the fire screen flush against the hearthstones and looked at the glowing embers. Then he returned to Nancy's bedroom and climbed in beside her. He was awake when she touched his calf with the bottom of her foot. He could feel her breath on his ear. Big drops of rain still hit the windowpane with an occasional hard slap. He could feel her breasts pushing gently against his back; she gripped his arm.

"I want to take you hiking in Newport State Park. Those were my plans. After you check a couple of things in the house. Or we could go look at the cherry and apple blossoms. I know an orchard."

"Yes."

"And the strawberries. The wild columbine."

"Yes. All of that would be good."

"But if the weather is still bad, we might have to stay indoors. What about that, mister man?"

"Yes, yes, all of that. We could find out if the roof is tight."

She curved her body around his. Sometime before dawn he slept.

Chapter 4

There were several phone messages waiting when he returned to Chicago two days later. The first was the official offer from Marion Hills Mennonite Church. He returned the call to the moderator and thanked him for the invitation and clarified the official start date. The last message was from Marvin Arnheim.

Marv. What could that possibly be about? Marv was one of his oldest, dearest friends from his first pastorate at Ebenholzer Church, but he didn't very often leave phone messages. John guessed he'd gotten the news that John was returning to the general Kansas neighborhood. Sure enough, it was congratulatory, but John sensed there was something more that Marv didn't quite know how to articulate.

John was also aware, after his idyll in Gills Rock, that he was pressed for time packing for this trip. He didn't want to start his morning with a raft of callbacks. Marv could wait. He padded into the kitchen of his apartment and brewed a pot of coffee. He poured a cup and cut it with a little milk, then carried it into the living room of his parsonage apartment to take stock of his things, of his life, the rapid upending of every routine.

What to pack when the trip ahead was not an overnighter and yet not exactly a *move*, either?

John stood in his study. He selected a few books from his shelves and stacked them on his desk. These included a couple of new things from Eerdmans and Westminster Press, and six Anchor commentaries: Genesis, Job, Ecclesiastes, Isaiah, Luke, and Mark. Best to travel light. It was just the summer and fall, six months, possibly less, he reminded himself.

He'd take sermon notes for about a dozen of what his daughter Sarah used to call his "greatest hits." But if he was completely honest, he wasn't sure anymore where the hits had gone. He wasn't duly impressed when he went back and read what he had written over the years. How much of it would last? Not much. Maybe nothing. No, revise that—nothing. *Then how should I begin. To spit out all the butt-ends of my days and ways?* Whose line was spinning through his head? Auden? No, Eliot. Eliot, droning wannabe Englishman from St. Louis channeling King Solomon while dropping the occasional antisemitic slur. Geniuses got the benefit of paradox and transgression, but who would want John's notes, scrawled on yellow legal pads in barely legible longhand, packaged in their fraying, soiled manila folders, clasped with paper clips mostly crumbling to rust?

He couldn't think of anyone. Certainly not his daughter. She had once made a crack about death cleaning. "You'd better do it, Dad," she told him. "I don't want to face a mountain of your shit when you're gone. I have no patience."

At times she showed the spirit of a ruthless scythe. He had seen the way she emptied her mother's closet a couple of years before when Vi moved downstate for full-time nursing care. No mercy. Sarah had dumped the dresses and belts and finery and shoes into six large open boxes. She finally consented to take Vi's jewelry case. "How long since Mom wore any of this stuff, Dad?" Sarah stood, brandishing empty hangers in one hand like a cluster of spears. There were price tags on a couple of dresses that had never been worn. John gave no answer.

"Dad, you have to stop looking back. I want you to live your life!" After a quick hug, she had resumed the closet clean-out. Now he told himself he needed to make a comfortable peace with his melancholy.

He noticed the phone was ringing.

"Hello, John Reimer?"

"Speaking."

"John, this is Marvin. Marvin Arnheim." The voice was faint. "I just left a message, but I'm glad to catch you live. I hear you are going to be back in Kansas soon."

"Where are you calling from, Marvin? Are you in Hillsboro?"

"No, as a matter of fact, I'm in Denver. And that's want I want to talk to you about." There was hesitation in Arnheim's voice.

"On business? You have a building project in Denver?"

Another pause. "You could say it's business. Of sorts."

That's when John knew something wasn't right. Arnheim was someone whom John had known for the better part of forty years. Marv had been chairman of church council at Ebenholzer when John had started his first pastorate, and when he and Vi left for another congregational assignment in Minneapolis, his friendship with Arnheim only deepened. Over the years they reconnected on a nearly annual basis at church conferences. But John couldn't recall ever getting a phone call from Marv, and here he was, calling from Denver. His voice carried trouble.

"The last time we talked was a couple years ago in Ontario."

"That sounds about right," Marv said.

"I'm starting to pack for Kansas, Marv. I'll see you in a few days."

"John—John, here's the thing. It's a bit of a situation. It's Jeffrey."

"Jeffrey? What's happened?" At the name of Jeffrey, John shook his head. He didn't like the feeling of heading down a dark path. Still, he didn't want to judge. But if history—and John's knowledge of the Arnheim family story—was any predictor, then this would take strange turns. Jeff had caused his parents enough grief already.

"Jeffrey." John said the name again flatly, waiting. "Tell me, Marv."

"Jeff is missing."

"How long?"

"Almost two weeks. His girlfriend got hold of my number. She said that after five consecutive days without contact, she got worried. It's a mess, John. I drove to Denver to look for him. Verla said I should go. She said we have to find our son. And honestly, I'm afraid this time." Marvin was speaking in a rush of words.

John wondered about the girlfriend. The last time he'd talked with Marv in Ontario, Jeff was getting divorced from wife number four. As Marv put it, the whole thing was especially "ugly" and "vexed." And there had been another divorce since that one.

"Marv, I am sorry. When did you last talk with Jeff?"

"I don't know, it's been a real long time."

"You've filed a report?"

"Yes, the missing person report, I did that already, but here's the deal," Marv said, his words tumbling out way too fast. "I wondered if you could come by way of Denver. I mean, I know you're on your way to Kansas, but maybe just treat this like a minor detour.

John thought, *How do we know he hasn't moved to Phoenix or Dallas? Maybe Denver's become too hot to handle for Jeffrey.*

He mentally added, *He's probably working his magic word trove to catch wife number six.* Marv wasn't making any sense. John didn't have the foggiest idea what he could do to find a fifty-year-old lost boy. He might be able to comfort the grieving father, but he couldn't very well say these things on the phone. "Look, Marv, I think I can make this work. Do you have a callback number?"

"Yes, I'm staying at the Best Western Motel on Colfax. Here's the motel number. I'm in room 224."

"I'll let Alan know we have a rendezvous in Denver with you. How does that sound?"

"Thank you, John. I can't tell you how much this means that you're coming. When are you leaving Chicago? It's a thousand miles to Denver. I'm so sorry."

"I think we can do it in a day and a half. I'll tell Alan to lay on the gas."

"Do that. Look, I'll pay for your gas. When are you leaving?"

"We'll get out of here first thing tomorrow morning, crack of dawn. I nearly have my suitcases packed up. And Marv?"

"Yeah?"

"Hang on tight. We'll find Jeff. Give Verla my love when you talk with her."

"I'm hoping Jeff just lost track of time. He did that as a boy, you know."

"I know. I hope you're right."

John knew all kinds of things about the boy Jeff, Marv's oldest son. Jeffrey was the first person John had baptized in his first parish. He remembered it all clearly, an early summer day at Marion Reservoir. In a sense, he was the boy's godfather. That's also how Marv saw it.

The boy would always be a boy to John. He thought about the boy. Even then, the star athlete and student had been a creature of fits and starts, ambitious achievement, stretches of brilliance interrupted by jarring lapses, the odd aporia.

How many times had Jeffrey already broken his father's heart? John stuffed the books into a couple of leather briefcases and set them on the floor. He dialed Alan about the change of plans. Alan said he'd be ready to go in the morning.

Chapter 5

At five in the morning, John was awake and facing the bathroom mirror. He looked at himself in the dark and then switched on the light to begin the rites of morning. He shook his head. During his middle age someone had once described his style of handsome as "craggy," but at this hour, his visage had all the grace of a crumpled towel. A couple of lines ran across his cheek. He must have ground his head into the pillow during the night. It was another case of what he had started to call the twisties. In a recurring dream, he was either being chased or doing the chasing. Either way, he awoke nauseous and sweating. He wondered whether he would tell Nancy or his therapist first about these dreams. Another decision that would have to wait.

Now he felt better than he looked, and the disjunction bothered him, but the thought *road trip* rippled through like a healing stream. Hours and hours of talk ahead, with Alan the entertainer. *We ride at dawn*, Alan had said. John took his coffee into his study for a few minutes of meditation.

A couple of weeks earlier, Sarah had sat at his desk, acting like she owned the place. She and Connor had driven to Chicago for Vi's memorial service. Sarah had pointed to the plaque on the wall with a medieval monk wearing a black eyepatch. The eyepatch had been crudely chopped out of a piece of cloth and taped over the left eye.

"Menno Simons as the pirate king?" Sarah had asked him.

"I thought it was the least I could do for him after he took a bullet for me."

Sarah had lifted the plaque off the wall, then ran an index finger over the hole in the plaster. "No kidding. Who told you to duck?"

"Pure coincidence. I was just sitting in that chair and bending over a book when the glass in the window shattered."

"So the book saved you."

"Maybe."

"All safety glass now?" Sarah had looked at the window.

"Yeah."

John sat behind his desk and imagined the conversation if Sarah were still here, now.

"Sorry I have to go so soon. But Marvin's in real distress."

"I get it. I'm sure the folks in Kansas understand you have to find the missing boy. Who did you say he was?"

"Jeffrey. Jeffrey Arnheim. He's fifty-some years old. And Marvin is from Kansas. He's presently in Denver driving himself crazy."

"Isn't fifty a little old for a boy?"

"Yes. I still think of him when I baptized him at Ebenholzer. Before your time. He was sixteen. I was twenty-five. Memory gets trapped in amber. But calling him a boy isn't inaccurate, either. He was a kid who never got his feet planted. Never quite figured himself out . . . There are actually lots of men like that."

Chapter 6

Alan put on a pair of Ray-Bans and tied a bandanna on his head. He spoke: "I feel like we're on a mission from G-yod."

"I'm enough of a fool to think we just might be," John said.

They entered the cockpit of Alan's Land Rover and buckled in.

Heading south on Ashland, they turned at Webster and took the ramp to 90/94 East. The morning traffic was already thick, trucks jamming the road, but Alan had a nose for the open lane. It was six o'clock. They shot past the Loop's massed skyline, picked up 57 South, and when they took the exit to I-80 West, Alan let out a slow exhale. The rising sun blazed behind them. A landscape of washed light emerged out of the billboards and power lines.

"The great American West beckons," Alan said. He slapped the dashboard. He could barely contain his exuberance. He set the cruise control at eighty.

John put on his sunglasses, leaned back in the leather seat, and let his thoughts drift. He worked to slow down his breathing.

"Now we settle in for seven hundred miles of mellow," Alan said. "That leaves us with a short hop tomorrow morning. ETA for Denver eleven a.m. Plus we gain an hour."

"Perfect," John said. "I'll call Marvin tonight when we get a motel."

"We'll stop somewhere past Grand Island. North Platte's too much of a stretch."

John hauled the road atlas out of the back seat and opened to Nebraska. "Maybe Kearney or Lexington."

"Yeah, that sounds about right," Alan said. We get a fleabag motel around six, by my calculations, find a steak house."

Alan put a CD into the player, and the quiet notes of a lone trumpet and snare drums spilled out of the front door speakers. John looked around the car's interior. Leather seats, wood-grain dash, a rugged and reassuring array of dials spread out in front of them. The vehicle thrummed.

Creature comforts for men of leisure, John mused. He said to Alan, "Why a fleabag motel?"

"Because I'm a cheap-ass Mennonite, that's why," Alan said.

"Though not cheap-ass enough to economize and Mennonite your way across the land. Don't you have relatives in Kearney? Any self-respecting Menno would. I mean, there's nothing like a fold-out sofa to break your back in the morning, especially if it saves you sixty bucks."

"No relatives I know of," Alan said. "That's not pronounced 'Carny,' by the way. I figure we'll live like kings at the Best Western on Colfax, so why not a dive before we get there? Now and then I feel a hankering for one of those shitholes with brown deep-pile, shag carpet, with the free breakfast bar that looks manufactured in Cold War Yugoslavia. Complete with fossilized Cheerios and white bread of death. The cracked-plastic sugar dispenser loaded with the most important food group. I like a bargain motel. Look, I'm a neat freak—consider my tidy vehicle. I got it detail-cleaned just for you. But I seldom turn down a good bargain motel on a road trip."

"You're not the first Mennonite with that problem," John said. "You seek ritual punishment. Please show me your full array of flagellant whips. The white bread of death sounds about right. Vi and I stayed at a Motel 6 near Cleveland once when the free breakfast thing was a novelty. In the morning, we went downstairs, and she motioned for me to look into the tiny closet that they passed off as a 'breakfast kiosk.' That was the reason I had decided to pull into the parking lot in the first place. That free breakfast. I still have nightmares about it. It was not a nook so much as a pit, an abyss. The nook was barely lit by a dying pair of flickering fluorescents. Pop-Tarts in a box on top of a little fridge. I didn't have the courage to read the date of expiration. What would have been the point? It looked like a corner of the box had been torn off by starving rats. The only coffee option was a hazelnut blend that spurted out of a crusty machine that moaned like a broken oil well. You pressed the red button to turn on that machine and your thumb felt violated by the indeterminate filth and fluid that covered every stainless steel and Corian surface. Vi told me if I ever brought her back there again, she would end the marriage. She called the breakfast nook the chamber of death. We went to Denny's that morning for eggs."

"Did you get the Grand Slam?"

"Yes. Although nothing could erase the memory of the death chamber."

"The worst motel I ever stayed in was the old Mandalay," Alan said. "Located in the broken part of the original Las Vegas. I didn't have to piss into the sink, but it was close. The motel had probably reared its young, glorious head even before the glory days of the Rat Pack. I was still married to Billie Jean. When we got to our room, she asked me what I thought had made the stains on the ceiling. I said they were probably residue from an exploding champagne bottle. She looked at me with pity and said, 'You poor, naïve piece of Kansas shit.' We stayed at that hotel three nights. On the third night I woke up in a sweat and noticed the layer of scuzz that covered all the bathroom surfaces and even the telephone and headboard. This layer of crap had crawled up and covered the inside of my mouth like an ambulatory biological organism. In the morning, I had to shave my tongue. My speech was strangely impaired. Whatever had grown on it retarded my ability to pronounce consonants."

"How bad was it?" John asked.

"So bad that Billie Jean discovered spherical accretions of lint and pubic hair bouncing across the tiled bathroom floor like tumbleweeds. Then, you know, there was a recessed bathroom ceiling fan. When you flipped the light switch, the motor came on like the engine of a Boeing Stratoliner. I nearly soiled myself the first time I hit the light. Very unnerving."

"That's rough."

"Listen, they didn't pick up room-service trays—at least not on any schedule I could tell. When we arrived, there was a plate with a half-eaten burger and fries on the floor in the hallway just outside the room. A spilled Coke on the plastic plate had started to dry out. It could have served as a sticky trap for mice. I'm surprised I saw no rodents writhing in the goo."

"I get the picture."

"The tray remained there *three consecutive nights*. On the second day I moved it to the center of the hallway to see if anyone in housekeeping would trip, but it was back beside our door in the morning."

"I wonder what you told the checkout clerk, but I am more puzzled why you would stay in Vegas that long. I mean, it is America's Sodom and Gomorrah."

"Meetings of the Qumran Dead Sea Scrolls Society of Scholars. We go for package deals because many members don't have the budgetary largesse possessed by Duke or the Divinity School at the U of C. The society is known to its members as QDSSSS. Admittedly hard to say. The old-timers just call it QDSS for short. I gave a paper that year on what we know about the sectarian squabbles within first-century Judaism and how those are reflected in several early texts, including the gospel of Matthew."

"How'd the paper go?"

"Smashing. It fueled my rise within the guild. But my marriage with Billie Jean was on the skids." Alan looked at his fuel gauge. "Win some, lose some."

"You've never told me how that unfolded. Your marriage, I mean. The end of it. The granular details. Mind you, don't talk about it unless you want to."

"And John, I'm grateful you've never asked in that kind of blunt manner. I'll tell you at dinner. I'll need a splash or two of bourbon to get myself started."

"I try to be a gentleman. Also, let me say I don't have any particular fetish for a brown-shag motel. I'm happy to pick up the tab for something decent. And I insist on picking up half the gas."

"I don't want to fight you, John."

"So be agreeable."

"Okay. You can pick up half the gas. We'll alternate."

"Thank you, Alan. But let me add one more field note to the brown-shag motel thread before we retire the taxonomy. One can't generalize. Especially on the differences in housekeeping. I stayed in a very clean brown motel once in northern Minnesota. I was traveling solo to a pastoral retreat near Mountain Lake, one led by your own uncle Waldo. Everything in that Comfort Inn had been coordinated in a tight color palate: Everything was tan or brown, the table lamps, the bathroom art, the towels, the bedspread. Knotty-pine walls and a brown TV set. The sheets were brown. The deep-pile shag was clean, scented even, like a pine forest. I expected tiny deer to emerge from the undergrowth at any moment. There was a brown scented candle on the back of the toilet called 'Rudolph's Cabin Essence.'"

"How was Uncle Waldo on that retreat? What was his topic?"

"I mean no disrespect, but I have only a vague recollection of what he talked about. He was starting to come out of his end times biblical prophecy kick, yet remained theologically offensive. But he'd attained a more generic quality of beige. There was exposition about Dad the Good Shepherd and the Lord's chain of command. Beyond that I have no details. Maybe it was the motel imprint that induced a kind of amnesia. On the other hand, let me segue here to the Moby-Dick Inn north of New Bedford, where Vi and I went the first time we explored New England, right after we had left Ebenholzer. We had a month off before starting our assignment with the church in Minneapolis. Anyhow, this place had a cutout plywood sign under klieg lights of the great white sperm whale himself. What were an Okie and a Kansas dirt farmer to do except feel charmed? That sign sucked us right in. We'd been reading Melville at the time. Vi was captivated by *Typee*. We tried Kusshi oysters and Kumamotos. On the Atlantic side, the restaurant menu offered the Lady Chatterleys from Nova Scotia. Viola went for those.

"But if the inn's food was extraordinary, the motel was a mistake. Even with my shoes on, I shuddered at the touch of that deep-pile shag. I was actually afraid. What kind of voodoo packet or bent, rusty needle would turn up in that waving sea beneath my feet?"

Alan reclined comfortably in his pilot's chair, his left wrist draped over the wheel, and said in a kind of professorial fugue, "John, we are both psychologically damaged human beings. You and I have real problems. But I feel already on this road trip as if we are escaping the demons' grip." As if for emphasis, Alan slapped the dash with the palm of his hand and gave his best Oral Roberts shout: "'Come out! I heal you!' Am I reading you right, Pastor Reimer?"

"You read me all too well."

⁓⟡

John looked out at the miles of Iowa falling away. The precision rows of the fields, soon to be packed with monocrops of corn and soybeans, receded as the Land Rover raced on. A crop duster paralleled them for a while, flying maybe one hundred feet above. It emitted a steady spurt of toxic weed killer, dipped its wings, and eventually turned and flew the opposite direction.

Alan drifted into the left lane and glided past three UPS triple-trailer rigs.

"Speaking of Denny's, did you want to stop for breakfast?" he asked.

"I had breakfast before we left. I'm good."

"You want a cinnamon roll? We have that Pyrex that Mildred sent along."

"I do, but I never eat in my car. No disrespect to Mildred, mind you."

"You are fastidious. You're serious about that," John said.

"Yes, I am."

"You like a clean machine," John observed. "I notice you even steam-cleaned the floor mats. If I were an analyst, I could say more. Very thorough."

"I always clean it up before a long trip," Alan said. Two minutes later, he resumed. "That was the other thing with Billie Jean. She had expensive tastes, but on road trips she indulged a fondness for Taco Bell and McDonald's that drove me fucking crazy. Dinners she wanted a four-course prix fixe layout even if we were driving through some godforsaken part of Wyoming. But fast food at breakfast or lunch . . . man, she was a maniac. And how she loved to eat in the car while driving. Food sprayed around the interior, the seat, the floor mats! She did it mainly to bug me. Sometimes after she took the car out for errands, I'd find the detritus piled up around the driver's seat and stray pieces of food jammed into the upholstery." Alan looked sideways at his audience. "This is true, John. I'm not exaggerating."

"Do go on."

"It came to a head when I found a punctured foil bag of Taco Bell Fire Sauce on the armrest. A giant schmear. Kind of spread all over the place, not to mention it stained the elbow of my favorite Oxford pin-point. I had to steam-clean the vehicle's interior. I went out of my mind. I reamed her out for that and that was the beginning of the end. Not a big philosophical, existential difference of opinion, not a quarrel about her Lacanian Left Bank politics. Not her ongoing belief that I was too obsessed with my spiritual direction and personal piety. No. It was a fucking Taco Bell sauce packet. A stake in the heart of matrimony. I told her I was through with her nasty habits, and she replied she was through living with a nitwit. Six months later we filed for a divorce.

"I ask myself this question all the time about the Taco Bell schmear. I loved my wife. And then I no longer loved her. I had the car deep-cleaned again after she moved out."

"She didn't get the car?" asked John.

"She got the other car in divorce court, an almost brand-new Camry. The alimony I paid, don't get me started. Maybe the lowest moment of my life happened in her lawyer's office conference room during discussion of the settlement. My attorney looked at me and said, 'Alan, you need to tone it down. Let it go.' *My own lawyer!* I felt like I was seven. It took only a nanosecond for me to lose three inches of my dick."

John looked out the window at the alternating geometric formations of soybeans and rapeseed going past. "I am sorry, Alan. I honestly didn't know it got this contentious. I should tell you that in marital counseling I've listened to a lot of stories. We've all heard the one about the couple breaking up because the guy slurps his soup and *loudly*. Or he doesn't pick up the popcorn bowl abandoned beside the couch, in the den, every night. The sound of dental floss twanging off the molars. It's often stuff like that. I've heard a lot of those. Now as for Billie Jean, I've always thought she was a sweet and exceptionally smart woman. How is she doing these days? Didn't she move to Nashville?"

"She's coming up for tenure at Vanderbilt. She's doing very well."

"Maybe you don't want to talk about her anymore. We just preempted the dinnertime talk. Maybe we can talk instead about Marvin Arnheim and his son."

Alan said, "Yeah, that's probably more fruitful. Just let me append a small postscript to the divorce topic."

"Go ahead."

"Did you ever do a church divorce ceremony?"

"No, can't say I have. Is that a thing?" John asked.

"One of Billie Jean's friends in grad school did it. She and her husband were very proud. They spoke about it with great excitement. They were both fresh-eyed California kids. When they were together and smiling, they reminded me of a toothpaste commercial that Karen Carpenter and her brother did, what's his name? A look that fairly screamed wholesome except it appeared incestuous. Anyway, this couple wrote their divorce vows themselves. Their minister was happy to pronounce them nonhusband and nonwife."

"A whole liturgy for divorce, huh?" John said. "What church?"

"Presbyterian."

"I would have thought Unitarian," John said. "Or Seventh Church of the Divine Light of Heliopolis. Did you go to the ceremony?"

"Why would I do that?"

"Just asking. No need to get hostile."

"Excuse me, but I think it's a travesty. Like all of us—and I will be boldly anthropomorphic, *pardon moi*—the deity is also disappointed with certain news items. Guess what? Not everything is part of his divine plan. And I'm not certain there's a need for God's blessing when we break our vows."

"Were they asking for God's blessing or God's forgiveness?"

The muscle at the top of Alan's cheek flexed. John could almost hear his teeth grind.

"Sometimes I worry you're going soft on me, John."

"No chance of that. No chance."

"Don't tell me you'd even contemplate doing it if some sappy dewy-eyed couple at Lakeview asked you to. You know, earnest folks who had buried the placenta with a sapling tree after their baby was born."

"I'd have to know the complete context to decide."

"There you go again, getting all squirrelly and situational."

John put out his hand and flipped it back and forth, thumb out, palm up—pause—palm down. Then he dozed. When he woke up, they were in downtown Des Moines.

⁓☙

They found a deli and stopped for lunch. They ate with singular concentration, as men often do after vital conversation and hours on the road.

"Let me tell you about Marvin's call," John said. "He knows you're coming to Denver, by the way." John finished his pastrami sandwich and forked a French fry, mopping up the ketchup. A waitress walked over with a coffeepot to give them a refill. She had straight black hair in a simple pageboy cut. She looked over her bifocals to appraise her audience. She appeared to be twenty-eight going on seventeen. John said thank you and then no to the pie menu that she had put out on the table.

She said, "I can't tempt you with just one little piece? That pie is what we're famous for."

Alan took the bait. "What's your favorite? I'm still a little peckish after that matzo soup. I don't mean that as a criticism, mind you."

She ran a polished red fingernail down the list as she spoke. "Oh, I'm listening. Now for scholars I always say the blackberry cobbler warmed up with ice cream. I don't think you're truckers, and you don't throw off a Rotary vibe, otherwise I'd suggest banana cream or the pecan. Who am I talking to?"

"We practice hermeneutics and explore texts," said Alan, gesturing with the plastic menu in his hand.

She said, "I had you pegged for a seminarian. Let me guess. Qumran? Nag Hammadi? Myself, I'm a sucker for the gospel of Thomas."

Alan's wolfish smile showed the shock of surprise. "Are you a psychic?"

"I'm a Scorpio," she said. "Name is Julie." She pushed the glasses up on her nose a little and pulled a strand of black straight hair away from her face and hooked it over her ear. "Does that work for you?"

Alan lost motor control over his tongue, a rare moment for him. "I'm Alan Wiebe. This is John Reimer. You talked me into that cobbler. Extra scoop of ice cream, please."

"You won't be disappointed," she smiled.

John watched her retreating figure and said, "I told Marvin you were coming along because my daughter thought I might need protection. You trying to get me into trouble?"

"It wasn't just your daughter who wanted me to go on this trip. Nancy was adamant about that too," Alan said.

"Nancy? What did she say?"

"She said she would hold me personally responsible to get you safely to Marion Hills."

John laughed. "What did she think could happen?"

"I don't know, but right now I just got mugged by a nubile siren. John, here's the deal. Your mysterious adventures and bodily injuries have gotten Nancy all shook up. Ever since March she's been on paranoid alert. What's the story anyway? Tell me if I'm imagining things."

John hesitated. "I don't know if there's a story."

"You and Nancy were both out of town recently."

"She invited me to Door County to look at a house she's thinking of buying in Gills Rock. She wanted my opinion on whether it was a good investment."

"Well, you're a spiritual guide for many of us when contemplating death's door, but I had no idea you also consult in real estate."

"Hey, Alan, I'm multifaceted. I check gutters, look at electrical and the fuse box, muck around in the crawlspace. I'm a man who gets his Levi's dirty. I tried not to fall off an aluminum ladder. I took my toolbox and played handyman."

"I'll bet you played handyman. Is this something serious?"

"No. I told her not to buy it. One entire corner of the house was infested with termites. We caught four mice in a couple of days. The critters are treating the residence as their personal Motel 6."

"I didn't mean the house. I meant you and Nancy."

The waitress brought back Alan's pie in a white ceramic bowl. It looked to be an extra-large portion, with two giant scoops of vanilla mounded on a hot wedge of berries. The browned crust sparkled with granulated sugar. "Enjoy!" she said, handing out forks and a couple of extra napkins.

They finally made their getaway and climbed into the Discovery. The doors chunked closed in unison and the men buckled in. John said, "You were a little taken now, weren't you?"

"Those librarian bifocals were not just for show. I almost fell over when she said Qumran. Did you leave a decent tip?"

John waved a finger in Alan's face. He said, "Don't even. I don't want you telling anybody I acted like a cheap-ass Mennonite. Did you get her number?"

"Yes."

"I noticed you talking."

"Yes. She wants out of the cornfields."

"What's she doing in Des Moines?"

"Master's in social work program, which she figured out last year wasn't for her. Starting a degree in comp lit."

"You work fast."

"We'll see." Alan hit the accelerator. "I told her she could do better in Chicago." Soon the on-ramp had them back in the flow of I-80.

Chapter 7

The soybean and corn fields of Iowa unspooled their machinelike rows into Nebraska, although after they crossed the border, the thick scent of feedlots filled their nostrils.

Alan wrinkled his nose. "The rural paradise."

"Yes, for much of the Midwest, the smell of money," John replied. "In western Kansas, outside of Garden City, the aroma of feedlots is overtaken only by the smell of slaughterhouse waste. IBP, huge operations. Chicago used to be the meatpacking center. It's now western Kansas. Open-pit bulldozing of acres of cow entrails. Enough to make you wake up in the morning with a case of dread. I lost my appetite for porterhouse ten years ago."

"The transition from the family farm to commercial feed lots has been rough. From the bodega to Costco in one generation."

"When I was a kid in Meade, we ran steers," John said. "Anywhere from thirty to sixty head. Had a few milk cows. Knew every animal by its first name. Now that sounds like something you hear on the Disney channel or NPR's *Weekend Edition*."

"Ever had an Omaha steak? You know, shipped on dry ice in a fancy container?"

"No. Have I missed anything? Was it better than Arby's?"

"Not really. And it was missing the little container on the side with gelatinous miracle gravy."

Past Lincoln, John said, "So tell me what you know about Jeffrey Arnheim. Let us speculate where he could be."

"Our missing man? The Denver kid?" Alan asked.

"Yeah. You should know some things. You went to Hillsboro High only ten years after he did. Surely the legend still lived on."

Alan began: "In my time at Hillsboro High he was still a presence. But the nickname 'Crazy Jeffrey' had caught on. If you wanted to be nice you called him 'Wild Man,' but it was usually 'Crazy Jeffrey.' People still talked about the risks he took, daredevil shit he'd do on his Honda, a kind of aspiring Evel Knievel. He moved to Denver when I was in high school. He'd been working in his dad's construction business."

John interjected, saying, "He was known for working three-day stretches with scarcely any sleep. Worked out of his car. Four to five-day road trips to western Kansas. Sublette, Liberal, further into the Panhandle. Guymon."

"Godforsaken country," Alan said. "I'm too young to know the Dust Bowl, but I saw a dust storm out there once, and it scared the living shit out of me. Wall of dirt a mile high, started out like a little pencil line on the horizon, then it grew. Towering cloud. I couldn't take my eyes off it. Sky turned black. It was the apocalypse, all right.

"But Jeffrey didn't know how to quit. He kept going. Down into Texas, Stratford, Perryton. I remember asking myself, *Where the hell is Texhoma?* It sounds like a malignant tumor. Jeffrey kept expanding Marvin's reach. No job too small, but he landed some big ones too. People wondered what Marvin paid his boy—privately held business and all that—but I suspect a finder's fee for every new client. Jeffrey seemed to make the most of it."

John spoke up, adding, "Or probably a percentage. Or a percentage on top. Then he walked away. First he walked away from Nell."

Alan continued. "Yes. He'd already gone through his first divorce. But in his high school, the name still carried a special aura. The trophies at the entrance to the high school gym. MVP this, MVP that. His coach called him the 'King of Hustle.' The old-timers said he should have played point guard for the Jayhawks."

"Yes," John said. "What happened to Nell after the divorce?"

"Surely you know. It was news. She moved to Pasadena and met some guy at a prayer breakfast. He was connected to the Crystal Cathedral dude."

"Schuller?"

"Yeah, that one. Best set of evangelical dentures in all of North America. Made for television. His fountain of positive-thinking Christianity made Norman Vincent Peale sound like Vincent Price. Anyway, Nell took her three kids along with her to California and married the guy, found her bliss. Apparently a great match."

John rolled back the years in his head and said, "Everybody predicted Jeffrey would be a superstar. But predictions based on high school performance are dangerous. Anybody who saw me when I was seventeen would have guessed I'd feed Mom's chickens and punch cattle for the rest of my life. Jeffrey peaked early. For men, this is often a sign of bad things to come. Until a couple years ago, he held the Kansas high school record in four-hundred-yard hurdles. His dad was maybe more excited about that than anything else."

Alan nodded. "Coach told us Jeffrey could shoot the ball like Earl 'the Pearl' Monroe, sometimes called the 'Black Jesus.' In profile he resembled Jerry West, the nose, the chin. Coach got a sad look on his face every time somebody asked why Jeffrey never played college ball. Then of course some smartass would say, 'Well, he decided to serve his country and went to Vietnam.'"

"There's complicated backstory there," John said. "Which we should get to. If we find him in Denver, I plan to ask. He was a good-looking kid, too . . . You're right with the Jerry West analogy. Even in junior high he had girls trailing him like he was a piece of scented patchouli. In the prebaptismal class at Ebenholzer, it was sometimes hard to keep their attention off the bright young boy asking all the deep questions."

"Did you mean patchouli?"

"That's what I said."

"Don't you mean patchooly? You said pudjouly."

"This is the problem with saying things from reading and not hearing them. I should keep more polite company. I'm a simple German pioneer, remember? Anyway, Jeffrey had a striking physical presence. He was homecoming prom king his senior year. Levi Schlegel's daughter Carol was queen. The best-looking couple Marion County has probably ever produced, though I hear Levi's younger daughter Julia and her husband Ken Dahlke now have the nicknames Ken and Barbie."

"Levi Schlegel as in Schlegel Motors, the car dealer in Marion Hills?"

"Yeah. His son Franz runs that business now. Levi has become more than a car dealer. Major holdings in gas and oil wells throughout Oklahoma, got a stake in the early going of Pizza Hut. A financier and investor. Some say he reminds them of the Koch brothers in their early phase. Something of a doppelgänger for Jeffrey's dad, Marvin, who we'll see tomorrow morning. Levi and Marvin, from adjacent towns, always competed to raise the best-looking offspring west of Chase County. Not to mention make the most money."

Alan pointed at a bald eagle on a telephone pole, then resumed conversation. "So Jeffrey was recruited by KU and Oklahoma State. Baylor and Texas came calling. But something happened," he said.

"He decided to take a year off after high school to figure out what he wanted," John said. "What do the kids call it now?"

"A gap year."

"Exactly. He needed the gap. He wanted to explore. He'd already been talking about that after I baptized him. He was sixteen. That was 1962. It seemed like an adult kind of inquiry. He liked to ask the probing questions. At least that's what I thought. Then he graduated in 1964 and everybody was talking about the Selective Service. I preached a sermon about it. Talked about our history as a historic peace church. Invoked Jesus, Saint Francis, and Menno Simons. I still remember people in the pews shaking their heads as if they were hearing it for the first time. Even went into my reasons for doing alternate service in Philadelphia right after Korea."

"What did Marvin think?" Alan asked.

"He didn't talk about it. Among our people there are a lot of taboos about certain conversations. I think he was afraid. Maybe terrified. Everybody worried what Jeffrey would do if he was drafted. Don't ever let Marvin know I said that."

"His daddy wanted him to be a superstar athlete."

"Yes. He was that good. I don't blame Marv for that."

"But Jeff had other plans."

"Always. He drove to Wichita and enlisted in the army before he even had a chance of getting drafted. Told his father he wanted to serve his country, that the dream of a basketball scholarship was a pretty selfish thing when boys his age were dying halfway around the world. Marv told me he tried to answer that but knew there was nothing he could say to make any difference."

"It's the genius of military recruiters and the presidential speechwriters," Alan said. "It's never about the killing, the rape, the destruction. No, it's all about the *service*, all about the *sacrifice* for your fellow citizens. The grand myths of civil religion."

"It's got quite a hold on people," John said. "You know where they're most fond of invoking 'servant leadership'? In the Marines. Didn't Wilfred Owen talk about it as 'the old lie'? To always make it about quote unquote 'service.' Dying for your country according to the lie is likened to Christ laying his life down for us. It's a very compelling, slick perversion . . . Augustine did quite a number."

"No shit, Sherlock," Alan said.

"So Jeffrey went to serve, as he saw it," continued John. "He climbed through the tunnels with a knife in his teeth, got a Bronze Star. He came back after a year in-country a changed man. Vi and I had left for the East Coast by then. I had one passing conversation with him by phone. He decided to do a gap year anyway to 'clear his head,' as he put it, after witnessing the 'furies of warfare.'"

"So he was not exactly gung-ho about the war," Alan said.

"No. But he wasn't turning against it either, like his firebrand cousin, guy in Enid, name of Warkentin. Warkentin also enlisted, worked in logistics for the army a year in Da Nang. Returned Stateside and turned into a full-blooded peacenik. He had also enlisted against the advice of his pastor. A lot of Mennonite boys got sucked in, especially in Kansas and Oklahoma. I spoke with a number of them. Most of them told me they thought alternate service was for pansies. One of them had the courage to use a more pungent term."

"Threatened masculinity makes us do the shit, doesn't it? How did Jeffrey's gap year turn out?"

"He wandered around in the Far East and his parents lost contact with him. He came back through Switzerland after spending a month at a place called L'Abri. It probably messed up the boy worse than Vietnam. When he got back home, he fancied himself a Swiss philosopher and said he didn't need college. Said he could read and interpret books on his own and preferred the Bible to the liberal humanism being spouted in secular universities. His younger brother said he looked like a dirty hippie, had a backpack full of strange literature, a well-worn Criswell Study Bible, and a sitar that he never learned to play. He talked a lot about the book of Revelation."

"Well, that is one easy rabbit hole."

"Yes. He told little brother James he thought JFK had a good chance at becoming the Antichrist had it not been for Oswald's marksmanship in Dallas."

Alan whistled. "That's a whole lot of insight for a gap year. Hey, not to interrupt the story, but I do spy a Red Roof Inn up ahead. And according to my odometer, we've covered seven hundred miles. I'm ready to stop. What say you?"

"Not much more to tell. Jeffrey went straight, according to his dad, buckled down, got to work in the family business, and helped expand the grain bin construction into machine sheds, airplane hangars, every kind of commercial steel building in the tristate area. His dad became a millionaire several times over. Jeffrey married a beautiful woman, had three kids, was set for life. I heard he was a great coach at the Y. Everybody's All-American. Then he snapped again."

"Right," Alan said. "He went to Denver and finalized his divorce. Proceeded to work his way through two or three more wives."

"Four," corrected John. "And he cut himself off from the family entirely."

"How did Marvin get word that he was missing?"

John shook his head from side to side and bit his lip. "Someone who works at Casa Bonita."

"What, the burrito palace with the cliff divers?"

"That's the one. And Marvin's source is one of the cliff divers. How she got hold of Marvin, I have no idea. He said she wasn't too happy."

"Let's check in the Red Roof. Then dinner—no steak. Maybe Italian. And I'll stop with the thousand questions."

"Good, we'll find out more tomorrow. We're outside of North Platte, by the way. I'm sure this is a bastion of northern Italian cuisine."

"Faith, my brother. Faith," Alan said.

They swung into the carport of the motel. "I'm booking us two rooms," John said, as they climbed stiffly out of the vehicle.

"We could share. Good stewardship. A room with two double beds. We could save money."

"Cheap-ass Mennonite," John said. "I always knew it."

John checked them in. He eyed the contract and asked Alan what his license plate number was. The form asked whether the purpose of the trip was business or vacation. John checked both boxes and signed his name.

The clerk pushed John's credit card and driver's license back across the counter while Alan stood looking at a loose-leaf binder with local restaurants and attractions. The men rolled their luggage through the lobby to their rooms, past a swimming pool and a hallway smelling of chlorine. The soaked industrial carpet squeegeed under their feet. Kids splashed around in the pool behind the sliding glass doors, barking like gleaming seals beneath the subpar lighting.

"Honey, we're home," Alan said.

"Alan, could you please explain to me exactly what a convenience fee is?"

"Ask the clerk."

"In the morning maybe."

"Right now, let's head over to the Eye-talian Kitchen. I have my eye on the carbonara."

"Good luck with that," John said. "How about chicken-fried steak with a side of warm gravy? I don't want to disappoint you, but I doubt if cacio e pepe appears on the menu."

Chapter 8

They were back on the road early the next morning, after breakfast at Denny's. Alan was quiet. After half an hour he asked John, "Did Marv have any more news about the mystery lady at Casa Bonita?"

"No. But we meet with her today."

John looked for the sign announcing the 76 split from 70. He didn't wait long. Ogallala sped past in a blur, and Alan lifted the Co-op Seed cap away from his forehead to smooth his hair back. He had ditched the bandanna. "Under four hours to go."

By noon they were grinding through Denver traffic on Colfax.

"The longest, wickedest street in America," Alan said. "My main memory of East Colfax is when I was a little kid. My cousins told me this was where the hookers were."

"How did you know Denver as a kid?"

"Aunt Edna's crew. The Voth boys. We visited them sometimes in summer. Denver was more interesting than Hillsboro, if you can believe that. We had a kind of low-level rivalry thing going with them. There were four of them and three of us. It was always a competition as to who could raise the most hell." Alan smiled at the memory. "Our mothers primed us with a good dose of sibling rivalry—frenemies, if you will. It was passed down to their boys. We continued the tradition. Mind you, I didn't even know what a hooker was when I first heard the word. I thought it was a fishing lure. The Voths knew their way around the taquerias, though, let me tell you. They were my first introduction to urban anthropology."

"Each day brings a new revelation of your special expertise," John said. "Sign me up."

They found the Best Western on a colorful and not completely broken stretch of Colfax. Marvin greeted them when they rolled their suitcases into the lobby. His face showed as an open book of unabashed gratitude, and he launched himself out of his armchair with the velocity and conviction of a stout torpedo.

"Boy, am I happy to see you, John," said Marvin, grasping John's hand, then embracing the preacher in a bear hug. John noted, maybe not for the first time, Marv's resemblance to the early Nikita Khrushchev, photogenic and avuncular. Marv's smile opened up his clenched face. His gapped front teeth made the smile seem even wider. He had a butt chin, a crewcut, and a trace of stubble on his jaw. At five foot seven, he could be called round but not soft. He was built low to the ground and had a torso like a pressurized metal tank mounted on a couple of short oak trees. He wore khakis belted at his waist and a Lacoste polo shirt with blue and white horizontal stripes. Completing the getup was a blue windbreaker and a black cap with a diamond logo and the words Arnheim Construction emblazoned in white brocade.

He pumped John's hand once more, and then Alan's. John went to the desk where the clerk pointed at Marvin and spoke and gave John two keys.

John walked back and said to Marvin, "You didn't have to."

"Well, I wanted to. You and Alan didn't have to reroute through Denver either."

"But—"

"Don't argue with me, John. The room is paid for. And let me say how much I appreciate seeing you here."

Alan said, "I guess that makes three of us."

"And if we find Jeffrey, that might make four," Marv said. His mention of his son cast a pall over the conversation and he switched gears. He looked at Alan, saying, "It has been at least five years since I saw you. You got rid of that ponytail thing hanging down your back. Have you been working on a custom-cutting crew?" He made a wavy motion with his stout hand. "Back home they just might stop calling you the hippie theologian." Marvin let the momentary pause work some mischief. "How is your Uncle Waldo?"

"W.W. is good. He says hello. We saw him in Chicago a few days ago."

Marvin looked quizzical. John started to speak but Alan interjected, "You know, things have been a little hot for John in Chicago recently."

"Yes, I heard you got into a scrape," Marvin said. "They even said it was life threatening, but you know, rumors about the big, bad city tend to exaggerate. What you need now is a nice, easy patch of Kansas and a little R&R."

"You may have to put up with me for more than just the summer," John said. "Waldo wants me to take an extended sabbatical. Honestly, if he gets his way, I may never see Chicago again."

"Trust me, we can handle it," Marvin said. "If Marion Hills bores you, we can find something for you to do here in the hinterlands." He looked at his watch, missing John's eye roll. "We have an appointment at Casa Bonita in half an hour," Marvin said. "Do you gentlemen have more of a preference for the Grand Vista or the Cliffside Area?"

"You're the connoisseur, Marv," Alan said. "I hear we will be speaking with a cliff diver. And if we can't see the diving up close, what's the point?"

The two travelers checked their luggage into their rooms and returned to the lobby. Alan had traded out his farmer's cap for a leather jacket and stocking cap. It was dry and gritty outside, and Denver's high-altitude air blew the dirt from Colfax into their faces.

John wore a light jacket. He squinted into the sun and put his sunglasses back on to protect against the dust. Marvin propelled him and Alan toward his yellow Cadillac in the parking lot. Offhandedly, Marvin told them that Delores, the diver, was the last person to see Jeffrey.

"For real?" John said.

Marvin nodded. "Yes, that also checks out with what Celeste says."

"Will she be diving during lunch?" Alan asked.

"No, Delores has moved into a part-time management position. She wants to talk with you, but I'm afraid she is in a very confused state of mind."

John and Alan waited for more. Marvin drove through a yellow light and kept talking. "Celeste is a bartender and short-order cook at a place called Brody's Lounge. And naturally you want to know what I am doing in the company of a bartender and cliff diver. Well, Celeste got me to drive to Denver. She phoned me just before Delores and said she was a friend of Doctor Jeffrey. When I asked her who she was, she said 'Surely as a father you might know where he disappeared to.' I said to her, 'Doctor Jeffrey? Doctor of what?'

"She told me, 'doctor of theology.' Celeste said he has a street ministry. Told me Jeffrey keeps his diploma in the glove compartment of his car. But in the next breath she told me he was very interested in her cousin Delores, and Delores was worried because she hadn't seen him in two weeks."

"Oh boy," Alan said.

"I asked Celeste how she got my phone number," Marvin said. He pulled up in the enormous parking lot outside the Casa Bonita palace, already filling up with the lunch crowd. "She said from Jeffrey's address book. I told her I hated to disappoint her, but my boy hadn't called me in years. Maybe I said too much. I don't know what these nice ladies really know about my boy."

"What have you told them?" John said.

Marvin was silent, and John wondered how much truth telling would come out in the next hour or two. They went inside. The cavernous space smelled of melted cheese, hot frying peppers, and chlorine. A slender brunette in a white bikini jumped off the ferny cliff nestled on top of a gleaming rock wall. To John's eyes, the wall looked slippery and dangerous. It reflected just enough illumination penciled in by floodlights to heighten a sense of crawling menace. And the diver did not disappoint. Like any accomplished athlete, she managed the illusion of slowing down time, did one-and-a-half turns and a somersault, then arched her back into form as she knifed the water. There was barely any splash. "Well, that was a ten," Alan commented. The diver's head emerged above the water. Her glance took in the room as she climbed out of the pool with the water streaming off her limbs. John couldn't help but think of Botticelli's *Birth of Venus* anyway. A small crowd poolside clapped and whistled then resumed their consumption of the burrito special on their trays. A couple of them called their server for another round of margaritas.

The men joined a line of docile tourists interspersed with an occasional leathery-skinned local. Metal barriers and chutes turned humanity into a single-file queue, and John suddenly imagined a feedlot. The food was dumped unceremoniously on fiberglass trays riding the metal rollers just before one paid the cashier. Another worker laid stainless-steel cutlery rolled up in hot cloth napkins next to the plates, in a bid for a touch of class. It was a little like positioning a caviar spoon next to a branding iron. A server took them to a table on the third floor, close to the rocky cliff, and returned moments later with their drinks.

"I only wish I had figured out your son a little better all those years ago," John said to Marvin.

"Don't beat yourself up, John. All of us wonder what we could have done different."

Two women appeared and asked if they could join the table. They said hello to Marvin, and he stood to introduce them to his friends. John watched the body language. The women trusted Marvin but considered him an emissary from another culture. Alan pulled out chairs for them to be seated on one side of the table.

The tall one, Celeste, could just as easily have been a bouncer. She had the build of a roller-derby queen and the delicate facial features of Jennifer Lopez. She was no taller than John but seemed to reach down to give him a firm handshake. John wondered if this was a sort of magic or just a young person's better posture. But it was Celeste's companion who held his gaze. He heard Marvin say, "John, this is Delores, the manager. She's the mother of the diver who just jumped off the cliff."

She had broad, sculpted shoulders like most professionals of the aquatic class. The button-down white Oxford under her red blazer did not so much obscure her muscular frame as highlight it. She was a diver who moved like a dancer and looked to be in her early thirties. He guessed the daughter had inherited her young mother's talent. Delores was Nancy's height and as John looked at her, his vision suddenly bifurcated to images of the cabin at Gills Rock while simultaneously drawn into the present tense of Delores's force field. The woman's eyes, in their slashing violent tinge, laid open the possibility of a world of pleasure, suffering, experience, and hurt.

Do we become our names? John wondered. This Delores could just as easily have been named Tristeza. Her welcoming smile disappeared off her full lips in an instant, as if not quite ready to relax. John's eyes went to her hands. They were working hands, nails cut short but well taken care of and adorned with flawless red polish. She wore an engagement ring that she periodically twisted as if it were an unfamiliar object. The rock on the ring was spectacular. John looked again and wondered if it was real.

The women ordered Diet Cokes. They avoided the plate of tortilla chips with red and green salsa bowls in the center of the table, and they watched the men eat.

"I had a late breakfast," Delores said. "You go ahead."

Marvin turned to the women, saying, "I told these friends I wished I had more news about Jeffrey, but I don't. I invited them to Denver because they are both good at asking questions. I hope they give us a few ideas." He paused and searched for more words. "They live in Chicago but share my Kansas history. I've known John more than thirty years."

"That long ago?" Delores said.

"Yes. He baptized my son."

"He baptized Doctor Jeffrey?"

John answered. "Yes. When Jeff was about the age your daughter is now."

Marvin looked at the diver preparing herself on the ledge.

"What's her name?" John asked.

"Areli."

"Pretty name."

"Thank you."

"I imagine you are very proud."

"She is a senior," Delores said. "She got a full scholarship to Regis University but is fantasizing about USC. She wants to study psychology."

John asked Delores, "What does Areli think of Jeffrey's disappearance?"

The question caught Delores by surprise. Her forehead wrinkled, and John became aware of the work she had done on her eyebrows.

"She tells me to be *realistic*." Delores emphasized the adjective with air quotes. Her polished fingernails carved the space above the table. "She says, 'Mom, he could be like . . . You know, men. Sometimes men disappear . . .'" Delores's voice trailed off, then she continued. "'Don't overthink it,' Areli says. 'He is probably in Reno or Las Vegas.'"

Delores's eyes lowered. "Then she tells me, 'Maybe if you are able to forget him you won't get hurt.'"

Delores turned a look of anguish in Marvin's direction, as if disturbed by her own words. "Please excuse me, Mr. Arnheim, I mean no offense."

"None taken," Marvin said. "Areli could be right."

"Areli got her toughness from somewhere," Alan said.

"She sounds like my daughter," John said with a wan smile. "Blunt but reliably straightforward. I would guess you raised her right." As if to answer, Areli vaulted out over the pool and did a double back flip before straightening her legs, feet pointed like a ballerina's, flawlessly piercing the blue water's depth.

Celeste said, "Delores can be fierce, if you want to know. Her daughter comes by it honestly."

Delores continued to watch Marvin. John asked her, "Do *you* think your daughter is right?"

Delores said, "I pray she is not. I hope this is the cynicism of youth. If she is right, I have been a fool."

John motioned the server over for a refill of coffee. He considered the possibility that Delores had no clue she was getting ready to become number six in Jeffrey's conga line of wives. He didn't know if he would have to break this news to her or whether it was Marvin's responsibility. Or whether Marvin was up to the task. How much history is a new fiancée entitled to?

John added milk to his coffee and stirred. He let his gaze settle momentarily on everyone seated around the table. It was a deliberate act. Their eyes met his and they waited expectantly for him to speak. Sometimes John paused in ways that reset the rhythm of conversation. Alan described it as moving from ordinary into ritual time. This was one of those moments. John chose his words with care.

"I have a friend in Chicago, a man by the name of Modeski. Arthur is proud to say that he is a pagan. He and I have been carrying on an argument of sorts for many years now. I suppose you could say we are close friends.

"He says the problem with ministers of the gospel is that we perpetuate illusions. And he bases this observation on a lot of hard evidence. It is hard to acknowledge that my pagan friend tells a truth I must seriously consider. But I have told Arthur that I believe my task is to strip away illusions, not to create them. 'And you will know the truth, and the truth will make you free.' That's what the apostle John said, but of course he was quoting Jesus. And I believe those words apply to what we want to know about Jeffrey in this moment. We need to know the truth about Jeffrey. We all want to find him. Marvin came to Denver because Celeste made an initial phone call. Thank you for that, Celeste. Establishing the truth about Jeffrey is important. Marvin, you said Areli might be right about Jeffrey. Why did you say that?"

Marvin looked like he had absorbed a stiff jab but he nodded. He rocked slightly in his chair and looked at Delores as he spoke. "Your daughter Areli has insight. My son has had several broken marriages. He divorced his first wife in Kansas many years ago. And he's gone through more marriages since. And I would hate—I would hate—for you to be hurt." His voice shook on the last sentence.

"He told me he had been in several relationships that didn't work out. Haven't we all?" Delores said.

Marvin looked at his plate.

Celeste said, "How many previous marriages, Mr. Arnheim?" As she spoke, she and Delores looked at him not with hardness but with unblinking patience.

"Including Nell, this many." Marvin held up his right hand with his thumb and fingers spread.

"Five," Delores said. "Nell—and who were the others?"

Celeste turned her face away from the table and John thought he heard her whispering to herself in Spanish.

Marvin answered Delores's question. "Patricia, Lucy, Terry, and Miriam. His marriage to Miriam lasted four months. He divorced her a couple of years ago, here in Denver."

Celeste spoke. "Do you know where Miriam is now?"

"No."

"You know quite a lot about your son who never spoke to you. Did he ever give you news about any other women between the wives?" There was some ice in Celeste's voice.

The question set Marvin back in his chair. He recovered and said yes. He was looking at Delores to avoid the steel of Celeste's expression. He said, "News trickles back to Kansas now and then. Please tell me, Delores, did he ever talk with you about these previous relationships?"

"Not in so many words," Delores said. "He said he was not perfect. He said that he had experienced God's grace and forgiveness and he hoped I would understand. I told him I would try. I told him I am not exactly perfect either. I mean, I'm not the Virgin Mary." She crossed herself, continuing, "I think we can be honest here." She looked down at the ring and turned it slowly on her finger. "But wife number six?"

A young woman in a short terrycloth robe over her bare legs and flip-flops walked swiftly to the table. The Casa Bonita label was embroidered in gold brocade on the robe. She pulled her wet hair back and rubber-banded it. "Well, hello," she said. When she smiled on the company before her, the dim wattage of the lighting seemed to increase a little.

"This is my daughter Areli," Delores said. "Areli, let me introduce Pastor John and Dr. Wiebe from Chicago."

The daughter nodded at John and Alan. "A pleasure to meet you. This looks like a very serious conversation. I hope I didn't interrupt."

"No, you didn't." Celeste said. "We were talking about your scholarship to Regis and your understanding of men's psychology. All the good stuff."

The young cliff diver blushed. She looked at her mother and said she needed to shower and change since she was working the afternoon shift and would be juggling torches on the Grand Vista level. As her long legs carried her away from the table, John sat up in his chair and looked around the table.

"Juggling *burning* torches?" he said to no one in particular. "That sounds like entertainment."

"I know," Delores said. "She learned to juggle because it raised her hourly pay by two dollars, and she could make bigger tips. I told her if she is not careful, she could get stuck working in a circus. 'And don't forget your dreams of USC,' I told her."

"May I ask a naïve question?" Alan said. "Has anyone filed a missing-person report or contacted the police?"

"I filed a missing-person report," Marv said.

Celeste quickly added, "Your questions are not naïve, Dr. Wiebe. But let me explain. Delores and I are in no position to invite the police for help. The first thing you know is they ask for proof of citizenship and various documents or the names of your friends. I know many people swept up in their dragnet when they asked for help. The next thing we hear is they are back in Guerrero after a long bus ride, courtesy of the U.S. Border Patrol. You seek help and they make you a criminal or an accessory. Are you familiar with this problem?"

Celeste possessed incantatory power. Alan and Marvin were nodding.

John said, "I understand why you are reluctant to contact the police. I have had recent experiences in Chicago with people who feel the same way. And I have my own reasons to be skeptical."

He looked at Delores, continuing, "There are other options if you don't want the police involved. You could hire a private detective. They cost money. But you might consider this if Jeffrey doesn't turn up. Do you want the detective to pursue any leads, even if it takes him out of state? You would have to decide how far to go with this strategy. Detectives I have spoken to guarantee privacy, with a caveat. If something illegal has occurred they are required to report it. In other words, they can't hide serious criminal activity from the authorities."

Celeste looked amused. "What you say by 'criminal' can mean so many things. Do you have opinions about Jeffrey's activity?"

"Not in the present tense," John said, looking back to Delores. "If you hire a detective, you need to state your questions and convictions up front." He looked at Marvin, whose expression gave nothing away.

John went on, "Delores, may I ask you a few other questions about Jeffrey's acquaintances in Denver? Anyone he knew or spent time with. Anyone we could talk to?"

"Sure. There were several people in the Bible study group that met in the library branch."

"Bible study?" Alan said.

"Yes. Doctor Jeffrey is a very interesting speaker and led a Bible study. He had been conducting a course on the book of Revelations, I think that is the Revelation of John, correct?"

Celeste broke in. "It was very popular. The librarian had to limit it to fifteen in attendance because the noise bothered other people in the library. She told us she didn't want it turning into a charismatic revival meeting and threatened to kick us out."

Alan smiled and said, "Getting boisterous with the book of Revelation. Imagine that. John, your namesake keeps popping up, doesn't he?" Alan motioned the server over to order another beer.

"Was there anyone in that group we could talk to?" John said.

"Maybe Fenimore," Delores said. "He sometimes helped lead the discussion. "Have you heard of Promise Keepers?"

Alan put a hand over his eyes, intoning, "To bring about revival through a global movement that calls men back to courageous, bold leadership." He took his hand away and gave John a blank stare.

John ignored Alan and asked Celeste, "Fenimore who?"

"Fenimore Ramekin," Celeste said. "He and Doctor Jeffrey sometimes eat lunch here."

"Have you spoken with Fenimore since Jeffrey disappeared?" John asked.

Delores wore trouble on her face. She corrected Celeste's pronunciation, saying, "It's Ram-kin, not Ram-uh-kin. As in baby ram. . . Fenimore Ramekin is also a realtor. He showed Jeffrey and me several houses after Jeffrey proposed. He said he knew a lender who could get financing for zero percent down. Jeffrey was pleased with that news. We went to a bunch of open houses in Commerce City."

"But have you talked with Fenimore since Jeffrey disappeared?" John repeated.

"No. I left him phone messages. The first time I got a message that he was out of town on a business trip. The second time his message box was full."

"Do you have his number or his address?" John asked. Delores took a pen out of her purse. John tore off a sheet from his yellow pad and handed it to her. She wrote down an address.

"Thanks. Are there other people we should try to talk to? And this is very basic: Where did Jeffrey live? Was he renting an apartment?"

"The Buena Vista Motel." Delores motioned for the paper she had just handed John. He handed it back and she wrote down another address. "I spoke with the manager there a week ago. She told me John had vacated his rooms a month ago."

"He was renting rooms there?" John asked.

"Yes, a one-bedroom apartment with a kitchenette."

"Sounds like the simple life. Renting by the week or the month?" John asked.

Delores didn't know. She looked down at her hands folded in her lap. The financial information embarrassed her. John thought that in America conversation about the end times was easy; what twisted people in knots was direct discussion of one's personal finances, a specter that galloped down on the unsuspecting like the fourth horseman of the Apocalypse. John changed the topic, asking, "Were there any other individuals who were important to Jeffrey that we might know about—and that we could talk to?"

Delores and Celeste exchanged glances. They simultaneously said, "Campbell."

"Campbell who?" John asked.

"Doctor Wyndham Campbell," Delores said.

Marvin scraped his chair loudly against the floor. He sat up very straight. "Well, that's somebody I know a few things about."

"How do you know him?" Delores said.

"Are you talking about the TV evangelist with a broadcast out of Wichita? He lives in Marion Hills, Kansas, one town over from Hillsboro where I live. The town, by the way, where Reverend Reimer will be this summer and fall. What a coincidence! You should know that Campbell is married to Carol Schlegel, a young woman who my son Jeffrey used to date in high school. Everybody calls him simply Campbell—even his wife. A big guy, right? About six-four, thick blond hair going gray. Slicks it back in a big whomp on top of his head. Likes the three-piece suit and always has that, that—hankie thingy in the front pocket of his suitcoat to match the tie."

Delores found her smile again. "That's the man. Do you mean a pocket square?"

"Yes, that's it," Marvin said. He showed a little bit of paunch in his horizontal-striped polo shirt as he leaned forward. He smiled good-naturedly in response to Delores, revealing the puckish gap between his two front teeth. "And it always matches the tie, am I right?"

"That describes the man exactly," Delores said.

"Marv," Alan said, "maybe you could call up Campbell and get his take on all this. Maybe he knows where Jeffrey went."

Marv appeared as though a second wave of troubling thoughts had overtaken him. He responded, "Yeah, you're right. I should call him. Maybe I'll dial him up tonight, though I'm not exactly on a first-name basis."

Celeste stood up and leaned over to give Delores a buss on the cheek. "Later, cousin. *Minha prima preciosa,* always in my prayers. Call me tonight." She shook hands with the men and said it was a pleasure to meet them but she had a shift to work. "I'm running late. I hope we talk again."

John stood up and walked away from the table with her. "You are at Brody's Lounge, the bar? Alan and I may drop by later."

Celeste said softly, "Please come by. I would welcome you. There is more to say. Just know that after eleven it can get a little loud."

John returned to the table and decided to say one more thing: "A thought is dogging every one of us, and out of politeness we are afraid to say it out loud."

He put his hands palms down on the tabletop. Then he turned his palms toward the ceiling. "But these are difficult circumstances and we cannot avoid considering all the possibilities. Jeffrey has not communicated with anyone here in roughly three weeks. That is my understanding."

He paused and waited for a response. There was none so he continued, "I think we need to visit downtown just to check off the possibility and put our minds at ease. I am not talking about going to the police. I am talking about a visit downtown."

"What are you talking about?" Delores's voice was small.

"The coroner's office. If Jeffrey has died, we should find out. If he was without identification, he would be held at the morgue until someone claims the body. And that normally requires someone with a photograph, preferably next of kin, to make the inquiry." John looked at Marvin and then Delores. "So, yes, I am suggesting a trip downtown."

"I don't know," Delores said.

"Delores, we are desperate to find him. No communication from him to anyone in your circle in three weeks." John made his voice as gentle as he could.

"Pastor, the truth might be unbearable."

"But you want to know it, don't you? Look at it this way. We can hope to cross the worst possibility off the list." John put his hand on Marvin's arm. Marvin appeared as surprised as Delores by John's suggestion. "Don't tell me you haven't thought about it, Marv."

"I have," Marvin admitted. "I think Areli might have a point about Jeffrey skipping town. But he has been in Denver more or less consistently for the past thirty years. At least as far as I know."

John looked at Alan. "Would you drive us downtown? Maybe that would be best." Marvin looked at John and handed Alan the keys to the Cadillac.

"Chauffeur at the ready," Alan said. He was eager at the prospect of doing something after all the talk. Just then another diver stepped out on the slippery black rocks above their head, a man sporting a black Speedo and a furry chest who leaped off the cliff in form befitting Acapulco. But the thrill was gone. John looked at the half-eaten chimichanga that lay in his plate like a broken boat. The server came by and asked if they wanted takeout boxes. Alan said no, thanks.

Delores said, "I'll be honest with you, gentlemen, the food here is not the main thing."

Alan grinned. "You don't say?"

The men were happy she was getting her sense of humor back. But she looked down at her lap. She put her hand out on the table, the one with the ring on the finger, and she extended it across the surface and found John's hand which she gripped briefly in a desperate, reflexive act. "We have to find him," she said. "Thank you for coming to Denver."

John watched her get out a Kleenex and dab at her eyes. She turned her gaze upon his face and looked for a sign. Her beauty and her faith aroused in him a certain sense of obligation, but she was also afraid of him because he had nerve to make her think about the dead body of her lover.

He thought that's what happens when you break through a taboo. You create the opening for new kinds of conversation.

Alan signaled for their server and paid the bill. Then he stood up and put on his sunglasses. "Are we ready?"

The group emerged from the cave of Casa Bonita into the mercilessly bright Colorado sunshine. John thought of Plato's allegory. They would find out the truth. He knew it. Alan got into the driver's seat of Marvin's Cadillac for the ride downtown. Marvin climbed into the back seat beside Delores, who held her purse on her lap. John sat up front with Alan.

There was mostly silence on the way. John looked back once at the passengers in the rear seat. Marvin was opening his briefcase and taking out an eight-by-ten glossy of his son. It was a picture snapped in Wichita by a professional photographer during Jeffrey's first wedding to Nell many years earlier.

Delores looked at the photo and held her face in her hands.

Chapter 9

The morgue did not deliver a match between the current occupants housed in refrigerated metal storage lockers and the pictures Marvin and Delores provided. That was the good news and also the bad news. No dreaded announcement, but no certainty either. The wait in the lobby took almost an hour, and then an attendant walked out, shaking his head. He reminded John of Jim Henson, but without the Muppets. The man extended the manila folder to Marvin and said, "He's not here. Best of luck locating him."

Marvin took the wheel and drove back to Casa Bonita, where Delores said goodbye and stepped out of the car, decidedly discouraged, judging by the slump of her shoulders.

"Will I see you before you leave town?" she asked John.

He reassured her that she would.

Back at the motel, the men got out of the Cadillac and Marvin locked it up. Alan and John walked over to the Land Rover. Marv walked in between them and said, "Thanks for all you've done. I need to gather my thoughts. I also need a nap."

"Should we wake you up for dinner?" John said.

"Don't bother," Marv said. "I need some down time. I'll call Verla. She wants to know if I'm taking my blood pressure medication. And she might have some ideas. We will talk with this realtor buddy of Jeff's, am I right?"

John nodded. "That is essential. And I also plan to talk with Campbell. When you call Verla, please say hello."

Marvin said. "I'll see you two at breakfast tomorrow morning. Meet you in the lobby at seven."

Alan turned the ignition. "So what's next, boss?" he said.

"Let's go to Brody's. Celeste has more to tell us. I say we go straight over there before happy hour gets too happy," said John, stretching and grimacing. He ran a hand under his sport coat. "That is if I can recover from lunch."

"Yeah, why did you even try to eat that desecration on your plate? Chimichanga, my ass! That thing looked deep fried, boiled, *and* steamed! They should rename it in the menu as the wreck of the *Santa Maria*. I tried to motion for you to cease and desist but you were drowning in Delores's beautiful eyes. Wasn't it a damsel in distress that got you into trouble in Chicago? For crying out loud, John, I may have to report you to Nancy as part of my ecclesiastical duty."

John laughed and said, "Go ahead, big fella! Make my day. Remember, I hate to see good food go to waste."

"Who the fuck is calling it good?"

"Okay, wise guy," said John, bumping Alan's shoulder with his closed fist, just hard enough to get a yowl. Then he asked, "Do you have the address to Brody's Lounge?"

"Yeah, I looked it up already last night at the concierge desk," Alan said. He pulled a note from his breast pocket.

"You're a smooth operator, Wiebe."

They drove another patchy stretch of Colfax, which was rapidly turning into the avenue of their Denver dreams. They pulled into a scruffy parking lot with a sprinkling of dented pickup trucks. Across the street the smell of charcoal and carne asada drifted out of A-1 Cabeza Taqueria. Next to it, a vagrant sheltered his cigarette butt from the gusting winds with his entire hunched-over body. He stood leaning against a cigar-store Indian inside the darkened doorway of what had once been a Rexall drugstore. The place had rebranded itself with a crayoned cardboard sign in the window that said, "For All Your Outboard Needs." Nearby, several hikers with leathery tans and draped in threads of outdoor chic that demonstrated allegiance to the apparel gods of North Face and Columbia, emerged from the doorway of a recently renovated coffee joint. They juggled Venti-sized smoking beverages and climbed into a Subaru with a hard-shell carrier on top. A smell of high-grade cannabis mingled with the taqueria scent.

John and Alan walked across an expanse of pitted, trashy parking lot. Bumper stickers announcing the Denver Broncos began to festoon the vehicles. Jesus fish proliferated. One beat-up muscle car showed CU overlaid on the profile of a charging buffalo, the entire decal basically obstructing the rear windshield.

Alan looked at the image and said, "Ever been to Lookout Mountain? Buffalo Bill's grave? Just twenty miles away, due west. Near Golden. You can pitch pennies into the wishing well."

"Let me guess. The Voth boys took you there?" John said.

"Sure did."

"You honored a great American hero. That guy understood show business and he would have made a great football coach. It's about the body count. Plus he had imagination. When he teamed up with Sitting Bull in the Wild West Show, he gave us something to be proud of. If Plato talked the talk of noble lies, Buffalo Bill walked the walk."

Alan said, "Yeah, mostly what remains is some really great taxidermy."

They went into the bar. The interior of the establishment was dim, except for a twenty-foot-long fish tank on the left wall, occupied by colorful masses of fake coral and a school of piranhas that darted as one in their beautiful, rectangular prison. Beyond the aquarium lay a row of four booths upholstered in sleek black Naugahyde. The deepest depths of the space held four billiards tables. Three dartboards at intervals adorned the back wall. Double doors to the right at the end of the long bar led to the kitchen. A solitary cowboy southpaw refined his throwing technique, his right wrist carefully bent and resting on his back hip as he launched his pointed missiles at a regulation corkboard. He was hitting near the center of the target on every throw.

Sports memorabilia adorned the walls, and drawing four spotlights at the center of the biggest display hung a large signed poster of John Elway. Alan looked at it and said to John, "You think the guy will ever break through?"

John said, "I hope so. The Tarkenton path is a hard one." He thought of Jeffrey, with his 0–5 record in the marriage game, embarking on yet another attempt.

The place smelled of grilled wings and frying jalapeno peppers but John was thinking more about Pepto Bismol. A chalkboard above the bar next to a TV announced a quesadilla special. Three sweaty guys sat at the far end of space, admiring Celeste as she wiped down the zinc bar surface with a cloth and a bottle of Windex. She had on more lipstick now, and metallic glitter highlighted one cheekbone. John looked at the junior executives. Had it been ten years earlier, they would have been wearing brown or powder-blue leisure suits. Now they wore blazers with all the abandon of North Dakota fraternity brothers who had ditched the necktie. The wall behind the bar, a solid mirror surface, showcased the liquor collection in a carefully organized display. More track lighting lit up the liquid shrine and created warmth within the larger chill of Brody's. Celeste glided behind the bar like a lethal knife fighter in tight jeans: at once gorgeous and terrifying. She had lined up a row of tall clean glasses in front of her and set down another stuffed with dollar bills. A bar cloth lay draped over her broad, bare shoulder. When she was tending bar, few customers watched the flat screen TV above the row of beer pulls. They watched her and were eager to be served.

Alan and John approached and sat down. She looked up. "Hello, gentlemen. What will it be?" She didn't show any sign of recognition. "If you have questions, I'll do my best to answer them."

Alan ordered a Coors Light. John asked for coffee and said, "You told me you had more information about Jeffrey. We're all ears. Any fragment, any clue."

"Yes, of course. You certainly didn't waste time, did you? Let me make you a fresh pot of coffee, Reverend." She fired it up and then pulled a Coors from the tap behind the bar and set it down on a coaster in front of Alan. A little foam ran over the edge.

She said to John, "There were things I wasn't sure about saying. Things that could have embarrassed Mr. Arnheim, or Delores, or both."

John said, "Such as?"

"What kind of man gives a woman a fifty-thousand-dollar ring but can't afford a down payment on a house in Commerce City?"

She turned her attention to Alan, whose Adam's apple bobbed as he consumed half his beer. "Doctor Wiebe, what kind of a man does that?" She put her elbows on the bar and leaned forward. He put the beer down and wiped his mouth with a napkin.

"Celeste, if I may. Please call me Alan. What do we know about Jeffrey to this point? Let me ramble a bit. He does have a lot of experience handing out rings, if his marital history is any clue. But, boy, Delores sure got excited about that zero-down option, didn't she? I'd like to meet the realtor, to be honest. He sounds like he's living in fantasy camp. But the jewelry. The rock. What about that fifty-thousand-dollar ring? If he actually delivered that to her, what could possibly be his reason for skipping town? Could be have lifted it somewhere? Was it hot? I don't know."

"My friend the professor has a vivid imagination," John explained to Celeste. "Like members of his guild, he is good at spinning hypotheticals. Maybe the rock is a cheap knockoff. Do we know if it's real?"

"You're a preacher and a skeptic. I like such combinations," said Celeste, freshening John's coffee. "I was skeptical too. I had Delores get it appraised at Capital Estate on the west end of Colfax because of my own doubts. It's the real deal, man. It's worth that or more."

"Celeste," John said, "have you met Jeffrey's realtor?"

"A number of times," she said. "Fenimore Ramekin is a close friend of his. As I think was mentioned at lunch, they lead these Bible study things and have a following. They call them the posse. Several come here Fridays. They're recruiting guys for an outfit they call Promise Keepers."

"And what do you think of this posse?" Alan asked. "You see these guys up close."

Celeste thought for a moment. "I would say this about men who talk real loud about protecting their women, or taking care of their women. The fathers who take their daughters to purity balls."

"Yeah, what about them?" Alan asked.

Celeste said, "They're usually the ones to watch out for."

"What else are these guys into?" Alan said.

Celeste said, "Fenimore plays a mean game of pool. He also loves to bet on the piranhas. He gets very excited."

"Bet on the piranhas? How do you do that?" John said.

She motioned with a glance and nod of her chin toward the fish tank. "On Friday nights the owner comes in and drops a live white mouse into the water. He gets the mice from the medical lab where his niece works. There's a betting pool set up for guessing how many seconds it will take before the fish strike the mouse. It's a very popular attraction here. Jesse's idea. He thought we needed a gimmick, and I suppose he was right. It's been a windfall for the bar's revenue," said Celeste, looking downward, with a kind of abject resignation. "The winners split half the pot, and the rest goes to the house. Wagers capped at a hundred bucks. Three or four rounds of betting. Jesse handles the cash."

"If Fenimore likes this, what else does he like? Cockfighting?" Alan's eyes showed some excitement of his own.

"I wouldn't be surprised," Celeste said. "The first mouse drop, as they call it, usually happens shortly after eleven o'clock when the house is full. Half the time we nearly have a riot on our hands. I always remove the pool cues before the shitshow starts."

"Do you have Fenimore's phone number?" John asked. "I'd like to talk to him. If Jeffrey checked out of the motel, where did he go? Fenimore might have an idea. Didn't he show Jeffrey and Delores a few listings?"

"Yeah," Celeste said. "Most of them in Commerce City. Delores liked those tours too much. Starry-eyed. I tried to warn her to lower her expectations, but after the ring she told me to shut up and stop being a spoilsport."

"So if he didn't get a new place, did he move in with Delores?" Alan asked.

"No," Celeste said. "I haven't seen him at her place. About some things she is . . . very *evangélico*, you know? She told me she is saving it for the honeymoon. If you want to know one of my wild speculations, I think maybe Doctor Jeffrey is living in his car."

Patrons began to drift into the bar in twos and threes. The boy-men at the end of the bar ordered another round. Celeste carried drinks to them and returned.

John said, "Living in his car sounds pretty sketchy. Then again, Jeffrey often bragged about his ability to live close to the bone. He started that kind of talk right after he returned from the Far East with nothing but a forty-pound backpack."

"Many people live out of their cars for a period of time. Many people do it. At least in my experience," Celeste said. "I did it in my twenties on a regular basis. I was trying to save up money."

"How did that work out?" Alan asked, as he pushed his empty glass forward for a refill.

"Okay," Celeste said. "I had a decent car and a membership at the Y, where I could shower. Then I bought a condo. A starter home, as they say. Kind of a shitty place, but I hold title. And the condo manager is solid." She crinkled her eyes at the corners. It was one of the ways she smiled.

She continued, "The working-class hustle requires many skills. People scramble. Kind of like that mouse in the tank, you know? But then again, not many of them dole out fifty-thousand-dollar rings."

"Exactly," Alan said.

"Who had the last sighting of Jeffrey on the day he checked out of the Buena Vista motel?" John asked.

Celeste poured herself a glass of seltzer water. "I've talked about that with Delores. She says it was her, but it seems it was me. Delores was in a manager's meeting much of the afternoon and Jeffrey came over here to hang out. He was here for at least three hours. Fenimore came in briefly, around two o'clock, and they talked. I couldn't quite get it all. Too busy that afternoon."

"How did Jeffrey look to you when you saw him that day?" John asked.

"You mean his physical condition?"

"Yeah."

"He looked wrecked, if you want to know the truth. I got the impression he wasn't sleeping well. He said something about sciatica. He was limping. I also remember him and Fenimore laughing and then not laughing so much. Jeffrey kept going outside to the phone booth next to the parking lot. He must have gone out there seven or eight times, either to make a call or to get one. Every time he came back in the bar, he looked a little more pissed off."

"Do you know who he was talking to?" John asked.

"No," Celeste said.

"Can you guess?"

"I caught a couple of phrases when he was talking with Fenimore," Celeste said. "Something about a note due, or a screwup with a dividend. I didn't hear any other details."

"How about the phrase 'earnest money'?" John asked.

"I can't be sure," Celeste said. "I was tending bar for forty people."

"So while he's talking with Fenimore here at the bar in an animated way about money, he is also on the phone outside with another party," Alan said.

"Yes," Celeste said.

"Maybe to do with a deal on a house?" Alan asked.

"Would make sense," John said. "Celeste, can you get Fenimore Ramekin on the phone?"

"Here, let me bring the house phone over."

She carried the phone to the bar and put it down. The other bartender came through the back doors from the kitchen. He wore a Nehru-collar cooking jacket and had the grizzled graying look of Southern gentry. The bar was filling up. Celeste punched the buttons on the phone and handed the receiver to John. He listened. The automated message announced that the box was full and no message could be left. John hung up. "Do you have Fenimore's address?"

"Yeah, I gave it to you at Casa Bonita," Celeste said. "Check your front pocket."

John looked flustered and said, "You're right."

Celeste picked up a black hardbound ledger beside the phone, opened it, and pointed at a line. She showed it to John. "Does this match up with what I gave you?"

"That's it," John said. "You're thorough."

"Good luck," Celeste said. "Call me if you need me."

"We will," John said. "Thank you for all your help."

Celeste rang them out and pushed the check across the counter. John left a couple of bills under his empty coffee mug.

"Thank you," Celeste said. "Call me, I mean it. Please keep me posted."

John looked at the fish tank again. He turned and asked, "Was there ever anybody else who came in here with Jeffrey to bet on the piranhas?"

"As a matter of fact, yes," Celeste said. "The big guy that Jeffrey's father knows about. William Campbell?"

"Wyndham Campbell," John said.

"Yeah, that guy. He came around here about once a month. He and Jeffrey acted like business partners. He bet big on the fish the first time he was here, and he won the pool. It went to his head. The following Friday he wanted to personally drop the mouse in the tank."

"Did Jesse let him?" Alan asked.

"No," Celeste said. "Jesse guards his privileges closely. He didn't tell Campbell to fuck off or anything like that—he was nice about it, but he was very clear."

On their way out, John said to Alan, "That woman is a Rock of Gibraltar."

"Yeah," Alan said. "Nothing gets by her. She made me almost completely forget about that librarian in Des Moines."

"Attention span, Alan. Attention span. I have a feeling that librarian in Iowa is a real treasure. Besides, I don't think Celeste has the slightest interest in you. I mean, in that way."

Chapter 10

Driving to Fenimore's place, his nerves singing with coffee, John sat in the passenger seat and struggled with the Denver map. Alan dialed the knob for NPR, but John was in no mood for Cokie Roberts. He reached out and switched off the radio. "Sorry," he said, "I'm trying to concentrate here."

They arrived in front of a vermilion ranch-style with a cracked driveway. Black tar patching material spidered across the surface. A black Ram 1500 pickup was snugged into the tiny carport stuck to the side of the house like a crooked Band-Aid. A decal on the pickup's rear window announced Promise Keepers: Staying True. Another decal carried the U.S. Marines motto: Semper Fi.

Alan said, "The man is at home."

The doorbell beside the front door seemed erased by colored wires sprayed like spaghetti out of the broken plastic cover. John knocked. The day's mail was still stuffed in the mailbox. John waited and knocked again. A man built like a wrestler finally came to the door. His feet were bare and his camouflage cargo shorts were cinched tight around his waist with a green canvas belt. He wore a black bandanna, and a little silver cross was buried in his bronzed chest hair. The V-neck sleeveless black T created the effect of a biker goth who'd met a very large Cub Scout, and the man looked more like an Oakland Raiders fan than a Promise Keeper. John thought that was maybe the point. A sprinkling of freckles crossed Fenimore's nose. He tried to brush a smear of taco sauce off the front of his shirt and only widened it.

"We tried to call first, but your phone's message box was full," John said. "I'm John Reimer and this is my friend Alan Wiebe. We're friends of Delores, and I go way back with Jeffrey Arnheim. I believe you know him. I hear he went AWOL three weeks ago."

Fenimore nodded, wiped his hand off on his shorts, and then shook hands with the visitors. "Marvin told me all about you two and said you were coming by. Where is Marvin?"

"He's at the motel taking a nap. We're here to help in any way we can." John furthered his introductions. "This is my associate, Alan Wiebe, from Chicago. He's a seminary professor in Chicago."

"Pleased to meet you, Professor Wiebe. What do you teach?"

"New Testament, Dead Sea Scrolls, first-century Judaism."

"Praise the Lord! I do something like that myself, but not as fancy. You guys come on in and make yourselves at home."

John and Alan followed Fenimore into his den. A wide-screen TV was on, and a Stouffer's dinner sat out beside a tallboy of Coors and the remote control. Fenimore shut off the TV and took the stacks of reading material off the sofa so his guests could sit. Realty brochures lay in a ragged heap on an end table. A big male buffalo, directly facing the viewer, framed in black and rendered in needlepoint, adorned one wall. John stood with his hands in his pockets and observed.

"We had lunch at Casa Bonita with Delores and Celeste," he said. "They told us you were close to Jeffrey and if anybody could help, you were the man."

"Yeah, a week after he disappeared, I was hoofing it up and down Colfax showing everybody and his dog my picture of Jeffrey. I got nowhere. He has tons of friends in the middle of Denver. He probably knows every Denny's waitress on the Colfax strip on a first-name basis. It was no good. It's like he evaporated. I thought for a while he'd been raptured, you know? Seriously!" said Fenimore, his smile crinkling a divot in his cheek to match the dimple in the middle of his chin. His face rapidly transformed from buffalo hunter into cute quarterback. "Jeffrey has been doing a Bible study of the Rapture lately. The man has charisma. He knows how to get your attention."

"He's been good that way since he was a boy. And Delores mentioned the Rapture, too. I guess it was fresh on her mind when Jeffrey disappeared." John paused at the word "rapture." Repetition of the word made it less familiar.

"Did you check out his super at the Buena Vista Motel?" Alan asked.

"Sure did," Fenimore said. "That guy, name of Michael, was the first person I talked to. He said Jeff checked out of there on Wednesday afternoon after we spent a little time at Brody's throwing darts. Our Bible study was scheduled as usual for Thursday at the branch library. Jeffrey was a no-show. That just wasn't like him."

"Celeste said Jeffrey made quite a few phone calls that afternoon at Brody's Lounge. Do you know what that was about?" asked John, sitting on the sofa and happy to manspread in the wreckage of Fenimore's front room. He crossed his legs, slouched, and made himself comfortable.

Fenimore's brow was impassive. "Jeffrey said it was about an investment dividend." "That's all he said?" John asked.

Fenimore skipped a beat. "Yeah," he said.

The hesitation made John skeptical. "One question I have is, Where was Jeffrey planning to live after he moved out of the Buena Vista?" asked John. "We figured if anybody would know, you would, since you were talking with him about a listing. Both Delores and Celeste mentioned you. Delores was very excited about a place in Commerce City."

"Yeah, she was enthused." Fenimore smiled. "Quite the little lady Jeffrey has set his eyes on, wouldn't you agree?"

Alan nodded. "No argument with you there, Mr. Ramekin."

"Fenimore, please. Can I get you guys something to drink?"

Alan said, "I'll have what you're having. A man gets parched in this dry climate."

John asked for a glass of water.

There was a grinding of an ice dispenser in the kitchen. Fenimore returned with their drinks and sat down. He said, "I wanted to file a missing-person report with the police after Jeffrey had been out of sight for a week. Delores and Celeste talked me out of that. I respected their wishes. I have a lot of respect for Delores."

John said, "We drove to the city morgue earlier today with photos of Jeffrey just to make sure the man hadn't shown up there unannounced. No match. Marvin was pretty relieved. But we're still not sure if Jeffrey is even in Denver."

"Yeah, if a missing-person report is filed, they'll also be on the lookout for his car," Fenimore said. "White Toyota Camry with rusting wheel wells." Fenimore finished his beer and crumpled the can into a small nugget.

"Delores was reluctant to go to the morgue with us, like she is skeptical of the police. I had to tell her the authorities would need confirmation of a match by his next of kin or close family. I convinced her she needed to come. Marvin was there, but he hasn't seen his son in years and there's no telling how Jeffrey's appearance has changed since his late twenties," said John, fingering his cheek. "We all think of ourselves as eternally youthful. Little do we know."

"So Delores was excited about a place in Commerce City," Alan said. "Can you tell us anything more about that?"

"Well, it's my listing, so I should know a thing or two. They came by during an open house in April. Delores fell in love with it. One thing you learn in the realty business is always watch the woman. What she wants is generally what they'll buy. If she's not on board, it's a no-go. Let me tell you, she was ready to get into that kitchen and bake tamales."

John paused. "So did they make an offer?" he asked.

"They did. And made the earnest money deposit. Right now we're working on a financing package for them. I've got a great banker in my corner."

"Zero down?" John said.

Fenimore started to say something, then changed his mind. "Yeah, we're trying for that."

⁓֍

They drove up to the property, at the crest of a hill. As he parked, Fenimore said under his breath, "What's this?"

Fenimore parked at the curb and walked over to the mailbox by the driveway. There was a square hole in the ground. John looked at the hole and at Fenimore.

"My sign has been removed. You know, the listing. It had a Contract Pending announcement on it. Somebody pulled it out of the ground."

Fenimore chose to enter the house by the back door. The front of the house presented as spanking new suburban split-level, but the back was janky. Access was by way of a makeshift, temporary set of seven ascending wooden steps with no railing. John looked down at the drop-off into a tangle of shrubs, then across to the backyard of the unfinished house next door. The tar paper on the roof had begun to tear, and several packages of shingles lay on a pallet in a yard of sawdust piles and spindly weeds. The house's warped soffits and trim hadn't yet seen a coat of primer.

"Jeffrey plans to build a wraparound walkout deck here," Fenimore explained.

When Fenimore unlocked the door on the landing, the musty smell enveloped them. Realty brochures were neatly stacked on the kitchen bar counter. A package of microwaveable ramen bowls lay open beside the sink.

"What the hell?" Fenimore said. "This is not how I left the place."

But he wasn't looking so much as following his nose. The scent came to them, steadily, a clear message from another world. Fenimore saw a closed door. "That was open when I left here. Somebody's in the master suite."

That's the way it is with doors, John thought. *They beg to be opened.*

Fenimore pushed through the door, and Alan and John followed. The chamber had afternoon light filtering in through the Levolor blinds that showed like thin slivers on the short-pile carpet. And here the olfactory message met the spectacle before their eyes. Alan grabbed a corner of his jacket and put the leather against his nose. Fenimore looked like he'd been smacked in the head. John's eyes took in the scene, starting with the man on the floor.

He lay flat on his back, desiccating in his Coleman sleeping bag on top of a stained foam mattress, eyes open, the whites of his eyes already the color of root beer. His hands inside the bag clasped each other for comfort and formed a mound atop his motionless chest. In the high, dry air of Colorado, his lean body had begun its alchemical transformation. Gray stubble had morphed into the hazy outlines of a beard, and his lips and gums had pulled back from the teeth to expose a feral grin. His nose had begun its inevitable declension into the middle of the skull.

A paperback lay beside his bag, on top of a thumb-indexed study Bible. The title on the cover read *Left Behind*. Its pages were marked with yellow Post-it notes. A reading lamp on the floor had been left switched on, casting a pool of light around the head and shoulders of the corpse. The effect was that of a modest piece of self-dramatizing show business: The man had staged his exit carefully. And yet—a ramen container had flipped over and spilled on the carpet, leaving the dry outline of a stain. A plastic spoon lay nearby.

John squatted beside the body. "He's been dead at least three days, maybe a week," he said, looking at Fenimore. "The cops are likely to treat this as a crime scene. The coroner will want to determine cause of death. Probably best not to disturb anything." He looked at Fenimore and said, "They'll ask how he got inside."

"I showed this listing to Jeffrey and Delores. Came back here with them after the open house."

"Looks like Jeffrey wanted to move in early," John said.

Fenimore wasn't listening. Ignoring John's suggestion to leave the scene alone, he stood up, holding Jeffrey's backpack. His hands rifled through the contents. He extricated a keychain. "I was wondering where this set of keys disappeared to."

"Now you know," John said. "Did you have any idea he was squatting on your property?"

"Of course not. I came by, what, five days ago, and everything was in apple-pie order." Fenimore and Alan went to check the garage. John glanced again at the paperback and he picked it up. Then he put it into the inside pocket of his jacket. Alan and Jeffrey returned moments later.

"There's no car. But he stowed the listing sign in the garage. He must have torn it out of the yard before he moved in," Fenimore said.

"I'm beginning to think that finding that car could tell us a lot," John said. He thought of Celeste's meditation about living in cars.

"Yeah," Fenimore said. "Excuse me, I need to take a look at the rest of the house."

Alan put on a pair of gloves he was carrying in his jacket. He went into the master bathroom and opened Jeffrey's Dopp kit and pulled out a pill bottle. He held up the open pill bottle to the light. Then he dug around for the remaining contents. He was glad to have something to do besides contemplate the corpse.

"What do you have there?" John said.

Alan held the bottles up to the light and read the labels. "Tylenol 3 and Paracod. A bottle of Paxil. Something called hydrocodone." He turned another pill bottle over in his hand. It was half full of pale green lozenges. "This is unmarked. I have no idea."

"A lot of prescriptions," John said. "The man was self-medicating."

"A lot of pain," Alan said.

Fenimore came back into the room. He said, "There's beer in the fridge if you guys are thirsty. A couple of six-packs." John and Alan were silent.

Alan said, "I'm not superstitious, but drinking the dead man's beer . . . I don't know."

John said, "It looks like he died in pain and alone."

John contemplated the Bible beside Jeffrey's makeshift bed on the floor, where the man's chemical dreams and visions of apocalypse had closed in for the last time. Fenimore slid open one of the closet doors. A black suit hung on a wooden hanger, and beside it a half dozen pinpoint blue shirts, still enclosed in the dry cleaner's plastic bag. On the floor beneath was a pair of Oxfords. A pair of silk socks lay crumpled on top of them.

"Sharp dresser, when he chose to be," Fenimore said. He stood frozen, looking.

Alan said, "Celeste told us he talked about sciatica. That can hurt like a motherfucker."

Fenimore said, "Yeah, he'd been limping the last couple of weeks I saw him. He was having trouble standing up from a chair. Told me it was an old injury flaring up."

John looked at Fenimore and asked, "Are you going to be all right?"

"I think so," Fenimore said. "It's hitting me now. Just give me a couple of minutes." He put a hand up to his eyes and with his thumb and forefinger pressed the bridge of his nose.

"I'm sorry," said John. "He would be glad you were the first on the scene."

John walked over and stood beside Fenimore. They both looked at Jeffrey. "I've just met you," John said, "but I know this: Jeffrey would be glad you're the one who found him."

Fenimore said, "Thank you," and walked out of the room.

"What's with the Post-it notes?" John said. The floor was littered with yellow rectangles sprinkled around Alan's feet. They had fluttered out of the Dopp kit when he found the pill bottles.

"Looks like phone numbers scribbled down."

"Keep your gloves on, please." John peered over Alan's shoulder. Alan shuffled through a couple of the notes.

"Do me a favor," John said. He pointed at a number on the note. "Write down as many of the numbers as you can. These are Kansas area codes, for instance. That one is central Kansas. And go through Jeffrey's Bible and his books for any other notes. When you're done writing the stuff down, leave everything here. We're not walking away with evidence. Got it?"

"Got it," Alan said, going through more of the Post-its. "I don't see any names."

"The numbers could be useful." John walked to the door and shouted out to Fenimore in the kitchen. "Was there any sign of an address book in that backpack?"

Fenimore replied, "No, but I'll look again."

John looked at Alan. "We have to call Marvin and Delores so they can come over here and see this before we dial 911. Once the ambulance and cops arrive, this whole thing will be taped off and the professionals will boot us out."

Fenimore stood in the doorway, blowing his nose into a handkerchief. When he was finished, he stuffed it into his back pocket. "Do you really think Delores has to see this? It could send her totally over the edge."

John replied, "Delores would never forgive us if she didn't see this. Fenimore, where's the nearest phone?"

"The phone in this house is disconnected. I have a mobile phone in the truck. Go ahead and use it."

⟶ℬ

Marvin arrived in his yellow Cadillac, and Celeste drove Delores to the house after John called her.

They filed into the master suite and looked at the man on the floor. John told them not to touch anything because the police would treat this as a possible crime scene. Fenimore winced at the words. The smell rose up to meet them and in a short time drove them from the room. Alan closed the door. Delores cried silently, and Celeste had an arm around her shoulders. They went into the kitchen.

Marvin's face was a perfect blank. John decided he wouldn't want to be the grief counselor trying to get Marv to forgive his dead son for fucking up this badly.

Alan stepped out the back door onto the landing to wait. Then he saw something in the shrubs beside the back steps. "What's this?" he asked.

Fenimore descended the staircase and reached into the foliage to pull out a pair of reading glasses. "They look like Jeffrey's. Wonder how they got here."

John looked down from the top of the landing to the ground and said, "Reminds me of that saying about falling off your back porch. When you reach my age, there's something about a railing. You might want to give those to the detectives. They'll want the whole picture." Fenimore handed the glasses to Alan and went to his truck and dialed 911.

Two police cruisers pulled up. The light was draining out of the sky when Delores and Marvin confirmed the identification of the corpse for the uniforms. A couple of detectives arrived shortly after. They asked Fenimore to wait outside. A little later they came back out and began their interview with him. Still later, the ambulance arrived and two men went inside with a stretcher and a body bag.

John waited outside the house with Alan, leaning against Marvin's car. They watched the zip-up parcel loaded for the trip to the city's medical examiner. At last, the women emerged. Fenimore let them out through the front door. They approached the minister tentatively, with steps that said they were ready to say goodbye.

Delores said to John, "They will do an autopsy."

"Please let me know when you get the report," John said. He gave Delores his card. "You can call me anytime. That's my Chicago number, but my secretary will notify me if I get a message. And I will call you right back."

"Thank you, Pastor John. And thank you, too, Professor Wiebe. You both are very kind—and . . . I will not forget. I am sorry and—it's crazy to say it, I know—a little embarrassed." She put her fist to her mouth. "Thank you for what you did. How could it end this way?" Then her eyes welled up. "But here's the bright side," she said. "This is something Jeffrey would say: 'Look, he was lost and you found him!'"

Then she went to pieces.

Celeste gathered her into her arms. John said, "This does not feel like success to me. I have done very little. I wish I could have done more."

Delores found her voice. "When I told my daughter Doctor Jeffrey was gone, she was not sad. She told me this man would have found a way to break my heart. And maybe this was not the worst thing to happen."

Celeste, nodding very slowly, gave Delores another Kleenex and said to John, her voice cracking, "What do you say to women like this?"

John was momentarily unable to speak.

"Keep them close," Alan said. He shook her hand formally and then managed to say, "Together you are very, very strong. You are as tough as they come."

"Take care of yourself, Pastor John." Delores leaned in and gave John a kiss on his cheek. Then she drove away with Celeste.

"I hope she gets a decent settlement for that ring she wasn't wearing," John said.

"How do you tell a woman in this situation that she dodged a bullet?" Alan zipped up his jacket and pulled his stocking cap down around his ears.

Fenimore dropped Alan and John back at his place before he headed to the police station to finish his interview. They said their goodbyes to him and took Alan's car to the motel where they waited in the lobby for Marvin. He arrived soon after.

John said, "Alan and I leave in the morning for Kansas."

"I'll see you there soon enough. I'm sticking around here for the coroner's report. And I want to find the car. Probably a couple of days."

The father of the prodigal stood in the middle of the lobby, unsure of himself, unsteady on his feet. But a stubborn belligerence rode over his face.

"John, it feels rotten right now," said Marvin. "For years I've had a bad feeling about how things would end for Jeffrey. But not like this. And now I have so much anger."

John waited for Marvin to continue.

"How is it possible that I hate my dead son for what he did? To himself, and to us? And to all the women he made promises to? What is the matter with me?"

"Nothing's wrong with you, Marv," John said.

Marvin said, "I think this terrible thought that gives me comfort! I think, maybe that woman is lucky my son died. Because he wrecked every woman who came across his path."

John raised his eyebrows and Marvin noticed. He said, "I told you I have anger. It makes me want to hurt someone. But I don't know who that would be."

John said, "Assure me you don't want to hurt yourself."

Marvin said, "No. But it feels rotten. It is so rotten that I have no words."

John spoke. "We will all get to Kansas. Maybe things will become clearer as we go. We have to give it time. Insight usually comes after the event. Go easy on yourself. I was thinking, also, before I forget, you should get the police to locate Jeff's car."

Marvin nodded. "They're working on that already." Then he paused. He put both his hands on John's shoulders. "Remember that sermon you preached at Ebenholzer right after Vi was diagnosed?" he said.

"Yes, I do," John said. "'For now we see as through a glass darkly.' I like even better, who was that composer who said, 'I have nothing to say, and I am saying it'? That was how I felt the day Vi was diagnosed. And now, too."

Marvin grasped his friend in an embrace. "You told me. It was John Cage."

"Right," John said. "Now find Jeff's missing car. And when you drive home, drive safe. Come by the parsonage in Marion Hills. Visit me."

Marvin forced a smile. He felt compelled to project victory. John reflected that the worst part of that impulse was you start to fake it no matter what. For a man like Marvin, the best part was it helped you refuse to give in to the demons.

There were plenty of those to go around on this sad stretch of Colfax. John felt the corners of the book pressing his chest inside his jacket pocket. The man on the floor had been left behind, all right.

Driving east toward their destination the next day, that image of skin drying on a skull stayed with John. Alan didn't talk much during the trip. John wrote in his journal as the Land Rover traveled eastward, from the high mountains and plateau of Colorado down to Kansas, to the cities of the plain.

Bleeding Kansas

Chapter 11

When you depart at four in the morning, five hundred miles don't seem like much. Out of Denver, I-70 was clotted with traffic and triple trailers but still reliably fast. America was in a hurry.

John watched the landscape. The Great Plains sometimes verged on the cusp of exaltation after spring rains had watered what would likely turn into a brown, baking crisp by the Fourth of July. To the eye, the green got greener. Under the sun, wheat fields rippled, the ground a single expanse of skin flexing in lazy, restless, sensuous motion. John kept count of red-tailed and Cooper's hawks perched atop the telephone poles strung out along the way.

In the early afternoon, Marion Hills came into view, just north of 56. A mass of giant machine sheds hunched their shoulders together like the defensive unit in a huddle. Above towered a sign announcing Halston Industries. Further on, the original settlement footprint showed itself with a verdant burst of trees fed by the North Cottonwood branch that ran through the heart of downtown. John thought about Marion Hills as he had first seen it. He couldn't quite remember that far back, but he didn't recall the town ever looking this green or prosperous.

It was not true, as some claimed, that money grew on trees in Marion Hills. But the town was blessed with both. Rising in the post-war boom on a tide of entrepreneurial cash and inventive tinkering, the town's most visible face to first-time visitors was still Halston Industries. Marion Hills had initially prospered on the bounty of agricultural innovation and technology. Its natural resources—primarily water flowing from the reservoir four miles north—also contributed. Leafy trees along its wide streets—sycamores, oaks, and the ubiquitous giant cottonwoods clustered in the park—made Marion Hills a deciduous palace. Those trees distinguished it from the surrounding arid towns of central Kansas.

There was an old hotel, the Eastlake, built in the 1890s and recently restored, spruced up in garish, decadent cowboy colors, chrome yellow with navy-blue trim on the soffits and details. It lay a block north of the railroad crossing and anchored the south end of Main Street. Across from it stood Marion County Courthouse, a brick and limestone structure that was still the largest building in the county. From there running north on Main, the street transitioned away from its industrial corridor into a leafy shopping and business district. Four long blocks of prosperity beckoned, again marked by sycamores and oaks. Intermittent benches invited pedestrians to lounge. Light posts done in a vintage Old West style came adorned with hanging plants in industrial copper planters that floated on gossamer chains. There was the Quick Stop gas station that enjoyed lots of traffic, mostly from the college boys who couldn't buy beer in the neighboring dry town. The police and sheriff's department came next, in a blond brick building flying an American flag. On the next block a hair styling salon was still decorated with a barber's pole and a sign announcing Paula's Place. The Copper Kettle Restaurant that had served ethnic German cuisine including verenike and Hillsboro sausage for Sunday lunch since 1963 was still there, as was Hepley's Hardware, a Mennonite Et Cetera resale shop with a rag-rug loom in the window, and the offices of the county's weekly newspaper, partially shuttered by Venetian blinds. Then John saw a sign: Little Pleasures.

"What's this town come to?" John said. "I can't imagine city council allowing a massage parlor on Main Street."

"Don't get too worked up," Alan said. "I mean, it makes sense, considering Marion Hills's reputation for creature comforts. But no. Coffee and pastries. A decent chicken-and-pesto sandwich at lunch. Owner is a recent transplant from Hawaii. An independent operator with attitude. Came here for a few weeks to help her daughter with a newborn and ended up staying."

"You know a lot about this woman," John said.

"I seem to have my ways with people in the food business," Alan said. "I connect naturally with restaurant help. Go figure. Anyway, Rachel decided she liked it here. When she opened Little Pleasures, a few locals were upset by the name, but nobody is complaining now. She has shaken up the Mennonite middlebrow in the best possible way. She lectures customers on the necessary toughness of a bagel and has begun to branch out into the bialy and the cruller. Their cinnamon rolls aren't quite Ann Sather quality, but they're close."

John nodded, absorbing the information. There was a store selling sports gear, hunting and fishing equipment, and western wear, a kind of miniature Sheplers. Tourists who came to enjoy the water sports and fishing at Marion Reservoir often remarked that staying in Marion Hills almost didn't feel like Kansas, and they said this with wonder in their voices: "I had no idea there could be so many trees this close to the Flint Hills." Locals nodded knowingly, not quite successful at concealing their swollen civic pride.

John thought the local Chamber of Commerce could do well with a new bumper sticker: It's Not Kansas—It's Marion Hills! He supposed whether such an aggressive slogan had any chance of success would all depend on the tenor of the local Rotarians. Maybe something to poll at a pancake breakfast.

John thought about the endless display of mammoth farm implements in the lots lining the industrial corridor just outside of town—all the stuff that made this prosperous, arboreal paradise possible. There were several acres of machinery. Rows of forty-foot-wide rigs crowded a field: seed drills, harrows, gargantuan baling rigs, combines. A fleet of shiny new semitrucks to haul grain, built by Mack, Peterbilt, and Volvo. There were plastic, semitransparent tanks the size of houses mounted on knobby wheels, implements designed to inject the chemical miracles of Monsanto and Dow into the thirsty soil of the American breadbasket. Grain augers in precision rows lined up like feeding Pleistocene storks. The economic backbone of the town was still Halston. Behind the phalanx of farm equipment lay the primary manufacturing plant, housed in a sprawl of buildings stamped upon the prairie. John observed that a couple of them were big enough to house airships, the German kind that used to make transatlantic flights.

In the Midwest, the company had become a brand to reckon with. Halston was to Big Ag what the Crimson Tide was to college football. The old man had taken out his first patent for a seed drill in 1939, and his two sons had joined him in the enterprise shortly after the United States entered World War II. Both studied engineering, Olaf at Case Western Reserve, Eric at the University of Texas. It wasn't long before the boys were running Halston Labs out of the firm's subsidiary branch, which they relocated from Emporia to Wichita. They had prevailed over their father's wishes, and he had learned to appreciate their vision. Revenue from patents fed the manufacturing, but no one was sure exactly how the money flowed, because the company was privately held. Innovation in agricultural implements was reputedly the main profit driver, but the Wichita labs branched into the aircraft and then space industry. Eventually they were also rumored to do U.S. government contract work, primarily in the manufacture of high-tech aerospace components, molecular switches, and circuit boards—all requiring rigorous security clearances. Eventually Halston Labs spun off a separate software division with locations in twenty-two different states.

"Peace and Prosperity" read the company motto under Halston on the giant illuminated white sign with red letters at the edge of town.

Several blocks on, Alan turned left on Elm past a handsome, low-slung series of buildings, all limestone slab and plate glass. These anchored the north end of the business district. The effect was prairie style, clean, inviting horizontal lines. Here there was more asphalt parking lot, though occupied by brand-new vehicles, sedans, SUVs, and pickup trucks. The showroom gleamed like a jewel. Inside, a black F-150 stood at the center of the floor on fat tires that elevated it like a burly sentinel above the multicolored Jeeps strewn around like pieces of PEZ dispenser candy. The marquee above the limestone tower was illuminated by floodlights—Schlegel Motors: Ford, Jeep, Land Rover. John said, "I have an appointment here tomorrow with Franz Schlegel. I'm supposed to get a loaner vehicle. He told me it was part of the church package."

"Good for you," Alan said. "You need a good church package, and I'm glad you get one. They're generous people. This all happened on short notice." He nodded at the Schlegel showroom. "Looks as though the Schlegels are prospering."

"When haven't the Schlegels prospered?" John said. "Levi figured it out about the same time Halston did."

Alan suppressed a laugh. "You mean to say he rode the Halston wave?"

"That would be correct," John said. "Why do you laugh?"

"I always laugh about Halston Industries," Alan said, "or whenever I see their sign. It's too much. This guy I know, Lenny, told me last year that Marion Hills has the most plastic surgery per capita of any Mennonite community in North America. It only stands to reason that such a place would house Halston Industries. I mean, how perfect is that?"

Alan looked at John, who appeared puzzled. "Lenny is a sociologist at U of I in Urbana," he explained. "Though recently he has moved sideways into the business school. Old friend of mine. Guy from Moundridge."

John said, "I don't follow. Maybe Nancy could explain it to me."

"Why, has she gotten work done?"

"Not to my knowledge," John said. "That's not what I meant. I meant about explaining Halston."

"Damn right," Alan said. "Does she buy the Halston label? I wouldn't be surprised," Alan chortled. "She does like the nice couture."

"Oh, Halston, as in *clothing* labels." John shook his head. "I'm slow, but if you give me enough time, I eventually figure it out. She is fond of clothes."

"You think? That's part of her damn Queen of Egypt act. I have a feeling she does it for you. Am I right?" Alan glanced sideways and gave John the inquisitor's look.

John kept a poker face. "I don't know what you mean by 'does it for me,' but she certainly doesn't disappoint when she wears a dress."

"You are a strange man of the cloth." Alan turned west off Main Street. "And I wouldn't like you any other way. But, come to think of it, when the hell does Nancy ever wear a dress?"

John chose not to reply. Six blocks away from Schlegel Motors, they pulled into the driveway of the parsonage on Sacra Via. The house—fully furnished as part of the package—was an understated but spacious ranch of painted white brick. A big hackberry stood between the sidewalk and curb and in the coiffed flowerbed under the front bay window sprouted a smoke bush and a Japanese red maple, the kind of trees that look good in paintings of Shinto shrines. Alan turned off the ignition. The men sat in the silence.

John said, "Thanks for all the driving."

"It wasn't exactly what I had imagined it would be," Alan said, "but boy am I happy we did it. Let me help get your stuff inside, and then I have to go."

"What, an appointment already?"

"The *Frintschoft* have a barbecue later this afternoon and I promised to show up. I'll be in Hillsboro all next week. Maybe I can catch you in the church office."

"That's perfect," John said. "I still feel bad not stopping in Meade on the way. But it's best I give them a decent chunk of time when I drive back out there to visit. Besides, they don't know I was arriving in Kansas by way of Denver."

"It's probably best they don't know, am I right?" Alan asked.

John said, "Going back to Meade is always complicated. Explaining what we did in Denver would be impossible."

"Relatives," Alan said. "You keep most of them at a distance, don't you?"

"Alan, you know me all too well."

John found the keys inside the mailbox and let himself in at the front entrance.

"Honey, we're home!" Alan exclaimed, following, a couple of suitcases in hand.

The inside of the parsonage was musty, close, and tinged with a scent of potpourri that was probably resting in a cute woven basket on the back of the toilet tank atop a crocheted doily. *A woman's touch*, John thought. The last interim pastor and his wife had moved out in February. Thankfully the weather had been cool through spring, and the place was not a hothouse despite being almost hermetically sealed. John looked around. There was a worn but inviting black leather couch and a set of matching Scandinavian sitting chairs, plus a couple of blond end tables with sharp edges. John opened the doors of a chipped china cabinet. It was stuffed with a random collection of coffee mugs and scented candles. The lamps on the end tables looked selected by someone raised on Lawrence Welk: red vellum shades trimmed with furry white balls, as if a team of miniature poodles had been sacrificed for the cause. One end of the room held a fireplace and a full bookcase. An antique TV set sprouted rabbit ears in crinkled tinfoil.

"Where do you want your suitcases and the garment bag?"

"The master bedroom at the end of the hall. Thanks." John dropped his two briefcases on the couch to sort out later.

After Alan drove away, John stopped and listened to the silence. His head felt like it was still in motion. He went out the sliding glass doors to the back patio, a cozy area marked by inlaid brick and a portable iron fire pit. The patio was enclosed like a courtyard and afforded privacy. Three Adirondack chairs bivouacked by a couple of tiki torches stuck into the ground. The lawn was cropped, green, and free of dandelions.

He went inside and poured himself a glass of ice water from a full pitcher he found in the avocado-colored fridge. He had another glass, tasting its strange mineral flavor, and then he sat down by the kitchen table to take off his shoes and socks. He padded down the hallway to the bedroom in his bare feet and stood by the wing chair.

He stripped down to his boxers and fell into the freshly made, king-size bed. *Take a pause on the adventures.* He felt his head sink into the down pillow.

All in all, not a bad pastoral package. *Six months to go,* he told himself.

Chapter 12

In the morning, John got ready to run. He laced up his blue Asics. He strapped on a leather fanny pack after putting the house key and a few dollars inside. He brushed his teeth and spit, leaned over the sink and splashed water on his face, and hauled sleep out of the corners of his eyes. In the bathroom mirror he tried to come to terms with his face, road-weariness written all over, the gullies and ravines of time roughing him up. His hair was a tangle of wiry white bedlam. No horror in the dream life, at least. He stretched his favorite terry-cloth headband over the mess. The front of the headband had a rainbow in the center with a single word, "Jesus," underneath, inscribed in simple Garamond. Sweat stains like rust marched across the stretch fabric.

His daughter Sarah had threatened to burn this article of running gear during a recent visit to Chicago. "Where do you find this schlock?" she had asked. When she threatened to pull the elastic off his head he had danced away from her threatening hand. "Frankly, I don't know if I'm looking at poorly designed swag for an early Pride parade or crappy low-brow Jesus wear from Cracker Barrel. You look like a leprechaun pervert. I mean, this looks like shit."

John asked, "Do I embarrass you?"

Sarah said, "In this, the answer is yes."

John held firm. "It was a gift from a very sincere senior citizen. She would be wounded if I didn't wear it. Besides, I get into interesting conversations because of it."

"I can only imagine," Sarah said.

In the sunlit kitchen he reread the typed note the welcoming committee had left for him. There was another set of keys that the sexton Buller had dropped off, including some for the toolshed out back, in case John was interested in tilling the garden bed behind the garage. Very subtle test of his character. Did he still have the agrarian touch? The church secretary, Linda Ebel, had signed off on the letter with a smiley face. John opened the fridge and made a more careful inspection of its contents. There was a bag of Thousand Villages fair-trade coffee and a half-gallon carton of milk. John looked at the expiration label. Fresh. A box of Cadbury chocolates. Fancy. These sweet people took care of every detail.

From the front porch he looked around. A wind chime sounded pleasant notes as John did stretches. The air was gloriously cool, the way Kansas mornings could be this time of year before the sun burns the comfort away. A woman across the street wearing a red scarf that matched her Camry backed out of her driveway. She waved then slowed to a stop in the middle of the street and rolled down her passenger window. "Reverend Reimer? Welcome to the neighborhood!"

"That's me," John said. "Happy to be here."

"Hi, I'm Karen Rempel. I want to drop off a welcome casserole later but have to run right now. We are thrilled to have you in Marion Hills!"

John walked west a block to Monroe Avenue and then north, crossing Teak, Hackberry, and Locust streets. He could see the high school a couple of blocks north. It was of recent vintage, apparently built in two phases (though the builders had done a good job of matching the brick). The first was during the energy crisis, hence the pillbox windows and joyless fortress structure partly built into the hill for temperature conservation, and then a second phase included a library with significant expanses of soaring glass. Twenty years after the oil embargo, the architects had rediscovered the joy of windows.

He started a slow jog to the football field and the track laid out around it. He walked onto the track to get the feel. A stout young man with a lick of blond hair hanging in his eyes came toward him from beneath the stands. The cargo shorts, camouflage tank, and flip-flops, plus the sunscreened nose combined for an impression of casual executive function. "Good morning, I'm Oscar. May I help you?"

John introduced himself and shook the boy's hand. "I'm new in town, John Reimer. I've heard good things about your track facility here. Franz Schlegel told me you welcome runners. I hope that's still true."

"Yeah, we work to keep it nice. And you're very welcome." The boy looked Reimer over and glanced at the headband. "Looks like you have the track to yourself until about eight this morning, when JV soccer practice starts. Enjoy!" The boy sauntered off.

John knew immediately the track would elevate his game. It buoyed him up. He wondered if the synthetics gave runners an advantage, and the sensation under his feet made him want more. Stopwatch in hand, he started a warm-up lap at the middle of the straightaway in front of the empty stands. When he made the complete circle, he thumbed the stopwatch start and picked up his pace.

On the second lap he spotted another runner ahead. She was dressed in purple shorts and a black-and-yellow Steelers jersey with the number 51 and the name Toews across her shoulders. She moved efficiently. Watching her and trying to match her stride for stride, John could see that she imagined herself as a younger woman.

She made John aware of his flawed running form. He tried not to chop the track with his stride—a tendency of his—and concentrated on lengthening his stride. More efficient horizontal energy, less wasted vertical motion. He tried to avoid the pain, but perversely, he knew as a runner that some kinds of pain were good for him. Effort. When he looked up again, to his surprise he had begun to close the distance. He held himself back and on lap four began a steady acceleration. Watching the runner ahead was like keeping a sleek pace car in focus. He tried to stay on his regular pace. She must have slowed down—was she encouraging him to catch up? By the sixth lap, he was running beside her. She was not even breathing hard.

"Morning," he said, powering ahead to avert the temptation of an appraising stare. He could hear her footsteps behind his. On lap seven she was still on his tail but at the beginning of eight, he turned on what remained of his nearly sixty-year-old finishing kick and began to feel the burn. He came across the line, clicked the stopwatch, and ran another half lap. He put his hands on his knees, bending over to get more air into his lungs.

She arrived at his side a few moments later and said, "You run real good, as the locals like to say. You always use a stopwatch?"

"On a track, yes. In Chicago by the lake, I measure pace by certain milestones."

"What do you do on a mile? Don't worry, I won't ask your age bracket." She stopped her steady stream of remarks and stuck out her hand. She beamed as if sitting in the back of a Rose Bowl parade convertible. "I'm babbling a little. Carol Campbell," she said. "Levi and Eva's oldest daughter."

He shook her hand and waited for her to continue the banter.

"And you must be John Reimer, if I remember a face. Welcome." She wiped a forearm across her perspiring brow. She had a pleasing scent, guava with a light sprinkling of pepper. He looked at her. The doctor who had wielded the knife had done so skillfully; the only sign was the skin on her cheeks, maybe more taut than smooth, and the Botoxed brow of perfection above a perfect nose. Her smile was tight and luminous over the shining dentistry.

"My friend Alan told me this track was worth a run. He wasn't wrong."

"We're so glad you're here," Carol said. "And just as sorry about the news of Viola. When did you arrive?" she asked, as they walked a cooldown lap together.

"Yesterday afternoon. Alan Wiebe and I drove from Chicago."

"Oh, that's right," Carol said. "Doesn't he have some family reunion going on? Franz said you were coming by the dealership this morning to pick up a loaner."

"Yes. I want to try out the breakfast scene downtown before I see Franz. What do you suggest?"

"Little Pleasures," Carol said. She walked with the same easy lope as her run. "They now offer eggs Benedict." She gave John a sideways look.

He said, "Eggs Benedict, huh? That's a big-city menu item for a small town."

"She's a big-city girl, that Rachel. From Honolulu. And we all know Marion Hills should not be underestimated."

"How'd she end up here?"

"She still doesn't believe she's in Kansas."

John laughed out loud. "I know the feeling. That touch of culture shock. I have the sense this town has gone cosmopolitan. Anyway, it's a pleasure talking with you."

"What's your normal run?" Carol challenged, wanting to continue talking. "You run every day?"

"When I'm in a good phase. Trying to work back to three or four miles. Totally out of shape and running above my head."

"You're doing fine," said the tall blonde, appraising him with warm approval. She put a manicured hand on his arm. "And again, please accept Campbell's and my deepest condolences about Viola. See you soon." She turned and jogged off the track toward the parking lot.

He found the locker room with bathroom under the stadium. The smells of witch hazel and commercial dryers tumbling uniforms floated through the complex. He heard water spraying a concrete floor and young voices, youthful horseplay, echoing down the hall. John walked back out on the field, past a trophy case filled with the achievements of several generations of Marion Hills athletes. He wondered if Carol had heard yet about Jeffrey Arnheim's death in Denver. Given the phone numbers John had culled from that split-level in Commerce City, it was clear there had been communication between Campbell and Jeffrey on a pretty regular basis. Jeffrey had even written the phone number on the inside cover of *Left Behind*. But there'd be plenty of time for that conversation, and John wondered who would bring it up. Now he watched the water boy pull his wagon on little rubber inflated tires up the ramp and onto the track. A couple of orange plastic bins on the wagon announced Gatorade. On the field, a few guys in a circle practiced one-touch passing in front of goal.

⁓⁊

In the time John was chasing Carol around the high school track, a steady stream of parishioners had dropped various food offerings on his front porch. When he returned to the parsonage, the door was blocked for days by packages, decorative tins, hot-dish Pyrex carefully covered with foil, and multicolored heavy Tupperware containers.

John made several trips from porch to kitchen, carrying the food in and depositing it in the fridge. When he ran out of room there, he slid several pans into the freezer. There were chicken-and-rice casseroles, a couple of tuna dishes, and lots of cookies. These people didn't skimp on dessert. There were stuffed shells in sauce and a lasagna. There was a pan of pork chops with instructions for rewarming taped to the foil. There was a tray of seven-layer dip covered with salsa. He was happy to see the chicken and rice had plenty of crispy bits on top. They looked like home-made croutons and not panko, not crushed potato chips or frozen Tater Tots out of a Sam's Club package, for crying out loud. *Such a food snob I'm becoming*, he thought. Nancy's influence had already begun to leach into his simple life. He thought of the sommelier at the Whistling Swan.

He had just finished packing the food into cold storage when the phone rang.

"Hello, John Reimer here," he answered.

"John, this is Marv. I don't want to bother you, and I can tell you're busy. I get back to Kansas tonight, a little sooner than I expected. Mind if I swing by?"

"I would be offended if you didn't." John stood holding the fridge door open, surveying the bounty. I have all kinds of food to make a hungry man happy."

"I want to talk with you about a couple of details. We got a coroner's report. No surprises. I met with the realtor, what's his name, Fenimore? Boy, was that interesting. And we found Jeffrey's car . . ." Marv paused, as if trying to find his voice. "Way too much to say on the phone. More details later. See you around seven?"

"Seven is good. Alan will be here, too. The casserole brigade has been unleashed."

Marv began laughing. "Good! I hope they're totally out of control."

John hung up the phone. The doorbell rang again. A leathery woman of diminutive size stood on the porch holding two plastic shopping bags. In her posture and the patient way she waited, she reminded him of his Chicago church secretary, Mildred. He felt a pang of homesickness.

The woman put down the shopping bags and took John's hand in both of hers. "Reverend John Reimer. God has sent you to us. Welcome to Marion Hills."

The woman was of indeterminate age. She wore a black scarf and no makeup or jewelry. Her eyes reminded John of a very smart crow. She wore a clean khaki jacket with lots of pockets with button flaps, almost like a Unitarian birdwatching coat, and her Levi's and a pair of sturdy work boots completed the outfit. She projected the countenance of a Sherpa guide or a Sioux medicine man. Hadn't he seen her face somewhere before, maybe in a conference directory? Sure enough, she introduced herself and confirmed it: Ann Hiebert, retired missionary nurse and midwife from Kodaikanal, India, the last old-timer of the famous family, several generations of which had inhabited India, Pakistan, and Ceylon for the past century.

"Please call me John—"

"Okay, John, let me clarify this situation. I have brought you a chicken tikka dinner with sides. There is dal and rice. Other things. Naan. Chutneys. Sometimes I get carried away with my directions, so I typed them up for the preparation and how to serve. I don't need to bore you with details or micromanage, which, believe me, I am capable of doing. All the food is in these two bags, and do you mind if I come in?"

"Please do." John led her into the kitchen but on the way, she surged ahead and arrived at the kitchen counter first. She swung the shopping bags up on the surface and began removing plastic containers, banging them in rapid succession as if to make a point. "I've labeled the contents of each container so you should not be confused. And these are directions. If I try to explain, you'll just forget everything anyway." She opened the fridge. "I see you are out of room. Have you checked your basement fridge?"

She proceeded to carry the shopping bags downstairs and returned five minutes later, saying, "Everything is in the basement backup fridge in the utility room. I plugged it in. I recommend you not freeze this dinner but eat it sooner rather than later."

"You make a powerful display," John said. "There are a few places on Devon in Chicago where I like the Indian food."

"Yes, I know Devon. There's a market up there where I used to go whenever I came through the city." She paused, as if remembering past lives. "For the condiments. The coriander and mint chutney. The lime pickle."

"Lime pickle is an acquired taste," John said. "I'm not quite there yet. But thank you for writing instructions. That's thoughtful of you."

"Food aside," Ann said, "I want to talk with you about your loss. About Viola. How are you doing?" She took his hands in hers and looked at him directly. Her look was hard to escape. "I don't know if now is the right time. I sense there are things you could talk about if I asked the right questions. You appear puzzled. A wise woman in Bangalore once said that to me."

"You see into the heart of things, Ann. Always have. And that talk would do me good. I meant to ask you, how is life treating you in Marion Hills? It must be a radical change from Kodaikanal."

"It is. I am getting used to it. At my age, I had better. Fortunately, one can escape now and then to Wichita or Kansas City. I really ought to visit you in Chicago."

"You would be more than welcome. Hop the train. And I understand your wish to escape. I know something about that."

She gave him a knowing smile and brought him in close for a hug. After consulting a man's chunky wristwatch on her forearm, she said, "I have a shift to volunteer at the Etcetera Shop. We will take good care of you, John Reimer. See you Sunday!"

Chapter 13

Franz, scion of Marion Hills, was Levi Schlegel's oldest son. He had run Schlegel Motors for more than three decades, building it into one of the heartland's most successful automobile dealerships. He rode out the recession in style after deciding to take on the additional management of a Toyota dealership in Hutchinson. That decision proved prescient. For a time, he was able to move more Japanese compacts and subcompacts than the bread-and-butter Ford pickups, SUVs, and Jeeps that triggered his traditional base. The bigger the tires, the more pumped the buyers, Franz liked to say. In the late 1980s he spun off the Toyota business because he was tired of the commute twice a week.

He surprised everybody by acquiring Land Rover for the dealership in Marion Hills. His detractors wondered why he'd embraced a snobby British import. He was unmoved by critics. He had an evolving customer base out of Wichita and Kansas City, even Oklahoma City and Waco, for that matter. His client Rolodex blew up with ranchers and doctors and lawyers—not to mention the engineers and management at Halston. Some of these individuals didn't care for F-150s or paramilitary vehicles that carried the whiff of Patton and, at best, unrefined creature comforts. These buyers wanted the feel of all-terrain and even global mastery but with a leather interior and genuine oak-grain dashboard. Grizzled old college boys, many of them, they thought of themselves as thoughtful conservatives who read *The Wall Street Journal* and George Will. There was even a smattering of aging success stories who didn't mind being called "liberal" so long as you still believed in American exceptionalism. They didn't apologize for their status. They simply wanted to cultivate a softer edge. Franz was there for them, too.

John thought about Franz as he entered the showroom. The heavy glass-and-steel door glided liquidly on its pneumatic hinge and closed without a sound behind him. It was quiet as a library, except for a faint backbeat of beachy-sounding pop that slid over the polished concrete floor. A woman's voice whispered plaintively about the "sweetest Shamu"—or was it "taboo"? The walls of the main showroom were finished out in layered slabs of rough limestone, culled from a quarry in the Flint Hills of Chase County twenty-five miles away. The stone showed the hand of an expert mason who knew how to lay rock down and preserve its raw, rugged beauty. He'd been hired by the original owner of the auto dealership, a man named Paulson, who had sold out his last financial interest to Franz's father, Levi Schlegel, in 1955.

Levi didn't need to change much of what Paulson had done for the business to succeed, but he had better financing. He had acquired a controlling interest in two local Kansas banks, added recently to his growing portfolio of assets. When Franz assumed management and expanded the business beyond Ford, the cultivation of careful aesthetics and attention to detail paid off handsomely. There was a main service desk in the center of the space, and a restored Stickley library table, which held a variety of brochures. Against the rear wall, a pristine metal drinking fountain hummed underneath logos for Ford, Jeep, and Land Rover, which, through some trick of lighting and the illusion of disappearing mounting bolts, seemed to defy gravity, hovering off the limestone wall. Nearby was another mission table that Franz nicknamed the "Teddy Roosevelt"; it featured a couple of fancy coffee machines and a small glass-fronted fridge stocked with foreign-named mineral water and Coca-Cola.

The overall impression conveyed was of aesthetics, luxury, history, and power, but understated. One sensed a sanctum where important transactions were meant to happen, and the effect on potential customers generated self-fulfilling prophecies. To buy a car at Schlegel Motors, a person entered a ritual space that drenched him in pride and self-worth. Doing business with Franz instilled confidence. Big men who entered the showroom with intent to purchase invariably exited with even more confidence after closing the deal.

Although the lot outside was packed with new cars and pickups, there were only six vehicles on the showroom floor: facing the door, a black F-150 mega-pickup with fat tires, Rough Country vertex shock absorbers, and plenty of attitude; a multicolored quartet of Jeeps, one with a roll bar, and one tricked out in pink highlights; and, at the far end, as if in brooding counterpoint to Detroit, a sleek silver Land Rover Discovery with enough wraparound glass to panel an air-control tower. It was a vehicle that might lift off from a launchpad.

At the back of the showroom, a door stood ajar. Franz sat behind his desk with a phone cradled against his ear, engaged in deep conversation. To bide his time, John climbed up on the running board of the F-150 and sat in the driver's seat. Then he looked at the showroom and tried to imagine it through Franz's eyes.

There were always rumors that Franz had bigger management offers to consider in Kansas City and Denver, but he had told more than one person in his "aw shucks" style that he wasn't interested—in much the same manner that his father, Levi, had shrugged off journalists' claims that the vast extent of his holdings rivaled the Koch brothers'. Levi liked to say that if he were twenty years younger, that might come true, but it was too late now. Plus, Franz had way too much flying to do, ferrying his dad to business meetings around the Midwest in the family's Beechcraft. Levi had given up his license when he turned seventy-five and preferred that his son take the controls.

The Schlegels were content in Marion Hills. Franz liked his Rotary and Elks Lodge memberships and the simple pleasures of doing business with local people. He had sold a used Chevy Impala to John many years earlier when the new minister at Ebenholzer needed wheels. It was a solid, reliable car in mint condition. John understood why Franz was successful. He didn't haggle or waste his customers' time. He priced cars fairly, and with used cars, he didn't make up stories. He took care of paperwork and didn't dump it on the buyer. He understood they wanted minimum hassle whether purchasing or leasing. He set up reasonable payment terms with First National downtown or the credit union or one of several banks in nearby counties. He made life easier, not harder, for his people. That was worth something in the car business. According to well-placed financial gossips, Franz's customer base—a closely guarded secret—had evolved to about 25 percent out-of-staters, a rather remarkable record.

Franz cradled the receiver and looked out his office door. A big smile creased his face when he noticed John watching him from the cab of the F-150. He came out of his office. John hopped down from the heights of the running board as gracefully as he could without hurting himself, and the men embraced.

"Welcome back, John Reimer," Franz said.

"Franz Schlegel, it is good to see you. And it's great to be back," John said. "Although the circumstances are a little strange."

"Yeah, I heard you've been butting heads with bad guys in Chicago. Why am I not surprised?"

"You talking about the thugs or Waldo?" John deadpanned.

Franz laughed with genuine glee. "Boy, you've still got it, don't you?" he said, gripping John's shoulder.

John sized up the car salesman. Franz still had that healthy head of graying, protein-rich hair characteristic of many Ukrainian Mennonites, of a density that practically made it a pelt. Combed back meticulously, it was the reason his buddies on the golf course sometimes called him "Michael Landon." He was dressed in khakis, tasseled oxblood loafers, and an expensive-looking knit black shirt open at the collar. He looked like a puffed-up version of Gary Player, more like a moderate Democrat than the small-town Republican he actually was. He liked Bob Dole and Nancy Kassebaum; he liked fiscal responsibility. Franz was a serene force for stability in Marion Hills, and although he had been invited to run for mayor several times, he'd always declined, saying he needed to look after his parents and run the business.

"Hey, Dad says he wants you to come by the house, and not to dally. Eva wouldn't mind saying hello, either."

"What's a good time?"

"How about tomorrow morning? Nine or so."

"I'll do that."

"He wants to ask about Vi. Her death hit him hard. He talked about it for weeks," said Franz, looking at John directly. "I'm sorry she had to go this way." Franz tried to control the crack in his voice. "I'm trying to imagine what the last fifteen years were like for the two of you." He shook his head and wiped his eyes unapologetically.

"I find it hard to describe even for myself," John said. "But it was her time. How about your dad? He's what now, eighty-one?"

"Almost. He says he wants to have the serious conversations while there's still light in the day. He never cared for small talk, but now he really doesn't. He's worried about his health."

John looked at Franz and asked, "Anything in particular?"

"We're all a little concerned. Some shortness of breath. It doesn't come at a good time. Says he feels lightheaded. Then he chalks it up to old age and says 'Forget about it' and puts in ten-hour days in the home office—same as it ever was."

"Your father was never one for small talk, that's for sure," John said. "He still traveling?"

"Not as much. If he wants to go somewhere, I fly him out in the plane. He let his pilot's license lapse after he upgraded to the Bonanza. Hey—I want to get you that car. Let me show you some things."

"Good. I was afraid you'd try to put me in this little number." John gestured at the Jeep with the roll bar.

"Quite the cherry bomb, isn't it?" Franz said. "Sort of like a rich man's toy in Pismo. But not exactly an executive vehicle. Fun, but lacking in dignity."

They sauntered out into the May afternoon. The staccato burp of an air compressor and speed wrench echoed from the service garage behind the dealership.

John asked Franz, "The family all good? Your kids still on the West Coast?"

"Justin is. Made partner in his firm and living in Palo Alto. Lucy moved out to New York a year ago. Susie is there right now with the daughter looking at condos in Brooklyn. Lucy's a senior loan officer at Deutsche Bank but has her eye on bigger things."

"Why am I not surprised?" John said.

"I told her if she gets the analyst job at Goldman Sachs, she should at least buy a house." Laughing, Franz led John to another part of the lot. "You still have the running bug?"

"I do," John said. "In fact, I tried out your new high school track this morning. Found myself in a foot race with your sister, of all people."

"I hope you showed her some mettle," Franz said. "Carol is pretty driven about her regime. She'll never admit it, but she's worried how she looks on TV." Franz caught John raising his eyebrows and gave him a sympathetic eye roll.

"I know," he said. "What with Campbell's speaking engagements and the small circuit talk shows, she obsesses."

"I understand Campbell is looking for a new network sponsor," John said.

"He stays busy," Franz said. "He's on the road much of the time, or should I say, in the air. Pushes himself."

Franz sauntered ahead of John, pointing out a red Honda Civic, with red velour upholstery and black rubber bumpers. It was trim, rhomboid.

"Last owner was a medical student in Kansas City," said Franz. "Became an oncologist. Took good care of it, though our cleaning crew complained about how much cat hair they had to vacuum out of the back seat. Five-speed manual transmission. Curious dashboard with these little sunken spaces. I call it the TV dinner design. You can pour your milk and Cheerios and eat it right off the top of the dash if you're in a hurry."

"Good thing I'm not allergic to cats," said John as he walked around the vehicle. He opened the vehicle door and got into the driver's seat. "Comfy," he said. "And the manual transmission isn't a problem. I'm open to a compact but—"

"I hear you," Franz said. They walked around the lot and passed a pleasant half hour. When Franz put his hand on the hood of a big boat of a white Ford, John prepared himself for the closing spiel.

"The Crown Victoria," said Franz. "When Detroit still knew how to build a sedan. This sat in Mrs. Ebel's garage for five years without being driven, and when she passed, we acquired it at the estate sale. It's like it was curated. Mileage is seventeen thousand, cross my heart on that odometer, and solid as a rock. Built like a tank. Very comfortable ride. The thing about the Crown Victoria is if you're ever in a scrape you probably walk away. Can't say the same about the Civic."

"Didn't police departments used to order these by the dozen?" John asked.

"Yeah, in some places they still do."

John needed to get over to the church office, where Linda Ebel would give him a tour of the place. Maybe she would have additional insight into her late grandmother's vehicle, which John drove off the Schlegel Motors' lot thirty minutes later. It was a beast all right, and it boasted a big, comfortable ride. He laughed—a cop car. It struck him as a little vain, but for Marion Hills, it was also properly pastoral. Franz called it "dignity."

John had just enough time to stop at Little Pleasures for coffee and a bagel with sun-dried-tomato cream cheese. He introduced himself to Rachel, telling her he'd already heard a dozen stories. Rachel shook his hand and said the bagel was in an experimental stage and still didn't show adequate toughness. "I had an assistant who kept wanting to turn them into muffins," she said. "Had to let her go. Girl didn't understand that a proper bagel should make your jaw ache."

John told her the bagel he was eating had "full presence" and made some more amiable chitchat before driving the eight blocks northeast to Marion Hills Mennonite. The car drove like a pliant, large obedience animal. He could barely hear the purr of the V-8. He found the minister's parking sign in a row of diagonal spots off the back alley and eased the beast between the yellow lines. When he exited the car and nudged the driver's door shut, it closed with an amiable *thunk*. He carried his bulging briefcase into the new workplace.

Chapter 14

The door to Linda Ebel's office was open, so John glanced in. She had her back to the door. Envelopes were stacked on her desk, and she was annotating a list with a pencil, intermittently leaning forward to enter data on her computer. She put the pencil between her teeth to type. Her blonde hair was rubber-banded in a ponytail, and she had the posture of a straight-A student or a 4-H winner. She was concentrating and didn't notice John, so he decided not to interrupt and walked toward the new copper nameplate affixed at the end of the hallway above a door that stood slightly ajar: Reverend John Reimer, Senior Minister.

The desk was massive and made of a walnut slab. John sat down and contemplated the row of reference volumes before him on the desk's surface, between carved-lion bookends in the style of ancient Assyria: Merriam-Webster's, a thesaurus, *The Chicago Manual of Style*, a fat Funk and Wagnalls unabridged dictionary and the two-volume condensed *Oxford English Dictionary*. *Gospel Parallels*, in a tattered blue dust jacket, stood next to four different English translations of the Bible, including the well-worn New Revised Standard Version. The desk was parked at an angle facing the interior doorway so John could meet visitors and avoid the glare of morning sun. Two walls of built-in bookcases were packed floor to ceiling.

Tschetter, longtime occupant of this office before his sudden death by heart attack, had preached in this church for more than two decades. He had cultivated a reputation for polished preaching and published regularly in the denominational periodicals. His death had occurred late the previous fall, only months before John managed to avoid being car-bombed in Chicago.

Who knew that a sedentary job came accompanied by so many lethal possibilities? John looked at the wall art. There was exactly one framed picture in the space, beside the office window, which was partly obscured by blue pull curtains. He didn't care for the drapes, and even less for the picture, a cheap reproduction of a painting in a warped frame probably fished from a Walmart sales bin. The shepherd—an outdoorsy Highland lad bearing fair resemblance to Sean Connery—was captured in the act of herding sheep with the help of a scruffy Scottish collie. John decided the painting would have to go. He'd wait a couple of weeks. No reason to rush changes to the symbolic order of things, find out first the provenance of the picture. Perhaps it had been a gift from a church member. Linda would probably know.

Right then she appeared in the doorway. She walked over and leaned across the desk to shake his hand.

"Welcome, Reverend Reimer, we meet at last. I'm happy to see you found your office. You're a little sneaky. How did you get in here without me noticing?"

"Years of practice lurking around churches," John said. "I could see you were fully engaged in your task, and I wanted to come in here and sit for a while. I find myself communing with Brother Tschetter's spirit."

Linda listened. "Did you receive any messages from him?"

"Yes. I learned about his superb ability to organize, his fondness for the NRSV, and the allegory of the flock and the shepherd. Was that a congregational gift?" John asked, pointing to the picture.

"I'm told it was a present from a Reedley nephew of his. He was fond of it. I have to say his death was quite a surprise. I'm sure you heard the details from Waldo."

"Yes, W.W. filled me in."

"No warning. Just another Saturday, late fall. Tschetter was mowing the lawn at the parsonage—he preferred chopping up the leaves rather than raking them—and he went inside for a glass of water. Ida asked him if he was feeling all right. He said not really . . . and just like that he was gone. They got him to the hospital within ten minutes, but a paramedic told me it was ten minutes too late."

"How is Ida doing?"

"She moved to North Newton and got an apartment at Kindred Bethel."

"I'll have to visit," said John. "That reminds me. I'm grateful for the membership roll you sent with your comments. Very useful. That short list of people I need to visit my first week. Anyone I need to see right away?"

Linda paused. "I'm not sure how I break this to you. Recent news directly affects several members."

"Who?"

"Doris Baumgartner. She is inactive but still on the roll. Her younger son Billy Ray was baptized and accepted into membership, too, though he was just a tyke then, maybe twelve years old. He hasn't been inside Marion Hills Church in a long time."

"And . . . ?"

Linda twirled her ponytail with an index finger and chose her words.

"Let me cut to the chase," she said. "Doris's two sons were involved. Billy Ray shot his older half brother, Dexter. Then he shot another guy, supposedly his best buddy. A double murder. This happened two days ago. It's the first double murder here in a hundred years. The old-timers are comparing it to the Clutter family killing in Garden City. That was before my time, but I've read Truman Capote. I'll bet you remember that."

John sat down in his chair. "I do. That happened close to where I grew up." He looked at Linda and said, "I don't know what to say. Honestly, I'm stunned to hear this."

"All of us are in disbelief. You might have to visit the whole town, if you want to know the truth. People are freaking out. I am so sickened telling you this on your first day here. I'm sorry."

John saw the box of Kleenex on the corner of the desk and pulled one out and handed it to Linda. "Any of this out yet in the local papers? You're the first to tell me."

Except for the tears, she maintained her composure. "Some folks are so spooked they're not sure what to say, I guess. We only have the weekly here in town. It made the *Wichita Eagle*, though. . . Do you mind if I sit down? Would you like a cup of coffee? I keep the coffee maker in my office."

"No, I'm good, thanks." John gestured to the compact sofa by the door that faced his desk. Linda sat down and looked at him with an expression of curiosity, as if speculating what he would say or do next. She clasped her hands around her knee. She wore black jeans and sensible flats, a pink sweater and a charm necklace, no earrings. She tapped her foot nervously on the rug.

John recalled what Alan had said about this secretary once, somewhat disparagingly. She was his third cousin and had grown up in Durham so Alan felt like he could talk freely. "She has learned all the gestures of meekness and submission," he said. *That is one of Alan's flaws*, thought

John. *That familiarity gives him license.* He had said Linda was "just like so many of these nice Mennonite girls in Kansas. You can't tell if she's dumb or if she was just trained that way."

John had nearly launched into a lecture against Alan's misogyny when he finished with a surprise twist: "Then she springs a remark on you, totally unexpected, that reminds you she is four steps ahead of whatever you were thinking."

John looked at Linda closely and thought about how she had presented her bombshell. She didn't strike him as dumb at all—in fact, he was speculating how many church secretaries in America had read Capote, and he read in her eyes that she had high emotional intelligence. She wanted to say more, but didn't know how to start—he could see it.

John leaned back behind his desk. "Can you fill me in on more details?"

"It happened yesterday—I mean the arrest. I am so sorry to hit you with this. It's not what I imagined telling you today. The story I first heard is that Sheriff Veblen picked up Billy Ray for a double murder. Billy Ray is in county jail right now waiting transport to Abilene. Baumgartner's son Dexter and Billy Ray's buddy Rufus are both in the county morgue on a slab. Dexter was Billy Ray's half brother. Did I already say that?"

"And who was this other guy?"

"Rufus was Billy Ray's best friend. They always ran around together."

"I still can't quite comprehend what you are telling me. Billy Ray killed his half brother and his best friend."

Linda nodded.

"Can you please give me Mrs. Baumgartner's address?"

Linda went back to her office and returned with a slip of paper which she gave to John. She also handed him a copy of the Wichita paper. "You'll want to read this."

"Thanks," said John. "Before I forget, about Sunday . . . I understand you want a fifteen-minute meditation. Something of a personal nature from me. I think you called it a reintroduction."

"That's right. We didn't think asking you to prepare the whole order of service made sense. The committee will continue to take care of that. You can join the committee next month." Her eyes showed a mischievous gleam. "We don't want to pile on the homework all at once."

She added, "I'm sure you know Reverend Tschetter was much loved. But his forte was not personal visitation, and he would have been the first to tell you that. So if you can give us something interesting to chew on

Sunday mornings, that's a bonus. Aim for fifteen minutes, and never over twenty. We've had a few pulpit supply preachers come in who loved the sound of their own voice. It didn't work out well."

"Understood. In seminary they school you on how to preach but not how to stop. I think I can manage that. And I think you said you needed a sermon title in advance. How about this?"

He dashed off something on a sheet of yellow legal pad, tore it off, and gave it to Linda. She looked at it and nodded her approval.

"Thank you. I'm working on the bulletin now."

John said, "I'll drive over to the sheriff's office and introduce myself and see if Billy Ray is talking to visitors. Then I'll pay a visit to Mrs. Baumgartner."

"She would like that, I think. Though she's not very sociable. This might just turn her into a recluse." Linda looked again at the note John had scribbled. "I'll get this title into the bulletin. It's such a pleasure to meet you. Is there anything else you need from me?"

"I like to come in early on Sunday mornings. I'll be here around nine or so."

"Good. I'll see you then. Oh, and here's the key to the outer door and your office in case you want to lock it up. Tschetter always did."

"Much appreciated." John grabbed his briefcase and left his office door ajar. He went outside and climbed into his Crown Victoria to drive off to the sheriff's office for his first official pastoral visit in Marion Hills.

Chapter 15

Veblen sat in an easy chair beside his desk with a book on his lap and a bulldog pipe in his mouth. His Carhartt duck vest over a checkered shirt was adorned with a tin star, and his bald head showed above his wire reading glasses. When John pressed the little bell on the countertop, the sheriff stood up and put his glasses in his front pocket. He was six feet tall and gave John a glance of stout appraisal.

"Good morning, sir, may I help you?" he asked, shaking the hand extended in his direction.

"Hello, Sheriff, pleased to meet you. Gustave Thorstein Veblen?"

"Yes. What can I do for you?"

"I'm John Reimer, new in town. Here on loan for a few months to Marion Mennonite Church."

"Ah, the new preacher from Chicago. Perhaps you've arrived to bring us a little excitement. Welcome to Marion Hills, Reverend."

"Call me John."

Veblen puffed on his pipe. "Come on back and let's visit."

Sheriff Veblen showed John to another easy chair in what seemed a living room behind the business counter. He appeared to do most of his work at the round table, with the desk mainly for show and manila folders stacked in alarming disarray. A pile of hardcover books sat at the desk's corner. John read the spines: local history and western lore, Chase County, Manifest Destiny, Sitting Bull, Fort Riley, Bleeding Kansas, Schlesinger's *The Age of Jackson*.

"I was expecting you, John. I hear you're famous for getting around and chatting up the locals. Everybody seems to have a story about you."

John said, "My gifts are modest and fading fast. I hear your life has been more exciting than usual. You're my second stop this morning."

"You read the *Eagle*."

"My church secretary filled me in."

"Linda Ebel, yes. Quick as lightning, isn't she?" Veblen leaned back in his chair and relit his pipe and a small cloud of smoke circled his head. "Do you mind?"

"Not at all," John said. "But I have a question, Sheriff Veblen. Any relation to the expert on America's leisure class? I ask because I recently visited his cabin on Washington Island in Door County, Wisconsin."

"Ah, yes, where he wrote many of his books during the summer. The glorious life of an academic," Gustav said. "I am related. He's my great-great-great-uncle, or something like that. Though you Mennonites with all your genealogical bullshit should be able to explain it to me. I'm still waiting."

"How did you end up in Marion Hills?" John said.

"I would ask you the same question," Veblen said. "I've been in law enforcement since I graduated from college in western Pennsylvania. Spent a decade in San Antonio. Then another in Traverse City, Michigan. Loved it except for winters. Decided to split the geographical distance and settled here in Kansas at the edge of the Flint Hills. It sounded more romantic than it is. So I hear you started out near Dodge. Meade, is that right? Suppose you're a font of information about the Dalton Gang, too."

"I could show you their hideout. Some things seem more important in books than in reality. Nondescript house. Dirt tunnel for the getaway. Not much to see. It's a sad little patch. You can almost feel the local resentment that the James brothers got more famous."

"I suppose that's why we need writers and philosophers, John. So, what in particular brings you to my palace of wisdom?"

"I hear you have an inmate here named Billy Ray. I hoped to pay him a visit since he's a member of my congregation."

Veblen raised an eyebrow. "The boy is a tough nut, on his way to Abilene shortly. And, sure, I can introduce you. Don't know how talkative he'll be."

"From the sound of things, he's in a world of trouble. Welder at Halston, am I right? Are you at liberty to fill me in a little before I ask him dumb preacher questions?"

"Granted," Veblen said. "He came in here by his lonesome and said he was turning himself in. Put his Glock and a silencer and some ammo on the counter and sat in that very chair where you're sitting now. That was evening before last. 'I killed my brother and my best friend a couple hours ago in my double-wide and I'm here to make a full confession,' was how he started out. He gave me an address on the west side of town and wrote down his full statement, which I have in a secure place. I had my deputy, Jerry, lock him up. Boy was meek as a lamb.

"I drove out to Billy Ray's house and checked out his story. Sure enough, everything lined up. He gave me the keys to his place. I went over there and found the bodies. The older brother was crumpled up, sitting in a chair. Had a hole in the back of his skull. The exit wound out his forehead looked like someone took a wrecking bar to him. The other guy, his buddy, was under the table. Had a couple holes in his face and had slid off his chair. I stepped gingerly around the puddles of blood and tried to make sense of it. The scene looked like a card game gone wrong. The most ridiculous, cheesy frontier cliché I've ever born witness to. The other two guys who survived Billy Ray's tantrum have been picked up by the cops in Junction City. I just got word on that. They may have more to say.

"Anyway, once I realized what I was looking at, I called in the Kansas Bureau of Investigation—Wichita. My deputy and I sealed off the building and waited till they arrived.

"When I got back here, I asked Billy Ray why he killed his brother and he said, 'He's been fucking me ever since I was five years old. This was a long time coming.'

"Did you say, 'Fucking me,' or 'Fucking me over'?" John asked.

"No. He seemed to think it was self-explanatory."

"What I'm saying is that sometimes meaning can hang on a vowel, know what I mean?"

"I got you—'ever' or 'over.' I'll think about that. I'm no analyst, I'm just a simple lawman. I'd take it at face value though. I think the guy meant it literally."

Gustav continued: "I also learned there was a woman as a point of contention between him and his brother Dexter. Girl named Trixie. 'Friends called her Trixie Mae,' says Billy. He had a picture of her in his wallet. Quite a looker. Billy Ray said she worked in the 'entertainment industry in Branson.'

"'Entertainment industry?' I asked.

"'Yeah, steak-house and casino hostess,' he said. 'Then an exotic dancer. She said it paid ten times as much, and she was nothing if not a gamer.'

"So, both brothers seem to have had a thing for her. Billy Ray said, 'Sharing didn't work out too well and it ain't supposed to, some things is against nature.' When Dexter started doing Trixie, that was the last straw for baby brother, I guess."

John sat and listened. After a moment he asked, "So there were five guys in the room, and two of them got away?"

"Yeah. They've just been picked up. According to Billy Ray, right before he started shooting, a mound of bills was piled in front of Dexter, next to his cards, face-down on the table. Texas Hold 'Em was the game. Dexter was on a roll and was cleaning up 'as usual,' said Billy Ray. And there was a stiletto stuck point down into the table by the cards."

"What set Billy Ray off?" asked John.

"He told me the last words his brother Dexter said to him were, 'I had you pegged for a loser, but I never thought you were a pussy.' Billy Ray had just returned from the bathroom and was standing behind his older brother who put his cards face down and didn't turn around and didn't look up. But as he insulted his little brother, he jammed his knife point into the table, thunked it real hard.

"'Don't threaten me, bro,' said Billy Ray. 'Put the goddam knife away or you'll be sorry.' Dexter ignored him. Billy Ray stood behind him and screwed the silencer onto the barrel of his Glock and stuck it against the back of Dexter's head and pulled the trigger."

"A silencer," said John. "That's an interesting detail. A big-city touch on a small-town crime."

Gustav gave John a stoic look. "Yes, that's what I thought. You have experience with silencers?"

"Some, indirectly," John said. "Did Billy Ray say why he used one?"

Gustav winced. "Yeah. He said he grew up hearing his mom carp about all the noise he and his brother made most of the time and she didn't like it that the neighbors talked. Billy Ray said he didn't want to disturb the neighborhood."

"Thoughtful," John said. "Mighty polite of him."

"Indeed," Gustav said. "After he was shot, Dexter thrashed forward and his forehead bounced off the edge of the table. The card game was pretty much over by then. Billy Ray's friend Rufus looked at the mess and said, 'What in the hell are you doing, Billy Ray?' And Billy Ray says he told Rufus, 'I don't need no sermon from you, neither.'

"Billy Ray claims Rufus reached for something in his pocket, so he had no choice but to act in self-defense. He sent two rounds into Rufus's face while shouting, 'Shut your goddamn piehole.'

"Rufus looked at Billy Ray and then at the ceiling for an instant before the blood from the holes in his cheek and forehead covered his face. He slid down in his chair to the floor. A pistol fell out of his pocket on the way down. This is what Billy Ray said.

"There were two other guys playing cards. Both threw their wallets on the table and stood up with hands in the air. Paul, the taller one, said, 'I'm out.' Then he said, 'Billy Ray, you can stop shooting now and claim self-defense, or else you kill us all and most certainly die in Leavenworth. So, me and Stevie are walking out of here now. Do you hear me?'

"And Billy Ray told him, 'You have a lot of nerve, big shot.'

"'You are scaring the shit out of me, Billy Ray,' Paul said. I don't know nothing about tonight. I don't remember being here. Listen up real good. Screw your head on straight. Stevie and I are walking out of here. Take the fucking money. You'll need it. Get the fuck out of town before it's too late. That's my advice.'"

John said to Veblen, "You tell the story in Technicolor. How do you remember so much detail?"

Veblen said, "I told you already. The man wrote a full confession. And in detail."

"If his welding is as good as his writing, he must be an all-around artist," John said. "What was his end game?"

"Billy Ray took the wallets Paul and Stevie left on the table and went through the other men's pockets and took their cash. He stuffed everything into his jacket and drove like a bat out of hell up Reservoir Road, all the way to the French Creek boat ramp, where he threw any evidence into the water. Decided to keep his Glock and the extra clip, though, in case he needed 'extra protection,' he said. He got back onto Reservoir Road and gunned it for the four miles back into town.

"He says around then he started to think deep thoughts about the rest of his life. He said it might have been the Lord talking to him. By the time he got to Main, he had reconsidered his options and says he pulled up in front of this office. He walked in and put his hands out for the cuffs and made a full confession.

"The Kansas Bureau boys are on their way out here to pick him up and take him to Abilene. With this written confession, he'll likely get charged and sentenced in short order. I'm not sure it will even go to a jury."

"What happens next?"

"You ask for my crystal ball. The best a public defender can do—if Billy Ray consents to one—is argue temporary insanity. They might also get the other guys who got out alive to testify. I'd be very surprised if he gets anything other than life."

"May I talk with him now?"

"Sure. Follow me. Right this way."

The door at the back of the sheriff's office led through a cinder-block hallway, a tunnel painted green long ago, stinking of nicotine and unwashed bodies. They took a right turn, then continued another fifty feet to another door, made of steel with a rectangle of thick glass at the top, more like a gun emplacement peephole reinforced with chicken wire. Veblen took out a ring of keys and unlocked the door. It swung open with a screech. Before them an open bullpen fronted three separate cells. Two of them were empty; the third housed Billy Ray. Veblen looked at John and asked, "Will fifteen minutes be all right?"

"That should be fine."

Veblen pointed to a house phone on the wall. "That connects to my office. When you pick up the phone, it rings on my desk, and I'll come and get you."

The steel door closed. John walked over to the cell. Billy Ray sat on the edge of a steel bunk reading a paperback. He didn't look up.

"Hello, Billy Ray Baumgartner?"

"That's me," said the man, turning a page. He had curly blond hair. He was wearing jeans and white gym socks. His blue work shirt was un-buttoned and showed a hard set of abs and a mat of golden hair from between his nipples to below his navel. He turned his head and hawked and spit accurately into the steel toilet at the back of the cell. He scratched his head. He dog-eared a page of his fat paperback. The title, *Left Be-hind*, appeared in bold slanted letters, superimposed on the silhouette of a jumbo jet. John realized it was the same book he had removed from Jeffrey Arnheim's room in Commerce City.

"My name is John Reimer. You're a member of Marion Hills Men-nonite Church, where I'm the new minister. I'm here to see if there's anything you need. Or if there is anything you would like to talk about."

"Yes, there is, matter of fact." Billy Ray put the book down on the lower bunk and stood up and stretched. He came over to the bars and grasped them and looked straight at John. He had cornflower-blue eyes. His face showed gentleness, but his eyes were too calm. "Yeah, there's something you can do for me. Can I get a goddamn TV set in this cell?"

"I'll see what I can do. Anything else?"

Billy Ray continued, "I want to talk with the judge."

John said Billy Ray would need to take that up with Sheriff Veblen. He asked Billy Ray if his mother had been in to visit.

"Tell my mother she can go to hell. Or maybe that's not so diplomatic, is it? Just tell the bitch I would prefer not to see her, okay?"

Five minutes later John picked up the wall phone. Shortly after came the sound of the key in the lock and the scraping door. John said goodbye to Billy Ray, but Bill Ray had returned to reading his book on the bottom bunk, his face turned toward the wall.

They walked the hallway back to Gustav's office. "What did you learn?" Veblen asked.

"I learned that I am still a naïve Kansas boy. I grew up in Meade and went to my small church college many years ago. I pastored the Ebenholzer Church nearby in the early to mid-sixties. I learned from Gustav Veblen that there is a double murderer in the Marion County sheriff's department holding cell, and I learned I am not always good at difficult conversations. The boy wants to watch television. He made that point emphatically."

Veblen laughed from deep down. He took short puffs on his pipe as the two reentered his office from the long corridor.

"John, did you know that the number one marker for schizophrenia in my business is memorization of all the *Andy of Mayberry* reruns?"

"No kidding?" John said.

"Yeah," Veblen continued. "They all think they're Opie."

"You going to get a TV for the boy?"

"Of course not. Too much of a security risk. He's better off doing his *Reading Rainbow*."

"Yes, but he needs better content."

"You have any suggestions?"

A baby-faced man came in the front door and went to the back hallway. There was a sound of a clock punching and then he entered the room and hung up his blue windbreaker on the hooks by the front door. Veblen introduced Jerry Siebert to John. Jerry went into his office, where a two-way radio crackled. A police dispatcher squawked in Abilene.

John resumed his dialogue with Veblen. "You could start him off on some of that stuff sitting on your desk—how about it?"

"History? I'll think on that. That boy has just created local history. First double murder in this town in a hundred years. That maybe marks him as more of an author than a reader."

"I defer to your wisdom," John said. When he walked out of the office, Gustav and Jerry were discussing the details of the prisoner transfer. Driving away, John looked in his rearview mirror and saw Gustav pull out of the parking lot in an unmarked brown sedan that looked an awful lot like a Crown Victoria.

John drove to visit Billy Ray's mother. He was relieved to find she was not at home so he was saved the task of inventing an opening line.

Chapter 16

Marvin watched John set the table. The preacher had located tall crystal glasses, fine china, and good silverware stored in a felt-lined wooden case. There were gray linen napkins in the dining room's sideboard. A candelabra with two burning tapers adorned the middle of the table that had been pulled away from the kitchen window. The blinds were down. Alan stood at the stove, flipping flatbread in a cast-iron skillet. Dal began to bubble in a Revere saucepot, and Alan peeled a couple of hard-boiled eggs.

He asked John, "Did she say slice them lengthwise?"

Alan opened the fridge door and took out a can of Coors and popped the tab.

"May I help?" Marv said.

"No, just talk to us," John said to Marv. He turned to answer Alan. "Yes. Consult her written manual, please. She said to nestle them carefully in the dal, sliced side up. A simmer, not a boil."

Alan set the bowl of dal on the table next to the rice. He put on oven mitts and returned to the stove for the double-handled saucepot full of chicken tikka.

John turned to Marvin. "Could you bring me a half dozen teaspoons from that drawer? I need them for the chutneys. Oh, and there's this yogurt and sliced cucumbers. A bigger spoon for that."

Marvin found the spoons. "Did you have this catered?" he asked.

"You Hilsboro peasants can dine fancy in Marion Hills," John said. "And I am glad you are my first official table guests. I entertained a mountain of food delivered to my doorstep this morning by a procession of eager citizens while I was out running at the high school. I have chicken-and-rice casseroles, something called tuna hot dish Blondine—don't ask me what that is. There is even Italian cuisine, including grieving lasagna. Apparently, I have a parishioner Cellini who grew up in New Jersey.

There are eight kinds of dessert. Frozen custard. Ice-cream cake. Cookies from a couple of identical twins, all according to my church secretary."

"The bounty overflows," Marvin said.

"But tikka, this is the true feast," Alan said. He sat down and began to pass bowls and dish out food. "Your congregation is a global village!" He leaped up to pull a flatbread off the skillet and put on a glove to carry it back to the table. "Marvin? Flatbread? This is, I believe, chapati."

"No, that's onion kulcha," John said.

"I told you the man had cultcha," Alan replied. "And he didn't even go to Hahvahd!" He started another flatbread on the skillet. The smoke filled the kitchen. "I mean no disrespect to the cuisine from Molotschna, but this is superior fare," Alan continued.

"Who brought this?" Marvin asked. He tasted the tikka. "What's this green stuff?" he asked. He spooned out a mound of rice onto his plate.

"That's coriander chutney," John said. "Try a little. See if you like it. But to answer your question, Ann Hiebert brought this. Retired missionary nurse and midwife from Kodaikanal."

Marvin nodded. "Okay, yes. Quite the lady."

"And you know her from where?" John asked.

"She was on a committee with Verla for the MCC auction in Hutchinson. I heard some things."

"Well, whatever you heard, that woman can cook up a storm. Hey, Alan," John said, "she told me to go easy on the heat with the flatbreads. Don't start a fire. Maybe dial it down to medium."

"Do you like it with a little char, or not?"

"Char," John said.

"Okay, then, for it to char, you need high heat. If I burn it, I'll eat it. Promise."

The men settled down to their food. There was spice. Marvin mopped his brow with the cloth napkin and poured himself another glass of ice water. John shoveled dal onto the flatbread and held it between his fingers like a slice of thin-crust pizza. It was uplifting food, elevating, it buoyed his spirits—in a way that tuna hot dish probably couldn't. He spooned more tikka over rice and tried a schmear of lime pickle. An acquired taste. Alan made himself a second plate. John leaned back. Marvin looked at John and said, "How is Marion Hills treating you so far?"

"I visited a young man in Marion County jail and tried to speak with his mother."

Marvin said, "You aren't talking about the Baumgartner boy, are you? I heard his mother went out of town for a spell. Something about being closer to Abilene."

"Yes, Billy Ray. The sheriff told me he killed his older brother and then a close friend, both with a Glock. Drove to the Marion Reservoir, threw the gun in the water, drove back, and had a change of heart while he was on the road. Said he maybe heard the voice of the Lord. Turned himself in, wrote a full confession."

"I suppose all before the lawyer showed up, am I right?" Marvin said.

"That's plain nuts," Alan said. "The Mennonite murders."

"He was a member at Marion Hills. Inactive for a number of years, but still," John observed.

"This is not how you want to put your town or church on the map, is it? What made him do it?" Marvin asked.

"The criminal psychologists will be interviewing this guy for the rest of his life. Sheriff indicated rage against his older brother, a card game gone wrong, probably a couple of fifths of liquor. A dispute over a woman. Add a weapon available and loaded. As far as I know, he's being transferred to Abilene."

"Did he talk to you?" Marvin asked.

"Pretty clenched. He must have spent all his personal charisma confessing to Veblen. He was in his cell, upset that he didn't have a TV. Reading the same book we found in Jeffrey's room in Commerce City. *Left Behind*."

"A member of the Marion Hills church?" Alan said. "Seriously?"

"Yeah. The newspapers are going to have a field day. Apparently already are. He was baptized when he was twelve. I tried to talk with his mother right after I visited him at the jail. She's also on the church roll. She wasn't home. I went back to the church office and managed to contact her by phone, at a sister's, near Abilene. She didn't want to talk. I could feel her resentment, like I was some kind of snoop. All she said was, 'One son dead and the other going to Leavenworth for the rest of his life.' I asked if I could call her in a couple of weeks. She said she was sick of being stared down by all the pious citizens in this fish bowl."

"Can't blame her for that," Alan said. "Small towns—community can be more often a tourniquet than a warm blanket. Can you imagine? I'm sure she's on several local prayer chains right now. And 'chain' is the right word. You can feel every goddamn link."

John said to Marvin, "Change of topic. I'm glad you're here. You must have more news from Denver."

Marvin looked at his plate. "What did you call this? Doll?"

"Dal," Alan said. "D-a-l. Sounds like the Mennonite name. Made with lentils. I've never had luck making this from scratch. Maybe Ann can visit Chicago and give me a tutorial."

John said, "I encouraged her to hop the train and visit."

"Delicious," Marvin said. "I was skeptical, but it's really something."

"What's the story on Jeffrey?" John asked.

Marvin pulled a folded piece of paper out of his shirt pocket and smoothed it down on the table. He handed it to John. "The coroner's office faxed this over this afternoon. They listed primary cause of death to be an overdose of several drugs. A combination of methamphetamines and codeine. 'Boatloads of codeine,' is what the guy said on the phone."

"So he was in pain," John said.

"Yes. A lot. The autopsy found a hairline fracture in his pelvis and he was malnourished and dehydrated when he passed. In terrible physical shape." Marv shook his head.

"Marvin, I'm sorry. Take your time," John said.

"It looked to me like he wanted to die alone in that empty house," Marvin finished.

John hesitated. He thought of the young man he had baptized.

"We found his glasses by that rickety set of back stairs," Alan said. "Did he fall off? Did the coroner say what could have cracked his pelvis?"

"Could be," Marvin said. "A fall like that would explain it. And that's probably when he really laid into the self-medication."

John paused over his food. He lifted his fork and put it down. He said, "This is a hard story."

Marvin continued, "We found his car. It was parked a couple blocks down from the house in Commerce City. Tucked into the carport of a vacant house."

"And?"

"It was almost worse than discovering his body. Where do I begin? It looked like Jeffrey had been living in that car a long time. I know his last address was a cheap motel, right? The Buena Vista. According to his fiancée, that was before he bought the house he died in. But the junk, the garbage, the amount of stuff packed in the passenger's side and piled up on the back floor mats, level with the back seat—we looked at it for half an hour in silence and tried to make sense of it. Then we removed the contents It appeared he started once upon a time using garbage bags as an organizing principle, then that broke down and he started shoving everything into garbage bags. It appeared by the body indentation marks that he had been sleeping on top of his own debris. We practically needed a front-end loader to pull everything out. When we first unlocked the car door and opened it, the smell knocked us over."

"Did you have help going through the car?" Alan asked. He spoke carefully, aware that his voice might convey his horror mingled with fascination.

"Yeah, his fiancée. Delores. A couple of guys from the county sheriff's department were also there. They took material of interest, which I'll get to."

"How did Delores deal with it?"

"Stoic," Marv said. "She was maybe in a state of shock. After half an hour I figured out she didn't know the first thing about my son. She looked hit by a Mack truck."

"He had concocted a whole new identity for her," Alan said. "He always had plenty of charisma and charm."

"Yes," Marvin said. "That's how he operated with each new woman he romanced. Actually, with every new person he met. He made a fantastic first impression."

"A brand-new guy, full of all kinds of potential," Alan said.

"I'm sure the ring didn't hurt any," John said. "And that ring was real. Where did he come up with the cash for that?"

Marvin hesitated. "Here it gets personal. I gave each of my three kids $150,000 a year and a half ago. I'd appreciate if that stays in this room."

Alan and John nodded.

"It was a way to move some of my assets before I'm gone. My accountant recommended it."

Alan and John waited for more. Alan retrieved a box of Kleenex from the kitchen counter and put it on the table. He took a tissue and noisily blew his nose.

Marvin pulled a couple of tissues from the box and did likewise. "Jeffrey probably bought the ring with cash. He had no bank account that I know of. Who knows how much money he wasted on payday lenders? Or he trusted someone to be his personal banker. If that's the case there's not going to be a paper trail. We found one journal from way back which I made a photocopy of. You both know Jeffrey was a conspiracy theorist.

One of the things he talked about incessantly was Social Security, which he called the International Slave System. We eventually found his Social Security card in an ancient briefcase. The words 'International Slave System Gog Magog' were written on the back with a ballpoint. We went through the briefcases in his car but found mostly odd scribblings on Post-its, like the ones we found at the house.

"There were documents concerning special trusts to fund Jeffrey's pet causes. I don't think he got around to setting them up. Lots of intentions though. One was for the Christian Sons of the Posse Comitatus. Another was something called NESARA. And the third was Wyndham Campbell Ministries, with a special designation for Campbell's antipoverty program in Mexico."

Marvin looked at John. "My son wasn't just a prophecy crackpot, although he was that. I know that 'Gog Magog' is something to do with Russia. But he was also interested in what he called his 'street ministry to the poor.' He had delusions of grandeur about the millions of dollars he was going to raise and the thousands of people he would lift out of poverty. Delores talked a lot about that. Although by the time I left Denver she had figured out my son was completely nuts."

"Well, this helps to explain why Jeffrey and Campbell were pals in Denver," John said. "Campbell's talk about ministry to the whole person no doubt tickled Jeffrey's theological sweet spot. Was Campbell scratching Jeffrey's back, or the other way around?"

"Pals," Alan mused. "That's a very interesting conglomerate of causes Jeffrey was into. "The Posse Comitatus folks hate the federal government. But I've never heard of NESARA. What is that?"

Marvin said, "I did a little digging. It's a crackpot organization headed by some university guy out of Louisiana. What is it with academics? I wonder." Marvin gave Alan a searching look. "Wants to return the U.S. economy to the gold standard, eliminate federal income tax, and replace everything with a national sales tax. The guy dreams of getting rid of everyone's credit card debt and completely restarting the economy. Believes compound interest is the root of all evil."

John interrupted. "I presume Jeffrey also used some of the cash to put a down payment on that house, am I right?"

"Yes," Marv said. "And there it gets complicated. I saw Fenimore again, the realtor. He didn't want to talk about the financial transaction. He told me he didn't think it was any of my business. 'What kind of father is still probing the business dealings of his fifty-three-year-old son?' And legally, I suppose it isn't my business. After we combed through Jeffrey's car, we found no record of a will, an executor, or named beneficiaries to his estate. It's all going to probate. I learned that as far as the house goes, Jeffrey put down a fairly sizable earnest money deposit—in cash. I asked what the status of that sale was. Fenimore wouldn't say."

"Did Fenimore indicate he knew Jeffrey was already living in the house?" John asked. "I got the idea that afternoon that he was as surprised as we were to find Jeffrey on the floor of the master suite."

"He didn't say as much. He clammed up. But if Jeffrey put down lots of cash they might have come to some understanding. Of course, that sale is suspended now."

"Here's a question: Did you find out anything about the seller?" John said.

"Funny that you'd ask. I did. And guess who it was. This might surprise you. It certainly surprised me."

"Who?"

"Wyndham Campbell. Fenimore says that Campbell has been buying and reselling renovated homes in Commerce City and Denver for the past couple of years. He called it one of Campbell's side hustles." Marvin looked at John. "You don't seem surprised," he said.

"I am," John responded. "But just a little. My sense is that Campbell is trying his best to imitate his father-in-law. Like Levi, he enjoys putting his finger into a lot of pies. This also explains the phone numbers Jeffrey had written down on all those notes we found in his room."

"How?" Marvin asked.

"They were practically all numbers connected to Campbell," John said. "I checked them out. His office, his several residences in Kansas City and Hillsboro, and even somewhere in Chase County. I wondered what is he doing with a listing in the Flint Hills?"

"He's got property out there," Marvin said. "An airstrip that he flies out of for business. I should know, I put in a bid to build his airplane hangar."

"I take it you didn't get the contract."

"No."

"This begins to turn into an interesting web," John said.

Marvin answered with silence. He spooned more dal onto his plate with yogurt. Alan flipped a last chapati onto the grill. He looked inside the fridge. "You guys up for dessert?"

"How are plans going for Jeffrey's memorial service?" John asked.

"I want to clear a few things up before I schedule it," Marvin said. "There's no rush. I need answers to a few more questions. They're shipping me his ashes by UPS early next week. Right now, I should head home to bed. Too long a day for an old man. Thanks for listening. And thanks for a wonderful supper fit for kings. This has been some kind of spread, John. Truly."

"Don't thank me. It was all Ann Hiebert. You want to take a few flatbreads home?"

"Maybe some of that onion bread, what did you call it?"

"Kulcha," Alan said, with a grin.

"Yeah, that. Kulcha. Lord knows that hanging around you guys I get more than my fair share. You're corrupting me. I don't want to take food off your table, though. Maybe two pieces? Wrap it up in foil? I think Verla would like it. She can even figure out how to make it."

Half an hour later, Marvin headed into the night with the package in hand. John and Alan went out to the back patio and sat in the Adirondack chairs, drinking tea and talking about the Baumgartner boys. Alan prodded John to reminisce about the Clutter murders in Garden City in 1959.

"You were a young buck, weren't you?" Alan asked.

"Yeah," John said. "I was living with Vi in Philadelphia then, working in the mental hospital and starting my first seminary courses. But like everyone else from Kansas, I knew something had changed. It's become a cliché to say that was when everybody started locking their doors, but it was true."

"Did Billy Ray spook you today? Did he say something specific?"

John asked Alan to pour him some more tea. "You picked up on that, huh?"

The wind rustled the leaves of the trees above them. John remembered the double murderer's plea for a television set. He still saw the cornflower-blue eyes and then felt the hair start to rise on his forearms. The comfortable feeling was gone. The vacuity of the boy's statements fell away like an abyss, and John tried to purge them from memory.

He looked at Alan leaning back in the patio recliner, laughing, asking questions, carrying the night on his comic performance and unstoppable curiosity. This kind of friendship was an antidote and balm. John wouldn't trade it for anything.

Chapter 17

The sun shot through the fleecy cirrus edges drifting high above, magnifying the morning light. John drove north on Main. He followed the long curve of the North Cottonwood to Reservoir Road, where old-growth cottonwoods, creaky giants, blew white seedpods through the air and the houses grew larger and spaced further apart. One subdevelopment that John didn't remember sported a lozenge-shaped artificial pond with a water geyser spouting in the middle. The aeration strategy resembled a baby whale stranded in the drink, struggling to breathe. Canada geese stood at one end of the pond on a closely cropped lawn colored Willy Wonka green. Further east lay the golf course, and beyond that, the grassy hills that turned into Chase County with the ancient grooves of the Santa Fe Trail.

An unmarked stretch of road continued north as Reservoir Road curved eastward outside the Marion Hills residential grid. John listened to gravel ping against the Crown Victoria's undercarriage. He slowed to look at the prairie passing by on the other side of the barbed-wire fence. The road sloped down into a little valley and then rose again and ran along a shelterbelt of burr oak and red oak, hackberry, and honey locust. There was a smattering of spruce and hedge apple shrubs. Then the road slanted through the shade of the shelterbelt and on the other side the Schlegel house came into view: magisterial, austere, as implacable as the eye of Levi Schlegel himself.

In the early 1950s, Schlegel had hired professionals from St. Louis to remove the house intact from its original site in downtown Marion Hills next to the Eastlake Inn. This was not the hard part. Moving it was. Schlegel had a destination in mind. A decade later, John got his first glimpse of the house, when the story of how it was moved over twelve days on a giant trailer was still a topic of conversation among local dirt farmers drinking their morning coffee at the Copper Kettle. Levi had found the resources to execute a monumental project. When he put his mind to something, there was little that could stop him.

Once bolted onto its new foundation, the three-story Victorian with the widow's walk looked as though it had been tucked into the landscape forever. It was surrounded by nearly four thousand acres of Levi's land; he didn't care for sightlines cluttered with housing developments. One could almost imagine old Judge Meacham, the house's original owner in Marion Hills, walking out on the porch with his ancient German shepherd and wondering where everyone had gone. Levi had purchased three adjacent farms about the same time that he acquired the car dealership in town. He consolidated the three properties into one extensive whole and razed every building and fence he didn't like. He understood the dedication required to design the wilderness of his choosing in a way that pleased him and Eva, and eventually their four children as well: Franz, Carol, Julia, and Franklin.

He had the big house painted dark olive green, with the soffits, cornice brackets, and window treatments finished out in black with white-and-purple detailing. The effect only improved and deepened with time, as the tall, straight black walnut trees and stands of chokecherry bushes and a couple of twin cedars grew up around the house like a protective shield. Levi's wife, Eva, the artist, had chosen the color palette. Later, as her paintings began to sell in galleries in Kansas City, Denver, and Jackson Hole, she moved her studio into a lofty carriage house almost a mile away from the main residence.

She had given Levi a sketch of what she wanted. Her youngest son, Franklin, already possessed of an architect's eye, completed the drawings. Levi had the carriage house built out of the deconstructed remains of the old barns and outbuildings he had torn down on the original properties that had been swallowed up to form the main Schlegel estate.

The Cottonwood branch, formerly an unruly channel that periodically flooded, ran across the northwestern corner of his combined property, and when the dam at the reservoir was eventually completed by the Army Corps of Engineers, it tamed some of Mother Nature's caprice. Schlegel's property value doubled—some said tripled—overnight. Eva planted an orchard and a big garden with raised beds and cold frames where she grew vegetables that no one for three counties had ever heard of. She let much of the acreage revert to tallgrass prairie, through which she carved a series of extensive walking trails. She called the stretch of land the Ramble. In complexity it was a labyrinth or maze—especially in late summer, when the tallgrass plants grew to twelve, sometimes fourteen, feet high. The land extended for miles and became her own personal refuge. She was not shy about her affiliations, and she proudly displayed Sierra Club and Nature Conservancy decals on the rear bumper of her Subaru next to the Jayhawks mascot.

At the far eastern edge of his property, Levi installed a metal machine shed that served multiple purposes: woodshop, airplane hangar for his six-seat Beechcraft Bonanza, and parking garage for his F-150, Town Car, and an assorted, constantly changing fleet of three or four vehicles, including a riding mower and snowplow mounted on the front of a Toyota pickup. Beside the shed, topped with a wind sock and weather vane, he had a professional crew carve out a mile-long grass airstrip.

John remembered the first time he had met Levi, at a Rotary pancake breakfast in Marion Hills in the early 1960s. This was before the mogul had begun contributing major gifts to the college in neighboring Hillsboro: first for a library wing that housed church archives and a center for historical studies, then for a business leadership institute, and finally, for a residential and alumni reception center where students, parents, faculty, and alumni could meet and greet. At the pancake breakfast, Marvin Arnheim had done the introductions. Even then, Schlegel's multiple quirks were the subject of continuous speculation. Whether he was crazy or merely had a hodgepodge of eccentricities was frequently debated. No one knew his net worth, but his investments were rumored to be vast.

With a reputation for driving hard bargains, he had gained controlling interests in several smaller banks in Kansas and the Oklahoma Panhandle. There were holdings in the Oklahoma and Texas oil fields. There were the restaurant franchises. One of Levi's big breaks came in Wichita, where he got in on the ground floor of Pizza Hut, just before it began spawning franchises with all the profligacy of a dandelion's puffball. Levi could spot opportunities of all kinds, and he amassed properties of every variety.

His gift, if one could call it that, did not always endear him to his neighbors. One cattleman friend of Reimer's, another John by the name of Schroeder who had been on the margins of Ebenholzer's community for years, once described it for John at a truck-stop coffee counter in Durham: "The death of a landowner, chronic illness, medical bills, flood, fire, and pestilence are all investment opportunities for him with his ready cash." And it was John Schroeder who had first suggested to Reimer that Levi was positioning himself as a slightly smaller version of the Koch brothers.

"How does he do deals?" John asked then. "What's his method of operation?"

"He has a familiar move," Schroeder had told John. "You're in a bind. You own a business or farm or a house, and you're short cash. You're about to lose the whole thing to the bank. Levi comes in and shows you more money than you've ever seen in your life. But it's less money than the business is worth. You know it, he knows it, and you still end up shaking hands on the deal. Pretty simple."

Reimer had told Schroeder at the time that he thought his assessment was a little harsh. To which Schroeder had replied: "All you have to do is watch Levi's social engagements. A visit from him often follows that of the undertaker or sheriff." Now John wondered how Schroeder was doing and decided he would need to pay a social call on his old buddy in the coming weeks, maybe sooner than later.

John had to admit that Levi could be aloof. He reportedly kept most of his records in his head. His Wichita attorney was someone nobody in Marion Hills had ever met. It was said he did his own taxes. In polite company, including dining events in the Marion Hills Mennonite church social hall and Rotary and Elks dinners, when he grew bored, he would often scribble rows of numbers on the back of a used envelope that he had pulled, slightly soiled, from his sport coat. He was a cerebral millionaire, not a backslapper. This habit suggested that he found his own musings of far more interest than most of the people surrounding him. Those he bothered to engage in actual conversation often interpreted this to mean they had somehow made the grade.

John remembered Schroeder as he pulled up on the gravel circular driveway in front of Levi's house, behind a black F-150 pickup. A bronze sundial stood on a pedestal amid a cluster of black-eyed Susans, and a couple of dragonflies dive-bombed the display. Before he could get out of the car, the front door of the house opened. A tall man, all of six-foot-four, white hair buzzed in a crewcut, stepped onto the porch. He had a pair of gold bifocals perched on his nose. He was more stooped than John remembered, but the smile on his face erased twenty years, at least from a distance. He wore a short-sleeved blue Oxford, tails out, and Bermuda shorts with sandals over black ankle socks. His legs were long and white and furrowed, stippled with the marks and veins of time. He met John with a hearty handshake and leaned over to grasp John's shoulder with his other hand.

"My friend, it is *good* to see you again! And we are delighted you will be with us for a few months this time, not just a drive-through. This is a homecoming!"

John gripped Levi's arms, old but lean and knotty with muscle. John said, "I am glad to find you in such good health. Franz said you wanted to see me. I got the impression there are things on your mind."

"Oh, there are, there are. When aren't there things to worry about? Eva jokes that I think of myself as a warrior when all I really am is a worrier."

"A modern affliction," John said. "One familiar to me."

Levi's thin lips parted over his even white teeth. When he stopped smiling, his eyes showed a pale, washed-out look, like ground that has withstood too many of the elements. "Well, she's right about the worrying part. I'm trying, John, I'm trying. Though to be honest, I haven't been myself lately. Chalk it up to this thing called age."

"We're all getting there," John said. "I've had a couple of interesting days in Marion Hills so far. I've been away too long. Most everyone looks at me twice before they figure out I'm not a stranger." He put a hand on top of his head. "When this goes white, even old acquaintances have to look again."

"Is Chicago doing that to you? Come on inside."

They entered a front hallway as big as a living room. It had a drop chandelier made out of deer antlers, and there was an expansive varnished coat rack against the left wall. A couple of windbreakers, a brown corduroy L.L. Bean hunting coat of indeterminate vintage, and assorted sports jackets in tweed and plaid hung on pegs above a long expanse of beveled Victorian mirror. There were hats on the pegs, too—Co-op Seed, Schlegel Motors, an old fedora with a feather in the brim, a couple of Stetsons. Below the coats on the parquet floor was a built-in storage locker. John followed Levi another fifteen feet to an open double-pocket door that led off on the right into the living room. Levi told John to make himself comfortable and asked how he liked his coffee.

"A little milk, thanks," John said. "The coffee is leaded, right?"

"As leaded as it gets," Levi said. He returned to the living room with two ceramic mugs and handed one to John. He put marble coasters on the coffee table and sat back in his recliner. Then he said, "Okay, that crack about Chicago doing it to you was unkind. What I meant to say was all these rumors have us worried about you. W.W. made it sound like you took a personal beating from the city itself."

"Well, that's one way of thinking about it, I suppose. You get into a scrape, and people want a familiar narrative. It works because people have already made up their mind Chicago is nothing but gangsters or ghetto. That used to bother me. By now, I'm used to it."

Levi squinted at John. "Yes, but Wedel also said your congregation was quite worried. And that was one reason you got this assignment in Marion Hills. I can't say I'm sorry. Whatever brought you here, I'm grateful. You're perfect for the assignment. I mean, we all liked Tschetter well enough, but you're a breath of fresh air. Tschetter could project ponderous eloquence from on high, but a lot of people are looking for someone who can actually *listen*."

"You flatter me," John said. "You tell me I have the common touch and all that horse doo-doo. Don't get me wrong. I'm glad to be here, Levi. And then of course—"

"I was going to ask about Viola," Levi said. "Her passing at about the same time as your scrape with the criminal class, well, that must have been a lot to handle. A rough spring in the Windy City."

"We did all right. Viola did all right. There was God's grace. Sometimes I don't believe in it, but there it is."

Levi was silent. Then he said, "Yes. And when you say things like that, I know you mean it. No one else can say things like that and be at all convincing. Oh, there is a lot of pretend piety. But I saw what Huntington's did to her—and to you." Levi reached for his coffee mug, and John noticed a slight tremor.

"That's where I have difficulty making sense of it, John. It makes it hard to get myself into the pew sometimes. 'Lord, help me in my unbelief...'"

John looked at Levi and drank coffee. He wiped his mouth with the back of his hand and said, "We scattered Vi's ashes at a bird sanctuary on the Chicago lakefront. I think it's a spot Eva would love."

"You should see her most recent paintings. She is finishing a couple of them right now. We'll walk over to the carriage house later. How much time do you have? She likes to keep her mornings for the work."

"I'm free till noon. And about Eva: Someone recently told me she is showing work in Kansas City and Denver."

"She calls it her late career surge. Now there is a gallery in Jackson Hole. Some guy out there by the name of Dick Cheney likes her big bird paintings."

"I like those pictures above your sofa," John said. "New?" He pointed at a couple of small oil paintings in ornate frames. He stood up and looked more closely at them. The frames bordered on gaudy and rustic. The figures depicted seemed to talk obliquely to each other. A cowboy held a skillet with his gloved hand on top of a little bed of coals. A horse stood in silhouette behind. In the other painting a Native American on horseback gave an awkward handshake to a cowboy on a pinto pony mount. The native man and the cowboy leaned reluctantly toward each other, and the cowboy offered his left hand.

Levi nodded. "Well, they're not new, but I just bought them. Not sure whether it was wise. They pushed up my home insurance policy some and made me install a new alarm system. The broker raised his eyebrows when he heard the name Charles Russell."

"I mix up Russell and Remington all the time," John said. "He was the Montana guy, right? Russell, I mean. Remington was the New Yorker."

"You seem to have sorted it out," Levi said. "I'm just a simple businessman. I leave the art history to others."

A door opened and closed in the rear of the house, then Franz appeared in the kitchen doorway. He rubbed his hands together. "Breakfast, gentlemen?"

Franz had a blue Schlegel Motors cap pulled down tightly on his forehead. His face was ruddy. "Pancakes and eggs await. I have strawberries."

Levi spoke. "Works for me. I'll take John over to the carriage house to see Eva around eleven."

"Okay, then," Franz said. "Breakfast in about twenty minutes." He stepped back into the kitchen and soon the sound of clattering skillets and a couple of gentle thuds of the fridge door merged with a radio voice that sounded like NPR.

Levi took John back outside. They stepped onto the front porch.

"I suppose you're wondering why I invited you here," Levi said. "There are several things I need to discuss with you in the next few weeks, if you wouldn't mind."

"Of course."

"I'm an old man, and I'm not getting any younger." Levi looked out over the circular driveway. "By the way, did Franz set you up with adequate transportation?"

"Yes, he did. You're looking at it." John pointed at the Crown Victoria.

"That's a nice executive car. I hope it works out for you. I heard someone tried to hurt you in Chicago."

John tried to make sense of the previous two sentences. A transition was missing, and Levi was repeating himself from just minutes before. "The vehicle is fine, Levi," John said. "Very comfortable. It meets all my needs."

"Carol tells me she ran into you at the high school track yesterday."

John laughed. "I don't know if she ran into me so much as proved she could outrun me."

Levi said, "You young people. Showing you can still do a full-on sprint. She is serious about conditioning. My oldest daughter lives in pursuit of eternal youth."

"Well, a lot of TV appearances will do that to you. At least that's what Franz said," John added with a laugh. "I would have to agree."

"Lord knows she and Campbell have enough projects to keep them busy for a couple more lifetimes. They just purchased an old house in Marion Hills that Carol wants to make over. I asked her, didn't she have enough other properties to nurture, or enough prayer breakfasts to attend? But then I reflected, 'Who am I to talk?'"

John let that one lie. He said, "And how are your youngest, Franklin and Julia? I heard Franklin was moving back to the area from out East, and I noticed Julia and Ken's farm outside town has a new theme that is mostly goat oriented. I actually saw a sign for the Schlegel Dahlke Running of the Goats. Last time I was out here they were raising Charolais cattle."

"Ah, yes, the goats. The Nubians and the Lamanchas. Julia is intent on branching out. First, it was the gorgeous French cows and, then, the Tennessee walking horses. Some of my children have trouble staying focused," Levi said. "Julia and Ken pampered those Charolais like movie stars. It all went to their heads when *Progressive Farmer* sent out a crew from Boston to do a photo shoot. 'Those are pretty cows,' the locals said soon after, 'but pretty for what?' It didn't sit well with Julia. One day out of the blue she began to disparage the herd. 'Dad,' she said, 'They are beautiful, but they haven't quite achieved what they were supposed to.' And I said, 'What do you expect? They're French. Beauty *is* the achievement. Beautiful cattle for the beautiful people. You're running a show farm. You don't make the money off the beef, girl. You make the money off the pictures.'"

"Ouch," John said. He tried to remember how far back it was when townspeople had started calling Ken and Julia "Ken and Barbie." It was pretty far.

"Yes, I wish I could have withdrawn that comment. It didn't please her. I don't know about your child, but my daughters have a real gift for reminding me of my shortcomings."

"The pattern is familiar to me."

"Julia told me I sounded like an ugly American. All I could do was shrug. Then she got a bug for Tennessee walking horses. Who knows when that cockamamie enthusiasm will wane? Ken is a nice boy but too compliant. My daughter runs him around. And now? They have the goats! I have to give Julia and Ken credit: They keep trying bold new ventures. Quirky stuff, bright ideas. They know how to make the farm a going concern. They believe an annual event featuring adorable baby goats next to gnarly old billies would complement the Hillsboro Sausage Festival. Julia says she wants to work the elementary school market a little bit harder, get tour groups coming through. Maybe write a goat cookbook. She's already thinking about a title, something like *Birria in the Heartland*."

"You're serious," John said. "Does anyone around here even know what *birria* is?"

"Julia has set her sights on bigger markets," Levi said. "Like both coasts. She thinks of herself as an educator. She's trying to get me to read some nonsense about a guy named Bromfield. Famous writer who was the envy of Hemingway. He turned farmer after World War I, ended up in Ohio, where he hobnobbed with all the celebrities. Hosted Humphrey Bogart and Lauren Bacall's wedding."

"When will I see the running of the goats?" John asked. "Are senior citizens allowed to participate?"

"You might have to sign a waiver. And bring body armor. But honestly, Julia is planning a goat sideshow at the Mennonite Central Committee auction in Hutchinson in a couple of weeks. You should come to the auction regardless, John. It will be a big one."

"An interim Mennonite minister who didn't go would be thrown out of town," John said. "And I have recurrent nightmares about being shunned. But seriously, Franz said you wanted to talk with me about something. Please fill me in."

"Yes. Oh, of course, now I remember. It's an element of estate planning. I have in mind a project that requires your insight, not to mention consent. I want to endow a neuroscience program at the college and name it after Viola. By the way, Eva also thinks this is the right thing to do." Levi looked at John, who was looking down at his hands.

"I know," said Levi. "These things make everyone go all somber. Don't. I've seen too many instances where wise men could not imagine what the world would look like without them, and when that happens, it's only the descendants who suffer. So this program named after Viola, I thought it was time to sit down with you and my legal team and hash the thing out."

"I would be happy to. And on Viola's behalf, I say thank you. I'm flattered."

"Don't be. This is an honorable thing. No flattery intended. It is right and proper. I'll let you know my schedule in the next week. You have plenty to keep you busy at the church, including a full visitation schedule, am I right?" Levi's eyes twinkled.

"Your sources do not mislead you," John said. "I have a lengthy list. Just let me know when you want to meet."

Franz called them into the kitchen. They sat down to short stacks of pancakes, fried and scrambled eggs, a plate piled with slabs of country ham. There were twin bowls of fresh strawberries and blueberries. Levi poured impossibly tiny glasses full of V8 low-sodium tomato juice. He exercised a delicate, firm touch, as if to prove he was still rock-steady. Franz brought out a wire stand with a troika of miniature syrup pitchers with stainless-steel handles, the kind with the thumb-operated slide on top.

John thought of his favorite pancake house in Lincoln Park, just south of DePaul. "Maple, boysenberry, and my own personal favorite, Mrs. Butterworth's. I hope I've covered the bases," Franz said.

The men ate with purpose. Levi and Franz conferred about preparing the Beechcraft for an upcoming trip. Levi handed Franz a manila folder. Franz opened it, leafed through several sheets of paper, and said, "Schedule looks good. I'll get her ready to go."

John finished his third cup of coffee as Levi stood up and said, "I think Eva is ready for us now. Let's go see what she has made this morning."

Levi and John crossed the yard under more trees and followed a gravel driveway next to a row of tanks marked Diesel, Gasoline, and

Water. The driveway continued another hundred yards east to the outbuilding and airstrip. A wind sock snapped to attention.

Three finches flitted overhead, two bright-yellow males and a female. John followed Levi back onto the trail. It dawned on him how immense Levi's compound was, how much upkeep it required, and he wondered about its actual boundaries. He knew the North Cottonwood Branch ran through it, but it couldn't extend all the way to the reservoir. They kept walking. Here the landscape changed: an expanse of lawn appropriate for croquet morphed into something wilder, freestanding tallgrass prairie, six to seven feet high and bordering each side of the path. The sight gave John a renewed appreciation for what it would have been like to come into this country on horseback: it would have been the only means of travel allowing one to see.

John was wandering through the grass, tantamount to entering a maze, a structure designed for surprise.

The landscape carried a charge. The scent of wildflowers and native grasses rose to John's nose and a swarm of tiny insects hovered above, accompanying the men like a hive of brightly lit energy beams. There was big bluestem and little bluestem, tufts of switchgrass. Asters and coneflowers exploded out of the ground; clusters of sunflowers with jagged stems rose twice a man's height above the earth, lifting their spiky golden heads toward the sun. Here the estate achieved a different dimension altogether.

When John and Levi emerged into a clearing a half mile on, a white, rectangular wood building rose into view like an apparition. John shook his head in a kind of gauzy recall, and as they walked closer, he absorbed its exterior details. It looked to be about fifty by a hundred feet. Several horizonal rows of windows wrapped around it, and a white cupola mimicking the building's outline jutted from the center of the gray-shingled roof. It was topped by a beaten copper weathervane in the shape of a heron in flight. Double sliding doors gaped open in the middle of the building, about twelve feet high and broadside to the two men walking, bringing the inside and the outside together. Through the doors, the other side of the building showed a matching sliding door, also open to the prairie that rolled away into the mounded distance of the Flint Hills.

A single figure stood working at an easel beside a table. She wiped her hands off on a paint rag and let the pince-nez, suspended on a fine chain around her neck, fall from the bridge of her nose. She approached and gave a little skip as she neared them. The woman leaned into John's arms. She was taller than he was, and as she put her forehead against his, cranium to cranium, he was reminded again that this was no petite greeter but more of a rib crusher, a human with feral sensibilities. Levi looked on amiably, then sauntered off in the direction of the airplane hangar.

"Eva," John said.

"How are you doing without Viola, John?" She looked at him. She wielded her blunt conversational skills without apology.

"Trying to get by," John said. "I am not quite peering into the abyss, if that's what you want to know. But what are you working on in this . . . what do you call this?" John looked up at the rafters.

"I understand if you want to change the subject, John. I really do. As to this—this is all Franklin and Levi's doing," Eva said. She followed his gaze from the doorway and contemplated the whitewashed, pitched ceiling. "Levi took down a couple of barns and Franklin put together a plan to recycle them into something else. I live among clever men! Franklin organized a couple of crews from Marion Hills and Cottonwood Falls and they hammered away. I requested modifications, the plans changed. I made both my husband and my son almost as crazy as I am. It is a good place to work."

John followed her inside the space. Light flooded in through the rows of windows that ran in a double band around the perimeter of the wall, twenty feet above. It was not quite a barn, but could double as a church. At one end of the building a sleek galley kitchen and a table were tucked along half the length of the wall, and overhead an open loft space connected to the main floor by way of a staircase angling down in the corner. It was painted white, with the oak banister and steps varnished for contrast. A sound system played a monotonal composition that John didn't recognize.

He considered the design. It was out of time, from another time, as if a pavilion from the 1893 Chicago World's Fair had been transported wholesale to the Kansas prairie. "The 'White City,'" John said. "That is your inspiration!"

"Right," Eva said. "But Franklin wanted something more like the 'decorated sheds' the critics hated. Not so much neoclassical. He ended up building it with almost no decoration, but I like the lines."

"What are you working on?"

She took his arm and led him toward a snowy owl on the canvas. A couple of library tables and a freestanding bookcase marked Eva's main arena of activity. Back issues of *Bird Watcher's Digest* lay scattered beside a stack of hardcover books and an open sketch pad showed several studies of owls done in charcoal. A pair of binoculars lay beside a camera with a gooseneck lens. John looked more closely at the owl emerging on the canvas. Next to the easel was a table with a taxidermied owl, perched on a branch that jutted from a heavy stone base. On that base lay another taxidermy project, a partly eviscerated prairie dog. One could feel the bird pausing mid-meal, the grip of its talons. On another table, a giant book of Audubon's birds lay open to a painting of a horned owl. Eva was working from multiple models. Her work in progress, an oil on canvas that stood five feet tall, was nearly complete. Its size was unsettling; it loomed almost as large as the viewer and appeared taller because of the easel. The bird had an inquisitive air about it and John could almost hear it ask, "Do I disturb you?"

"How is Franklin?" John asked. "Levi tells me he has moved back from New York and is working on a place in the Flint Hills."

"Yes," Eva said. "My youngest. Franklin is still finding out what he wants to do. Maybe just his version of the midlife crisis. I mean, I'm not surprised. I think I've had at least three of those. He comes by it honestly. He worries about his estranged wife and his daughter Samantha in Rhode Island who is about to get kicked out of boarding school."

"Franklin had two commissions in Connecticut and one of them fell through," Levi said, reentering the studio. "Normally he would say that is not uncommon and he would have rolled with it. But this time was different."

Eva said, "Franklin is no longer content drawing blueprints. He talks more about landscape. Therefore, what better place to try out ideas than in the Flint Hills? You'll have to visit him there. He is building a house."

"He acquired an abandoned quarry that sat empty for forty years," Levi said. "It's north of the Tallgrass Prairie National Preserve tract, right on the edge."

"He needs a new challenge," Eva continued. "That is how my boy— or I should say my boys—function."

"Or your children," Levi corrected.

"Or my children." Eva's lips closed in a narrow horizontal straight line in her weather-beaten face. John noticed the fine network of vertical grooves that emerged above her upper lip when she was deep in thought. Now anger had hijacked her thoughtfulness. "My only concern is with the crazies in Strong City. They could make life difficult for Franklin. As they have for us."

John wore a puzzled expression. "What do you mean?"

"We have certain citizens opposed to the tallgrass park. They're making a fuss that could get ugly." Eva crossed her arms. Her hands were covered in paint and she had a smear of gray on her left elbow that matched the background on the canvas. The smell of turpentine drifted in the air. She continued, looking at John, "I should have known when I read Heat Moon. Have you read him?"

"Do you mean *PrairyErth*? I brought it along on the trip. I thought it would be useful if I was at Marion Hills for the next six months. I started reading it on the drive into Kansas with Alan Wiebe."

"You're darned right it is useful," Eva said. "I should have known what we were in for when I first read him three years ago."

Franz entered the carriage house through the open double door with his hands in his pockets and sauntered over to the table where his parents and John stood.

Eva looked at Franz. "I was talking about Heat Moon."

"Yes, Mother's favorite seer," Franz said. "Mom buddied up to that rancher lady Jane Koger immediately after she read Heat Moon's book."

"Do you want to explain her for us, too?" Eva inquired sweetly.

"Sure," Franz said with a wide grin. "And I quote, 'In this county I'd rather admit I'm a feminist than an environmentalist.'"

"I don't know," Eva said, "but I have total admiration for a writer who can get people to trust him enough to say things like that. Or that rancher who was incensed when they reintroduced a few native wildlife species. 'What the goddamn hell are they doing putting antelope back in here for?' he said."

Levi enjoyed his wife's performance. He said, "I had to think about restraining Eva so she wouldn't drive over there in her Subaru and tie his ears back. But Eva is right, the fringe is getting more vocal not just in Strong City but in Marion County proper. Some of these people are even willing to identify with Terry Nichols and Timothy McVeigh."

"That's not so long ago," John said.

"Just a little over a year," Eva said. "Did you know the last place those guys refueled their Ryder truck full of explosives was in Kansas? On their way to Oklahoma City, where they killed all those people and kids in a nursery school?"

"The antifederalists," Levi said. "Crazy lunatics. Some of them iden-tify with the Posse Comitatus. Others with a movement called We the People. One of them said he was sorry innocent folks died along with the guilty at the Federal Building in Oklahoma City, but he personally believed Terry Nichols deserved a medal. He actually said that."

A barn swallow flew through one open double door and straight through the space overhead, then out the other double door. It seemed a harbinger. Its flight momentarily halted the conversation.

John said, "Yes, the Posse Comitatus. I dislike the word 'robust,' but that would describe the health of the Posse in western Kansas already ten years ago. My brother Andrew introduced me to the county weed sprayer, a buddy of his, who believes the biggest unit of legitimate gov-ernment area in the United States is the county. Which means the highest executive power in the land resides with your local sheriff."

"What did you do when you met the weed sprayer? I mean, what did you say?" Franz asked.

"What was there to say? I was embarrassed. And I didn't drop into my finest rendition of the 'Star-Spangled Banner,' if I rightly recollect."

John wondered where the cowboy elocution issuing from his mouth was coming from. He imagined it was the surroundings. He wondered what he would turn into if he stayed in Kansas for any length of time.

"That sounds like you," Levi said. He found all this quite amusing. "I wonder if Sheriff Veblen knows about that. It might make his day. John, I won't ask you which county you were in, but was it Meade or Grant?"

Levi's own joke seemed to get the better of him. He looked at Eva, who showed her impatience.

"All right," said Levi. "On a serious note, let me explain how some of our local politics hook up with the madness in Oklahoma City. A lot of folks are angry. I bid on a farm last month at an auction in eastern Colorado. Didn't buy it, which is probably one reason I got in on the conversation with some locals afterward. They didn't know who I am, and I have a feeling if they had, they wouldn't have talked to me. They hate the banks, they hate the Jews, they hate guys like me who buy them out when they go bankrupt or are in arrears on back taxes to the state and federal government. And, any more, those financial conditions describe about three-quarters of your family farms. It's a lose-lose proposition for most of them these days. I understand why they're mad. Unfortunately, mad can get dangerous."

"We have a group in Marion County called We the People," Franz said. He took off his cap, smoothed down his hair, and put his cap back on. "They are mailing affidavits to county officials that they claim exempts them from any laws set by the federal government. They call the feds fraudulent for issuing paper currency and not using actual silver and gold bullion—I kid you not. This is medieval. They don't think the feds should have any jurisdiction outside of Washington, DC. Here I am, sounding like them just by my pronunciation of the words, 'the feds.' Nichols did one of these affidavits. He called the federal government a 'fraudulent, usurping octopus.'"

"How does this play out locally?" John asked.

"If you're not opposed to the tallgrass park over by Strong City and Cottonwood Falls, they hate your guts," Franz said. "They call you a collaborator with the enemy. I've received three separate anonymous letters at the auto dealership. One of them threatened to burn me down if I didn't sign up with We the People. Dad's been getting similar mail here. You sit in the Copper Kettle for a cup of coffee and wonder who's got you in their sights."

"Did you say something to cause a flare-up?" John asked Franz.

"I think so. It was at an Elks meeting. I said I supported the Bob Dole and Nancy Kassebaum bill that preserved local ownership of the tallgrass preserve. I thought they had come up with a real creative compromise to quell the anger. And it wasn't enough. Now it's common knowledge that all of the preserve, or almost all of it, will be purchased by the Nature Conservancy when the whole package is wrapped up. That wasn't good enough for some of these guys. 'Unique private-public partnership, my ass,' one of them told me. 'It's collusion with the feds, who will have complete control. It's still going to be managed by the National Park Service,' was how he put it. He called Dole and Kassebaum socialist wolves in GOP clothing.

"I asked him if he'd like a more moderate Republican Party in Kansas. And he said, 'What I'm saying is they're no longer reliable Republicans. Just whores like all the rest of those Washington politicians and their Jew bankers.' Then he made a crack about Franklin. He said, 'Might your very special little brother who's moved back to the Flint Hills support this sell-out as well?'"

"What does Campbell think of all this?" John asked Levi. The question seemed to take Levi off guard.

"He's watching and waiting but says it will blow over. I think we try to share that attitude. That it's mostly huffing and puffing."

"Yes, and then you get Oklahoma City," Eva said, picking up her brush and paint board.

"Yeah, maybe huffing and puffing," Franz said. "But did you notice Campbell's started carrying a couple of rifles in his pickup gun rack? I asked him about that and he didn't want to talk about it."

"He's got new property over in Chase County, I hear," John said.

Levi looked at John. "You're right. I bought a place off a bankrupt sunflower farmer out there and decided to sell. It eventually went to auction, and it turned out my son-in-law was the high bidder."

"What does he need a ranch in Chase County for?" John said.

"Beats me," Levi said. "What does anybody need a ranch in Chase County for? I think he wants to save time. Said he needs to get on his plane and fly sometimes at the drop of a hat. His recording studio is in Kansas City. He's got investments in Denver, also down in the Mennonite colonies in Mexico, likes to shoot over to California now and then so Carol can go shopping. He put in an airstrip. Couldn't see driving all the time to Wichita and hiring a charter. Said he didn't have the patience. I mean, I'll be honest—"

"Sounds like somebody I know," Eva said, finishing his sentence for him. She applied a big daub of gray paint to the background of the snowy owl canvas. She used her thumb and the brush in a combination that only she could do and the result was an expert smear.

Levi said he felt tired and needed a nap. "Let me say, 'So long,' here, John.'" He put a hand on John's shoulder and leaned toward him. "Don't forget about those plans I mentioned earlier. I'll call your office with a couple of possible times we can sit down."

Levi walked out of the carriage house with Franz beside him. John paused by the easel and watched the men walk on the path back toward the house. Levi stumbled, and Franz gripped his elbow. Then they disappeared into the tallgrass when the path angled. Eva looked at her painting, put down her brush, and wiped her hands on a rag. "Pull up a chair, will you, John? Visit with me."

"How is Levi's health?" John said. "Do you mind if I ask? It seems a little early for a nap."

"He's slowing down," she said. "We all are." John watched her. She wanted to say more but had decided against it.

John told her about Viola's last days, and Eva reminisced about Vi as a little girl in Enid. She said she hoped she'd see John at the MCC sale in Hutchinson.

John promised to be there. Eva picked up her brush.

"I like your owl, Eva. Are you painting something besides a bird?"

"Say more. Are you saying it's maybe a parable? What does it need? What do you like? What is it missing?"

"The prairie dog adds another element, too," John said. "Are you putting any prey into your painting? I am reminded of the peregrine falcons that nest all over Chicago now. They have adapted to the city."

"They are beautiful when they dive, aren't they? Though they do destroy an awful lot of beautiful songbirds," Eva said. "They have a special appetite for warblers—nature at its most perverse. Last time Franz took me to Chicago we went up to the Hancock. The Signature Room. We spent two hours watching the falcons fly around the top of the building. They were quite a sight, dive-bombing the pigeons. I did not want to leave. On the way back home to Kansas that is all I thought about. I sat in the back of the plane with my sketchbook while Franz flew and Levi chatted him up."

John wondered which boutique hotel off Michigan Avenue Eva had stayed in. It took him a while to realize that she probably knew certain Chicago details better than he did. Her long trips away from home likely made her an expert. *She keeps her cosmopolitan identity well under wraps,* he thought. *Like her snowy owl, with its perfect winter camouflage.*

After saying goodbye to Eva, he took his time walking back to the Crown Victoria in front of the house, picking his way along the path. Next time he would politely request a guided tour of the Ramble, so he could lose himself in the tallgrass waving above his head.

Chapter 18

I was born on a ranch in Meade, Kansas, during the Great Depression, a couple of years before Adolf Hitler sent his Panzers into Poland on their way to Russia. I was the youngest of twelve children. My father, a deacon, died when I was six. Mother carried on.

Before bedtime, my siblings and I gathered around the table and read the Bible. We would go around the circle and read one verse each. Then we paused for silent prayer. Until I went to grade school, I had never heard an audible prayer. Prayer was so sacred it could not be uttered out loud. That is what Mother believed. Before the brothers and I climbed the stairs for bed, she would say, "Boys, think of God. *Denkt an Gott*."

I grew up in the Kleine Gemeinde church. This body of Mennonites had originally split from the larger Mennonite community in Russia in 1812. They believed their way was a better way, a more holy way. They sought purity. Their leader was Klaas Reimer. I can claim him as a distant relative. The historian P. M. Friesen described Klaas this way:

> The religious disposition of Klaas . . . although a sincerely pious one, was devoid of any joyous knowledge of God's grace, while his confessional stance in educational and cultural matters was indescribably narrow. Reimer even considered the reading of books published by people of other faiths to be a sign of apostasy and of the coming Antichrist. Extreme severity in matters of dress, residence, and furniture . . . complete the profile of this new church.

I will let you be the judge of whether Klaas would fit in at Marion Mennonite, or whether he and I would have very much to agree on. Let me say this as I stand before you on this first Sunday in this church: You are a handsome and well-dressed crowd. You are beautiful people. "Do not let my flattery go to your head," I hear Klaas saying to you in the background. Perhaps my Kleine Gemeinde spirituality is still at work, at least on certain subconscious levels. May we all listen to our inner Klaas. Be humble.

One of my older brothers, Pete, once got into trouble for buying a pair of fly nets for his horses. I remember that if a newly purchased car had a nickel-plated radiator shell, that radiator shell had to be painted black, because nickel plate was worldly. The elders enforced the rules.

Hell was real to my elders, as it was to me. That focus on hellfire was not accompanied by an understanding of God's grace as the means to salvation. The preachers told us, "To know for sure about your salvation is heresy. It is a sign of pride."

During the eighteenth century, the Puritan preacher Jonathan Edwards, of Massachusetts, anticipated Kleine Gemeinde doctrine when he preached his famous sermon, "Sinners in the Hands of an Angry God." He said:

> The God that holds you over the pit of hell, much as one holds a spider, or some loathsome insect over the fire, abhors you, and is dreadfully provoked; his wrath towards you burns like fire; he looks upon you as worthy of nothing else, but to be cast into the fire; he is of purer eyes than to bear to have you in his sight; you are ten thousand times more abominable in his eyes, than the most hateful venomous serpent is in ours. You have offended him infinitely more than ever a stubborn rebel did his prince; and yet it is nothing but his hand that holds you from falling into the fire every moment.

Such a message drove me to rebellion. I was a teenager, and I turned against the elders. My rebel ways involved sneaking away to a revival meeting at another church, one that involved a different kind of Mennonites. I had been forbidden to go to their church because of their piano, a worldly musical instrument. The girls at that particular church were also wildly good looking, and they curled their hair! Imagine! I met several of those girls, and one of them, someone's cousin visiting from Oklahoma named Viola, looked me directly in the eye. And I will not lie to you: She made eye contact with me repeatedly!

And I thought, *If this is temptation, I am all in!* Her cousin was the president of the youth organization. I learned a different way to read the Bible at their meetings. Their teaching was different. They said the gospel means we trust and follow Jesus. It is about grace. It is not about rules.

I decided to become a preacher. Feeding Mom's chickens was the one thing all my brothers and sisters could graduate from, but since I was the youngest, it appeared I would never graduate. I felt family pressure to stay home and take care of Mom. But I knew I had to go to school, and to do that, I had to leave home. I said to God, "I don't know how to get away from this farm. I have to take care of Mother." My brother Cornelius once told me, "Sorry, John, but we can't relieve you to go to school because we don't want to come and live with Mother." But after my prayer that day, he returned and said, "John, if you still want to get an education and go into the ministry, we are willing to come live on the farm."

I proposed to Viola shortly after, and we got married and enrolled at the college. I finished my degree in three years and served in Civilian Public Service during the 1950s as an aide at Morristown Psychiatric Hospital in Pennsylvania. Then I completed my seminary degree in Kansas City, and Viola and I moved to Ebenholzer Mennonite Church nearby, where I met many of you for the first time.

Several years later, while we were in Minneapolis, a different moment engulfed our family, which by then included my daughter, Sarah. Viola would show the first symptoms of an incurable neurological disease that would eventually kill her. To be precise, it did kill her, a few short months ago. I still remember that moment, so many years ago, when I first heard the diagnosis of Viola's condition. And I thought, "My God, why have you forsaken me?"

My friends, there was no healing. But there was grace to cope with the inevitable path of illness. There was grace. There were also friends who told me if I just had more faith, Viola would be healed. They had the best intentions, but they used the language of faith as a bludgeon, and in the years since, I have recognized their advice as a common heresy in American life. The gospel I preach does not promise health and prosperity. It does not promise great riches and miracle cures. Least of all does it promise the absence of suffering in this world.

How absurd such claims sound when we consider the path of Jesus! The gospel as I understand it is the call to follow Jesus and obey his teachings. These are not complicated. In the gospel of Matthew, chapter 22, Jesus tells us "to love the Lord your God with all your heart, and with all your soul, and with all your mind. This is the greatest and first commandment. And a second is like it: 'You shall love your neighbor as yourself.'" Then Jesus summarizes, speaking in the words of a Jewish rabbi: "On these two commandments hang all the law and prophets." I said earlier that Jesus's message is one of grace and forgiveness, not of rules. Let me amend that: The only rules we obey are the rules of love. Love God, and love your neighbor.

What I know is I found the ability to cope in the midst of Viola's illness. I remember Mother telling me that when you start to feel sorry for yourself, get busy! Among other things, I took up running. Where I live in Chicago, I normally run four or five times a week, usually three or four miles each time. I have already met some of you running your laps at the high school track here in town.

How do I spend my days? In activity and contemplation. I perform marriages and dedicate babies. I preside over the funerals of those who have passed. I write letters and sit with people in diners and listen to their stories. I visit the sick. I watch the news, which most of the time leaves me depressed. I read the Bible and also many books that Klaas Reimer would not approve of. I read in order to prepare my thoughts for Sunday morning.

And I have received personal condolences from some of you. Thank you. I have received gifts of food from many of you this past week to the point that my fridge is overflowing. And I will confess that while I have great affection for the old country's verenike, I look forward to wolfing down the grieving lasagna that originated from a recipe at a diner on Route 46 in the Garden State of New Jersey. The chicken and rice. The curry dinners. Blueberry muffins. Cake. Your love is acknowledged and deeply appreciated. You know who you are.

I will visit with you while I am here in Kansas. I will listen to your words and your experience, both as a native of Kansas and as a native who got away and has now returned. I can tell you I am a very different man from the one who left his home in Meade, even from the man who left Ebenholzer. Life inflicts its share of damage on us as we travel. It also provides the greatest, most amazing experiences. This is how life has come to me. And this helps me imagine what some of you have experienced. I want you to tell me your stories—all of your stories.

On this Sunday morning, I stand before you with a heart full of joy. I am glad to be here. And as my mother would say: Brothers and sisters, boys and girls, think of God. Find it within your heart to love your creator. *Denkt an Gott.* And may we love our neighbors as ourselves. All of our dogma, all of our learned theological discourse, means nothing unless we heed the words of Jesus. Or, as Paul told the church in Corinth, and I close with his words:

> If I speak in the tongues of mortals and of angels, but do not have love, I am a noisy gong or a clanging cymbal. And if I have prophetic powers, and understand all mysteries and all knowledge, and if I have all faith, so as to remove mountains, but do not have love, I am nothing. If I give away all my possessions, and if I hand over my body so that I may boast, but do not have love, I gain nothing.
>
> Love is patient; love is kind; love is not envious or boastful or arrogant or rude. It does not insist on its own way; it is not irritable or resentful; it does not rejoice in wrongdoing, but rejoices in the truth. It bears all things, believes all things, hopes all things, endures all things.

Chapter 19

It was a seething mass of plain people, and plain people of every kind. Coming from as far away as California and Pennsylvania, they churned their way through the middle of the Hutchinson fairgrounds, where the annual Mennonite Central Committee Relief Sale was going full tilt on this Saturday in early June.

But the weekend of events was hardly just a sale. It was a series of transactions and auctions and raffles and thousands of conversations, of musical entertainment both live and recorded, of myriad gustatory pleasures, an orgy of consumption conducted under an aura of virtue and sobriety—a paradox for which the plain people are known. All was designed to support the keystone work of transformation: Mennonite Central Committee's mission to assist global refugees and sufferers of every kind of human conflict and natural disaster. The raising of cash was of paramount importance. This served as a release valve for the more buttoned-up and repressed behaviors that plain people are more accustomed to displaying. It was a giant Mennonite virtue package wrapped in bonhomie, pulsing with joy and uncharacteristic festivity. Tightly wound human packages of virtue could gather and let go. And if virtue was the thing, the thing was accomplished by pure, unadulterated buying and selling. The relief sale was part shindig, part promotional carnival, jamboree, circus, fete, and frolic. There was no need to feel bad and a thousand reasons to feel good, including handmade top-shelf quilts and fourteen varieties of verenike of both the boiled and fried subgenres.

The day was perfect, at least by Kansas standards, with no clouds on the horizon and chances of a thunderstorm or tornado hovering at only 20 percent in the mid-state area. So said National Public Radio's weather report from the University of Kansas studios in Lawrence.

The event was most palpably rooted in the quilts and the food, which this year showed what kind of bacchanalian range the plain people were capable of. But the relief sale was on a bigger order than usual this year. The vehicle and tractor auction, scheduled for late afternoon, featured a vintage 1964 red convertible Triumph TR-6, a green 1932 John Deere tractor, a restored New York yellow Checker cab, a blue 1959 Chevy Bel Air sedan with tail fins looking brand-spanking new, and a reconditioned white Mercedes all-terrain vehicle dating from 1940—it had a battered luggage rack above and a spare tire bolted to its rear. It was the kind of vehicle that cried out for a couple of surfboards lashed to the top or at least a grizzled Indiana Jones riding one of the running boards, whip in hand.

Garnering the most attention, however, was a late-model silver Land Rover Discovery that sat sleek and massive on its fat tires. It shone on a dais under a spotlight, and John thought of the golden calf. The Discovery had recently occupied center stage at Schlegel Motors in Marion Hills. It would be raffled off at five that afternoon, and the tickets for the drawing, at fifty dollars apiece, with no number limit per customer, were flying out the door. Seated behind a long folding table, Franz Schlegel's assistant Tom, also a member of Marion Hills' Mennonite Church Council struggled to process the transactions. Demand was fierce.

Immediately outside the vehicle shed, the pilgrims traveled Soup Alley. This packed concourse featured at least two dozen church groups serving a smorgasbord. The organizers of the sale this year had planned the event under the theme Many Lands, Many Flavors. Visitors to Soup Alley had embraced that spirit. There was borscht in several varieties. The Moundridge Women's Auxiliary was pushing what they called Kosher Red Beet Vegetarian Borscht, claiming it was descended from the *Moosewood Cookbook* and an obscure deli in Warsaw. Alan remarked with enthusiasm, "Redder is better." There was Thai green-chili coconut stew with an optional side of basmati rice; several varieties of Texas chili, with and without beans; and Grandma Goossen's Famous Farmhouse Split Pea, served by the Ladies' Sewing Circle from the Freeman Old Order Communion of South Dakota. There was vegan wedding soup and Hungarian stew and miso, both spicy and regular. There were ruddy farmers with their caps on, supervising the coffee machines hauled up from church basements, slicing bread and putting out dishes of fresh butter on the picnic tables under the sun umbrellas. Women, some of them in traditional head coverings and others in stretch tights and sweatshirt hoodies, tended to the Crock-Pots and thirty-gallon saucepots atop hot plates and portable stoves. Farther on, the booths featured ham, gravy, verenike, bierrocks, zwieback, and shoofly and apple pie.

The Hillsboro Sausage Company had its own booth loaded with seven kinds of links that were grilled over charcoal. These could be consumed with verenike (for the traditionalists) or a hot-dog roll (for the venturesome). A giant of a man sporting the jet-black hair of Bobby Knight and wearing size 18 running shoes presided over four concurrently running Weber grills, plus a couple of wood-burning, commercial-size flatbeds. His chef's toque made him even taller and was adorned with neat embroidered letters across the front—Hillsboro: Sausage Capital of America. Jars of grainy mustard and little wooden spoons lay close by the serving area in neatly arranged rows, ready for action.

John Reimer and his friend Alan Wiebe shouldered their way through the crowd. John felt the mood of the people bubbling like an uncontained loaf of rising dough, an effervescent wave of good feeling and excitement. There was love here for every kind of neighbor. Most of those in attendance looked like any Kansas fairground crowd in their ruddy and predominantly Caucasian cast, but the distinctive tribes sprinkled throughout signaled something different and gave the event, rooted in piety, its oddly carnivalesque flavor: the Holdemans, the Kleine Gemeinde, the Bruderhof, the Amish with their goaty chin beards, the Beachy Amish, and let us not forget the Hutterites, whose women sported the big polka dots on their bonnets and full-length dresses and whose men abjured sunscreen, their faces notched and carved into gargoyles by ultraviolet rays and frost suffered through decades of work in the field. Most of these had driven from the Dakotas. There were Swiss Mennonites and Russian Mennonites, a sprinkling of Black Mennonites and a few more Latino Mennonites, mostly from California and Chicago, and one group that had traveled all the way from the Old Mennonite colonies in Mexico. There were liberals and conservatives here, the biblical literalists and the critical theorists and hermeneuticists, the cosmopolitan Mennonites in jewelry and sporting successful cosmetic surgery, as well as people eschewing deodorant and trailing their musky scent. Some dressed as though they were in sixteenth-century Austria. There were pacifist Mennonites and a surprising number of flag-waving closet militarists, and those moderates who sometimes grumbled that MCC's peaceniks and activists could pass for commies given their ironic inflection and barbed rhetoric and "Can't we all just get together and sing wonderful praise music and work on our four-part harmony?" There were poor and threadbare Mennonites who grew rice in steamy Louisiana fields, and poor and threadbare graduate students wearing second-hand sport jackets and black jeans they'd picked up for a few dollars at the nearest Etcetera Shop. A prosperous Ohio black-bumper Mennonite in his midforties stroked a handsome chin beard; he had driven to the event in a new BMW with appropriately painted-over chrome. He was rumored to be a top financial adviser for Edward Jones. Definitely of this world, but in his own way unworldly.

Alan looked at the crowd and said to John, "It cries out for a *National Geographic* photographer. You know, the amateur anthropologists."

"Why amateur?" John said.

"The guys who dream of publishing a big, lush coffee-table book filled with romantic portraiture. The kind you put next to the mint dish beside the cute volume of inspirational poetry by Anne of Green Gables Swartzendruber. Convey a people's vitality as they bustle through their marketplace. Kansas exotica. Ten pounds of art book worth eighty bucks a pop. Another way to convert the heathen to the way of the meek."

"Convey all the varieties of Anabaptist virtue," John picked up. "Kodachrome color, high production values. Show a skeptical world how a utopian vision of living in harmony with our fellow creatures is possible." The men strolled by the booth for the five-hundred-voice Kansas Mennonite Men's Choir. A couple of Bose speakers on tripod stands blasted out the especially lovely harmonics of "There Is a Balm in Gilead." Two graybeards in polo shirts and jackets hawked CDs of the choir's spring concert recording made on tour in Germany, France, and Switzerland. Next year's tour, they informed John, would take the choir to Russia and Ukraine.

John's eyes danced. "Well, that makes sense," he said. "You know it's just over seventy-five years since Mennonite Central Committee was founded in Chicago. In 1920 it was all about getting starving Mennonites out of the Ukraine. Stalin had other ideas."

"That chronology is what we had in mind," one of the graybeards said. "Where are you guys from?"

"Chicago," John said. "John Reimer, pleased to meet you. Currently interim minister at Marion Hills. This is Alan Wiebe, professor of intertestamental studies in the Divinity School in Hyde Park. I'll buy one of your CDs. Actually, make that two." He handed the man a twenty-dollar bill and took the CDs and deposited them in his jacket pocket. "Thank you very much!"

"Of course. A pleasure to meet you, Reverend." The man looked at John more closely and said, "I think I heard you preach when you were a very young man. Weren't you at Ebenholzer once upon a time?"

John laughed. "I try to go incognito around here, but you know how it is."

"I sure do," said the graybeard named Ben. "We remember our own."

People were already sampling the food even though lunch was an hour away. This was Mennonite carnival. Rules and protocol could be played with, and the women running the verenike stations wanted to get a jump on the crowd's appetites. They cranked out the dumplings. John slowed down but Alan nudged him on.

"Hey, there's something," Alan said. He pointed at a sign ahead: "The Birria Bodega. Brought to you by Schlegel Dahlke Farms."

"I see," John said. "Levi Schlegel told me to look for this."

"The goat stew," Alan said, pointing ahead. "Now I'm on a mission. But will it equal the birria found in the Pilsen neighborhood of Chicago? We'll see. Dahlke Farms seems to be betting on it. They brought maybe half their herd, practically running a Wild West show in their corral. All they lack is Buffalo Bill."

John said, "I'll meet you there in a little bit, but first let me say hello to the big billy goat."

Alan gave him an inquiring glance, and John continued. "Campbell. Give me about fifteen minutes."

Alan looked over at the Campbell tent and nodded before entering the surge of third and fourth graders who stampeded toward the goat pen.

John walked toward the tent, perplexed. What was Campbell Ministries doing here? Were they partnering with Mennonite Central Committee? Was the relief sale turning into a big tent for parachurch fundraising entities? Of course, the Mennonite investment outfits were here, eager to sign up people for their plans and get a cut of the national Medicare pie. The Mennonite Foundation had a presence with half a dozen emissaries trying desperately not to look too corporate, and the private Mennonite high schools and colleges had personnel fanning out across the event, portfolio cases bulging with recruiting literature. But Campbell Ministries?

John wondered if Campbell was making a pivot away from *Hour of Power*–style evangelism and end-times prophecy toward a more socially engaged message. The man had obtained his degree at Oral Roberts and later attended Dallas Theological Seminary but would appear to be transitioning. If anyone could wrap the Four Spiritual Laws—or John 3:16— in a towel and bar of soap and sell it, Campbell could. Campbell had set up shop under a striped white-and-red awning. He relaxed in a blue canvas director's chair in front of a large video screen that was alive with images. Mexican farm laborers were bent over in a sunlit field working side by side with farmers who seemed to be auditioning for a Stuttgart folk festival. The film was narrated by a mellifluous male voice explaining the economic development projects currently carried out by Campbell Ministries among Old Colony Mennonites in Zacatecas and elsewhere. John recognized it as Campbell's own voice, at once folksy and polished, more Frank Deford than Billy Graham, the kind of voice that instills confidence and can open hearts, hands, and wallets. The soundtrack segued from music not unlike that of the Mennonite Men's Choir to the thrum of Mexican guitars and a drum corps that imparted just a touch of *sazón*.

John watched the screen and tried to decipher the message. Carol sat in the back of the booth on a little sofa, thumbing through an issue of *Architectural Digest*. She looked up and smiled for John. A black scrunchie secured her thick blonde hair, and she wore the faintest hint of lipstick. "How are you doing, Mister Marathon?"

John waved. Campbell walked out on the concourse to shake John's hand. "John," he said. "Good to see you."

Campbell's handshake was thick and meaty, a statement of man and master. He had the angular moves of a retired quarterback who understood raw power. The graying hair at his temples was coiffed to perfection. John thought he could have been a Rogaine model.

"I wanted to come by and say hello before I go over and eat goat," John said. "I'm hearing a lot about these goats."

Carol spoke up from the couch. "Yes, Julia is excited about the herd. She might talk your ear off. Dad calls it her latest enthusiasm."

"You know what they say," Campbell said. "Where there are goats there might also be sheep."

"I'm not a mutton man myself," John said, "though some have tried to cast me as a shepherd." He glanced again at the screen. The infomercial had shifted from the fields to a shop where artisan craftsmen carved and painted small figures of animals—horses, llamas, arboreal monkeys so cute they needed a hug. Nearby, three women who looked to be of Incan descent worked at looms. The words Thousand Villages appeared across the bottom of the screen.

"You might be wondering whether I've embraced the social gospel," Campbell said with a smile.

John volleyed back without hesitation. "Is there any other kind?" A part of him enjoyed watching people's reactions when he said that.

A pained expression crossed Campbell's handsome face, then he recovered. "Well, you know what those of us who claim the fundamentals sometimes say: 'I'll call you a Christian if you call me a scholar.'"

John sensed the conversation might get prickly. "I never thought you had scholarly aspirations, Campbell. You're more of a great communicator."

"I'll take that as a compliment."

"Please do. I meant it that way. You mind taking a stroll with me down the concourse?"

"Sure. What can I show you?"

"I wanted to share a recent experience in Denver."

Campbell's eyes blinked once. "Let's hear it," he said.

Carol looked up. "Go ahead." She put down her magazine and moved smoothly off the couch into the director's chair. Campbell and John strolled into the crowd. Three Hutterite teenagers in black pants, blue shirts, and suspenders walked past, eating hot dogs with mustard.

John said, "I'm trying to answer a few questions that Marvin Arnheim brought up in Denver. I drove through there at his request a couple weeks ago."

"How is Marv?" Campbell asked.

"To be honest, not too good," John said, choosing his best farmer grammar to deliver the news. "I think he's struggling with Jeffrey's death. You know about Jeffrey, right?"

"I heard he passed. Terrible news. But how can I shed light on this?"

"I learned in Denver that you were a close associate of his."

"Really?" Campbell said. "Who told you that? I occasionally saw him when I passed through town. We had mutual acquaintances in the Promise Keepers."

John waited for Campbell to continue, but it was clear the big man didn't want to offer more information. John said, "Yes, Jeffrey's fiancée and her friend both spoke of that. They were enthusiastic about Jeffrey's ministry. He was a popular figure in a local bookstore on Colfax. Bible studies, book discussions. A popular series of talks he gave about the end times. They called him Doctor Jeffrey."

"He did have a following," Campbell said. "The man's charisma was larger than life. Carol has told me he had it already in junior high. You know Jeff and Carol were homecoming king and queen once upon a time, right?"

"I know that ancient history pretty well," John said. "I baptized Jeffrey at Ebenholzer when I was starting out as a preacher, still in my twenties. I feel partly to blame for getting Jeffrey interested in the book of Revelation. Losing him hurts in a strange, uncanny way that I still can't accept. He was reading *Left Behind* when he was left behind. I knew him before he worked with his dad in the construction business and before he joined the army. I knew him before his five divorces and before he was living out of his car with the back seat piled high with dirty clothes and binders full of wishful thinking. When we found him dead in his sleeping bag in a house in Commerce City, it was something of a jolt."

"You what?" Campbell said. "You personally found him?"

"Yes. Some people put me in touch with a realtor, guy by the name of Fenimore Ramekin. Jeffrey's fiancée Delores introduced us to him and Celeste, a friend who tends bar at a place where Fenimore likes to go for the occasional beer and betting entertainment. Jeffrey had been missing, and people were worried. Especially his fiancée, who was wearing a diamond the size of Texas. Mind you, it was real. Not something you see every day at Casa Bonita. Anyway, it turns out Fenimore was in the process of selling a house to Jeffrey. And here's one place where I thought you might have a little information."

"I don't get it. How could I?"

John looked directly at Campbell. It was a look he had practiced on his daughter, Sarah, when she was a teenager and could blithely claim that she *really had* cleaned her bedroom. Campbell returned the stare.

"Fenimore told us you were the seller." John paused for effect. "He claimed he didn't know Jeffrey was squatting in the house before the deal had even closed. Jeffrey first saw the property during an open house."

"What's your point exactly?" Campbell said.

"Fenimore was there too when we found Jeffrey. He seemed surprised."

"How long had Jeffrey been living in that house?"

"The coroner estimated between a week and two weeks."

"Look, I have a modest investment in a few Colorado properties, though I'm not entirely sure what is in the portfolio. But me the seller? I think Fenimore is yanking your chain. Dropping you a load of bullshit."

John's voice was sharp. "I agree that Fenimore can produce bullshit. But maybe he told me what he did to yank *your* chain. And you should know it's in the public record that you're the owner of the address where Jeffrey Arnheim died. I confirmed that with a lawyer. The coroner's report listed cause of death as opioid overdose and dehydration. He'd cracked his pelvis, unclear how, but a pair of his reading glasses were found in the bushes by the staircase off the back deck. A rickety affair, don't you think? He probably fell off the porch, dragged himself inside, and self-medicated. He had eaten almost nothing except a little ramen for several days."

"Like I said, it's a terrible thing," Campbell replied.

"Yes, and it was clear Jeffrey was trying to reach you."

"How would you know that?" Campbell's body language showed his impatience. The man really wanted to end this conversation. They had strolled into the parking lot and were leaning against a black Tahoe with vanity plates: ruready.

John measured his words. "The dead man left a lot of scribbling behind. Mostly Post-it notes with your various phone numbers. It was clear he tried to reach you. By the way, I've called you several times and left messages. You are a busy man. If you answered Jeffrey's calls the way you've answered mine . . ."

"Do you have any other relevant questions I'm supposed to answer?" Campbell said. His tone was icy now, all the false amity gone.

"Yes, I wondered whether you had any idea where Jeffrey's fifty thousand in earnest money disappeared to."

"Where did you hear that figure?"

"From the source. Jeffrey had received a family settlement from his dad and you know how dads get sometimes. He was curious what his boy did with the money. There was also an engagement ring on Delores's finger that looked like it had come from Cartier's. The fiancée was quite interested to know what happened not just to Jeffrey but to the wad of cash he liked to carry around."

"That's a lot of earnest money. I wouldn't know. If that's what Jeffrey actually paid, Fenimore would be required by law to hold it in escrow."

"Yes, the law requires so many things, but realtors sometimes make up their own rules. Not that I'm suggesting anything about Fenimore, but . . . you know. It would be a special temptation with a client who didn't have a bank account because he believes banks are a tool of Satan. I thought maybe Fenimore spread the largesse around a little. No ideas, huh?"

"Look, Reimer, I have nothing else to enlighten you with. You'll have to talk to your lawyer buddy in Denver."

"I had one other question," John said.

"You're wasting my time," Campbell said.

John wondered what kind of bully Campbell had been as a teenager. It wasn't hard to imagine, so he said: "Have you ever seen a mouse dropped into an aquarium full of piranhas?"

Campbell's eyes narrowed and flickered side to side. "Is this a fishing expedition? If so, that's quite the fish story. Are you inventing parables? You're talking crazy talk. I'm as troubled by Jeffrey's death as you are, but I don't understand your agenda or what you're driving at."

John looked at the big man. "Campbell, that's a lot of words with no answers. Something is rotten about Jeffrey's death and you know more than you're letting on. So, hear me on this. I ask questions until things make sense to me. I'm stubborn that way. Sorry if that bothers you."

John let the silence ride to allow the discomfort sink in. Then he put his hands in his pockets and sauntered away from the Tahoe. "Think about it, Campbell. Maybe something will jog your memory. But I understand there's a lot you don't want to say."

"You can shove it, Reimer."

"Now, now, Reverend Campbell, that's no way for a preacher to talk."

John turned and walked away. He had to admit he took pleasure seeing the big quarterback sacked way behind his line of scrimmage.

Chapter 20

For John, putting in the verbal shiv was a recurrent temptation, and his tongue had given him trouble before. But at this moment, a felicitous interruption erupted on the concourse, some sort of melee. *Maybe divine intervention*, he thought later. The noise level by the Schlegel Warkentin Farm tent had risen, even above the majestic harmonies of the Kansas Men's Choir. A scramble of people moved jerkily past, at once anarchic but also gripped by singular purpose and direction. They moved down the center of the relief auction corridor. A group of older men streamed out of the machine shed. One of them stopped John and asked, "What happened?"

"I have no idea," John said. He began to jog toward the epicenter of the chaos.

The source of the action came into view: A crowd within the crowd was attempting to corral a breakaway herd of diminutive livestock. The acoustics of the hoofed fur balls cut through the other sounds: earsplitting, panicky bleating. It was the sound of goats, a mixed herd of Nubians and Lamanchas, maybe thirty in all. A magnificent Nubian animal, deep bronze in color, raced ahead of her companions. Her ears rippled in the wind like streaming pennants, and her eyes were two golden orbs completely spooked by the crowd closing in. She also had a voice: a powerful alto in full goat register. A distinctive woman's voice answered: "Brat! Come here! Somebody catch that goat! She'll break for the highway! Someone please stop that animal!" Brat's companions pounded their hooves in pursuit of their leader. They also gauged their pursuers. When the crowd slowed, they insouciantly slowed to a saunter. When the crowd sped up, they accelerated with an instant burst of speed.

The woman who shouted orders wore khaki jodhpurs and leather boots, and a black cotton jacket adorned with brass buttons. Her jet-black hair streamed out from beneath an unbuckled dressage helmet. John remembered seeing *National Velvet* at a theater in Philadelphia with Vi at what now seemed like the beginning of time. If the goats were built for running this concourse, their master was built for the runway. And at this singular moment, her authority was under attack by a rowdy gang of four-footed beasts. John sized up the situation.

This was Julia Schlegel, the show farmer and Levi's youngest daughter. There was no telling how the animals had escaped, but she was making the clear and present danger apparent. She needed help.

To the junior high boys who led the chase, the running of the goats was a party. Their joy was instant and richly distilled by the unexpected chaos. And the boys appeared to have the best chance of making the catch. A couple of them had already launched themselves in heroic flying tackles but had narrowly missed, ending up ass over teakettle on the turf. John found himself plotting a direct path of interception, slanting toward the concourse runway to head off the hoofed leader. He dodged through the jumble of parked cars and turned his jog into a sprint.

"Grab that goat!" Julia Schlegel screamed.

John heard her voice as personally meant for him. He threw off his coat and vaulted the rail fence separating the parking lot from the concourse. He was running in relatively open space. But halfway between him and the highway, he saw four people form a line across the empty concourse. He wondered how they had anticipated taking this strategic position and then holding it. One of the figures sat in a motorized wheelchair. There were a couple of women crouched in a sort of wrestling profile, arms stretched wide, body language that precedes going to the mat. All four of these people were ancient. John did quick calculations and realized the collective age of this quartet possibly totaled three hundred years. The women looked ready, and with their arms spread, they presented a formidable gauntlet. How could these people move with such confidence? The geriatric squad of linebackers looked ready to cut the goats off at the pass. They weren't fooling around. The white-haired man in the wheelchair made a feeble whooping sound as if to compete with the goat chorus.

"Bring it on!" he shouted. He waved a cap at John, as if he knew him.

John stalked toward the thundering herd of animals and humans. Brat, the lead goat, made a direct line for him, closing the distance in a flash. John crouched low and made himself wide. He prepared for Brat's swerve. He feinted left and lunged right. Sure enough, Brat hit him in the chest but squirted through his arms. He got one hand on her neck but she was slippery. He hung on, losing his balance and being dragged across the concourse. He got another hand on her hind leg, but she started kicking and her hooves were sharp. Then she broke free.

The Mennonite spectators stopped surging forward and went silent as they watched the goatherd thunder toward the crouching Gang of Four, ready to practice their clothesline moves. The seniors, near the end of the concourse, were prepared to make their last stand.

Brat ran directly into the lap of the man in the wheelchair, who had executed a startling reverse move that even the supple goat did not fully anticipate. It was like a game of red rover. "Gotcha!" the white-haired gentleman shouted. He was premature—he wasn't strong enough to hold her. She squirmed out of his lap and came thundering now in the opposite direction, a streak of barreling bronze fur.

The running of the goats now entered the end game. John was ready. All the instincts of mastery came to a head in the farm boy from Meade and he told himself he would not be denied. This kind of mental framework had made John a good breaker of horses, and it served him well. Brat recognized she was surrounded, nowhere to go. On one end of the concourse the old people were lined up like a wall, and coming from the other direction, a phalanx of Mennonites advanced with a laughing preacher at their head. All they lacked were pitchforks and clubs. Brat's wisdom deserted her and she panicked. She practically leaped into John's waiting arms. He grabbed her around the middle and held one leg in a vise-like grip. She kicked furiously but his hands were too strong. John knelt down on the runway and she blatted pitifully as he whispered into one of her long, floppy ears. The boys gathered around to pet Brat, who struggled a little in John's arms and then settled down.

Julia Schlegel walked up, slightly flushed. The other goats meekly followed her now that Brat was under control. She looked at John. "Do they call you the goat whisperer, Reverend Reimer?"

"Never before today. Who knew?" he said. He sat on the concourse getting the seat of his pants dirty, with the goat wrapped up securely in his arms, but he didn't care. This animal was his, and he had no intention of losing her. He felt as charming and triumphant as a seventh-grade boy. He looked at the black polished boots of the master farmer and followed their tight line up her legs to the jodhpurs and jacket to her glowing face. She blew a strand of silky black hair out of her eyes and tucked it in under her velvet helmet.

"Thank you. I don't know who opened the gate, but when Brat sees an opportunity, she takes it. And she has her followers," Julia added, with the smile raising her upper lip over her very white teeth. "She is a natural leader. And you have done me such a great service, thank you *very* much!"

"Happy to help," John said. He got to his knees, goat in his arms, and stood. He turned toward the old people who had bottled up the concourse and enabled him to capture the Brat. Ann Hiebert, the medical missionary, came running toward him. "That was a determined animal," she said. "I have seen the running of the bulls in Pamplona, but I must declare they have nothing on these Kansas goats."

Ann brushed off her blue jeans with her hands. "Did you audition for this part?" She beamed a smile on John and her face wrinkled into a crabapple of wizened joy. Then she nodded to her companion who had motored up alongside her in his wheelchair. "This is Caleb Epp, retired professor of physics and chemistry."

Epp doffed his hat. His Ray-Bans were still askew from his recent tussle. John nodded. "It is good to see you, Professor Epp." He remembered Epp covered in chalk dust at the front of a classroom, the blackboard covered in numbers and letters. Now the man sitting in a motorized chair spoke with undiminished power.

"I hear we have a few months to get reacquainted, Reverend. Welcome back." He wore a Tabor Bluejays cap. "Come visit me at the Village."

"I will," John said.

"And this is Katie Nikkel," Ann said. "I'm sure you have met before. Retired professor of German and Russian. Katie, John Reimer."

"Pleased to see you again, Professor Nikkel," John said. "I would shake your hand but am afraid this goat would make another break for freedom."

"Well, you seem rather taken with your new friend," Nikkel observed. Her eyes moved from the goat to Julia Schlegel, who stood watching. The professor of languages cracked a smile that conveyed multiple meanings.

"It is understood, I think," she said, "that you are an uncompromising jailer." Nikkel's thin lips drew a straight line on her face, and John found himself searching for clues to the joke. She had always had this effect on him in class. She was as severe and inscrutable as ever.

The fourth member of the entourage stepped up and put a hand out. Reimer shook it and returned quickly to his two-handed grip on Brat.

He didn't want to take any chances. The man spoke. "I'm just a poor dirt farmer out here keeping company with the Brain Trust. Good to see you again, Reverend Reimer. I'm the other John. John Schroeder. You might remember me from Ebenholzer. I'm not master of the data like Epp here, but I can tell you a few stories."

"Of course," John said him. "Hello, again. It is very good to see you."

"I need to run, but you can find me most afternoons at the Copper Kettle," Schroeder said, winking as if he had some secret. "Let's get reacquainted."

Schroeder doffed his Co-op Seed cap. John watched him disappear into the crowd. He walked with a twisted, tough gait, from the pelvis down sinuously gliding like an eternal sixteen-year-old while his thick powerful arms sprouted from the upper body like stiff, ancient branches. *The bonsai cowboy*, John thought.

The goats docilely followed their master, Julia, who walked beside John as he carried Brat back to the pen. Julia unlatched the gate for the wayward goats to follow her inside. John deposited Brat on the ground. The reunited herd jumped together. Julia handed John a handful of tickets that she took out of the inside breast pocket of her riding jacket.

"What's this?" John said.

"It will get you a free bowl of birria at our food concession on the concourse. Goat stew. We teamed up with Tata's Birrieria and Taco Stand in Wichita. I recommend the stew with a couple of plain tortillas. Then you should chase it with our gelato. Made with genuine Nubian goat milk. You can't go wrong. Thanks again."

"Is the goat meat from your farm?"

"Possibly. We castrate all the boys and ship them out to another farm here in Hutchinson shortly after birth. Jared's outfit handles the meat side of things. We're more focused on dairy, the goat cheese and gelato. All our goats at Schlegel Dahlke are girls."

"I see," John said. "I was wondering about a girl named Brat."

"Many people do, John. I'm so sorry I have an appointment now. I have an informational talk and the petting zoo in five minutes. It's the life of a farmer. We'll have you over for dinner one of these days."

"I would like that," John said. After all the adventure, he felt like doffing a cowboy hat and taking a bow. He walked away laughing and looking at the tickets.

And at that moment he felt a familiar hand grip his right bicep from behind and heard laughter like music mingling with his own.

"I see you get a kick out of pleasing Marie Antoinette. She is quite fetching when she plays the peasant farmer, no?"

Nancy stuck a subtle elbow into his ribs and then put her hands in her pockets and marched on. "You know, Antoinette built the Hameau at Versailles so she could milk goats when she wanted to identify with the people."

Nancy wore a tan trench coat and boots, not quite as high or as polished as Antoinette's, but they cut a pleasing line nonetheless. She had on a black linen button-down blouse. John inhaled her scent and felt part of his chest fall away. He did this sometimes when triggered by a pretty woman. At heart he knew that he was nothing more than a high-minded spiritual leader trapped in the body of a sniffing dog. He wanted to wrap Nancy up in his arms right here in the middle of the concourse and take her home—maybe after swirling her around in front of the verenike and sausage. And, of course, that kind of thing would never do. Still, the thought pleased him.

"Discretion, big man. People are watching. You don't want this to get back to Waldo." She fell in step beside him and gave him a sideways glance without turning her head. She had a new haircut, and with the collar of her coat turned up, her sculpted head achieved near perfection. She turned her gaze fully on John. He visually lapped up the pools of her eyes, rimmed with a light touch of violet. Any darker and she could have passed for a Spiders from Mars backup dancer. The woman wasn't even trying to pass for Mennonite. What on earth?

"Here on business in Wichita?" he asked.

"Yes," she said. "We're dealing with an unruly client, and the firm sent me down to put out the fire. Fortunately, I had extra time. I've never been to the Hutchinson MCC Relief Auction before. I had to come."

Then John noticed another stealth figure coming up at on his left and felt a hand grip his arm. Alan Wiebe had gone full cowboy as the day wore on, sporting a Carhartt jacket lined with sweat stains, torn jeans, and cowboy boots. A stem of grass rode thoughtfully in his mouth. He had a red bandanna knotted around his head. John tried to remember if he'd been dressed this way an hour before.

"Mind if I join you two?" asked Alan. "I thought maybe lunch. Impromptu council meeting. I mean, they're going to ask what the hell she's doing here"—Alan pointed a thumb in Nancy's direction—"and I don't want people gossiping. Can't let them get the wrong idea. We need some cover."

"Are people talking?" John said. "I've been chasing wayward goats."

"You are a true man of the people," Nancy said. "I'm hungry."

"Well, I am just pleased as punch to meet up with the two of you like this," Alan said.

"I have tickets for birria and gelato," John said, flashing the paperwork Julia had given him. "Consider it my treat."

"You're a true gentleman, John boy," Alan said. "That's what I need. Some goat in my life. What do you say, Nancy?"

"Well, I'm all in for goat," Nancy said. "I want the full low-down on the goat princess, name of Marie Antoinette. Can anyone tell me why she is outfitted for a dressage competition?"

"Myself, I thought she was about to walk onto a Mississippi foxhunt," Alan said.

"Her father says she's running a show farm," John said. "French Charolais cattle. Tennessee walking horses. And now, goats. She poses for magazines. Her farm is very photogenic."

Nancy rolled her eyes. "I'll bet it is."

Again, John felt his chest hollow out. He accompanied Nancy into the Schlegel Dahlke tent, extracted his tickets, and joined the line for the order station. He presented the tickets and waited. He and Alan watched the staff assemble lunch on their tray: coffee, three bowls of birria, a stack of tortillas, a salsa bowl, and sour cream. They carried the food and plasticware to a table in the corner where they could look out at the crowd. They sat on either side of Nancy and tucked into the food. As they ate, Nancy said, "What's on the docket this afternoon?"

Alan said, "I don't know about John, but I will be at the main auction tent at four when they announce the winners of the silent raffle. I bought a couple of tickets. Maybe my lucky day."

"How perfectly gendered," Nancy said. "I'm going to be a nice Mennonite girl and frolic in textiles. I saw a quilt this morning that caught my eye. A blue Amish shadow design, but with a twist. Unfortunately, it seems to have drawn the attention of a couple of other bidders as well."

"Do you know who they are?" Alan said.

"A museum curator from Akron and a millionaire fruit farmer's wife from Dinuba, California. The farmer's wife is actually a hoot. She was limping. Said she was on her way to a wedding two days ago and hooked her shin on the corner of a cornhole game that her husband forgot to put away in the garage. 'Just like a man to leave stuff lying around,' she said. She tore her leg wide open on the plywood edge. Nasty wound.

She talked a little rough for a Mennonite woman, and I liked that. We discussed the possibilities of leg makeup. But I want to bid on that quilt. I have to go back to Wichita this afternoon for a meeting with the client, unfortunately."

"This quilt you're looking at. Who made it?" John said.

"Verla Arnheim."

"You should buy it. She's getting collected lately by serious investors," John said. "At least that's what Marvin said. He told me she was even more withdrawn than usual since the news of Jeffrey's death in Colorado. 'Woman does nothing but sit in the basement and stitch,' he told me. 'She's very depressed. I think I need to take her to Palm Springs or something, maybe Morro Bay to look at the big seals. We haven't vacationed in way too long,' he said."

"What are the options on the gelato?" Nancy said.

Alan recited. "Salty caramel swirl, blueberry horizon, and Krakatoa chocolate."

"Let's get some," John said. "Salty caramel for me." He handed Alan a pile of tickets.

Nancy said, "Same for me. Make it a double scoop with one Krakatoa."

Alan moved in the direction of the counter, as John turned to Nancy, and said, "Are you flying back to Chicago after your meetings in Wichita?"

"I think so. It depends on the client. But listen, just in case plans change, please keep your porch light on. I might have a delivery to make."

"I'll leave the back light on, patio courtyard," John said. "That makes more sense."

"Okay." Nancy's eyes were moving over John's face.

"It's a small town," John said.

"I understand. I am the soul of discretion."

"Oh, I know. And you draw no attention," John said, eyeing her chin and lovely mouth above the collar of her blouse. As if to answer, her hand found his leg under the table after Alan brought back the gelato. John concentrated on the salty caramel. He put his tongue on the mound of dairy pleasure balanced on the wooden spoon. Maybe Julia Schlegel was right that the future of her farm lay with the goats. But now it was definitely Nancy pulling John in like a tractor beam.

Chapter 21

John had been accosted so many times that afternoon that the weight of another hand on his shoulder didn't surprise him.

He was drinking weak, lukewarm coffee with Keegan Ratzlaff in the Mennonite Disaster Service booth. Keegan asked him, "Why can't Mennonites brew a decent cup of coffee at events like this? It's shameful. Why?"

John was about to respond with Alan's all-purpose answer, the unified-field theory of cheap-ass Mennonites, when Keegan abandoned John to seek a refill of the terrible brew.

John thought of his mother. She would have called it dishwater. Carol Campbell, sitting nearby, was reviewing with John her use of weight training and Suzanne Somers's ThighMaster, topics of greater interest to her than prattle about beverage quality. John asked her if Levi was at the auction, and she said no, he was feeling under the weather.

Then Sheriff Veblen appeared at the periphery of the concourse entrance to MDS and hesitated. John invited him to sit down because his presence afforded a nice buffer. John was not sure how he could avoid the subject of Campbell in Carol's presence and he imagined just what it would be like to break the hard truth to her here and now: that evangelist-entrepreneur husband of hers was a grifter without a soul. Then the pressure on his back repeated itself. John turned around.

It was Schroeder, bonsai cowboy and member of the recently infamous Gang of Four. "You need to get over to the machine shed, John. They're pulling raffle tickets for the roadster and the Land Rover in about fifteen minutes."

Everything seemed to happen at once.

Schroeder grabbed John's arm to get his attention and bent down to speak in his ear. "Let me repeat. You are wanted at the machine shed," he said. "Your buddy Alan Wiebe said you can't miss it. They're drawing raffle tickets."

"Why would I care?" John said. "I don't have any skin in that game." The raffle tickets were fifty bucks apiece. John had briefly thought about buying a couple, then decided against throwing away cash.

"Oh, I think you do. Alan can be stubborn," Schroeder said. "He said you had at least twenty tickets riding in that raffle and he has a good feeling."

"Alan is an emotional guy," John quipped. "But twenty tickets? Impossible."

"John, that coffee water must have put you to sleep." Schroeder leaned in. "Some people around here love you, man. They bought a few tickets in your name. You probably have a lot more than twenty tickets riding. Now let's go."

"Okay," John said. "Excuse me, sheriff. Excuse me, Carol. I am being summoned."

He followed Schroeder across the concourse. When they arrived at the machine shed doorway, it was congested with men and boys eager to follow the action. The public-address system had broken down so from the inside came a low babble of voices and, every once in a while, a shout. Someone had just bid twenty-two thousand dollars for the roadster.

The auctioneer was a slim mustached youth who looked barely out of high school but had a baritone voice that made him sound twenty years older. He stepped up on the dais to call audibles on the 1959 Chevrolet Bel Air. The starting bid was five thousand and that rapidly climbed to eight.

"Eighty-one hundred? Eighty-two hundred, I see that hand, we have eighty-two from the cowboy hat on my right. Come on, now, people, come on, now, this is Detroit golden age engineering, when GM was king. Do I hear nine thousand dollars? Come on, now press your pedal to the metal, I don't care if you're a sorry dirt farmer in overalls or some city slicker Menno who keeps it fancy. Do I hear nine thousand? If you're black bumper I'm happy to pass you a can of spray paint.

"Come on, now, ten thousand, I see that hand, thank you, thank you, you in the back row there who needs a shave. Going for eleven! Are you good for eleven? For this glorious piece of engineering, perfectly reconditioned by Unger Motors in Henderson and *donated*, thank you, Unger Motors! Show this machine *respect*, my brothers and sisters! Eleven now, I ask. I see a hand, the gentleman with the handlebar mustache. Wait! I see two hands, with all the fingers outstretched, plus a victory sign. That must mean twelve thousand dollars! I have a twelve thousand dollar bid for this sweet ride! Let me confirm that bid, ladies and gentlemen! I have a bid of twelve *thousand* dollars! People, you are doing the Lord's work here, you are working a mighty deed. Do I have thirteen? Can someone give me thirteen? Reach deep, people, listen to your heart, reach deep and seek the wisdom!"

The Bel Air went for sixteen thousand to a sturdy tree farmer from British Columbia dressed in a Hawaiian shirt and hugged by his very tan wife. The auctioneer invited him to the podium to take a bow. Afterward he posed with his family next to the teardrop tail fins of the Chevy. A photographer from *Mennonite World* snapped their happy picture, and the *Wichita Eagle*'s photographer let his camera's motor drive do some talking, too. The businessman wrote a check for twenty thousand dollars, donating the extra money because he said the joy of the moment made him "want to round it up to the right amount."

The drawing for the Land Rover was, by contrast, anticlimactic but came prefaced with a touch of show business, beginning with a bluegrass band from Moundridge who brought their best game. Their vocalist had a voice clear as handspun glass. By the time they finished their second tune, half the crowd was in tears.

Then the auctioneer invited Franz Schlegel, president and chairman of the board of Schlegel Motors, to the podium. Franz wore a button-down black shirt under his black blazer. He ascended the podium and lifted both his hands to silence the crowd. He didn't need a microphone. His voice carried clearly through the space as he read from a card in his hand.

"I am pleased to tell you," he began, "that 2,483 tickets were purchased for the raffle of a 1995 silver Land Rover Discovery cruiser located under the lights to my left. That is $124,150 that will go to Mennonite Central Committee. Thank you, friends, brothers and sisters, for your generosity. Yes, please go ahead and give yourselves a big hand now." The crowd applauded with vigor. "And at this time, I want to invite the co-chairman of this MCC Hutchinson auction to the podium for the drawing of the winning ticket."

Two teenage women carried forward a bushel basket brimming with the red-tinged tickets. The auctioneer raised his hand. Franz Schlegel resumed his speech. "I am pleased to introduce to you, Mrs. Frieda Loewen of Goessel, Kansas. She has served in many capacities at this event since 1955. This year she was cochair with Doctor Irvin Plett of Cimarron. Mrs. Loewen, welcome to the podium. We are grateful for your administrative gifts and the superb organization of this year's MCC Relief Auction, the biggest and best in our fair state of Kansas. For that, you have the honor of drawing the winning ticket for this brand-new, four-wheel drive Land Rover Discovery."

More applause ensued. A blue-haired woman of seventy stepped carefully up the steps and grasped the handrail. She was in a calico dress and wore her hair in a bun covered by the most modest of head coverings. She was slightly taller than Franz. She waved to the crowd, then spoke out: "You know that I never play favorites, although Doctor Plett tried to give me instructions."

More raucous applause rumbled through the shed, mixed with laughter. The auctioneer brought out a scarf with something of a magician's flourish. "Frieda, you can't play favorites because you must draw blindfolded."

"Billy, you will spend the rest of your life seeking a submissive woman," Frieda said. "I wish you luck."

There were reasons she was popular with the crowd. She let the scarf be tied around her head. The auctioneer adjusted it in a band across her eyes. From the width of her smile, she seemed to be having some fun. The two teenagers tossed the bushel basket of tickets like a salad. Frieda stepped forward, plunged her right hand into the basket, and came out with a ticket. The auctioneer pulled the bow tied at the back of her head and the scarf dropped away. She held the ticket in front of her and brought a pair of bifocals out of her apron. She adjusted them on her nose and read in a clear voice.

"The winning ticket is number zero, five, two. That is number zero, five, two."

Alan stood by John, shuffling through a stack of ticket stubs that he fanned out in his hand like a straight flush. He smiled. Then John realized Marvin was standing on his other side, beaming like a big happy cat.

"Ticket number zero, five, two is held in the name of Reverend John Reimer," she said in a clear voice, as the crowd began to clap. John stared at Alan, who handed him the winning stub. "Take that up to the podium, John. They'll need a match."

John didn't move. Alan leaned sideways and said, "Get up there, John. Congratulations," as the crowd began to applaud. Somebody whistled.

"Are you here, Reverend Reimer? Please bring your matching stub to the podium." The auctioneer spoke in a secretive voice into the microphone, "I hear maybe the goat whisperer is still busy out on the concourse." More laughter. The crowd parted so John could pass.

"I'm told the Reverend has a solid set of farm skills and wants to stay in practice. Are you out there milking the goats, Reverend? We need a match." The auctioneer was now speaking to him personally. "Glad you could make it to the party, sir."

John stood by the auctioneer, faced the crowd, and took a modest bow as he listened to the applause. Alan stood in the back of the shed soaking up the scene. Marvin gave John two big thumbs-up.

John gave the winning ticket to Frieda, who read it and shook his hand. She held the ticket above her head and then showed it to the auctioneer and Franz. They stepped forward in turn to shake the preacher's hand.

John listened to the noise, a kind of low, contented roar. It felt like a revival meeting where he had just been washed in the blood of the lamb. He reminded himself it was only a car.

He exited the machine shed fifteen minutes later, after saying hello and shaking hands with all the people who professed to know him. When he was able to find breathing room, he looked up at the sky. He looked at the moving clouds, at the way they were starting to churn. He was still enough of a native to take note and try to interpret.

Chapter 22

The Land Rover enjoyed pride of place in the parsonage garage while the Crown Victoria stood at the curb. The sedan absorbed a thorough soak under the jagged lightning bolts blistering the dusk. The thunder crunched in successive waves. John worried about hail. He checked the weather station again. One special worry: He wanted to return the loaner to Franz and worried that a cottonwood would fall on it before he could drive it back to the lot. One of the earliest pieces of advice he had gleaned from his oldest brother, Andrew, was simple: After a good thing happens, be careful.

Marvin and Alan had decided to leave only minutes earlier. Thank goodness. He looked at his watch and wondered if Nancy was driving through this storm right now. Or worse, flying back to Chicago. He hoped she had flown out before the weather hit Wichita. Then again, he had other hopes.

The men had come by to celebrate another splendid free supper at his table and could barely contain their joy when he began heating up the lasagna and stuffed ricotta shells. He had left the lasagna out on the counter during the day to thaw. If there was one thing he knew how to do, it was to set an oven to 350 degrees, standard Mennonite cookbook temperature.

With the red sauce and a garlic baguette served on the side, the enterprise had been a success. John enjoyed hosting these dinner parties when he didn't have to cook. Marvin said it was as good as Ann Hiebert's curry dinner. Alan pulled a bottle of Valpolicella out of his briefcase and found a corkscrew in the utility silverware drawer. The men feasted. They agreed that the Halston engineer from New Jersey had learned a thing or two cooking at that diner on Route 46.

"What's his name again?" Marvin asked.

"Cellini. Tom Cellini." John wasn't his normal conversational self. He didn't want these guys to get too comfortable.

"I drink to Tom," Alan said, refilling his glass. John and Marvin had sparkling water. Then Marvin went to the kitchen cabinet and got a little glass out. He brought it back to the table and held it in his thick paw. "Actually, just a smidge, Alan. Medicinal value, you know."

These buddies were making themselves at home. John hoped he could get them out the front door before ten.

They decided not to tell him how they had raised two grand for raffle tickets all signed in John's name. "Why do I suspect you guys pulled off some kind of heist?" John asked. "Or that this whole thing was rigged?" They shook their heads.

"No," Alan said, "it was no caper. We just increased your odds, fair and square. The Lord's blessing comes to those who plan."

"Hey, no prosperity gospel for me," John insisted.

They filed into the garage after they had cleaned their plates. Sitting in the Land Rover, they admired its oak burl dashboard and inhaled the fresh new smell of spacious leather seats. Marv looked under the hood. John read their body language and figured they wanted to go for a ride, but he'd had enough adventure for one day. And besides, the day, which was not yet over, was threatening to turn into a raging storm. A second, bigger storm cell was arriving. And he was afraid that if they started talking vehicle details, he might sound ungrateful. He had made the mistake of opening the manual and noticed the numbers for estimated fuel mileage. A pretty beast of a machine—and a thirsty one. A question about insuring it in Chicago felt like a rock in his shoe, so he decided to stop thinking about it. All problems could not be solved on a dark and stormy night. At nine o'clock, John sat in his Barcalounger and began to yawn. He decided there was no point in subtlety.

The men sat in the living room and watched John take off his shoes.

"I'm beat," he said. "I think it was the goat chase."

"You want us out of here. I get it. I mean, tomorrow is Sunday, isn't it? You probably have to put the finishing touches on your sermon," Marvin said. He was disappointed. He didn't want the evening to end. "Let's get together Monday then and talk about your chat with Campbell."

"I already told you, Marv, I wish I had more information. He was pretty clammed up," John said. "He played dumb."

And then, changing the subject: "And here's the deal, guys, I promise to take you for a joy ride, but tonight cannot be the night." He turned up the volume on the television. The weatherman was talking about wind shears.

"We'd better go," Alan said, "before this storm turns ugly."

After they left, John rinsed plates and loaded the dishwasher.

Then rain poured from the sky as if out of a giant pump. A lightning bolt hit a telephone pole a block away from John's place on Sacra Via and lit up the world. The thumping crash that followed several seconds later dwindled to a fuzzy grumble followed by a smell of burning metal and rubber, as the power grid went dark. The aftershock rattled the windows. John stood immobile and thought, *This is why most Midwesterners believe in God.*

Then in the darkness came silence broken by the wicked hiss of rain and more thunderclaps that shook the house's foundation. Through the mayhem John heard something else: a faint knocking on the back patio door that opened onto the inner courtyard.

He didn't look because he already knew who was there. He opened the door and Nancy burst inside, soaking wet in a black hooded garment. A flash of light lit her up. Her hair was streaming, and her face washed by rain. Her eyes were bright under the running mascara. She was barefoot and held her boots in one hand. Slung over her shoulder was a soft tote bag and a rectangular plastic parcel on a carrying strap. She dropped both items on the floor beside her boots and stepped into John's waiting arms.

Her mouth moved over his face. "John, you have no idea. I want you back home. In my house." She smelled of rain and perfume.

He gripped her wet head in his hands and savored her. He leaned his full weight into hers, and she pulled him in closer before she said, "Take me to bed, John, and put your hands on me. Talk to me like that poet, the way you promised."

A short time later he offered:

> License my roving hands, and let them go,
> Before, behind, between, above, below.
> O my America! my new-found-land,
> My kingdom, safeliest when with one man mann'd.

Nancy said, "Don't stop," and later she heard him say, "All joys are due to thee, as souls unbodied, bodies unclothed must be."

They rested together. Nancy turned on her side and said, "Mmmm. That was very nice. I like it dark like this. But shouldn't we light a candle or two? I'm afraid of tripping over something."

John said, "I'm loaded with candles. And let me ask, are you hungry? I have leftover lasagna. If the power comes back on, I could heat up a piece."

Nancy snorted. "Oh, you could heat it up all right. Come here, old man. Let me taste your ear."

John found a flashlight and procured a couple of column candles from the china cabinet. He lit them and set them beside the master bathroom sink. Nancy stood behind him. He said, "I can smell your candy." In the wavering light she bent over to scratch her ankle, and he watched her lean down in the near darkness. She wore a towel around her waist. She took hold of his hand to keep her balance.

She stood up, saying, "Let me show you what I bid on this afternoon. While you were winning the Land Rover, I was buying this."

She walked across the room to the rectangular carrying case she had dropped on the floor beside her purse. "This is ours," she said. She unzipped the package and unfolded what was inside. It was the Amish shadow quilt that had hung in the barn earlier in the day. She draped it over the back of the sofa and went into the master bathroom, returning with one of the burning candles, which she set on an end table. The design rippled through geometric waves of cobalt blue. The stitching created an effect of cubes ambulating in a latticed grid, and it also created an illusion of three-dimensional depth, like an Escher print. Even while still, everything tumbled in motion. *One could get lost in a quilt like this*, John thought.

"What do you mean 'ours'?" he said. "It's yours. You bought it."

"John, you're a bit dense sometimes. If I have anything to say about anything, you will be sleeping under it with me on a regular basis, and very soon, I hope."

"Oh. I see."

"John, I'm approaching middle age. I am a woman with goals."

"Are you sure of your math? I thought you were thirty-two."

"Don't fuck with me, John. Thank God I'm not half your age." Another blast of thunder shook the house and lightning lit up the sky. More sheets of rain blew against the windows and rattled them. The drops hit with the force of little projectiles.

He recovered his voice. "You are barely over thirty, young woman, and I am Horus, ancient and mighty sky god, and I ordered this storm with my hammer."

"Don't you mean Thor?"

He made a grab for her but she dodged out of his grasp. She retrieved the quilt from the living room. She spread it out over the bed and then pulled back the corner of the covers. She sat on the bed and said, "Come here."

"What are you going to do?" he asked.

"How about this . . . and this . . . and this?" she said. Her hand moved expertly. He realized she was touching all the fingers of his left hand. She grasped his ring finger.

He said, "What do you mean?"

"What on earth could I possibly be talking about?" she said. Her kisses rained down.

At two she sat up. Their legs were intertwined. John's hand rested on her smooth hip.

"I need to go," she said.

John looked at the clock. "Now?"

"It won't do for me to walk out of this house in the bright light of Sunday morning. My plane flies out of Wichita super early, and I have to pack the rest of my things at the hotel."

She folded the quilt and pushed it into the zip bag. He watched her adjust her skirt on her hips and button up her blouse. "Mind if I borrow your toothbrush?" she asked.

He looked at her in the bathroom mirror, with toothpaste suds at the corner of her mouth. She bent over the sink and spit. Her eyes met his for a moment in the mirror.

"I'm a real treat at two in the morning, don't you think?" she said. She pursed her lips and applied lipstick. "I think I'm ready," she said, digging through her handbag. "Just let me check for my keys."

"Where are you parked?" John said.

"Around the corner."

John opened the front door. "The power is still out," he said.

She said, "Lucky me. And listen. I want to bring you back to Chicago in one piece. Go easy on Campbell. Avoid Marie Antoinette." She pulled on the hoodie. The thin black garment transformed her striking figure into something inchoate. She walked into the dark, a shadow in the larger shadows.

He went back to bed. Later, he heard a truck grind slowly through the alley, then came the sound of a chainsaw. They were cutting down fallen trees, replacing downed wires. He imagined they'd switch out the transformer on the toasted telephone pole. He tumbled down a maze of cobalt blue chairs that morphed into an orderly grid.

Chapter 23

Monday morning John ran three uninspired miles at the high school. Neither Carol nor Oscar the water boy were in sight. By mile three John had slowed to a labored jog. He tried to push through the wall, achieving something like a geriatric kick on the last four hundred yards. It yielded the familiar cleansing, winded feeling. He put his hands on his knees, and after getting his breath, stood up and walked to the railing by the bleachers. He toweled off his face. Water still lay puddled on the outer edge of the track. A maple had blown over near the edge of the parking lot from Saturday night's deluge. Given the storm's intensity, Marion Hills had been fortunate.

That word—"fortunate"—could also describe his weekend. The parishioners had warmly congratulated him on their way out the foyer door at the end of the service—mostly about his skill at running down goats and acquisition of a Land Rover. "The Lord is good," Mr. Nuss said. He wore a buttoned-up, dark-green flannel shirt and removed his black-rimmed plastic glasses as he shook John's hand. "The Lord saw the need and He provided."

"I got lucky," John said, smiling, and decided it wasn't the time or place to interrogate Nuss's theological premise.

Ten parishioners said they appreciated his sermon. For John, who kept track of such statistics, that was close to a record. Diminutive Ann Hiebert, dressed in a black pantsuit and sporting her chunky man's watch and a quartz pendant, cradled his hand in both of hers. "Good message," she said, like a speech coach to a schoolboy. "Keep telling the stories. Especially the Chicago stories. They are more unpredictable and less didactic. I appreciate that."

John didn't tell her it was mostly a retread of a sermon he had first preached in Minneapolis twenty years earlier, with material from

Chicago sprinkled in. He leaned over and said to her, "Your curry dinner was a smash hit. Thank you."

"I'm very pleased to hear you say that. And look, John, if you liked the tikka, wait till you taste my butter chicken. I'll bring you some."

John Schroeder came through the line, and Reimer appraised him carefully. The man resembled a bent, gnarled coat hanger moving with fluid grace, and John still wondered how he did it. He said to the cowboy, "I didn't expect to see you here, but thank you very much."

"I'm not much of a churchgoing man anymore," Schroeder said, "but I was darned curious what you'd have to say for yourself this morning."

"I hope I didn't disappoint. Maybe I can bring you back," John said.

Schroeder replied, "Don't get cocky. The deal is coffee tomorrow morning. Tell me, are you a Copper Kettle kind of guy or more of a Little Pleasures type?"

John imagined Schroeder winked. "Well, that's a loaded question. Maybe I'll answer you tomorrow."

"See you then, Reverend." John watched Schroeder take a cowboy hat from a peg in the foyer and head outside into the sun.

When Julia Schlegel greeted the minister, she showed demure gratitude. John marveled at her finishing school perfection. She moved with a slightly pigeon-toed gait in fancy high heels and a sheath pencil skirt. She wore a riding jacket to perfection in keeping with the dressage look of the day before. She shook his hand and held it just a moment. "You're a preacher and a gentleman, Reverend Reimer. If you hadn't caught Brat, we would have required the local police or a ranching posse. Thank you." Her husband smiled and let her do the talking. John reminded himself that Ken was actually named Ken.

Linda had come by his office shortly after the congregation had all exited the foyer. He was sitting in his office chair, feeling drained but content. She closed his door behind her and said to him, "Reverend Reimer, do you have any idea how you just knocked it out of the park? We had almost six hundred in attendance! Everybody loved your sermon."

"Don't get too excited. A few of them told me it was all right. The novelty will wear off. They don't care about the personal yarn spinning or even my sad collection of spiritual nuggets. They just wanted my comments on the goats and the new car. The thrill of big-city anecdotes. They think they want to be edified but they really prefer entertainment."

"And you delivered!" Linda said. "Why so grumpy?" She seemed worked up. She was attired in a professional pantsuit with a black ribbon necktie at her throat. Was she aiming for a more formal appearance of late? Was John imagining that she had ditched the pink sweaters?

She kept talking: "More farm-boy stories from Meade!" she said. "All that detail about how to gentle a nasty horse! Even the kids listened, and our kids don't listen well. They're a bunch of entitled little spit ballers. The entire pulpit committee is walking around all puffed up because they decided to bring you here."

"Well, Waldo had something to do with it, too," John said.

He sensed something stronger in Linda as she gave him the pep talk. She was beginning to speak her own mind without fear. He thought about this quality that certain individuals develop in life. Vi had most certainly had it. And Nancy possessed such an ability, in spades. Ann Hiebert had probably possessed it from the time she was four. His own daughter, Sarah, delivered truth without fear of consequences in a blunt diplomatic vocabulary.

Now as he toweled off the back of his neck beside the high school track, he removed his rainbow Jesus headband and put it in the pocket of his sweatpants. Then he walked back to the parsonage. On the way, a tree crew was running downed branches through a wood chipper behind their rig. He waved. Half an hour later, after he showered and dressed, he drove to Little Pleasures.

Chapter 24

Most of the customers at Rachel's place were ordering the Eggs Benedict Breakfast Sandwich, served with a side of frisée lettuce dressed with
lemon and balsamic. Veblen was there and raised a hand of greeting to
John, pointing at his plate with approval. A sidewalk chalk signboard
advertised the daily special. The eggs came with an extra dollop of hol-
landaise in a miniature paper cup.

"What will Reverend Reimer have this morning?" Addressing John,
Rachel had a distinct burr in her throat, as if she'd been shouting too early
in the kitchen. Combined with the full wattage of her smile and a blue
silk scarf twisted into a special knot atop her head, the effect was striking.

John pondered his options. "The breakfast sandwich, I think," he
said. "Eggs Benedict? Is this a real breakfast sandwich?"

Rachel puffed out her cheeks in a small pout. "Okay, I'll admit I'm
trying to attract the pickup and gunrack crowd. If I did not put 'breakfast
sandwich' in the title they wouldn't bite. Coffee?"

"Please. And I'll take that sandwich with a knife and fork, thank
you."

She brought him coffee. John looked at the Monday morning paper and saw from the center photo section that he'd made the news at
the MCC auction. In the photo he held a Nubian goat in his arms and
grinned for the camera.

Rachel looked over his shoulder after putting the plate in front of
him. She pointed at the picture of Marie Antoinette who stood by his
side, projecting beatific calm. "You and Julia Schlegel make quite a pair
now. You appear with her in a photo spread, you'll get real famous. Maybe
even achieve notoriety."

John said, "I want to clip this and send it to someone I know." He
gave Rachel a look.

A figure outside with the posture of a bent piece of barbed wire pushed through the door and made the bell ring. He tilted the cowboy hat back on his head to expose the visage of an ancient sea turtle. His skin had the consistency of flogged, charred leather, and the age spots marring his face were map and testament to decades of sun damage. Schroeder saw John and walked over.

"Mr. Schroeder," John said, extending his hand for a shake. "We meet again. Please sit down. You absolutely want the breakfast sandwich."

"Breakfast sandwich, my ass," Schroeder said, taking a seat. "I read that sign on the sidewalk and figured you might be attracted to this French decadence passing as local cuisine." He nudged the little paper cup beside John's plate with a grubby index finger. "What's this, Holland-easy sauce? Oh, all right, I'll try it."

After the men devoured the last morsels of English muffin on their plates and mopped up the sauced egg yolks, Schroeder didn't waste any time.

"I wanted to see you for a couple of reasons. One being that it's been way too long and reconnecting seemed the right thing to do. The second is that there's talk among some of the cattlemen I spend time with at the Copper Kettle."

"About what, exactly?"

"I'll cut to the chase. Talk about the Schlegels putting you in their pocket."

"What's that about?" John looked at Schroeder. "Sorry to tell you this, but gossip never held any veto power over my choice of friends. Besides, isn't that what the big money always does? Put you in their pocket?"

"You haven't lost a step, have you, John? You were always pretty skillful trading on gossip. I just want you to know the cattle association isn't duly impressed. You might be getting such a big hug from the Schlegel outfit that you're going blind."

"You know you're not the first person to suggest that. I'm listening. What else has Levi done to raise your hackles? He was never that popular among the farmers or the ranchers, as I recall it thirty years ago," John said. "Already then, he was buying out more than his fair share. Financial success has a way of creating enemies."

"Now you're talking straight, preacher. On top of that, some of my neighbors are in a lather because he's actually colluding with the feds in this cockamamie scheme for a national park."

"You mean Tallgrass Prairie?" John said.

"That's exactly what I mean. Some of my acquaintances in Chase County asked Schlegel to sign on to a document to the county commissioners. The letter raised a few questions about the feds' encroaching authority. Schlegel refused to sign. He said it was no encroachment, and he called it a Nature Conservancy lease done with full compliance of the owners."

"You have a problem with that?" John said.

Schroeder was chewing the last of his breakfast sandwich. "Some of my acquaintances see this Nature Conservancy lease on the land as a smokescreen. I don't necessarily agree with all of them, but I think they raise several legitimate questions. How much acreage do the feds want to control? What about local ranchers and farmers? Shit. What's next? Marion Reservoir run by National Park rangers? Next thing you know these effete wine sippers will ban ATVs and V-8 engines."

Rachel came over and refilled their coffees. John looked at Schroeder, an old friend from way back, and felt the yawning abyss of the culture gap separating him and the rancher. He also felt pity, and pity never made him feel good. The man had tipped over into the hoary Kansas pastime of conspiracy theories, embraced some rather predictable redneck stereotypes, and John believed he was better than that.

"What else?" John asked. "I could ask you about your views of Jewish bankers on the East Coast taking over Cottonwood Falls, but I'm interested in what you say at a more local level. It seems to me the most ancient rivalry was between the ranchers and the farmers. That's what the story of Cain and Abel was all about. God seemed to favor the itinerant herders initially. But it was the farmers who nailed down property rights to grow grain that built the whole modern system of ownership, maybe banking itself. Look, for instance, at all the big cattle operations in the Flint Hills. All the would-be tycoons went under, overextended. Nobody, and I mean nobody, could make the numbers work."

"Are you talking like a landowner," Schroeder said, "or trying to school me in a history lesson?"

"I still have a few parcels in Meade, actually, if you're curious."

"A preacher full of surprises. Keep talking."

"I know from experience the cattle business is tough. About all those big ranchers left behind in Chase County were a couple of overbuilt limestone barns big as castles. Those things will still be standing after World War III. But I digress. Let me recap what you and the dirt farmers have decided," John said to the bonsai cowboy. "You're telling me now that the ranchers and farmers have made common cause against the people they see as outsiders: the federal government and big banks, not to mention wicked environmentalists like the Nature Conservancy folks. Do I read you right?"

"Look, John, I despise the fake cowboys and the Branson trash. They're not real. I also am not fond of show farms, by the way. They're a pain in my ass. I'm just a simple dirt farmer who runs a few head of cattle on a narrow margin. I'm trying to get by."

"Exactly. And now you see the outsiders as encroaching on your local right to run cattle or plant wheat. You're even more pissed off that the local financier and his bird-loving family are concerned about the plight of the snowy owl in the Flint Hills and half a dozen other liberal pinko causes while they continue to buy out failing farmers and businesses. A few thousand acres set aside to run a few buffalo or maybe longhorn Texas heritage cattle, some land where the grass can grow and not get overgrazed—for you that spells trouble. What's next, the United Nations and their black helicopters flying overhead?"

John stopped talking. Maybe he was going a little too far.

"No," Schroeder replied. "But funny you should mention black helicopters. I can show you unmarked black semitrucks if you're interested in a little night excursion. There is all kind of speculation right now about what the hell is going on out there. Maybe you should take a look yourself."

"Entire convoys?" John said. "Tinted windows? Rigs with Russian mafia drivers?"

Schroeder finished his sandwich and wiped his hands on the napkin which he crumpled up and dropped on the table. He threw down a ten-dollar bill beside his plate and stood up to go. "I've seen two, sometimes three, parked out at an airstrip in Chase."

"Well, you know the saying, where two or three are gathered—"

"Don't yank my chain, John. I'm shooting straight here. I can show you things."

"Whose property?"

"Come along and I'll provide the show-and-tell. I don't read the big-city newspapers and I can't do the fancy exegesis—am I pronouncing that right?—but I know what I've seen."

"Connections to Levi?"

"Could be," Schroeder said. "That's one of the things I want to find out." The look he gave was not warm. "You push me too hard, John, and I don't mind walking away from the conversation."

John made a tent with his fingers and put his elbows on the table. Without looking up, he said, "I might have some open time on my evening schedule in a week or so. Stay in touch. Call me if you want to keep talking." He imagined Nancy shaking her head and he heard her voice distinctly: *No, no, you fool. You crazy fool.*

Schroeder jammed his hat down hard on his crusty brow. He said, "Maybe I'm getting too old for stupid arguments. See you around. Don't get too close now to those damn goats. You might suffer a headbutt." He lurched out of the door, got into his pickup truck, and roared away.

Rachel came by. "More coffee?"

"No, I think I'm through. It was very good. You're setting new standards of culinary excellence for Marion Hills."

"That Schroeder fellow is an angry man, isn't he?" Rachel said, clearing the plates.

"He has his moments," John said. "Let me ask you: As someone who's come to Marion Hills with a fresh perspective, do you ever pick up on the rage that percolates through this town?"

"Every day, Reverend. Every day."

John paid his bill and headed for the front door. At a table in the corner, three farmers sat together and watched him. He didn't recognize any of their faces, and they didn't touch their caps in the standard local signal of greeting. Their eyes were stone cold.

Around here, you didn't even have to be Mennonite to practice the fine art of shunning.

Chapter 25

The voice on the other end of the phone came through as a screech, a tone of strained protest, a muffled shout with too much wind at its back. It crackled with age and malice. There was an utterance of garbled words ending with "happy."

"Say again? This is John Reimer. May I ask who is calling?"

"Are you happy, John? Tell me. Are you happy?"

"Happy about what?"

"With the vehicle? The Land Rover! Goddammit, do I have to spell it out?" John doubted this was a customer service satisfaction survey.

The voice continued. "Did you hear me? I said, are you happy?'"

John detected a note of hostility. *Is this a prank?*

"May I ask who's calling?"

"It's Levi! Dammit, John, don't you recognize Levi Schlegel, you old coot? Fucking hell."

John had never heard Levi talk this way. This was either a demon impersonator or an episode of *The Twilight Zone*. "Levi, you sound a little worked up. Is everything all right?"

"It sure is. Just dandy. Like I'm standing next to a lucky lady, you know? How do you like the new vehicle?"

"Levi, I feel like the luckiest man in Marion County right now."

"Well, John, maybe you are, maybe you are. Share some of that luck with me, for crying out loud, because I need it. I'm calling to make sure you come in to the dealership and sign all the paperwork."

"Okay," John said, "I will do that." He hesitated. Franz had told him in Hutchinson that all the paperwork was already taken care of. Maybe there was more. But wouldn't Franz take care of that? Why was Levi suddenly micromanaging?

"John, the state and county licensing process gets more convoluted each passing year. I don't know what else to tell you. Nitwits and morons. Wish I could sweep them away. And the insurance companies! The worst! Always one more fucking form to sign and notarize. One more lawyer or sissy-boy bureaucrat to pay. It's worse than dealing with the federal government. I'm tired of it, and I'm so sorry to inflict it on you. Sorry if I sound impatient."

"I understand, Levi. Don't worry. I'll be by this afternoon to sign whatever you need me to sign."

"I'm running out of file cabinets for the paperwork, I swear I'm up to my ears—"

John heard background noise and another rising male voice. Then came breaking noise, something heavy, metallic. Static crashed through the phone. A woman said in notes of low, pleading desperation, "Oh, Levi." Franz's voice cut through the chaos, and John could make out the last two words, "Attending nurse."

John said, "Levi, where are you calling from?"

"Oh, yes, John, there you are. Surely you know I'm at Marion Hills Hospital."

"I'm sorry to hear that," John said. A click sounded and the line went dead. John's phone rang again a minute later. It was Franz.

"I apologize, John. I'm calling you back from the hospital front desk. Dad's here. The noise you just heard was him dropping the phone."

"This is very sudden," John said.

"He fell down in the driveway this morning. They're keeping him under observation but haven't figured out anything definite yet. They're running tests. Elevated heart rate and blood pressure."

"He asked me to come by and sign additional paperwork."

"Ignore that," Franz said. "Dad is confused. Doctor Thiessen says he is also dehydrated. They hooked him up to a glucose drip. He's none too happy. It was a bit of a struggle."

"Was that what I heard falling over?"

"Yes. Besides the phone."

"Franz, I am sorry. Please let me know what I can do."

"They're not allowing visitors. Obviously, he's in no condition to receive any. He just needs to get his blood sugars evened out. At least that's what I'm told."

"Give Eva my regards," John said. "How is she doing?"

"She's solid, John. Thanks, I'll keep you in the loop."

"Thank you, Franz."

Levi was shouting in the background when Franz hung up. John couldn't understand it, this voice of an enraged animal speaking Low German.

Chapter 26

Reverend John Reimer, "When the Ground Opened Its Mouth"
(Genesis 4:1–17), Marion Hills Mennonite Church

Now the man knew his wife Eve, and she conceived and bore Cain, saying, "I have produced a man with the help of the LORD." Next she bore his brother Abel. Now Abel was a keeper of sheep, and Cain a tiller of the ground. In the course of time Cain brought to the LORD an offering of the fruit of the ground, and Abel for his part brought of the firstlings of his flock, their fat portions. And the LORD had regard for Abel and his offering, but for Cain and his offering he had no regard. So Cain was very angry, and his countenance fell. The LORD said to Cain, "Why are you angry, and why has your countenance fallen? If you do well, will you not be accepted? And if you do not do well, sin is lurking at the door; its desire is for you, but you must master it."

Cain said to his brother Abel, "Let us go out to the field." And when they were in the field, Cain rose up against his brother Abel, and killed him. Then the LORD said to Cain, "Where is your brother Abel?" He said, "I do not know; am I my brother's keeper?" And the LORD said, "What have you done? Listen; your brother's blood is crying out to me from the ground! And now you are cursed from the ground, which has opened its mouth to receive your brother's blood from your hand. When you till the ground, it will no longer yield to you its strength; you will be a fugitive and a wanderer on the earth." Cain said to the LORD, "My punishment is greater than I can bear! Today you have driven me away from the soil, and I shall be hidden from your face; I shall be a fugitive and a wanderer on the earth, and anyone who meets me may kill me." Then the LORD said to him, "Not so! Whoever kills Cain will suffer a sevenfold vengeance." And the LORD put a mark on Cain, so that no one who came upon him would kill him. Then Cain went away from the presence of the LORD, and settled in the land of Nod, east of Eden.

Cain knew his wife, and she conceived and bore Enoch; and he built a city, and named it Enoch after his son Enoch.

Thus ends the ancient testimony.

A short time ago, when I spoke with Billy Ray Baumgartner, he sat on his bunk in a jail cell, not far from this pulpit. Before my interview, he had confessed to Sheriff Gustav Veblen that he had murdered his brother Dexter. He fired a pistol into the back of his brother's head. This followed a disagreement over a card game in Billy Ray's house on the west side of town. His friend Rufus was also playing. When he said something that upset Billy Ray, Billy Ray responded by shooting him twice in the face. Dexter was Billy Ray's brother. By all accounts, Rufus was Billy Ray's best friend.

Billy Ray was transferred to the Abilene jail and then the federal penitentiary in Leavenworth shortly after we spoke. He has been charged with two counts of murder and he does not deny the charges. He has refused a lawyer. Our church secretary, Linda Ebel, and Sheriff Veblen both informed me that this was the first double murder to occur in Marion Hills in more than one hundred years. They were not wrong.

Many of you follow the newspapers and are talking about it. I know. All I have to do is go into the Copper Kettle or Little Pleasures in the morning for breakfast and listen. And I hear about it directly from you.

When I met with Billy Ray, he asked me to help him get a television set for his jail cell. The sheriff denied his request because he said it would pose a security risk to the inmate. They had taken away Billy's belt and shoelaces to prevent him from harming himself. I went to visit Billy Ray's mother shortly after I saw him at the jail, but she had left town. When I reached her by phone, she was grieving and didn't want to talk. I can't say I blame her.

Some of you know Billy Ray from childhood. He grew up in this town, went to school here, and worked as a skilled welder at Halston Industries. As a schoolboy, he attended vacation Bible school at this church during the summers. When he was twelve, he confessed Jesus Christ as his Lord and Savior and was baptized by your late pastor, Reverend Tschetter.

As I grapple to understand these events, there is mystery here, the mystery of a soul in distress. Perhaps it will take a skilled journalist to interview Billy Ray, someone who can ask the right questions and describe his life fully and fairly. To comprehend the motivations that drove him to commit this crime. To understand his principal life experiences and tell his story the way it should be told.

I remember when the murder of the Clutter family occurred in Holcomb, Kansas, outside Garden City nearly forty years ago. That was seventy-five miles from my birthplace of Meade, which I had left only a couple of years earlier. This event delivered a seismic emotional shock to everyone living in this state, and to many in our country. Everyone was talking. The account by writer Truman Capote in his book *In Cold Blood* partly explains the events. In other ways, it only deepens the mystery of facts that elude comprehension. This recent event in Marion Hills exists on that same plane of terrible mystery.

Now listen carefully. Billy Ray was a part of this body. If we take his early testimony and baptism seriously, he is part of the body of Christ. And he still is, although according to this church's membership roll, he had been moved to the category of inactive. In my conversations with members of Marion Hills Mennonite, a question repeatedly emerges: How could Billy Ray have reached such a point of desperation? Some of you might have better answers to that question than I do.

The two earliest stories in Genesis about humans set a grim stage for us. The first story, in chapters two and three, narrates the fall of humans from grace because of Adam and Eve's disobedience of God in the Garden of Eden. The second story, in chapter four, which we heard Linda Ebel read earlier, is an account of the first premeditated, cold-blooded murder. Murder in the first degree. Cain kills his younger brother.

From a perspective of Christian theology, these two stories set out a view of the world that is shockingly grim. "The only empirically verifiable doctrine of the Christian faith," Reinhold Niebuhr once famously said, "is the doctrine of original sin." I can't argue with Niebuhr—at least not on this point. Such a harsh, dark truth does not blend easily with our inclination to seek joy. But bear with me for a few minutes. If we hope to find our way to the light, we had best be ready to wrestle with darkness.

I understand that Billy Ray had a certain amount of rage against his brother Dexter, and that is one of the issues the psychologists will no doubt argue about. In the case of Cain, we know that rage was part of the reason for the fratricide. The story is tantalizing but ambiguous. Cain offers God a portion of his crops, while Abel offers God some butchered livestock. The text indicates that God prefers Abel's offering. "And the LORD had regard for Abel and his offering, but for Cain and his offering he had no regard." No wonder Cain is angry! The story relentlessly proceeds: "So Cain was very angry, and his countenance fell. The LORD said to Cain, 'Why are you angry, and why has your countenance fallen? If you do well, will you not be accepted? And if you do not do well, sin is lurking at the door; its desire is for you, but you must master it.'"

God speaks to Cain in a series of questions. He does not directly tell him he's in danger until the last assertive phrase, when he says, "Sin is lurking at the door; its desire is for you, but you must master it." There is warning but also empowerment here: Cain, you're entertaining dangerous thinking. I know it, and you know it. "But you must master it," God tells him. In other words, Cain, you still have the power to avert disaster. You have agency.

Cain can give in to anger or try to master it. Note that throughout this passage Cain remains silent. He doesn't attempt to answer. He is marinating in his anger. Maybe he thinks God is taunting him, and he feels like a dumb student listening to his teacher browbeat him with rhetorical questions. Then we have the expression: "his countenance fell." The phrase is repeated when God observes, "Why are you angry, and why has your countenance fallen?" We can picture Cain looking down at the ground, refusing to meet God's look. That's a grown man pouting. Watch out. Everything is about to crack wide open.

The fateful turn in the story's plot begins after God has left the scene and Cain tells his brother, "Let us go out to the field." The text is blunt: "And when they were in the field, Cain rose up against his brother Abel, and killed him."

Enter God, again, the ruthless interrogator: "The LORD said to Cain, 'Where is your brother Abel?' He said, 'I do not know; am I my brother's keeper?'" Cain compounds the murder with a lie and then a lame rhetorical question: "Am I my brother's keeper?"

God thunders in reply: "What have you done? Listen; your brother's blood is crying out to me from the ground! And now you are cursed from the ground, which has opened its mouth to receive your brother's blood from your hand." Notice that God also delivers words parallel to that judgment leveled against Adam and Eve: "When you till the ground, it will no longer yield to you its strength; you will be a fugitive and a wanderer on the earth."

"The ground has opened its mouth." What a phrase! That line, pregnant with meaning, also offers another way to read this story, not only as an account of the first murder but also as a parable about land management. Many commentators read the story of Cain and Abel as the first allegory of conflict between ranchers and crop farmers, something that in our own local history is no mere abstraction.

Cain and Abel have very different ideas about how to use the land. One wants to grow things and would prefer to fence his property, and the other wants his animals to have free access to graze on the open range. Of course, this way of framing the story has limitations; I don't think this passage tells us that God has special love for livestock ranchers and disrespects the growing of grains and vegetables. These range wars between cattlemen and farmers have generated hundreds of stories, novels, and films, usually mixed up with rustlers, gunfighters, stampedes, and dramatic shoot-outs. Who will control the land? Who will get access to water and water rights? How will power be shared or not shared? These are basic questions at the root of many, if not most, human conflicts since time immemorial.

"The ground has opened its mouth to receive your brother's blood from your hand." The phrase could be applied to the range wars that have afflicted the history of the great American West. New skirmishes are happening in our own backyard about the ownership of the Flint Hills and what the Flint Hills are for. The last remaining stand of tallgrass prairie is still there, 4 percent of the original tallgrass footprint because it was simply too rugged to till. The name Flint Hills is not a misnomer.

Maybe I digress, but hear me out. Sometimes a dogleg in the road allows us to slow down and think more deeply. Consider our own beloved Flint Hills angle. A big rancher stepped in and built the Spring Hill Ranch in 1878; it was eventually bought out and turned into the Z-Bar in 1955. And several successive big ranchers couldn't make the finances work, so it was eventually turned over to the National Park Service. That enraged certain neighbors, ones who detest the prospect of federal ownership or management. Some hate the idea of a national park in their backyard, period. And so, compromises are floated by politicians who hope to keep the peace. The park, we learn, will be owned by a private corporate entity and comanaged with the federal government. And still not everyone is happy. They murmur about "the feds." The talk turns dark, there are threats of violence.

The heartland of America has experienced that violence in its history, and we have seen it erupt very recently. Places come to mind such as Ruby Ridge in Idaho, and Waco, Texas. And Oklahoma City just last year, where a couple of terrorists bombed the Federal Building with a Ryder truck packed with fertilizer and fuel oil, killing 168 civilians including children, and injuring 850 more. These are places marked by blood. *The ground has opened its mouth.*

The human race has not evolved ethically since the story in Genesis. God grieves. He tells Cain: "What have you done? Listen; your brother's blood is crying out to me from the ground. And now you are cursed from the ground, which has opened its mouth to receive your brother's blood from your hand." And there is that moment when Cain is reminded that he can master his anger. We can be mastered by our anger—or try to master it.

The end of the story of Cain and Abel is such a puzzle that most retellings of the story glide right over it. After God delivers his judgment of Cain, the man finally shows remorse. In verse thirteen, Cain says (or maybe he whimpers): "My punishment is greater than I can bear! Today you have driven me away from the soil, and I shall be hidden from your face; I shall be a fugitive and a wanderer on the earth, and anyone who meets me may kill me."

And God listens. He puts a "mark" on Cain. This is often considered part of the curse on Cain, but in fact, if we read on, God does this *expressly* to protect Cain from danger. God assures Cain that anyone who kills him "will suffer a sevenfold vengeance."

The end of this story paradoxically shows God protecting a killer and a fugitive, ensuring his life. God does not put Cain's neck in a noose. Anyone with simpleminded notions about murder deserving automatic capital punishment might do well to reread this story. God does not execute Cain. Cain will live to see the future. To be sure, God has pushed him off the land, telling him he will not succeed as a farmer. Verse twelve says: "When you till the ground, it will no longer yield to you its strength." So what is left for him to do?

Quite simply, Cain gets on the road. He makes a road trip! He becomes the first migrant in the Bible. He "went away . . . and settled on the land of Nod, east of Eden." Cain has found new land that he will call home! More astonishing, "Cain knew his wife, and she conceived and bore Enoch; and he built a city, and named it Enoch after his son Enoch."

Cain will not make it as a farmer, so he journeys to another land and builds a city. If the story of Cain and Abel begins with a murderous rural feud, it ends peaceably in an urban place! Cain names the city and his son Enoch, derived from the Hebrew name Chanoch, which means "experienced" or "dedicated." In the next chapter of Genesis, we meet another patriarch named Enoch, who, we are told several times, "walked with God."

I like to think that Cain, too, learned to walk with God in the city that he built, years after he killed his brother. But on this Sunday morning in June in Marion Hills, my thoughts are with our brother Billy Ray Baumgartner.

May we hold in our hearts our brothers Cain and Billy Ray.

Like them, we live in the light of transcendent grace, all our quarrels and our crimes covered, by a God whose mercy is everlasting.

Let us pray.

Chapter 27

The wide front glass door of Marion Hills Hospital slid open and John entered the lobby. Filtered air washed across his face. He knew too well the funk of hospitals, nursing care facilities, and retirement villages, the bad ones masking the aroma of illness, death, and assorted bodily fluids with plug-in deodorizers studding yellow wall outlets. If you wanted better, places like Marion Hills Hospital were a good place to start. The chief administrator, Edna Koslowsky, RN, JD, disliked unwanted smells, and she understood that a hospital was more than a repository for patients filling beds. It needed to inspire confidence. She hated shortcuts and cheap materials. The reception area had a new hardwood floor. John took note. Mingled with the smell of potpourri was the sharp scent of new hardware and solid oak. It was real, not plastic veneer laid down on puddles of glue.

A young man with a post earring and tortoiseshell glasses greeted John at the front desk. The name tag announced Richard and smaller beneath, Intake Specialist. He had a high mop of curly hair that rose above the shaved sides of his head. It reminded John of haircuts in the 1940s, and he unconsciously ran his hand through his own shock of unruly white crested above his craggy brow.

"That's a good look, Reverend," Richard said. "The new preacher, am I right? Reimer, is it? You should see Paula downtown, she's a great stylist. Have you met her yet?"

"I need to," John said. "Just call me John."

"Pleased to meet you. Call me Rick."

"I'm here to see Levi Schlegel. Is he available?"

"Yes, he's having breakfast. Here's a pass. Room 217." Rick wrote "Rev. John Reimer" on an adhesive name tag. John stuck it on the lapel of his sport coat and thanked the man.

He followed the odd numbers to the left. Ahead a door stood ajar. Voices trickled out, increasing in volume. An argument devolved into disconnected monologues. John heard a man say, "What the hell does Franklin think he's doing?"

Then a woman's voice, pleading, "Now is not the time, Campbell."

Underneath these threads came an older, quavering voice: "These plastic forks aren't worth shit." Something sharp hit the floor, followed by the sound of breakage. A momentary pause, then another voice cut in, gently forceful: "Dad, calm down."

John hesitated to knock.

As he debated whether to move forward or tiptoe away, Carol Schlegel burst out of the room and nearly ran him down. She wore a bronze velour track suit and high-end running shoes. A sun visor was clamped down tightly around her puff of platinum hair. "Excuse me, John," she said, "but I had to get out of there." She put out her hand as if to steady herself on John's arm. He saw that she had a wadded-up Kleenex in her fist. Her eyes were red.

John covered her hand with his own and patted it. "Carol. I've come at a bad time."

Someone in the room shouted Franklin's name again, louder, and stripped of any kindness. Campbell was talking. John watched Carol's expression. She tried hard to put on her lovely, professional face.

"John, your timing is fine," Carol said. "I'm always glad to see you. It's not you. It's Dad. No one understands what's going on with him. Not the medical people and certainly not his own family. I have never heard him curse like this. It's like he's a different person."

The voices inside the room went silent. Franz poked his head out the door. "Hi, John. Carol is right. It's not a bad time. You are needed. Maybe you can calm him down."

When John entered the room, Campbell was seated in the corner underneath the TV mounted in the corner near the ceiling. John couldn't believe the set was switched on to an episode of *Let's Make a Deal*. Thankfully someone had turned down the volume. Campbell barely made eye contact, and his hello arrived as an afterthought.

Levi sat up in bed. The blue hospital gown drooped at his white stubbled neck and the effect was shocking. He looked like a tom turkey dragged across a farmyard, making a final desolate protest before the hatchet came down. A purple bruise marked his forehead and a food tray rested in his lap. Franz was cleaning up the floor, returning to the tray's wreckage an oversized slab of pink ham. An overturned bowl and a limp slice of canned pineapple lay nearby. Levi pulled the broken tines of a plastic fork out of the seared flesh and then he gave up.

Levi seized John's arm and addressed him. "John, I apologize for the mess. Plastic cutlery, for God's sake! Not worth a rat's ass! Is there a set of real silverware in the house?" He looked at John as if trying to fully recognize him. The look of petulance changed to regret. "Are you here to rescue me from this hellhole?"

"You're not enjoying this," John said.

"This is not hospital food. But you're right. The hospital food violates everything that is holy."

"I brought him breakfast from the Copper Kettle," Franz interjected. "The western omelet the way he likes it. Unfortunately, the plasticware is not making the grade." Levi's oldest son walked around the other side of the bed and deposited the remaining debris and food on the floor into the trash can.

Carol returned to the room with silverware wrapped in a brown linen napkin. "Courtesies of the hospital kitchen." She handed it to her father.

"Where did that ham go?" Levi said. Franz found the ham and pineapple which he'd put in the bowl and returned it to the tray on the old man's lap. Levi began slicing the ham into chunks and resumed breakfast. He gradually calmed down. Between bites he delivered commentary. "So, John, the hospital food. A nonstarter. The Jell-O is a desecration. No fruit cocktail at all, just a lot of colored marshmallows that make me want to puke. And why can't they serve a man a decent piece of Hillsboro sausage? Franz, who's that lady running this place?"

"Edna Koslowsky. Dad, I've conveyed your concerns to her."

"Yes, but does she listen?" Levi said. "I think it's going to be takeout as long as I'm here. And where is Thiessen? He told me he was ready to discharge me two days ago."

"Thiessen?" John asked.

"Doctor Thiessen," Carol said. "The attending physician. Dad, small correction on that. He didn't tell you any such thing. They're still running tests. They're trying to figure out what's the matter."

Levi got a look of delinquent mischief in his eyes. "Of course they are."

"We'll see what we can do, Dad," Franz said. He poured orange juice into a glass for his father. There was a knock at the door. A balding man with a shiny forehead and pronounced puffs of black ear hair stepped in. He was maybe five seven in his loafers. He wore a blue lab coat and a long stethoscope was swinging from his neck.

"Good morning," he said. "I see I've interrupted a family gathering."

"Dr. Thiessen, this is Reverend Reimer," Franz said. John shook the doctor's hand.

"How are we feeling this morning, Levi?" Thiessen said.

Levi simmered, then he quietly said, "You told me two days ago I'm ready for discharge."

"Now, Dad—" Franz began.

"I want an answer from the doctor," Levi said.

Campbell, who had been quiet in his corner all this time, looked at his watch and stood up to leave. "Good to see you, Levi. Listen to the doctor, you hear?" He moved out of the room, trailing a scent of soap and Brut. Carol kissed her father on the cheek. "We love you," she said, following her husband.

Levi continued to talk. He was ramping himself into another fit of rage. "Doc, I need to have a word with your CEO—"

"Dad—" Franz began.

"What's her name, Franz? Edna, right? The Koslowsky woman? What's she doing in charge?"

"Dad, please try to relax, this isn't—"

"The *food* isn't acceptable, and I'm not getting answers, and I'm *tired*. If they draw one more blood sample, I'll shoot somebody."

Levi made a sudden move. It was not well thought out. He brought up a knee under the covers. The tray tilted and the foil containers and the cup of orange juice jumped two feet. "Shit!" Levi shouted, holding his knee in pain.

John watched the juice tip in midair. A bright orange spike spurted sideways and down the side of the bedcovers.

"Oh, come on, Dad," Franz said. His hands went up.

Thiessen spoke. "Don't let him get out of that bed." Talking fast, Thiessen sounded like he was hyperventilating. "He has no balance. He'll fall again, and we can't let that happen." Thiessen picked up the room phone to page the front desk for help.

John met Franz's eyes. Franz held his father down by the shoulders. "Do you need me here?" John said, taking a step toward the door. "Or do you even want me here?"

Franz, physically restraining his father, said to John, "It's probably best if you go. We have the situation in hand. I'll call you later."

Levi cursed his son. For a moment John wondered what medication he was on. What had Carol said? "It's almost like he's a different person."

As he walked out of the hospital into the main parking lot, John saw Franklin Schlegel climbing out of his battered red Porsche. The youngest Schlegel had trouble on his face.

"Carol told me Dad was in a *very* foul mood this morning and wanted to see me." Franklin pushed his sunglasses up on his forehead. He wore steel-toed work boots over gray socks and a ragged pair of cargo shorts. Dust flecked his salt-and-pepper beard and blue work shirt and he appeared to have been working outdoors in the sun for the past week.

"You might get in on the tail end of the party," John said. "Campbell and Carol just left. Franz is wrestling with your father, and the doctor seems panicked."

"Yeah," Franklin said. "They don't know what the hell's going on, do they?"

"Franz is patient. Thiessen looks lost in the woods. Your dad is treating this like a jailbreak."

Franklin nodded approvingly. "That's a concise report, thank you." He put his hands in his pockets and scuffed the parking lot with the bottom of his boot. "Say, I need to get in there, but may I call you this afternoon?"

"By all means. Or come by my office."

Franklin loped to the front door of the hospital. John drove away, wondering whether Carol and her snarling husband had exited to avoid an awkward meeting with Franklin. John also reflected that Franklin didn't have much confidence in small-town doctors, and found himself nodding in agreement. He'd have to ask around about Thiessen. He was even more curious to know exactly what kind of dirt Campbell had been dishing on his wife's little brother.

Chapter 28

Later that afternoon John drove east on Highway 50 and slowed for the tight curve past the broken faded town called Elmdale. There the last untilled portion of the Flint Hills gradually rose up like the back of a vast, ancient animal dotted with the occasional scrub tree. In the far distance stood scattered herds of Angus and Hereford cattle. John cracked the window a bit. It was starting to cool off. The world smelled of grass and recent rain.

He remembered a long time ago driving through this landscape late at night. Vi was with him then, head on a pillow, dozing in the passenger's seat.

John had gradually crept up on the taillights of another vehicle when he realized he had been following a black Cadillac hearse for fifteen miles. He wondered about the driver: was he carrying someone home or going to pick someone up? When he grew tired of wondering, John waited for a passing lane and with some relief was finally able to pass the hearse at seventy miles an hour.

Now he turned south on I-177 at Strong City. Cottonwood Falls was a couple miles down the road. On this stretch of 177, the Atchison, Topeka & Santa Fe railroad tracks danced parallel to the pavement. He glanced at the directions he'd scribbled down during his phone call with Franklin. He drove past Bazaar, not quite a ghost town, but getting there. He passed the field on his right where Notre Dame legend Knute Rockne had died in 1931, when a Transcontinental and Western Super Fokker Trimotor airplane crashed during a thunderstorm, killing everyone on board. Just beyond that point, marked by a simple limestone obelisk, the tracks crossed from the left to the right side of the highway, and he started to look for the next turn. Matfield Green lay straight ahead, but

Franklin had said if he drove into that town, he'd have to double back for the turnoff.

He followed a weathered sign for Steak Bake Creek, and three turns later, the pavement turned to white limestone gravel. He eventually found a point in the road with a mailbox marked F. Schlegel and crossed over a metal cattle gate. The lane wound through the hills like overgrown moguls. Finally, a sweeping, mile-long gravel driveway transitioned to macadam as it inclined slightly into a saucer-shaped expanse marked by massed clusters and slabs of limestone block. These at first seemed randomly scattered, but as he drove around them in several sweeping S curves, John saw that they had been carefully arranged.

How does one achieve ballet-like effects with tons of limestone? Franklin had done it. The largest rectangular stones were a couple of car lengths long and ten feet high. John could only imagine the machinery required to move all of this, and he also imagined the designer had intended for people to think about that. The chunks of rock loomed like small buildings, interspersed with recently planted stands of oaks and cottonwoods that thickened as he drove into the basin.

From the flat plain an incline rose gradually to the crest of a flat-topped hill that showed jagged outcroppings poking through the grass lining a cliff. At its peak, the cliff rose fifteen feet above the basin of the long-abandoned and now reclaimed rock quarry. Tendrils of foliage had started to climb at various points on the cliff's face. A couple of trees sat out on a flat chunk of rock the size of a road grader awaiting placement, their root balls still encased in burlap. Nearby a battered white Bobcat crouched silently, its front-end bucket resting on the ground. It was roll-proof, with a rusting cage of metal guarding the driver's seat. A bundle of oxidizing rebar, as if to match, was braceleted nearby with a loop of heavy chain. A pyramid of topsoil ten feet high had been dumped recently on the flat.

When he lifted his eyes to the house that hovered on the lip of the cliff, John thought of Daniel Burnham's motto that had defined Chicago in the dawn of its heyday: "Make no little plans." High above the quarry bed, and unmistakably grand in its midcentury modern vernacular, the structure displayed sheathing of slivered horizontal layers of limestone. These emanated gold and yellow hues against the afternoon sunlight. A wide horizontal expanse of glass overlooking the landscaped quarry was divided by a couple of vertical I-beams painted white. The effect was of a vast, all-seeing eye that hovered above the shadowed front yard basin, like a starship command console. Above rose an escarpment of solar panels swept back like scales on a big breaching fish.

A man came out of the house and stood near the edge of the cliff. Then he raised both arms in greeting. Franklin's gesture seemed familiar to John, who recognized a perfect imitation—or parody—of his own Sunday morning benediction.

John followed a final hairpin turn in the driveway that swerved away from the rock wall and switched back up the slope to the parking spaces behind the house. Franklin came around the side of the house to greet him.

—❦

The back door off the trellised patio opened onto an expansive kitchen finished out in white subway tile and white cabinets. The center island had a butcher block surface that could accommodate an entire boar or a buffalo. It focused the room directly beneath a skylight. John noticed the six-burner Wolf stove and the way the double-door fridge had been hidden behind a panel of walnut veneer blending with the rest of the wall. Franklin offered John a drink and poured him a Pellegrino and himself a refill of Macallan's. He dropped a couple cubes of ice in both glasses and then he showed John around.

Franklin had been hanging art on the wall behind a slab table possibly of medieval provenance. The figures in the paintings were crude renderings of a man and a dog, which seemed in motion, dancing even, as if about to pop off the wall. John looked again.

"You like Haring?" Franklin said. "He left us too soon." John followed Franklin through a plastic tarp hanging between the kitchen and a hallway leading to the back of the house. There was a finished high-ceilinged loft with several skylights and a bank of windows that made the walls seem to melt away. An expanse of open shelving displayed stacks of oversize books, all laid horizontally. John saw they were mostly art and architecture. A ladder on a track allowed access to the upper reaches, and a drafting table in the middle of the room, underneath pendant lights, showed several sketches in progress. One depicted Franklin's front-yard quarry bed.

The hallway was unfinished, Sheetrock nailed in, but no light fixtures yet. Most of the rooms still awaited the plasterers. The master bedroom was not yet complete. Franklin said he was modifying the master bath and walk-in closet design. On the wall by the dresser hung a small portrait of a brunette wearing a peasant dress. She looked up with eyes melancholy, dark, and utterly transfixing. She reclined in a wooden chaise lounge against a backdrop of ivy growing on an ancient stone wall. A girl of perhaps five stood at her side, twirling one of her pigtails.

"My wife, Felicia, on vacation in Romania. That's our daughter Samantha with her, though Sam is older now, and trying very hard to get herself expelled from boarding school. Felicia isn't too happy with me presently. She's a fashion photographer from Bucharest."

"I see," John said. "I hope I will have the pleasure of meeting her."

Franklin said, "She's deciding if she wants to stay in the marriage."

John did not continue the questioning but Franklin rattled on about his missing women. "Wife number three," he added. "It breaks my mom's heart. Just say the name Felicia and she'll give you the complete story. But let me show you the lower level. Thank God I have the house roughed out," Franklin said.

He didn't bother to make a transition between wife number three and the house, thought John.

"It's all finish work now, the floors, the plastering, lighting, and painting. The biggest problem is the damn subcontractors."

Hardwood floorboards lay in long boxes wrapped with loops of metal tape: lots of oak and one sizable package labeled Brazilian Rosewood. John followed Franklin around in the basement that had two sets of sliding glass doors. These opened onto a terrace on the side of the house featuring a hot tub and deck furniture, all nicely enclosed behind a trellis screen. There was a pool table and a wet bar under construction in the main recreation room, then another inner sanctum where Franklin kept an antique rolltop desk. Overhead flood lighting in metal canisters illuminated architectural drawings spread out on a drafting table. One wall was covered with photographs of houses. John recognized one of them as Farnsworth, but the picture was from an unfamiliar angle. The rest merged in a jumble of straight horizontal lines, tasteful arrangements of glass and steel and stone.

⌐✦

They sat in the leather furniture. It was more than a living room; it embodied aspirations and vistas that induced dreams but haziness. John took it all in, and the landscape that opened beyond the glass. A bonsai sat on a low table by the window, and on the floor next to it, a concrete planter box held a profusion of ferns and grasses. Franklin turned on the stereo; the sound of a muted trumpet and single snare drum emanated from a couple of big speakers in the corners. The blocks of stone down in the quarry bed cast shadows across the earth, their rectangles and cubes mimicking the house that stood above.

"Refill?" Franklin said, holding up his glass. There was another wet bar in the corner of the room. He went over and poured a little. John said, "What's that you're having?"

"Macallan fifteen-year double cask," Franklin said.

"Let me try a finger of that. Thanks."

"At your service, sir," Franklin said. He brought the drinks back and clinked his glass against John's. "I'm glad you could come out here. This morning was not a good time for talk." He leaned back in his Eames chair and put his feet up on the hassock. John took a modest swallow of the whiskey and sat up straight.

"Thank you. I'm happy to drive into the Flint Hills. How do I deserve this invitation?"

"Well, maybe I can get you out here more often. I'm planning to make this a weekly rental come fall. I have a commission in New Orleans that's going to tie me up at least a year. Maybe you and your lady friend would be interested." He raised his eyebrows for emphasis with the words "lady friend." He continued, "I'll give you the ministerial rate." His eyebrows lifted again.

John noticed how Franklin accelerated his diction when he was on a roll. Though a native of Kansas, through his years away in college and grad school and then career, he had picked up the East Coast rhythm and speaking cadences, unlike his father and older brother. It was one reason he defined himself as an outsider, John thought. This was the Mennonite kid who got away to the big city and could now pass for Jewish with his graying curly dark hair and gift for a wisecrack. In his old age the kid would probably resemble Groucho Marx. John had observed on more than one occasion how much this verbal acuity amused his father.

"My lady friend?" John said. "And who do you speak of?"

"I believe I met her at the MCC auction," Franklin said. "She told me her name was Nancy. The attorney, the one who likes to talk about Columbia. She and I were chatting while you wrestled down that Nubian goat and continued to build the legend of John Reimer. I could see that Nancy perceived my sister Julia as a direct threat to her interests."

Franklin grinned. "I mean, Nancy obviously has some feelings. And she is a woman of considerable intelligence and beauty. Just saying. She told me she was on a work trip." The smile widened.

"Were we that obvious?" John said.

"John, I know passion when I see it. Lord knows I've been through it enough times already."

"You make it sound like a travail," John said.

"My second wife said I was very good at spotting love but I had a problem keeping it, you know what I mean?"

"Tell me about your second wife," John said. He took another sip of the scotch and felt the trickle travel like a burning flame down the back of his throat.

"Sheila," Franklin said. "A six-foot field hockey player from a wealthy family in Westport. She was an emotional Godzilla. I was rebounding off a petite flower, and at first it was great being married to a woman of her ample gifts. But by the time we were done, she made me feel like a third grader trying to escape training wheels. She bullied me into joining the Unitarian Universalists as a last-ditch try for religion. The minister was a feminist alpha blonde who checked all the right progressive boxes but operated like a Nazi corporate trainer. Sheila was deeply attracted to her, but I wasn't. I eventually discovered that the coffee and fellowship at most Starbucks outlets on Sunday morning is just as meaningful as the standard Unitarian brand of spirituality. Plus, I got more insight because I usually had *The New York Times* in hand. What you see before you now is a backslid Unitarian." Franklin beamed. *This kid has been to Harvard,* John recollected. *And he wears his Ivy lightly.*

John said, "I've been pleasantly surprised to see you at Marion Hills Mennonite. What brings you to our humble congregation? And three Sundays in a row? I've noticed. And you're wearing a tie. Are you having a spiritual rebirth?"

"I will ignore your mocking tone and tell you I've enjoyed the sermons, John. And I'm not just there for your special brand of vaudeville. People show up on Sunday morning because they want to be surprised. People here still believe in hearing a message from God. Your line about God protecting Cain and refusing to execute him for murder jolted a few of us. Not to mention building a prosperous, peaceful city. They were still arguing at Little Pleasures yesterday about it when I went in for a bagel."

John nodded. "I had one parishioner look me in the eye and say, 'I know Billy Ray is still a member of this church, but frankly he should be excommunicated, and I hope he fries in the chair.' I told him Kansas doesn't use the chair, and he said, 'Okay, the noose then. And make sure the rope is new.' Then he slapped me on the back and said, 'Reverend, we can agree to disagree on this, can't we?'"

"There are times when I wonder whether it was wise to buy this property and build this house," Franklin said. "You know what *The New Yorker* said about moving to Florida, right?"

"No, what?"

"The only problem with moving to Florida is living in Florida."

"I sympathize," John said. "This is one advantage of doing an interim pastorate. I can audition certain lines of interpretation knowing I'll be back in Chicago by summer's end, or at least by Thanksgiving."

"You ever get in trouble? I mean, been forced out of a church?" Franklin looked at John's empty glass. "You need a refill?"

"Make that some more fizzy water, thanks."

Franklin went to the little wet bar across the expanse of the room and brought back a glass brimming with Pellegrino. He gave it to John, who resumed his story.

"I was forced out once. In South Dakota, church after Ebenholzer. I had a group of Full Gospel charismatics who wanted me to preach more about the gifts of the spirit—they thought I was lukewarm on healing and speaking in tongues. I told them I wasn't interested. The only thing I've ever seen happen when people get caught up in the so-called gifts of the spirit is a lot of one-upmanship and bullying. Meanwhile, another member in that same church wasn't happy unless I mentioned blood atonement every time I opened my mouth. He blew up when I preached about Jesus and nonviolence, something I did on occasion. I suggested there were people who would do well to 'believe in Jesus' less and pay attention more to what the man actually said. I thought I was pretty clever when I said that. Chalk it up to youth. I resigned before things got completely ugly. Had to follow Vi's advice. That was a smart woman."

"Yes, that's what everybody says. Is that church still in the conference?"

"No. They split years ago. What I mean is, they split from the Mennonite conference and then afterward they had a church split."

"Ah, the usual, the perils of the Reformation," Franklin said. "Splits and endless splintering. The next thing could be disputes over sugar-free grape juice in the communion tray—for or against? You created quite the stir talking about the bomb shelter that Marion Hills Mennonite installed under the sanctuary. Did you say 1956? I think I remember going inside that thing during preschool. Some kind of field trip."

"Yes. It was a church trustee who worked at Halston who convinced the rest of the board that a bomb shelter made sense. I heard about it when I first went to Ebenholzer."

"John, half the congregation had no idea what you were talking about. I mean, absolutely no idea. I don't think you're supposed to talk about a sanctuary built over a bomb shelter. But I hear there's a group lobbying for you to organize a tour. Like I said, people want to be surprised."

"I'm afraid it would turn into a tourist attraction. Although it could be an educational opportunity. Could bring some of our Halston employees who are church members along for the ride. They certainly know more about it than I do."

"John, sometimes you have a way of making the people's blood *pulse*."

"Don't flatter me. Some self-knowledge can be useful. One of our dirty Mennonite secrets is we sucked on the Cold War tit like everybody else. What I want to say is Halston is getting deeper and deeper into what Eisenhower warned us about. But, look, other parts of my sermon didn't go over at all."

"True," Franklin said.

"Do you know what parts I'm talking about?" John said.

"Let me try," Franklin said. "For instance, I couldn't believe some of what I heard you saying, though I was happy you said it. Like pro-lifers wanting to kill doctors and thinking of it as just war."

"I know. But it's already happening. Revise that. Already happened. A couple of doctors have been murdered in Florida. Family planning and abortion clinics bombed. The pro-life fantasy of Jesus is that he's Dirty Harry with a big pistol who will take out the bad guys. That's why so many evangelicals love the book of Revelation. Warrior Jesus."

"Jesus as Judge Dredd," Franklin said. "They're going to come after you if you don't watch out. You're treading on dangerous ground."

"That's possible," John said. "I learned a lot from many conversations with a pro-life chapter in Minneapolis. A few outspoken members of our church there were part of it."

"What did you learn?"

"Although they claim the sanctified worship of the zygote, they have precious little regard for actual women and children. And they hate it when you bring up rape or incest or both, as if these are statistically insignificant. Of course, they're all too common."

"How common?" Franklin said. He was unfurling himself from his Eames chair and making a move toward the kitchen.

"Maybe ask Billy Ray that question," John said.

Franklin was in the doorway to the kitchen but stopped and turned and said "What?"

"Ask Billy Ray Baumgartner about rape and incest," John said. "Sometimes it's the unfortunate recipe for a loss of life."

The expression on Franklin's face transformed like a couple of two quick solar eclipses crossing the moon. "You mean he shot his brother because—?"

John nodded slowly. "I can't even talk about it," he said.

"I won't ask any more questions," Franklin said. "But back to your comments about abortion and the killing of doctors. You're saying we live in an imperfect world. Wasn't that part of Niebuhr's argument against pure pacifism and his rationale for just war?"

"Yes, it's a fallen world, and all of us are fallen creatures. That keeps me awake at night. If you're a Mennonite who has pat answers to Niebuhr's questions, you're a fool. It's a world where only the fanatics believe in moral absolutes. I believe in the moral imagination and I believe that cruelty is the worst thing we do. We can try to prohibit cruelty but we can't eliminate it. All we can do is mitigate or minimize it."

Franklin rattled the ice in his glass. "John, did I say something earlier about you being full of surprises?"

"Franklin, I have seen hearts of darkness in Chicago. And now I am finding them in the land where the deer and the antelope play. But you were on a pilgrimage to the kitchen. Please let me help."

Chapter 29

"How did you end up in architecture?"

Franklin tossed arugula in a wood bowl, squeezed half a lemon over it, and tossed the greens again. He said, "I'll get to your question in a minute. There's a water pitcher on the kitchen counter. Could you pour us some?"

John came back with the pitcher and poured water. Franklin plated the steak he'd finished grilling and opened a bottle of wine. He brought out a bowl of baked potatoes and smaller bowls of minced chives and sour cream, then he filled two wine glasses with Tempranillo. He put on a heat glove and carried a little skillet full of sautéed mushrooms to the table under the trellis on the back deck. The men sat down. Franklin asked John to say grace.

"We are grateful, Father, for the bounty of this table and for your medium agnostic servant Franklin who has prepared it. We give thanks for this land and the beauty of these hills. Amen."

Franklin was smiling when John finished. "So, to your question. How did I come to architecture? I wasn't into team sports, to start with. Everybody expected me to follow in Franz's footsteps, get that letter jacket and make them proud. I had no interest. The basketball coach told me I had better potential than my big brother, more intensity. Said it was a terrible waste of talent if I did not go out for the team. I didn't give a shit. This is the problem of the small town. Two categories that they slot you into: jock or faggot. Mind-numbing stupidity. I discovered I'd rather drive out into these hills with my sketch pad and draw landscape and abandoned grain elevators. Everyone in the community, my dad especially, said I had my head up my ass.

"I was immune to negative public opinion. I left when I was seventeen. Two years at Wesleyan and then three more at Harvard. I liked literature and art criticism but preferred to draw more than anything. I kind of fooled around. Ended up at Yale for my grad program. Dad paid my way. The longer I lived out east, the more alienated I felt here. I started my own firm and screwed up financially five years after licensure. I got fucked over by a subcontractor who inflated his charges at the last minute. Still not sure I could have done anything differently, though I still kick myself. Declared chapter eleven and regrouped. Can I pass you anything?"

"I'm doing fine, thanks," John said. "Delicious."

"In Marion Hills, whose opinions I no longer cared about, they called me the prodigal son. The spoiled progeny. Now I'm working on a couple of projects in New Orleans and Bangor, Maine. But this house is where I plan to spend half my time going forward. I've always wanted to come back to the Flint Hills—on my terms. People in Marion Hills have been a little surprised that I returned at all."

John carved away at his steak, a fillet expertly nestled on a bed of mushrooms. He took a small bite and then a forkful of potato topped with sour cream and chewed thoughtfully. He swallowed some wine.

"You've built a beautiful place here. I want to call it Shangri-la. Friendly neighbors?"

"You've been talking with my brother, haven't you?"

"Some. He says a few folks are worried. About the feds and all that. He told me he was pressured to join a coalition that opposes the park."

"Yeah, that bunch of whiners. They're up further north of Strong City, where the park will be established. The people from the National Park Trust are getting the old Spring Hill Ranch house and barn ready for the visitor center. The troublemakers, and I think there are about ten of them all told, are just boiling about the feds moving in. They thrive on the attention. Unfortunately, the county sheriff, Mingus, hasn't discouraged their pissing and moaning. Posse Comitatus nutjobs, some of them. They consider Randy Weaver a hero. They hate environmentalists, and when they hear the word 'biodiversity' they practically puke. The smart locals who have been here a while understand that the biggest landowners in these parts are mostly absentee oligarchs. It's strange—a lot of the so-called moderates I meet up with in Cottonwood Falls give the Texas oil and cattle crowd the benefit of the doubt, but they choke when they hear 'National Park Service.' They think of me as a candy-ass East Coast liberal. Which maybe I am. Did you read Heat Moon? *PrairyErth*?"

"Yes, as soon as I got the call from Waldo Wedel that I was spending a few months back here I decided to read it. You like him?"

"Well, you love him or you hate him, right? Actually, this guy Ed Bass, a Texas two-step bazillionaire, has thousands of acres. Though I expect he'll donate it all to the Nature Conservancy or some such outfit for the park so long as he can keep his precious grazing rights."

"That sounds like a winning compromise," John said. "What does your dad think?"

"He thinks the prairie park is the smartest thing to happen in Kansas since Dwight D. Eisenhower. He says it's good for the land, and it's a winner because, long term, it means more capital flowing into the region. 'A no-brainer,' he calls it. He's puzzled by the hatred for tourist dollars. There's a lot I've fought about with my father over the years, but I've never questioned his financial wisdom. But I haven't talked with him about the Flint Hills very much lately. The whole family is focused on his health. I'm pretty worried. We all are."

"Your dad has not been himself in my last two conversations with him, once by phone and once at his bedside."

Franklin didn't want to continue this thread of conversation. They ate silently for a couple of minutes and then John said, "Your cooking"—he held a piece of steak on his fork and pointed at it as he resumed chewing—"is first-rate."

"Thank you, and you're welcome. How about let's walk out back. Then I'll make coffee." Franklin gestured in the direction of the hill sloping away behind the house.

"Sure."

The path cut through the grass around the machine shed where Franklin parked his vehicles. It followed a long, straight line down the hill through a little dip and climbed again to another hilltop. It was dusk, and the sun's yellow orb was enlarging like a round, fat pear as it dropped toward the horizon.

"I love Kansas in June," Franklin said. "Always have. Especially out here. All kinds of grass. It's almost poetry." As if it heard the man speaking, a Cooper's hawk drifted off a fence post and soared vertically a hundred feet. It cast a long swooping shadow on the ground. Franklin kept talking. "Big bluestem. Little bluestem. Indian grass. Switchgrass. All these native flowers that bloom through the entire summer. At its peak this meadow will grow eight, ten feet tall with flowering plants. And we've had a good bit of rain so everything is happy. Next time you come out here, I'll show you the buffalo wallow. It's about two miles over."

They walked down another slope until the house was out of sight. They came toward a stand of cottonwood and Osage orange. The footpath led to a rivulet of water visible only from up close. It fed the trees and wound through the hollow like a lazy snake. Something scuttled in the underbrush. "Prairie dog?" John said.

"Deer mouse or ground squirrel, most likely," Franklin said. "Maybe running from that hawk." His eyes swept the horizon. "But you were talking about my dad. He's not in a good way. When I met you at the hospital this morning, he was a mess. They sedated him shortly after I arrived. I gather he had just had a throw-down with Campbell, is that right?"

"When I arrived there this morning, people were talking loud," John said. "I heard Campbell take your name in vain a couple of times. Carol tried to calm him down. Your brother was trying to calm Levi. He had broken his plastic fork in a piece of ham and was none too happy. Franz did his best to restore order. Doctor Thiessen came in and Levi upended the tray."

Franklin said, "What a festival. That's about where things stood when I arrived. I helped Franz clean up. They put a needle in dad and he went to sleep. But before they did, he was saying nasty stuff about Campbell. Very angry. What was Campbell saying about me when you walked in?"

"I heard him mention you twice before I got into the room. Then he went kind of sullen. It was something to the effect of 'What does Franklin think he's doing?' I didn't get any more detail.

"That's been the drumbeat from Campbell for the past five years. It's complicated. He's never liked me much. He's probably questioning my investment in this house and the costs. As if it's his business to ask me questions about personal finance."

"What do you mean?" asked John.

Franklin turned back on the trail and gestured to John to lead the way back to the house.

John said over his shoulder, "I hear Campbell has acquired property in the Flint Hills."

"Yeah," Franklin said. "I get the impression he's not pleased I'm in the neighborhood. I'm not sure what that's about. He's flying in and out of his airstrip over by Perkins Spring on a pretty regular basis. Either going to evangelistic rallies or his TV sound studio in Kansas City or flying to Texas for the charity or economic development project or whatever the hell racket he's running in Mexico. He went in on the airstrip with a business partner."

"What does Carol think?"

"She is busy hosting prayer breakfast fundraisers for Campbell, including events in Washington, and feeding the man Viagra. Okay . . . that was cruel and gratuitous. Seriously, I get the feeling she's not happy doing what she does and would rather be a full-time interior decorator. She talks to me, you know. My sisters, they're talkers. So she's not necessarily fulfilled doing this stuff, but it's pretty clear she's a big reason Campbell enjoys his two bits of fame. She's part of the team, and it's too late for her to quit. She attracts the donors. For a while now, I've sensed that Campbell is polished on TV, but she's better at authenticity. I mean, charisma works in different ways, don't you think? She's got way more of it than Mister Big Man."

"I know almost nothing about charisma," John deadpanned. "I'm a simple country preacher."

Franklin laughed out loud. "I call your bullshit, Reimer! Anyway, the other thing about Campbell is he's developed a real estate bug. As we get older, some of us focus more on what we love and others develop multiple interests. You know, to some extent we've all sort of imitated our father, I guess. Dad can't keep his hands off anything that looks like a moneymaker. He's invested more widely than anyone knows. Including a jazz lounge in Wichita some years back where he really caught the bug. Franz and I agree that was a turning point. Heard of a place called Lancers? He likes the big-band sound, not to mention the three-piece combo."

"Well, I knew he liked all kinds of music," John said. "Like the art. He's a Renaissance man. What's next? Part ownership of an NFL team?"

"Don't joke," Franklin said. "You might be onto something. Half the time I don't know where Franz is flying Dad around the country. A lot of the business is very hush-hush, even in the family."

John decided to take a chance, so he asked Franklin, "So what was Campbell lobbying your father for?"

"Perhaps a bigger line of credit? For years he's been angry about Dad's investment in my career. He was especially critical after my bankruptcy."

"Where does Carol stand on this?"

"She tries to stay clear. I should be careful how much I say. A little context for what you heard this morning. Dad has hurt Campbell in the last year or two and he was yelling about him when I walked into the hospital room, what, eight hours ago.

"The biggest quarrel happened last spring. Dad was about to write him a check and asked him, 'Is this a charitable contribution or an investment in your Mexican economic development project?' Mind you, this was according to Franz. Apparently, Dad said the word 'project' like a slur. Campbell tried to explain to Dad that if he read the brochure, he'd see that it all depends on which box you check. Then Dad lost it. He said the brochure's explanation of dividends left him more confused than before he read it, and told Campbell if he didn't watch himself, he could get sniffed out for a Ponzi scheme. 'At least make a respectable effort to distinguish between a dividend and a kickback,' Dad told him. Franz said that when Dad told him that, Campbell wanted to punch him in the face. He didn't talk to Dad for six months."

"And what do you think?" John asked. Franklin poured coffee at the kitchen counter, and the men carried their mugs into the front room and sat in facing easy chairs next to a broad limestone fireplace. John could see out through the expanse of front glass. The shadows had lengthened in the former quarry bed below them, and John thought about how much audacity it must have taken to turn that debris and waste into a front yard.

"What I think is that Campbell is overextended," Franklin said. "Carol has hinted at it. And even if she didn't say anything, her anxiety is a tell."

"I ran across Campbell's trail in Denver when I was on my way here a few weeks ago," John said. "Didn't you say he's developed an interest in real estate?"

"Yes. How did you run into him in Denver?"

"I said I ran across his trail. But let me back up a bit. This has to do with a semifamous young man one town over from Marion Hills who was once upon a time destined for greatness. His dad is a friend of mine, Marvin Arnheim. We go way back. He's a builder."

"Of course. He built my machine shed behind this house," Franklin said. "And you must be talking about his son Jeffrey. Everybody called him Jerry West when I was a kid."

"Exactly. That might have happened if he had gone to college. But things turned out a little different. Pardon me if I tell you things you already know. After his brief career in the construction business with his dad, Jeffrey divorced his first wife and moved to Denver. And in Denver, he disappeared eventually, vanished. Before his disappearance he had become something of a cult figure on Colfax Avenue. Semi-destitute but still in possession of his charisma, and quite the snappy dresser, at least to a certain population. He liked to preach about the end times. Lived in a rundown motel, and toward the end, he sometimes lived in his car. But he had the ability to shape-shift, I suppose you could say. And quite the ladies' man. His fans called him Doctor Jeffrey.

"Footnote here: I baptized Jeffrey in Ebenholzer many years ago. So I feel some connection. Obligation, in fact.

"Marvin had been estranged from his son for a couple of decades. Then out of nowhere he gets a phone call from a young woman who works at Casa Bonita. She'd been a cliff diver there and then went into management."

Franklin interjected, "Excuse me, did I pour you too much of that Macallan earlier? Am I hearing you right? Casa Bonita?"

"Stay with me, Franklin. This is all true. I drove through Denver on my way here. Alan Wiebe was with me and we spent a few days there, scoping out the situation at Marvin's request.

"And the young woman was desolate. She was wearing a ring with a diamond as big as my thumb. But no recent sign of Jeffrey, the man who had put it on her finger. Marvin doesn't have the heart to tell her—at least not right away—that if she ties the knot with his son, she will be wife number six. I know, I know, I'm praying you will salvage your own number three, Franklin.

"We found Jeffrey. This was after we'd exhausted other possibilities, including an inquiry at the city morgue. Turns out Jeffrey had been squatting in a real estate listing, a split-level house in Commerce City. We traced him by contacting the realtor who'd been one of his Bible study buddies and claimed to be part of the Promise Keepers."

"This isn't a tall tale? I heard Jeffrey was deceased."

John shook his head. "This is all true."

"What was Jeffrey doing when you found him?"

"We called the cops. He'd been dead several days. We found him flat on his back in a sleeping bag on the floor of the master suite. It was one of the realtor's listings that Jeffrey had seen during an open house a month before. He either stole a key or else broke in and made himself at home. Somehow, he broke his hip, probably fell off the back deck that had no railing, and then dragged himself inside, self-medicated, and died of an overdose. Exposure and dehydration likely didn't help either. When the realtor took us to the house, he had no idea Jeffrey had been squatting there. At least that's what he claimed. He seemed clueless. But he told us Jeffrey had put earnest money down toward purchasing the place earlier that month."

"Sounds like one crazy real estate transaction."

"Yes. And the owner of the house was none other than Wyndham Campbell."

"No way."

"Hear me out. When we asked the realtor a few more questions he conceded that Campbell is buying up distressed houses in Denver and the surrounding suburbs, using cheap contractors, and selling for a fat markup. I had to wonder. And what was he doing selling it to Jeffrey, who didn't even have a bank account, so far as his father knows? It struck me as an odd line of work for an evangelist and economic developer appealing to the faith community."

"Look," Franklin said, "this microloan stuff for the campesinos is all the rage. Campbell is working the angle. The Mennonite churches in Canada and in the U.S. Western District are eating it up like the Lord's Second Coming. Did you talk to Campbell about his Denver operation? He must be desperate for cash, that's what I think."

"I asked him a few questions at the MCC auction. He wasn't interested in a real conversation. Then I got tangled up in the goat stampede."

"How is Marvin doing?" Franklin asked.

"He is angry, and as you can imagine, depressed. He loved that boy. He's put off the memorial service until he gets more answers. His wife, Verla, has withdrawn into an emotional cocoon."

"And Jeffrey's fiancée?"

"I was tempted to tell her she was lucky to avoid marriage with the street preacher. Marvin went ahead and told her something like that himself. I hope she makes bank when she sells the ring."

Franklin shook his head in disbelief. "As I was saying, Campbell is working on a bigger line of credit from Dad. Dad and Franz are both hesitant. It puts Carol in a tight spot. I sense she wants to tell me the whole story, but she's holding back. I understand. Of course, both my sisters confide in me. It's been like that since I was three. They love the little brother who's been spending Dad's resources but doing it with style. They know Franz holds the whole financial winging together but they prefer to talk to the smallest bambino. Meanwhile, Campbell seethes. He more or less hates me." Franklin went over to his wet bar and poured himself another finger of whiskey. "More coffee?"

"No, but let me join you for a nightcap and then I need to head back."

"Rocks or neat?"

"Neat, thanks."

Franklin brought the drinks over.

John asked, "Why does Campbell hate you?"

"Because I laugh at him. To his face."

"Why do you laugh at him? That's not nice."

"He's a fake all the way through. When you spend any amount of time in his company, it's also clear he is something of an oaf. In his heart he wants to work the grift but deep down understands he isn't quite smart enough. He's raising most of his money right now off his standard PowerPoint show about antipoverty relief work in the Mexican colonies. Even evangelists have to name a cause when they pass around the offering plate, am I right? His hit single is the orphanage work. Some guys raise millions off of so-called Bible distribution. But for Campbell, the orphanage is a fucking winner every time."

"What does Eva say about all of this?"

"Mom keeps to herself and stays busy painting in the studio. She's been more productive this past year than she's ever been. I mean, she's in there all the time. It's her way of staying sane."

"How is her mental health?" John said. "I know Levi was concerned years ago when I was at Ebenholzer."

Franklin skipped a beat and then said, "Yeah, there was a tough patch." John sensed a trace of defensiveness in Franklin's tone.

John felt embarrassed. Mental illness, like abortion, was one of those mostly taboo topics among the Mennonites, even the most enlightened among them. He rued his clumsy word choice. Then a memory flashed into his mind so vividly that he couldn't manage a reply to Franklin. He recalled driving by the Schlegel home when they still lived in Hillsboro. It had been around eleven at night, and John was driving home after a church council meeting that had gone late. A woman was on the front porch, energetically sweeping the welcome mat, holding a dustpan and hunched over in a housecoat, totally focused on the task. She was so intent on the work that she didn't notice John's slowly passing car. When she stood up straight, John saw her face. It was Eva. She looked scared, and her look scared him. It was more than odd; it had raised the hair on the back of his neck. There were community whisperings around that time. Levi had told John at the Copper Kettle later that year that she was especially "fragile" and "not herself."

And in the hospital room earlier on this very day, John had heard Carol say identical words about her father: "He is not himself." John remembered how Eva had disappeared from Hillsboro for six weeks. The story circulated that she spent that time at Menninger's in Topeka, in treatment. John wrenched himself back to the present. Franklin looked at him and said, "Penny for your thoughts?"

"How does Eva feel about Thiessen?" John asked. "Is she happy with the medical care he's giving Levi?"

"No, not completely, and I mean to talk more with her and Franz about that. I think we need to consider a different physician, at least get a second opinion. You ask about her mental health. We're pretty jumpy right now. We're all mystified. The rock is suddenly crumbling. I mean, the old man is almost eighty-one, but he's had the energy of a much younger man for so long. None of us are prepared for the inevitable."

"How are you dealing with all this?" Watching Franklin talk and gesture, John knew part of the answer: The man was comfortably inebriated.

"I work on the house. I talk with Julia a lot. That's been helpful. But she's beside herself. She says he's not getting any better. These little things, these what do they call them? The nurses and social workers talk about it this way. 'Activities of daily living.' He's falling apart. They're afraid to let him go to the bathroom alone because he's liable to fall. The bump on his forehead happened at the hospital. He blacked out and keeled over. The last time I talked with Julia she was crying. She said he's always been so proud and independent and now this. But I tell myself, Franklin, get a grip. Calm down. Dad is an old man. He's had a good life. How will we be doing when we're pushing eighty-one?"

Franklin took a sip of the whiskey and wiped his mouth with the back of his hand.

"I'm pushing sixty," John said. "I have my own doubts."

"You run because you're afraid. You think about your mortality."

"Of course. You know your Freud. I also run so I don't lose my mind."

"They want Dad to cut out coffee," Franklin said. "Because of his heart. There is some arrhythmia. But that's just pissing him off even more. I've seen him so angry his hands are shaking. And something has happened to his speech. There are times he can't seem to start a sentence.

We need to get him to a specialist in Wichita or Kansas City, but so far, I've been ignored."

John looked at his watch. It was eight thirty. "I need to mosey." He stood up.

"May I—"

"Bathroom is down the hall on the left," Franklin said. John avoided the long packages of hardwood flooring that cluttered the way. Franklin said, "But stick around a while longer. I've been holding back the good parts. The night is young. I thought we were just getting started."

John laughed and flipped on the switch in the bathroom and closed the door behind him. He flipped another switch and heard the ventilator fan go on. The floor tiles, black-and-white octagons in a pattern John had seen before, maybe in an Italian restaurant in Andersonville, had already been installed, and there was an expanse to walk across to the new commode that stood beside the window. Apparently, Franklin liked a view from that vantage point. Sometimes a man needs a view.

Below John and to the right, the redwood deck, on two levels, was spread out with the hot tub sunk in its floorboards and the surface of the water rippling. John imagined it would be a comfortable place to soak about this time, sundown on the way, with someone he loved. Shangri-la indeed. As he zipped up, he looked at the bathroom sink vanity, the long white marble counter built for two. Then he stood in front of the expansive medicine cabinet. It occupied six horizontal feet between the industrial-style wall sconces. He washed his hands in the sink and toweled off.

He hesitated only briefly, then flipped open the four doors of the medicine cabinet. It didn't take him long to register the contents. The middle shelf in the center cabinet got his attention. A bottle of Depakote, something called Stavzor. A bottle of Lithobid, 400 milligram tablets. He thought that was lithium. He looked at the spelling. Another bottle, hydrocodone/acetaminophen, 325 milligram tablets. That was serious pain relief, he knew, an opioid, and there was also a bottle of Tylenol 600s. John wondered how many varieties of pain Franklin was experiencing. He extracted a little address book from his front pocket and took out a ballpoint pen and turned the sink tap back on. He wrote down the names of the drugs. He flushed the toilet again and quietly closed the medicine cabinet doors. He returned everything to its proper place.

He maneuvered his way back down the hall. Franklin was rinsing dishes in the kitchen. John sat in the easy chair. When Franklin returned to sit down, John said, "Thank you for a splendid dinner. I haven't had that kind of conversation in a long time."

"I need to thank you," Franklin said. "There was something else I wanted to say and I apologize for being slightly tongue-tied."

"What are you talking about?" John said. "You're one of a rare breed of people who can actually carry a conversation."

"A few minutes ago, you mentioned Eva's mental health. I wanted to say something about that but your blunt phrase caught me off guard. As I said earlier, you surprise people around here with the way you talk."

"I can be abrupt. Sorry about that. It was insensitive."

"No, that's the way you work. You jar stuff loose. You're as good as my former analyst. But here's the deal." Franklin looked down at the floor and put his fingertips together. He leaned forward with his elbows on his knees. "It's like this. What they said about my mother they're saying about me now. That I'm the crazy one in the Schlegel clan. That I have the artistic flair of my mother but lack the financial savvy of my dad. I'm the bipolar, crazed designer and architect who goes through money like water. I've been in bankruptcy once in my thirties, and it was no fun. In Connecticut. My first firm got burned on a commission in Stamford. I'd been out of Yale just a few years. At the time I was depressed and suicidal and thought seriously about jumping off a bridge. So now I have my town and country house, nearly finished, in the Flint fucking Hills. I'll admit I'm something of a libertine. I've been careless. And now my third wife is running around somewhere in Eastern Europe on a photo shoot with an animal rights activist. I tell her I'm working hard in Kansas, and she snorts over the phone. When she laughs, she does this snorting thing."

John sat impassively and waited for more.

"Designing and building that studio for Mom, her so-called White City painting shed, that was the best thing I've done in my life, better than all my commissions, all of it. Listen, John. My mother is the real achiever in the family. Dad buys a lot of shit, but where has it gotten him? He is an empty shell on his last legs. Mom is a creator. Eva Schlegel will be a name to reckon with long after she's gone. Dad, not so much.

"The big family secret that no one can admit is that *she* is the rock, not my dad. But Dad is an old-school patriarch. Good at bluffing, at creating layers of confidence. Confidence, or fear, actually. And that's why he's such a good dealmaker. He has acting skills, and those have brought him wealth. I'm guessing Dad told you so many years ago over a nice cup of coffee that she was frail and needed help and all that bullshit, am I right? It doesn't hurt that she simpers around half the time when people come by and acts like a vintage version of Emily fucking Dickinson."

John raised a hand and slowed Franklin down, stopped him. "I didn't think it was bullshit, Franklin. I understood that she might have needed treatment at that time. There is no stigma in mental illness, believe me. Remember, I lived with Vi for many years when her symptoms included dementia. Days when she was full of brilliant insights interspersed with obsessive-compulsive stuff, and toward the end, before twenty-four-seven nursing care, a lot of agoraphobia. And terrifying falls, including down an entire flight of stairs in Lakeview. I understand Julia's terror about your dad falling."

"Well, what I'm trying to tell you is about Eva. You should know she has a—somewhat different version of those events, when she presumably went away for treatment."

"What's that?"

"She went away for a while, all right. But she told me she was deciding whether to stay in the marriage. She had to get away to think it through. And she told me if I ever revealed this to my father, she would call me a liar and deny it to her death."

"Do your sisters know about this?"

"I don't know. I haven't asked them."

"Does Franz know?"

"I think so. But we haven't talked about it."

"Did she do this thinking about the marriage while she was at Menninger's?" John asked. Franklin sauntered back to his wet bar and poured himself a sloppy couple of fingers of Macallan's.

"John, hold it right there. You presume *she* was the one getting treatment at Menninger's."

John looked at Franklin and processed. Then he said, "Oh."

Franklin let the thought sink in. Then he continued. "I'm not sure she went to Menninger's at all. I've never asked her. I could call over to Menninger's and find out and dig up their historical records, but I really don't care one way or another. I personally believe she got on a plane and spent six weeks in New York at the Pierre, going to the Metropolitan and Guggenheim and living in some precious solitude of her own making.

To get perspective. She still likes the long trips away. They're her lifeline to sanity because she has to live with the crazy old coot. I don't think she could live without those trips. And in an odd way that part of the myth about her mental fragility has bought her additional privacy here at home to get her work done. People around here leave her alone. It's part of the pose. Her mystique. Dad might have lied about her but she used the lie to her advantage. All you have to do is invoke Menninger's and people get very hush-hush."

John sat and wondered about the contents of Franklin's medicine cabinet. He wondered whether only Franklin or the entire family was medicated. He stood up. There was too much to absorb. He still wondered if Franklin had invited him over with a special agenda. Sometimes, in John's experience, people wanted company, nothing else. Or they were unconscious about their agenda.

"What can I do for your father right now, Franklin? Anything?"

"Wait and pray. Talk to Eva about getting a second medical opinion for Dad."

"I will do that. And I'll have you over to the parsonage. I owe you one," John said. "I'm not much of a cook but I have a deep freeze and a fridge full of bounty. The people here bring me food. Of many kinds and in great quantity."

He walked a step toward Franklin, who stood up from his easy chair.

"John was the apostle of love," Franklin said. "But he was also a Son of Thunder."

"Yes."

"You are a man true to your name." Franklin wrapped his arm around John's shoulders and saw him out the back door. "Thanks for coming over. Thanks for listening."

John's vehicle slowly tooled down the road to the hairpin turn at the bottom of the quarry bluff, and then onto the sinuous driveway out of the estate. The man in his castle stood on the cliff above the cut stones of the stylish ruin. Again, but this time in farewell, he lifted his two hands above his head, against a sky shot through with the spectacular dying rays of the sun. John drove on across the cattle gate and made the requisite turns toward I-177 and eventually back to Highway 50.

Then it was westward to Marion Hills. There was too much to tell Nancy right now, and he anticipated his bedtime telephone conversation with her would delay sleep for a couple hours yet. He imagined her tucking herself in under that new blanket, then he accelerated to sixty and set the cruise control.

John's head was whirling with information. The sky above turned starry black and the Milky Way spilled out like a sheet of diamonds across an inky tabletop.

Chapter 30

Marvin pulled up in front of the parsonage in his yellow, mud-encrusted Cadillac. He emerged from his vehicle. His hard hat matched the color of his sedan, and he was showing his age. He hobbled painfully onto the porch and rang the bell.

John opened the door. He had just come in from the track. He had his running shorts on and a towel around his neck. He was barefoot and shirtless and showed a thin patch of salt-and-pepper hair pasted down on his chest. His hair was cropped short after his recent visit to Paula's salon.

Marvin wiped grime off his face with a red bandanna. He inspected his work boots for mud and decided to leave them on. He walked into the kitchen.

"I have a fresh pot of coffee and caramel rolls with pecans," John said. "Want some?"

"Don't mind if I do. Pardon my appearance, John, though I can't say you're making a very pastoral presentation at the moment. I just got back from Peabody. Been out there since six a.m. Work crew stripping off forms on a foundation we poured yesterday."

"Everything all right?"

The old man grimaced. "I have a do-over. New hires still learning how to use a level. Gung ho, but not so bright. The result is a wasted day of work and dumpster rental to haul away a footing we botched. I should have supervised more carefully. But I'm looking over that new fancy vehicle of yours out front and have to admit, those Schlegels know how to take care of their preacher, don't they?"

John ignored the gibe. He poured Marvin coffee and motioned toward a stool by the kitchen counter for him to sit down. He pulled a pan of rolls out of the oven where they had been warming, plated one of them, and pushed it in Marvin's direction.

"What brings you to my humble abode?"

"I have news from Denver."

"Yes?"

"Our friend Campbell is out of the real estate business there."

"Did Fenimore tell you that?"

"Yeah."

"Any more details about Jeffrey's last transactions to buy that house?"

"No. There our boy Fenimore is like a vault. I think he imagined he was setting my heart at rest when he said Campbell was no longer flipping property."

"Did he give a reason for sharing this golden information with you?" John said.

"No. I asked him how Delores was doing. And Celeste. He clammed up. He said he was sorry about my boy." Marvin was finishing his roll and removed another from the pan.

"Fenimore wasn't the brightest dog in the litter," John continued. "I have a feeling he would also need instruction on how to use a level."

"Yes," Marvin said. "But, John, here's something. I think Fenimore felt relief about being done with Campbell. It felt to me like he was sharing good news—and I was supposed to share his joy. And—surprise, surprise—it left me feeling a lot worse about Jeffrey."

"Campbell has come across my radar in several conversations recently," John said. "He's doing a lot of flying in and out of Chase County. Has himself an airstrip near Perkins Spring and a new business partner."

"I believe I told you about that airplane hangar, John. I originally put in a bid to build it for him." Marvin took an enormous bite out of the cinnamon roll. He grasped the pastry as if it could save his life. He slugged down more coffee. "Your memory slipping?"

"Always," John said. "Day by day. Seems this hangar is a little bigger than a standard single airplane bin. At least that's what I hear."

"Whatever for?" Marvin said.

"Beats me. A bigger plane? A woodshop where he can unwind? John Schroeder says he is running semitrucks."

"Have you asked him?" Marv said.

"Look, I am not on easy speaking terms with Campbell. In fact, I asked him one too many questions at the MCC auction and he flared up like an angry ferret. Hot temper, that man. There we were, two men of the cloth, facing off like it was an ultimate fighting championship."

Marvin went to the sink and rinsed off his hands. "That's not your way, John." Then he dragged them across his khakis for drying. "Well, all this jawboning about Campbell gets me nowhere. It won't bring back my son. What I wouldn't give to ask Jeffrey what he was doing in that man's company to begin with."

"Any discoveries from the paperwork in Jeffrey's car?" John asked.

"Wish there were. But the answer is no. It's not a valuable archive. I've incinerated most of it."

"I wish I could talk longer," John said. "I have an appointment in about forty-five minutes and need to prepare, not to mention shower. Let me know when you're ready to do Jeffrey's memorial service."

"I will. I'm waiting on Verla for that. She'll make the call."

"I understand."

"I know you do, and I appreciate that, John."

"Let's do another potluck soon. I have a new installment of gourmet cooking waiting in the fridge. I have a Chinese stir-fry kit and a Pyrex full of enchiladas. *Muy picosas*, I am told."

"So many options," Marvin said. "Let me know when. I'm back to the work site this afternoon. Need to knock noggins together on this crew." Marvin put on his hard hat and tilted it back at a rakish angle. His head looked even more massive when crowned with the yellow plastic. "Oh, one other thing. Verla told me she met the buyer of her quilt at the auction. She was very impressed with her knowledge." Marvin's face broke into an impish smile.

"Really?"

"Yes, really." Marvin couldn't resist. "You have been rather mysterious. We want to hear all about her when you're ready to talk."

"All in good time, you rascal."

Marvin showed a light step heading to the door and John snapped the towel in his direction.

John whistled in the shower. When he got out, the phone was ringing. It was Franz.

"We need you here at the hospital, John. *Now.* We're in real trouble."

Chapter 31

It took but a moment to see the sick man was sinking. Levi's eyes were closed and his skin the color of bluish clay, already a good way down the road toward the embalmer's art. His hands were outside the thin hospital blanket, curling in on themselves like the front appendages of a large mantis. He had lost weight since John's last visit. His fingers occasionally fluttered over the bedclothes, like a pianist reaching for the right chord.

Levi's breathing was still steady. John thought there were days or at least hours to go. Then he reminded himself that predicting the end is something even the best physicians don't do. Years of visiting the terminally ill had taught him this. Living with Vi had taught him this.

John stood by Levi's bed. The children, Julia and Carol and Franz and Franklin, gathered close by. John noticed that Carol and Julia, the track star and the show farmer, wore dresses. Franz's shiny gray suit showed a few wrinkles. Eva was there, too, at the head of the bed, smoothing Levi's temples. Her eyes were spooked. When Doctor Thiessen entered the room, he looked at the heart monitor and brought out his stethoscope. The spouses of the married children retreated into the hallway. Franz's wife Susie, also dressed up as for a social occasion, led the way, as if she were a docent in charge, followed by Campbell and Ken.

Doctor Thiessen asked Franz to help him turn Levi on his side. He applied the stethoscope to various parts of Levi's back. He turned to Franz. "His lungs are starting to fill up. We'll stop the medications. There's really no point."

"What's he taking, if I may ask?" John said.

Thiessen looked at John and said, "His blood pressure pills and a mood stabilizer."

"I see," John said. "He looks like he's been knocked out."

"He's been hard to control," Franz said. "Remember that tray he threw off the bed a week ago? The Haldol calmed him down. He's been pretty cooperative since. Although he was talking Low German when I called you to come by just a few minutes ago."

"He's been speaking in Low German a lot more, hasn't he?" John said.

"Yes, he has," Franz said. "He's in a lot of distress."

"He's been in distress ever since he entered this hospital room," Julia said bitterly.

The man in the bed opened his eyes and looked directly at Franz. He turned his head the other way and looked at John. "Hello, John. How are you doing?"

"I'm fine, Levi. Talk to me."

"I want you to pray for me, pastor. Would you do that?"

John took one of Levi's hands. Eva held his other hand. John spoke, more loudly than usual, because he wanted Levi to hear: "Dear Lord, we commend Levi's health to you, and we pray for his recovery. We give thanks for this family. We ask for your wisdom and grace to be with the medical team. Amen."

A metal pushcart in the corner of the room was piled with trays and food remnants. Dirty metal cutlery lay in an oblong plastic bin. John recognized the takeout containers from the Copper Kettle.

"How was lunch, Levi?" John asked.

"Not good," Levi said. "Couldn't taste a damn thing. Taste is going. Smell is going. I'm in a bad way."

"It was chicken-fried steak, his favorite," Carol said. "He had a couple of bites and lost interest." Julia stood by Carol and gripped her hand.

"What can I do to make you more comfortable?" John said to Levi. He noticed the intravenous tube and needle secured to the inside of Levi's elbow, and the restraints on both Levi's wrists and forearms. Levi thrashed against the heavy Velcro bands. John saw his despair.

Julia turned away and said quietly, "Oh, God, this is killing me." Franz put an arm around her shoulder.

Levi spoke a guttural phrase in Low German, peeling off a string of angry words.

"Say that again, Levi. Slow down," John said.

"*Cun all mien Frintschoft mol in baet dim Ruem, filoti?*"

"What did he say?" Franz asked. "I sort of understand. He wants the family out of here?"

John spoke slowly. "Yes, something like that. He said he wants to speak with me alone."

"Dad, do you want to speak with John alone?" Franz said into his father's ear.

"Yes. Go," Levi said.

"Let's go," Franz said to his siblings.

"Give me ten minutes," John said. "Thanks."

The siblings left the room and closed the door.

"You, too, Eva. I want to talk with John," said Levi, brushing her fingers away from his head.

Eva left the room.

John looked directly into Levi's eyes. He grasped the man's biceps. There wasn't much there anymore. He was momentarily reminded of holding a struggling goat in his arms. He saw a tired, desperate animal fast losing comprehension.

"Danke," the old man said, and breathed heavily.

"What is on your mind, Levi?"

"Something is happening to me, Pastor John. Something is not right."

"Yes. You are in medical treatment. Your heart. The heart gets tired. Do you want a drink of water?"

Levi's eyes began to focus. He was concentrating, trying to track John's speech. "Something, John. Something is—happening to me." Levi hesitated now. The ataxic speech pattern was a new development. He struggled to start a sentence. John had seen very old people decline, but this was steep. The changes in Levi's appearance and enunciation left John stunned.

"Listen," Levi said. "I know I'm not sick. I was in Mexico."

"In Mexico, Levi? When were you in Mexico?"

"Our people have a hard time there. I think somebody stole from us."

"Who stole from you, Levi? Are you talking about the Mennonite colonies?"

Levi's head bobbled on his stringy neck. John thought he was nodding but couldn't be quite sure.

"To see our people there," Levi continued. "My mom was so mad at me." He unleashed another unintelligible torrent of Low German. John decided Levi was confused and then he thought of his own mother. Levi was maybe right on that point. We all make our mothers mad at us at one time or another.

But Levi wasn't letting go of his story so easily. He repeated, "To see our people in the colonies."

"Is that where you went in Mexico?" John said.

"My mom was so mad at me," Levi said.

John pressed Levi's hand in his. "I will speak with your mother."

"No, John. Listen to me. You think I'm crazy. I am not. My mother is gone. Don't let them get by with it. Don't let them do this to me."

John pressed his hand again. He was out of words.

Levi wouldn't let go of his hand.

"Who are they?" John asked him. "What are they doing to you? Tell me who they are."

Levi's hands balled into fists. The sinews in his forearms stood out as he struggled against the restraints. His head lifted off the pillow, and he spoke.

"Don't leave me." And then a second time: "John, don't let them do this to me."

John leaned down and whispered into Levi's ear. "Try to sleep, my friend. I will be back."

Then he walked out of the room and to the lobby where Levi's family had gathered. They saw him approach and stood up. "Let's gather together," he said. They instinctively formed a circle and took one another's hands.

"He might need another sedative," John said, looking around at the faces in the circle. "He's trying to break out of those restraints."

"It's okay, John. I'll page Doctor Thiessen," Franz said.

John hugged each family member goodbye. Julia was unable to stop crying. Eva held onto him for a long time. He said to Franz, "A sedative. I hope Levi can get comfortable."

"We'll see to that. Did you have a good talk?"

John paused. "I'm sorry to say Levi didn't make a lot of sense. I wish he had." Franz nodded bleakly. John went outside the lobby and walked into the bright sunlight. It was a glorious seventy degrees. In a couple of weeks, the custom combine crews would be driving by, about to start the harvest in Marion and Chase counties.

He pulled out on Highway 50 driving west.

It wasn't but a minute before a fast-approaching pickup loomed in his rearview mirror. He was on the outskirts of Marion Hills when the flashing headlights appeared. He decelerated and pulled onto the shoulder where he stopped. He didn't recognize the driver of the red F-150 braking suddenly behind him, and for a moment, he reverted to Chicago mode and wondered if this was a carjacking. Then the driver ran up beside his window and John rolled it down.

The man was Don Seibel, a Branson-style cowboy in a ten-gallon hat who was also the forty-year-old boyfriend of his church secretary, Linda Ebel. Seibel seemed winded, and he hunched over to look John in the eye. His message was terse.

"Levi Schlegel just coded. Eva and Carol asked me to try and catch you. They want you back there right now."

"Thanks," John said. He was already looking both ways on Highway 50 as he did a quick U-turn and tromped the accelerator.

<hr>

The *fwap-fwap* of the intercom Code Blue alarm was sounding when he entered the hospital lobby. A nurse and a nurse's aide scrambled in the hallway. They were pushing a crash cart. John looked at Rick, the intake receptionist. The kid pointed down the hall and said, "Follow them."

John ran. The entire Schlegel family was outside the room. The nurse motioned the cluster of people aside and opened the door so she could run the crash cart in. The noise, frantic and disorganized, poured out, and Franz, following the cart, said to John, "We're going in."

Franz nudged John ahead of him through the doorway and a half-muffled voice behind a blue mask snapped, "Shut the door." The nurse didn't want to argue with anyone and handed masks to Franz and John.

Thiessen used a device to suction out Levi's mouth and throat. Electrodes, snaking from the man's four extremities and the center of his chest, were plugged into the monitor on top of the cart. The patient's head was tilted back, and Thiessen looked down the throat briefly before plunging a tube straight into the tracheal passageway. The tube resembled a J-shaped clear segment of stiff garden hose. John looked away.

"Okay, intubation complete," Thiessen said. The respiratory therapist attached a melon-sized bag to the endotracheal tube and began to apply rhythmic pressure to the bag, taking his signals from the doctor who was applying chest compressions five at a time. The clay color of the skin on Levi's face showed distinctly gray. A nurse injected something into the intravenous feed via syringe, pushing the plunger steadily. Then she administered another dose from a different syringe.

Thiessen looked at the jagged, erratic line on the screen of the heart monitor and said "vee fib."

"What's he talking about?" John said to Franz, who stood beside him.

"Ventricular fibrillation," Franz said. "See that jagged line on the screen? The heart has electrical activity but no effective pumping action. I think they're starting with the defibrillator. Thiessen has to restore the pulse."

The nurse flipped a switch on the cart. Thiessen picked up two paddles.

"Here we go," he said. "All clear." The man doing chest compressions stood back. The paddles came down on Levi's chest and the machine barked. The body jumped off the bed but not like anything living. The legs were straight out and rigid. The irregular sawtooth line continued its march across the screen.

Thiessen waited a moment and said again, "All clear."

Levi's body levitated off the bed once more. Thiessen looked at the monitor. A repeating, regular pattern appeared now, as if a series of moguls was stepping in formation. "We have a pulse," Thiessen said. The other doctor resumed the chest compressions.

After a few seconds, the sawtooth line ruined the order of the marching moguls.

"Okay, here we go again," Thiessen said, the paddles held up above Levi's chest.

"All clear," the nurse said.

Bang! The paddles came down, and Levi jumped once more. The pulse resumed and held up for all of ten seconds. Then the ventricular fibrillation took over. This pattern repeated again and again.

Thiessen kept up the effort for half an hour.

Franklin nudged his way through the door to join Franz and John. The nurse's aide handed him a mask. The men watched the doctors sweating. Circular stains darkened the underarms of Thiessen's blue coat. The space started to smell like a locker room. There was another smell, too, and it reminded John of an overheated electric toy train set from his childhood. Levi's shaved chest wall was mottled and developing scattered blisters. At almost two that afternoon, Thiessen took the paddles off

Levi's chest and parked them on the cart. The other doctor stepped up to resume the compressions.

Thiessen pulled him back. "We're done here, Luke. I'm sorry." He looked at the clock on the wall. "Time of death: 1:56 p.m." Thiessen looked at his audience and said, "I'm sorry, gentlemen." He left the room.

A nurse turned off the heart monitor and began to detach the wired electrodes on the body. She unhooked the intravenous line from the catheter taped into Levi's arm. Franklin and Franz walked out of the room. At the door, Franz looked back. John said, "Give us about five minutes. The family will want to see him." Franz quietly shut the door.

After the commotion came the silence broken only by the hiss of the air-conditioning system. The nurse was sorting equipment and threw discarded supplies into a big red plastic bag and a plastic tub. John looked at her name tag that read Betsy Grace, RN.

She looked at John. "Is there anything I can get you? You seem a little lost." She prepared to roll the spent crash cart out of the room.

"You're right, I am," John said. "Betsy Grace?"

She nodded. "That's me."

"You're right. Lost is the right word."

"But I'll bet you've seen this before. Sheriff Veblen tells me you have all kinds of chaplain experience in Chicago."

"Never like this," John said.

"I've worked in ERs for twenty-five years, including before I moved to Kansas," she said. "Every time is different. You guys were pretty smooth slipping in here like that."

"Should I take that as a compliment?" John said.

"Yeah. I read it as determination."

"Does Thiessen normally push it this long?" John asked.

"Let me tell you a story, and I'll keep this brief. I once saw the paddles applied for nearly a full hour. At Cleveland Clinic. When the doc finally called it, we were relieved. The room smelled like charred flesh. Patient was a fifty-six-year-old man who'd already had two open-heart surgeries. Stubborn doc. I thought he had lost his mind."

She was pulling the sheet from the foot of the bed over Levi's body and face. Then she uncovered Levi's face and said, "Eva will want to see him. I think they're waiting out in the lobby."

"Please finish your story," John said. "What happened?"

"So the doctor calls it, right? Pronounces him dead. The respiratory therapist detaches the Ambu bag from the endotracheal tube and begins to pack up. Then he looks back and notices something truly eerie: the rhythmic appearance then evaporation of condensation in the lumen of the tracheal tube. He puts a stethoscope on the guy's chest and says, 'My God, we have spontaneous respirations and a heartbeat.' The attending physician and respiratory therapist both almost shit their pants. The guy was alive." Betsy Grace looked at John. "No one knows what's going to happen. It's different every time."

"It sounds like a medical miracle."

"Well, yes and no. I personally don't put much stock in miracles. The patient suffered brain damage, likely from lack of oxygen flow during intubation and the resuscitation procedure. I saw him half a dozen more times in the five years after that. His wife was severely depressed. The long struggle at the end of his life destroyed his family. So not quite a clean victory."

John looked at Levi, with the sheet snugged up to his neck. His arm stuck out from under the sheet. John couldn't be sure, but the man's white, stubbled chin seemed to jut out more aggressively than usual. His eyes were slightly open and his hand pointed at the floor. John carefully moved Levi's arm back under the sheet.

"Thank you," Betsy said. "He's really gone, Reverend. We all have to let it go."

"This never gets easier, does it?" John said. "You've been very kind. And it's been a pleasure to talk with you."

A knock came at the door as the nurse opened it and rolled the cart through. Eva was waiting impatiently outside and led her family inside. They gathered around the bed. Julia did not want to look at her father. "Can you pray?" Carol said. She stood to the right of John; Franz was to his left.

John extended his hands to Carol and Franz. The family joined hands. John spoke with his eyes open: "Merciful God, we grieve the death of this man Levi Schlegel, father, husband, brother, a creative spirit whose energy was boundless and whose vision was clear. Please be with us in the hour of our grief."

The family dropped their hands and he raised both of his. He felt the energy pulse through him, and then he spoke again: "For this beloved family now we ask for your grace and peace that last forever. In the name of the Father, Son, and Holy Ghost. Amen." An hour later, pulling into his driveway, John was still thinking about Betsy Grace's story.

But as the evening wore on, it was the patriarch's last words, spoken to him earlier that day, that echoed loudest: "John, don't let them do this to me." He tried to make the words go away.

Chapter 32

The arrival of June was painful because it made John ache for Chicago in summertime. He imagined what he would do there: Run the cinder trail at the lakefront. Stop at the Melrose for breakfast. An outdoor table with the newspaper spread out before him, a coffee and tall tomato juice with a slice of lemon and a shake of Tabasco. Alex would come around to make small talk.

Or he could meet Nancy on Halsted for a special brunch in Lincoln Park. They would sit on the same side of the booth and look out at the world. At the right moment, she would reach for his hand under the table and interlace her fingers with his and put their joined hands together on top of her warm, slender thigh. He could be leaning forward right now, to consider her profile and catch the scent of her citrus and cinnamon perfume that drifted off the nape of her neck like a whisper, as they contemplated their next move in a world of crazy possibilities. Her candy, she called it.

Instead, he was here in central Kansas, almost dead center in the middle of the Lower Forty-Eight in the thick of wheat harvest. To be exact, at the gritty entrance of the Copper Kettle restaurant on Route 50 on the edge of Marion Hills, where he was waiting for John Schroeder. It was the day after he conducted Levi Schlegel's funeral in a packed church. John felt like he needed at least two days off for recovery. He had sensed the tempestuous undercurrents of the event; it was not often that a local mogul was consigned to the earth. The familiar hymns and magisterial organ music and biblical passages did little to quiet the unspoken sentiments of Levi's neighbors as they filed past the coffin in the foyer before it was closed up and wheeled to the front of the sanctuary.

While waiting for Schroeder to arrive, John thought about the stark message the man had given him in the parking lot, not too long after Levi was buried beneath a grove of cedars in the church cemetery. Almost everyone had gone home. Then Schroeder leaned over and said in his ear: "Half the people came out today to hold a mirror under his nose and make sure the asshole was dead." John wondered why he put up with Schroeder.

A couple of custom-cutting crews crowded the Copper Kettle this morning, a dozen guys, mostly young and busting with attitude, over-size belt buckles (Lone Star Proud, superimposed on a Mack truck; the Eighty-Second Airborne patch fashioned in bronze; Merca), and noisy banter. They had started in Texas weeks earlier and were working their way north through the wheat belt of Oklahoma, Kansas, Nebraska, the Dakotas, eastern Montana. They had a long way to go before the harvest ended in the middle of August up near Malta, but in the present moment, they were busy stoking energy for the day's work. Their noise contrasted the taciturn local-dirt-farmer caucus camped out at their usual corner table against the back wall, partly obscured by a blue haze of cigarette smoke.

Schroeder stood up from the table and came over to say hello. "How about we get a booth?"

"Yes, let's take something up front here by the window," John said. "I don't want to interrupt the important conversations swirling around me."

Schroeder raised his upper lip in semblance of a smile, exposing his nicotine-stained teeth. He had a toothpick in the corner of his mouth and he worked it around to the other side.

"You eat already?" John said, glancing at the dirt farmers' table.

"Nah. I was waiting for you."

Members of Ella Eitzen's kitchen crew were slinging the hash browns and omelets, the country ham and bacon, stacks of toast and griddle cakes. A couple of waitresses came through the back double doors with platters of food that they deposited in front of the custom crew outfit spread out among four adjacent tables.

"I've been thinking about what you said to me yesterday in the parking lot. I even wrote it down," John said.

"Wow," Schroeder said. "I made it into your journal. Now I feel like a big man. What did I say?"

"You know what. Half the people? Did they get the satisfaction that Levi is truly gone? In your words, are they glad the asshole is dead?"

Schroeder sipped coffee. "I reckon they are. Half of them know someone he bought out or screwed over, or both. The other half are just human."

John countered. "Levi Schlegel was a generous man. He underwrote MDS, the Mennonite Foundation, and the MCC relief auction for years. He supported development projects in Mexico, Bangladesh, and the Chaco. He gave to environmental causes and was a major donor to Doctors Without Borders. He was a humanitarian, for lack of a better word."

Schroeder said, "Not to mention his rumored twenty-million-dollar bequest left to the college in his will. You're beginning to sound like a public relations flack, or someone in the college development office, for crying out loud. I know all the official bullshit. And of course, his son is also quite the philanthropist. He likes to give nice vehicles to the clergy."

"I'd still be driving that Crown Victoria if not for a raffle," John said. "It wasn't a bad car. Part of the interim pastoral leadership package."

"Okay, donates generously to Mennonite raffles," Schroeder said. "Makes Catholic bingo look tame. And let me say something about the esteemed Schlegel giving. One of the truths about Schlegel philanthropy can be summed up in a simple saying."

"What's that?" John asked.

Schroeder was laconic: "Where there is a gift, there is also a tentacle."

"You're a man of stern judgment," John said. He remembered Levi's last conversation with him, the broken sentences about Mexico. He thought about where Campbell was flying and caught himself wondering. He thought about his conversation with Franklin at the limestone quarry mansion, and the bathroom cabinet full of antipsychotic medications, and Franklin's talk of suicide. He thought about too many things and tried to pull back from all thoughts altogether: He was drawing many imaginary connections, and the mess of vectors had scrambled his brain. He noticed Schroeder was trying to ask him something.

Did you see the Flint Hills newcomers at the service?" Schroeder waved a hand in John's face. "Are you with me?"

"No," John said. "I didn't notice the Flint Hills newcomers. Guess I was too focused on my funeral remarks. They must have driven out before the burial and fellowship meal. You know, burying millionaires among the Mennonites is hard work. How did you spot these bad guys from Chase County?"

"Bumper stickers on a couple of jacked-up pickups with Chase County plates. 'Feds Out of Flint Hills.' Something like that. They came to Schlegel's funeral to send the message loud and clear."

"You think Franz got the message?" John said.

Schroeder answered. "They've been giving him hell, I know that much. From time to time, I stop through Strong City at a little coffee klatch. I rent a parcel of pasture near there for some of my cows. You should listen to Sheriff Mingus when he gets going. They love that man and he's pretty clever ginning up the rage. Frankly I'm surprised those bumper stickers were as mild as they were. I kind of expected Confederate flags."

"Come on, these guys aren't happy with their fine upstanding Kansas Republicans?"

"Are you kidding? These guys think anybody seeking common ground with a Democrat is licking the Antichrist's boots."

"Say what you really think," John said.

"You worry too much, Reverend. Now let me tell you more about those black semitrucks in Chase County."

John rolled his eyes. "Something has really managed to spook you."

"Reverend, I don't live in a world of fantasy," Schroeder said. "If it makes you feel better, I've not seen any black helicopters. But there is questionable activity some have noticed on and near the Campbell property. Lots of night flying. Trucks in and out. We should drive out there some late evening and poke around. You could take a break from your learned commentaries about the Good Book and we could book an adventure."

John perked up. "You are a craven local rancher who likes trouble," he said. "I know about booking adventure. Just remember I ran into trouble in Chicago. Which is why I ended up in Marion Hills. Don't you try to tempt me."

"Don't brag until you provide the details. You never told me what happened in Chicago, did you? You know, you're all ears when I say Campbell's name," Schroeder said. "Like a coyote that just sniffed some gamy rabbit roadkill. Gets your fur up, doesn't it? What's that about?"

John had to admit Schroeder piqued his curiosity. He was like an extra shake of pepper in the tomato juice. John knew the man sometimes functioned merely as an amplifier or echo chamber for what he'd heard around the community. Maybe that was why John found him interesting—and useful. And he could have whetted Schroeder's suspicions further had he mentioned Campbell's real estate shenanigans and Celeste's account of the evangelist's sadistic streak on display in Brody's Lounge. John knew Campbell was not on good terms with his father-in-law toward the end. What else was possible? The details John knew about the man pointed to more than merely grubby; a kind of genuine rottenness emanated from him. If the man's hide showed scabs, maybe a closer look was advisable.

John said, "What were you thinking? Some kind of night excursion?"

"You read me," Schroeder said.

John mopped up the runny egg on his plate. He spread strawberry jam on a last bite of toast and put it in his mouth.

"We'll take my pickup," Schroeder said.

John said, "Not so fast. Let me do a little more exploration before I commit to your bold venture. I might know more by the time we go. And that could be useful."

"Suit yourself, preacher."

John's focus turned inward again. He thought about the Schlegel fortune and its direction now that the patriarch was dead. He thought about Levi's last pleas: Get the *Frintschoft* out of here. Don't let them do this to me.

Something is not right.

Alan Wiebe called him that evening from Chicago. His words about Levi carried, in a strange sense, echoes of Schroeder. Alan pronounced: "The last of the petty robber barons is dead."

When John called Nancy that night at nearly eleven o'clock, she asked him, "Did you give him a good send-off?"

John said, "It's complicated burying a rich man." He didn't elaborate for Nancy, and he sensed she wanted him to. Oddly, he didn't feel as if he'd exactly sent him off, at least not yet.

"You stay out of trouble. Do you hear me, you crazy man? I need you here."

"When am I coming back home?" John said.

"I'm working on it. I want to see you naked at least one more time, and I will consider myself lucky if I do. You are the number-one priority on my project management schedule."

Chapter 33

After Levi's funeral, Eva decided to host a dinner for John. She had run into him on the sidewalk downtown in front of the hardware store, where she confessed she had not expected to cry during the funeral but broke down when he recited the Psalms and that lovely poem. "Was it Tennyson?" she asked.

"No," he answered. "The Book of Common Prayer." He told her a lot of Anglican writers were influenced by Tennyson, whether conscious of it or not. She had blushed. At her dinner party, she presided with a firm presence that John hadn't noticed before. Now that the patriarch was gone, some sort of veil had fallen away.

John arrived at the front door shortly after seven. He gave Eva a fresh spray of flowers wrapped in green tissue.

"The funeral is over, John. You didn't need to," she said, accepting the bouquet from him. She took his hand and kissed him lightly on the cheek. She had a modest but sparkling clip nestled in her white hair.

"Consider it for the sideboard," John said. "Something for a brand-new day."

"That's something Vi would have said," Eva said.

"What?"

"'A brand-new day.' Vi liked that expression. She said that the first time I met her," Eva explained. "When she was still a child."

"Watch out," John said. "Don't make this grown man cry."

All her children were already there: Franklin; Franz and his wife, Susie, who seemed even more gregarious and full of hilarity that evening; Carol and Campbell, who was uncharacteristically quiet, and, John thought, maybe pouting a little; and Julia and Ken. Adorning his embroidered, western-style shirt, Ken wore a bolo tie of braided black leather with a little silver goat nestled under his Adam's apple. Julia showcased one of her *National Velvet* pantsuits that exaggerated her willowy height and black-patent-leather heels. John looked at her feet and noticed something that he had been educated about very recently: Shoes—like blouses—could be low-cut and designed for "toe cleavage," as Nancy put it. John made his eyes move back to Julia's handsome face. Franklin was freshly shaved, wearing black jeans and a black felt jacket, button-down white shirt and a skinny, glittering green tie. Everyone had dressed up for the occasion this evening.

Franklin grasped his hand first. "John, before I pour the Beaujolais, let me say, you did our daddy proud three days ago. Thank you." Murmurs of assent rose up from his siblings and in-laws. Even Campbell said "Hear, hear!"

"May I invite you into the kitchen?" Franklin said. Then Susie interrupted, "Champagne first. The Beaujolais can wait."

The party moved into Eva's kitchen, which was redolent of roasting meat. John picked up notes of rosemary, fresh dill, sage, and thyme. Julia arranged a charcuterie board. Susie emerged from the pantry carrying a couple of bottles by their necks. She went back for a tray of glasses. Franklin popped the corks and poured while Susie and Eva handed the glasses around.

"I toast our beloved friend, Reverend John Reimer," Franklin said. "To your honor and health."

"And I toast this family," John said. "All of you have shown me friendship that I can never forget. We remember Levi." He hoisted his glass and drank. The family followed his gesture. Campbell said "Cheers!" before draining his glass. He ignored Franklin and reached for the bottle. John noticed he liked a big pour. Minutes later, Susie brought out another bottle of champagne.

John found himself with an angle to look into the pantry. Four empty bottles stood on the counter there. Someone had apparently already motored through them before John's arrival. The group circulated out to the living room and John again reconsidered Levi's twin Charles Russell paintings. There were little lights in brass fixtures on the wall above each, providing special illumination. Franz stood beside John and asked, "Do they shine brighter now that Dad is dead?"

"I don't know," John said. "What does your mother think?"

"She's indifferent to the cowboy thing," Franz said. "She's more Sierra Club than Future Farmers of America. But she'll hang onto them for his sake."

The group was hungry. Campbell swooped down on the charcuterie plate and half the cheese-and-cracker supply disappeared in his sizable paw. Ken and Julia talked with John about the goat dairy and building a market for goat cheese. John asked why so many things had suddenly become "handcrafted." He admitted to his weakness for gelato and the delicious samples at the MCC auction. Franklin sat in his father's favorite chair and looked around with a contented smile on his face. Eva and Carol monitored the contents of the double oven and called Franz into the kitchen to pull the porterhouse steaks. Susie replenished the hors d'oeuvres. She returned with the plate piled high with more cheese and homemade pickles, red pepper slices, and banana peppers, and directed John not to hold back.

Eventually they all sat at the polished walnut expanse of the dining room's Chippendale table. The space was loaded and austere in the way of the absent patriarch; a double-wide china cabinet with two sets of glass doors loomed at one end, housing a lifetime of collectibles, including high school trophies and award medals. A massive buffet sideboard across the room supported two ornate silver candlesticks and a 1950s silver fondue set and chafing dish that looked polished but unused. Through the window, John could see the lengthening shadows cast by the yard trees. Over the table hung a chandelier chosen to match the furniture: ornate, heavy, dark with the stains of time and imparting an aura of an eighteenth-century coffeehouse.

Franz stood at one end of the table, holding a meat fork and carving knife. The chopping block at his elbow, standing a little apart from the table, might have served a Tudor trencherman, and it presented two-inch thick slabs of porterhouse. At the other end of the table Franklin served portions of a side of salmon laid out on a ceramic platter on a bed of fresh dill and parsley. Julia and Carol brought out more dishes of food. John found himself beside Eva, and eventually Carol sat on his other side. The Schlegel women plied him with food. The brothers insisted John partake of surf and turf. Susie ran in and out of the dining room and replenished wine glasses. She uncorked a bottle of chilled Chablis. John watched her handle the corkscrew and could see she had the benefit of a lot of practice. "Maybe you prefer this with the fish, though the Beaujolais works," she said. "Let me get you another glass."

"I'm fine," John said. "That's okay." He put his hand over his glass.

"The potatoes!" Julia exclaimed. "How could we forget the potatoes?" A short time later she entered the dining room with oven mitts on, bearing a smoking hot heavy Pyrex dish. "Potatoes au gratin," she said proudly. John thought of them as scalloped and tried to remember how to pronounce the French. Julia followed up with another serving dish of jumbo yams roasted in their skins.

Eva put her hand on John's arm and apologized. "This is a traditional and unimaginative meal, John. But it's the way Levi liked it. Meat, starch, vegetables. Repeat. He was a pretty simple man at heart. This is what he would have ordered if he were still alive, although I think Carol and Julia made sure the vegetable part was more than adequately covered."

Roasted carrots were dressed in a sauce that John learned was called "harissa." A roasting pan came piled high with broccoli rabe and cauliflower florets. For good measure there was a big wooden bowl full of dressed Boston lettuce. Franklin lifted the bowl as if to send it in John's direction.

"I don't think I have room for it yet. But I promise to eat salad. I have been schooled about the importance of eating salad."

"Who has schooled you?" Carol asked, leaning over and bumping John slightly with her right arm.

"That would be Nancy Huefflinger," John said.

Julia clapped her hands and opened her eyes wide. "I knew that woman was looking out for you! You lucky man! Isn't she the moderator in your church in Chicago?"

"Yes," John said. "I must introduce you. I didn't get around to formal introductions that day in Hutchinson. She was in and out from a business trip in Wichita."

"We felt a bit slighted that there wasn't a formal introduction," Eva said carefully. She reached for the bottle of Chablis and poured herself a separate glass. She watched John's face fall and then gave a low giggle. "I'm toying with you, John. But I can tell when a man is serious. You tried so very *hard* to appear casual."

"You mean it's not casual?" Franklin quipped from his end of the table. When he grinned, the light from the smoky chandelier caught his front teeth. He looked like a friendly pirate asking for a modest donation.

Campbell spoke. "I understand she bought the prize quilt, the one Verla Arnheim made."

"That was quite a prize," Carol said. "I put in a bid myself."

"What does she do?" Campbell asked. He sawed off a chunk of porterhouse in his plate and put it in his mouth. "Nice job on this steak," he said to Franz.

"She's an attorney," John said. "Estate planning, divorces, trusts. Some corporate law."

This information brought an awkward pause to conversation. John wondered whether anybody else was thinking about the Schlegel estate. He said, "But these carrots! I like this salmon very much, but I could live on these carrots. What do you call this sauce, again?"

"Harissa," Franklin said "A North African dish. Rhymes with 'Clarissa.'"

"What on earth are you going on about now, Franklin?" Carol asked.

"*Clarissa*," Franklin said. "A book I read in a class at Wesleyan, assigned by a crazy prof. Longest novel in English. Almost a million words."

"What's it about?" Carol asked.

"A damsel in distress. She is ravished and ruined by an evil man named Lovelace. Very sad ending. She dies without justice. I told Dad about it at the time and he said, 'What in hell's name are you doing wasting my money on this shit? You call this education? What is wrong with the people at Wesleyan? Do all of them have their heads up their asses? Why don't you study something of value to the human race? Like learn how to build something, make something, be a credit to your family and community!'" Franklin waved his hands around his head dramatically, an inspired cartoon impression of Levi throwing a fit.

John listened to the youngest son but watched the others around the table. Franz had a benign smile on his face, as if he had heard this story before. Campbell refilled wine glasses and tuned out the storyteller. Eva rose from the table to fetch another bottle of wine.

"So, in response to Dad, I took up the study of architecture." Franklin loaded his fork with a morsel of salmon, steak, and a chunk of sweet potato, sculpting the mass with the edge of his knife. He guided the medley into his mouth. He thoughtfully chewed for a moment. "I give all the credit to Clarissa. That woman saved me."

"Would you like a refill?" Susie asked John, holding up a bottle.

"Maybe just another skosh," John said.

"You are fond of the skosh," Eva said. "And please forgive Franklin," she added. "He gets this way sometimes."

"Woman, his sins are already forgiven," John said. "And about the skosh, the apostle Paul was also fond of it. You know, he constantly exhorted his people to moderation. How does he put it in First Corinthians? 'All things are lawful, but not all things are beneficial.' That is commonly called 'the skosh chapter,' at least it was when I went to seminary."

Franklin interrupted. "Now you're really yanking our chain, John. And I think it was the Greek philosopher Hesiod who said 'Moderation in all things.' Not Paul."

"Hey, little brother, now you're showing off," Julia said.

Eva apologized: "He is our dancing monkey."

"The skosh chapter," Campbell mused. He turned to John. "I might preach something on that topic if I may borrow your term. Although to be quite honest, no disrespect meant to Paul, I wonder if a man of moderate appetites can achieve anything at all."

Campbell sat in his chair, a light sheen of sweat on his brow, slightly stunned by his gustatory intake. Carol looked at him and stroked the back of his head, as if he were a large house pet in need of attention. John watched them and tried to understand the relationship.

They finished the meal with generous wedges of hot apple pie baked by Julia. She served the portions in white porcelain bowls with a side of vanilla ice cream and optional whipped cream. She handed the bowls around the table. Carol poured coffee. The party broke up with an abrupt burst about an hour later. It had begun to crash on the shoals of its own excess. John excused himself from the table. He felt sluggish.

He went to the bathroom and again found himself opening the medicine cabinet. Nothing of note here. Aspirin, Pepto Bismol, Band-Aids, a jar of nail clippers and tweezers. Four different kinds of sunscreen. If there were serious medications, they were probably in the master suite. He closed the medicine cabinet and flushed the toilet. He washed his hands and walked down the dark hallway. In the dining room, he stacked dishes and carried them into the kitchen by the sink. He opened the hot water tap. He repeated the trip several times.

Eva walked over and put a hand on John's shoulder. She said quietly in his ear, "If you have a little extra time, I want to show you a few things in the studio."

John cleared the dining room table while the children took leave of their mother. He pushed in the chairs and, back in the kitchen, rinsed the bowls and plates, stacking them on the counter. He found the Tupperware drawer and brought out containers and lids. After he had stored the leftovers in appropriate containers, he refrigerated the works. Then he wiped down the dining room table, and carried the crumbs back to the kitchen on the sponge cupped in his hand. When he rinsed out the sponge, he ran the sink disposal. The sound of it brought Eva into the kitchen. She watched John take a tea towel to the dining room, where he wiped the water marks off the walnut surface.

Eva spoke from the doorway: "John, you really don't have to. Please."

"But I want to, if you will indulge me. It's the least I can do," John said. "I know I'm slightly eccentric. But this gives me a sense of serenity. I didn't load your dishwasher, by the way. In my experience, everyone has a particular method." He gave the sponge a final rinse and squeeze and put it in the soap dish.

"Does Nancy not like the way you stack her dishwasher?"

John turned to look at Eva. Buried in that question were several layers of presumption and probably a double entendre. John had to give Eva credit.

"Where do I begin?" John said. "Nancy believes I need to refine my housekeeping."

"From the looks of things, she already has you house-trained. I look forward to meeting her," Eva said. "I'm about due for another trip to Chicago. Now that Levi's gone, I have scheduled more flying time with Franz. He likes to fly. Please leave these dishes. I'll take care of them."

"Okay." John dried his hands. He followed Eva to the back door. "Where are we going?"

"To the painting shed."

They walked the familiar route through the property that John had traversed earlier in spring. The wild grass in parts of the yard was taller now. Everything smelled of summer dust. Late April seemed distant when John thought of Levi's rapid decline.

"I have to ask you, John, what did Levi want to talk about with you on that last day?"

John waited to speak. He noticed she had traded out her bejeweled hairpin for a rubber band that sensibly gathered her swatch of gray hair in a ponytail. She moved swiftly. He reframed her. When she was part of the entity known as Levi and Eva, he had always thought of her as much older, like the patriarch she had married, but he recognized with a kind of delayed reaction that she had more youth than he had given her credit for. John tried to interpret her gait, her body language. He picked up a little bit of anger and tried to keep pace with her. An automatic yard light came on as they approached the studio. "You mean the day he coded? When he sent everybody out of the room?"

"Yes, all of us except you. What did he say?" Eva stood outside the sliding door of the painting shed. She didn't open it yet. John was surprised by her speech patterns. No starry-night artist here. More of an alpha executive.

John said, "He spoke about Mexico. It was disjointed. He said, 'Don't let them do this to me,' at least twice. I asked him who they were. He didn't say. I got the sense he felt he was being taken advantage of."

"What did he say about Mexico?" Eva asked.

"He said, 'I know I'm not sick. I was in Mexico.' Then he said something about 'our people are having a hard time there.' And he said, 'I think somebody stole from us.' The last thing he said to me was, 'John, please help me. Don't let them do this to me.'"

"Strange," Eva said. "My last conversation alone with him followed something of the same sequence. But he said nothing about Mexico. I wonder why he was talking about it with you."

"Maybe medication?" John asked. "I mean, Franz said he was on a mood stabilizer after he started throwing food trays. And they had him in restraints so he wouldn't pull out the IV. It all seemed rather extreme to me. I thought he was being hospitalized for a case of lightheadedness and arrhythmia. Julia told me he fell at least once at the hospital."

"That was a hard fall. He didn't want to leave us," Eva said, with a stubborn set to her jaw. "Levi was naturally always looking out for his interests. Always looking over his shoulder. Franz, who is closer to the business details than I am, has said more than once that if Levi weren't so paranoid, he could have been much more successful."

They went into the painting shed. Eva turned on a couple of can lights nestled in the rafters that created a pool of illumination for her work area in the center of the space. Four under-the-counter lights also flooded the running countertop along the far wall. She led John to a couple of easy chairs in a corner of the shed. Underneath their feet was a Berber rug. "Please sit down. I will brew tea. This conversation is long overdue."

She sauntered back while the teakettle warmed. "Strange, this business about Mexico," she said. "That's puzzling to me because, so far as I know, Levi never flew to Mexico. He flew mostly to California, Oklahoma, and Texas, to look after his 'energy investments,' as he called them. However, Campbell has business interests in the Old Mennonite colonies in Mexico like he has in the Chaco, and Carol tells me his office staffers in Kansas City are almost completely dedicated to the relief work there. She says he's talked about starting up a Latin American division to Campbell

Ministries. Carol seems to be all in." Eva paused as if deciding how much more to say.

"I don't completely understand what she sees in him," she continued. "But it's not for parents to judge their children's choices. Of course, Levi allowed himself to get talked into investing money with Campbell. Sort of like he's invested in so many other projects. The man liked to spread his money around. You don't know how often I tolerated the spiel about portfolio diversity in the early years of my marriage."

"But it has served you well," John said.

"What? The spiel?"

"No, the diverse portfolio."

Eva stepped back and crossed her arms. "You're a smart aleck like my boy Franklin. I can see why you two get along."

John said, "Pardon me for asking, but how thorough was your understanding of your husband's business interests?"

"That's a personal question, John. But I understand why you're asking."

"You opened the topic," John said. "Levi said something else to me. In rapid Low German that I didn't fully understand. I figured he was reverting to Low German under stress. And he spoke about making 'mother' angry. I know nothing about Levi's relationship with his mother."

"It wasn't good," Eva said. "Maybe he was thinking about his mom close to his death. Is that so surprising?"

"No. You do know the story about soldiers dying in combat?"

"I think so, but tell me."

"The last word most of them say is 'Mother.'"

"Let me show you my new paintings," Eva said.

She had four canvases in progress. The largest was the snowy owl gripping a rabbit in one of its talons. The smallest was of a cowboy squinting into the evening sunlight. Wind blew a bandanna tied loosely at the cowboy's throat.

John looked closer. The face was Levi's, maybe sixty years ago. "That's a portrait of your late husband. Franz told me you're not very much into the 'cowboy thing,' but that's rather convincing."

"Franz doesn't know everything about his mother. But, yes. I've been working on it since the funeral. Which, by the way, you handled with tremendous dignity. I am so grateful. I am giving you one of these paintings. I should have these completed very soon."

"You don't have to."

"I want to. This is not an argument."

"I am fond of the owl."

"Something of the predator bird appeals to you. Notice I switched out the mouse for a rabbit. I wanted the prey to look more substantial. Let me add that you are a man in touch with your animal nature. Like a poacher. That's not something I say very often about preachers."

"How do you know that? I have lately been watching the peregrine falcons in Chicago."

"You see? I am a trained observer of life," Eva said. "Poachers, preachers—it's all my wonderful world to explore. I'm about to start work on a coyote. Maybe a series of canvases. I would say this: there's something of the dog in you, too, if I may be so blunt."

"Well, it's not like I haven't heard that before. Nancy says all men are dogs."

"Treasure that woman. Humans are just another kind of animal. You're the kind who sniffs around. Like all these questions you are suddenly asking me. And you disarm people. You make us comfortable. We are fine with saying things we should maybe not say. I notice you are sensitive to smell, too. I've watched you."

"When did you watch me?"

Eva ignored his last question. She said, "I could do your portrait, if you want."

"When you paint that coyote, give him my personality."

"Oh, I will. That's what I plan to do."

John looked at the cowboy portrait again. "Let me explain what I meant earlier about Franz. 'She's indifferent to the cowboy art,' is how he put it. And here you go with a classic cowboy painting." He pointed at the young face of Levi. "Franz mentioned your Sierra Club interests. What do you think about the proposal for the tallgrass prairie national park?"

"I think it's great. It's sort of what I'm trying to do on this property on a smaller scale. I just wish they'd move some of the cattle out and let the native species back in, is what I think. But that doesn't endear me to the ranchers."

"I had a couple more questions about Levi."

"Go ahead. My defenses are down. You are a predator."

"This is personal. It goes back to when I met Levi in my first go-around out here in the early sixties. When I was at Ebenholzer."

"That's a real long time ago, John. I have forgotten so much."

"Maybe. There was a night when I drove by your place in Hillsboro."

"Is this a confession?"

"It is, kind of. I drove by, late on a weeknight. I had been in a church council meeting that went too long. You were on the front porch in your housecoat, vacuuming off your doormat. You were focused on the task. You didn't notice me driving by."

"Why were you driving by? How late was it?"

"Must have been ten or eleven o'clock. But all I can remember is you out there, vacuuming like your life depended on it."

"Okay."

"And then you and Levi were gone for a spell. For several weeks. There was talk in the community about you, a counseling situation that had to be taken care of. That is what I heard. I wasn't sure if it was Prairie View or Menninger's. You know how small towns work. The story got clearer. People exchange information. Sometimes part of the story is true. Weeks later at the Copper Kettle, maybe a couple months, Levi confided to me that he had taken you to Menninger's for a bit of rest. That was his phrase: 'a bit of rest.' He told me you were 'fragile.' That you were 'not yourself.'"

Eva clasped her hands behind her, and her face hardened into a sort of sculptural durability. John had the impression that she was acting before an audience. She reached up and redid the rubber band on her ponytail. She looked very directly at John. "That's the story all right. That is the story Levi wanted to tell."

"What are you saying?" John said. "Was the story not true?"

"I went along with it. And I sort of kick myself for that. The fact is that I took Levi to Menninger's, and not the other way around. He was convinced we were going for my sake. I indulged him. I decided it was all right if he wanted to tell the story that way. If people wanted to think of me as the crazy bitch, that was fine. It would give me more privacy and more time to devote to painting. In a strange way, my alleged fragility allowed me more freedom to pursue my art. I've always loved Kansas. You have no idea. I'm just not so much in love with its people. And Levi could pass himself off as the powerful financier on track to match the Koch Brothers. If his bipolar problem had been made public, his career would have been over. If we were outside of Marion County right now, I would say his career would have been fucked. Vi always chided me for my bad language. Pardon my French. What I'm trying to tell you is that the whole story worked out, at least for Levi and me. But understand it was a lie of convenience. We cultivated it for a purpose. We made a pact. It allowed both of us the freedom to pursue our careers without impediments."

"But I . . . but I always thought—"

"You thought I was the hysterical woman that the family revolved around. That's what all of Marion Hills still believes, John. The lie was perfect because it was so predictable. Doesn't everyone just *love* a hysterical female? And it's ten times better if she's an *artist*. I fulfilled everyone's notion of the myth. I was slightly touched, *oh God bless her heart*, and needed to be treated as a *very* delicate flower. You were taken in like everyone else. But I was not the bipolar wreckage looming over everything. Levi was."

"Did your kids know?"

"Gradually. I let them know when it made sense to tell them. They figured it out."

John said, "Franklin told me you were fond of doing your Emily Dickinson impersonation." He decided not to share that he had found Franklin's bathroom cabinet full of medication generally associated with the treatment of psychotics and bipolar disorder. He wanted to, but it wasn't the right time. He waited for Eva to resume her story.

She said, "Franklin was the most perceptive about what was happening. Here is how I would sum it up for you, John, and I prefer this not be made available for public consumption, or even for my children. As something of a dog yourself, you understand when to let sleeping dogs lie. Levi was the bipolar piece of the puzzle. He was in treatment for six full weeks, close to seven. He had a really bad spell there. They stabilized him with lithium. The therapists were stellar. They made Levi right as rain. I thought it was a medical miracle."

"I'm familiar with lithium," John said. "You know during Civilian Public Service I worked in a mental hospital in Philadelphia when Vi and I were first married. The straitjackets were coming off and the lithium was going in. That's how one resident psychiatrist explained it to me."

"Vi loved to talk about Philadelphia. She said you both had some of the best times of your life there."

"We were young," John said. "We were kids off the farm. We started going to the movies. There was nothing like it, not before, not since."

"There's nothing like being in your twenties, John," Eva said. She put her hand on his arm and squeezed it. "Nothing like it."

She was nodding and her eyes began to tear up. She pointed at the portrait of the cowboy. "I had a hard time when they put restraints on

Levi during the last few weeks. My heart sank like a stone when they did that. But he was out of control. They had to do it."

"I wondered why Thiessen mentioned he was medicating Levi with Haldol," John said. "I thought that was a strange prescription for arrhythmia."

"Well, his heart was shot to hell, too. He'd been lightheaded for a month and they'd been monitoring his heart pretty closely. Had he been only sixty, I would have medevacked him to Denver for a transplant. But he was past that point, wasn't he?"

"What do you call your portrait of Levi?" John asked.

"'Headwinds,' she said. Then she walked over to the sliding door and hit the switches to extinguish the interior lights of the painting shed. John followed her.

"It has been a long day," she said, "and thank you for coming to dinner." She closed the door behind her. "It's my bedtime. I'm sure you understand."

They walked out under the stars of the Milky Way, side by side now, not in single file. John got into his Land Rover and drove home to the parsonage in Marion Hills and wrote several pages of notes in his journal before he went to bed.

He dreamed about Delores diving off the cliff at Casa Bonita. Another woman was diving beside her, synchronously. But he could not identify who she was. It might have been Nancy or a very young Eva Schlegel who looked almost like Georgia O'Keeffe. Or maybe Carol.

Often he lay awake after a dream and tried to break it down. He wondered why his dreams were so often full of beautiful women, but on this night, he decided the dream was more about Mexico. He was sorry he had never learned Spanish.

Chapter 34

At the college, John parked outside the library in a new paved lot. The campus was deserted. He reminded himself that it was June but still wondered where all the students had gone. He walked to his destination, found the familiar entrance, and pushed on the glass door, which swung open. A big aquarium in the front lobby had been converted to a terrarium. Less maintenance, John supposed. He remembered the first time he'd entered the library at the college. Back then, in the year of Sputnik, it was a brand-new temple to the life of the mind. Now the lilies looked like they could use water; they appeared to struggle in the thin soil deposited in the bottom of this shrine, built into a cinder-block wall painted baby blue. It was early afternoon. A maintenance man drove a green John Deere lawn tractor across the lawn in front of the Ad building, and the sound of its engine spurted distantly through the silence.

There was no one at the front desk, but it didn't matter because he knew how to rummage through a card catalog, still available for old-timers like himself. He found a single call number on a slip of paper and meandered into a distant, isolated part of the stacks. He found a brown accordion file folder with a label affixed to the front with an industrial-size patch of yellowing scotch tape: "Wyndham Campbell Ministries: documents, brochures, misc.: 1972–present." John took the folder to a carrel buried deep against a far wall and spread its contents on the desktop. He pulled a chain hanging from the interior of the carrel and a tube fluorescent came on above his head.

He had used this space as a young man, and its familiarity pleased him. It was as if he hadn't left. He recalled coming off the farm and launching himself with furious intensity into the life of scholarship at this "worldly" center of learning. That was how his brother Andrew had characterized it, partly because of its proximity to Wichita. This was the carrel where he had read Hemingway and Hardy when he was supposed to drill down in the commentaries on the book of Romans for a course in early Christian community. This is where he had read both Karl Barth and Karl Marx. Where he picked up Heidegger and tried to plumb the being of beingness. The heady smell of scholarship. Dangerous ideas. The fumes of treated paper floated up to his nose. Dusty books and acidifying paper. He took off his sport coat and hung it over the back of the chair. Then he settled in for close reading.

What he saw in front of him was mostly brochures and fundraising publications that showed the size, range, and evolving theological aspirations of a Protestant ministry emerging in Kansas after World War II. He was surprised that Campbell hadn't produced a paperback bestseller yet. But the man's gifts lay elsewhere: as an evangelist, as a builder of organizations, and more recently, as a media personality. He was maybe a Johnny-come-lately to the evangelical TV party, but he had certainly arrived there now. The publications were mostly glossy trifolds, with a few staple-bound items that featured pages of donors. Pages and pages of mostly small print. The earliest brochure presented Campbell as "a soul-winning man interested in the whole man." There were references to Explo '72 in Dallas and the PROBE Mennonite conference in Minneapolis that same year.

John removed a yellow legal pad from his briefcase and scribbled down notes. There were pictures of Andraé Crouch and the Disciples, and Larry Norman with his long blond hippie hair belting out "I Wish We'd All Been Ready." There was a full-color centerfold of a very young Campbell and Carol with their celebrity friends on stage in front of packed stands of stadium seating.

The later brochures showed a shift in emphasis. The musical celebrities were switched out for Washington politicians. The prayer breakfasts showed well-groomed bowed heads in hotel ballrooms and fewer sweaty stadiums, and this literature carried pledges to take the good news to "The Whole Man," now capitalized. In the 1980s, relief projects in Mexico and the Chaco began to figure into the mix. These were explained as part of a mission to "lift up God's people." Economic development became a theme. The list of well-heeled donors, American and Canadian, grew. "Help people help themselves" was a slogan. John took more notes. He looked at the end-of-year rosters of donors that began to fatten in the mid-1980s, and he ran his thumb down the alphabetized names. For 1990, he found one he was looking for: Jeffrey Arnheim, recognized as a

"Good Steward" sponsor, a category reserved for any donation between five hundred and a thousand dollars. John thought it was a generous gift coming from a man who divided his time between a rent-by-the-week Denver motel and the back seat of his car. *Oh, well, maybe it was trickle-down from Marvin.*

John went further back, to a summary dating from the late 1970s, where he knew he would find his own name on a list. There it was. He tried to remember what he'd been thinking when he wrote the check, and didn't remember why he'd stopped writing them. His mind wandered. There was the matter of saving for Sarah's college tuition. There was Vi's illness, the bills, the neurological consultations. He could go on. He wondered at the fuzziness of his historical memory when he contemplated that period.

John read the key at the top of the last couple of lists. If the donor categories were described accurately, fundraising for the organization was more significant than he'd initially guessed, in recent years averaging consistently in sizable multiples of a million dollars. He found Levi Schlegel's name, too, in the "Nicodemus" level of gift givers for 1992. That was the high-bracket, million-dollar club. There were short articles, more like thumbnail sketches or inspirational nuggets, John thought, that stressed the ministry's good works and skillfully tied in the altar call to giving at the end of each nugget. More interesting to John was the slogan "God Rewards the Giver" and a toll-free number for donors to inquire about investment and dividend opportunities.

He thought about Levi's quarrel with Campbell: Was this a charity or an investment pyramid scheme? The brochures did not say. They invited interested parties to phone in for "dialogue" and "to have all your questions answered." He wrote down the phone number. It was something he would send on to Alan Wiebe. Maybe Alan would enjoy the experience of making a few strategic cold calls. Chalk it up to research.

John put the assorted contents spread across the carrel desktop back into the accordion folder. He folded the flap down and secured the string to secure the package. He wanted more information.

One thing he knew for certain was that Levi had died unhappy and afraid. And his ravings had suggested money was at the center of it. Then again, for a man of his wealth, how could it not be? He wondered about the Schlegel children and their dealings with their father's financial empire. If Carol and Campbell had benefited to the tune of millions in just one year, who knew how many transactions were out of the public record? And what about Franklin and Franz and Julia? Money was the lingua franca of this family's affairs, and with the death of the patriarch, surely there were seismic changes underway. The darker possibilities crowded at the edge of John's mind.

Why had Levi invoked Mexico on his deathbed? Why had he told John, out of earshot of his family, "I think somebody stole from us." Who was he talking about? If Levi was being defrauded by his son-in-law, how would the details leak out?

John packed up his briefcase and put on his sport coat. Then he walked the accordion file to its lonely spot in the stacks. He wouldn't make some undergraduate assistant go to the trouble of reshelving it. On his way to the main door, an owlish desk clerk nodded at him by the checkout and he smiled and said thank you. He didn't have time for chitchat. He drove across town and took the Thirteen Mile Road past the Pioneer Adobe House and the golf course. He turned left and the asphalt street meandered after a couple of blocks into a cul-de-sac of apartments arranged around a courtyard. A sign read, Welcome to the Village.

He found the apartment he was looking for. The name on the mailbox: Caleb Epp, PhD. *Just a nice pastoral visit,* John told himself, *and a few questions.* He recalled what Schroeder had said about Epp's grasp of the "data," and he sincerely hoped the bonsai cowboy hadn't exaggerated the scope of the man's powers. What did Caleb Epp know about Campbell? It was time to find out exactly what the so-called Brain Trust was made of.

Chapter 35

Caleb Epp came to the door almost immediately.

The very old man sat in his motorized wheelchair, a Jayhawks cap on his head and a black shirt buttoned up on his gaunt frame. A furl of white chest hair poured out of his open-neck collar like a spume of smoke. He had on a pair of powder-blue slacks that resembled those Arnold Palmer wore in his prime. His white sneakers occupied the chair's footrests; white gym socks bunched around his hairless ankles. He cackled when he recognized John. The sound was joyous, that of an ancient warbler still in command of his powers. Epp was pushing ninety.

"Come in, John. I was just on the phone with Katie Nikkel, talking about you. I was beginning to wonder when you would pay a visit."

"Dr. Epp, you are very high on my list right now."

"Don't Doctor Epp me. Call me Caleb. You're no longer a sophomore, John. You've aged well, I must say. Katie tells me you stay fit. And don't forget I saw how you tackled that goat."

John laughed. "Professor Nikkel makes it her business to know things."

"Let me say a few things of my own," Epp said. "I am glad you are back in these parts. We enjoy your sermons. Thank you for throwing in a few surprises. Not that I should speak ill of the dead, but your predecessor was such a comfort that he put many of us to sleep. Rest in peace, Brother Tschetter."

John noted the collective "we." He looked around at Epp's living room. An array of diplomas adorned a wall in one corner, and facing them were framed photographs of Epp's family. The earliest of these had been taken in the Ukraine. Epp's parents had sailed out of Odessa on the eve of World War I and found their way to Kansas. Caleb had been an early graduate at the newly established college, then went east for a doctorate, and a few years later for a second doctorate—this one in chemistry, to complement his first in physics, at the University of Rochester. Katie Nikkel had once defended his reputation against district pastors accusing him of being an "elitist." "Not an elitist," she told them. "Just a completist."

Now Caleb lived in simple splendor. There were four jade plants in ceramic pots lined up on the window sill that appeared to have been curated for several decades. The furniture consisted of a couple of Scandinavian wing chairs and a loveseat arranged around a shabby oriental rug. Two walls of the room were covered by stark, floor-to-ceiling metal bookcases packed with books, mostly science, including several shelves of textbooks and a lot of popular astronomy. There was work by E. O. Wilson and Stephen Jay Gould. Carl Sagan. There was also literature: Thomas Mann, Rainer Maria Rilke, Günter Grass. *Maybe Katie Nikkel was an influence on the old scientist*, thought John. The wall art included a tattered, fading print of Monet's water lilies and a poster of Michael Jordan gliding midair, high above the rim.

"Bulls fan?" John said.

"I wonder what the odds are they win another championship. I foresee a dynasty. If I come to Chicago, can you get tickets for me?"

"I'll see what I can do," John said.

"Don't be flippant. I mean it. I have a nephew who has offered to drive. Any recommendations for hotels?"

"Well, there's always the Palmer House," John said. "I could meet you for lunch at Miller's Pub on Wabash. There is also pizza, although let me steer you clear of the deep dish, which is tourist fare and vastly overrated."

"I will rely on your local knowledge," Epp said.

"I hope you visit," John said. "I would like to host more visitors from Kansas. I'm trying to talk Ann Hiebert into coming up."

"Excuse me a moment." The wheelchair whirred out of the room and into the kitchen. Caleb returned shortly after and put a tray of cookies on the coffee table. John bit into one.

"These go down very easy," John said. "What are they?"

"Compost cookies."

"Do you bake?"

"No, but I know some people who do." Epp smiled slyly.

"I know that you know the right people. John Schroeder told me if I ever had any question about anything, you were the man to ask."

"You have been very busy lately. Putting Levi Schlegel to rest must be a herculean task."

"Yes. Funny you should say that. That's the main reason I'm here right now, eating these fine compost cookies. Please know I trust you and come in strictest confidence."

"You understand how to get a man's attention." Caleb raised his Jayhawks cap, smoothed his white hair with one bony hand, and resettled the cap.

"I need to know something specific. Did Levi Schlegel ever go to Mexico?"

Epp said, "Why do you ask?"

"I had a scrambled conversation with him a few minutes before he died."

"How was it scrambled?"

"He was talking half English and half Low German. My Plautdietsch is rusty."

"You might consult with Katie Nikkel."

"I might, although I am hard pressed to recall exactly the words he used. The strings of German. If I had only put it on tape. The man was in distress. They had him in restraints because he was throwing food trays and trying to rip out the IV. He was heavily medicated. He said he wanted the *Frintschoft* to leave the room so he could talk with me."

"What did he say?" Caleb asked.

"It was something like, *Cun all mien Frintschoft mol in baet dim Ruem, filoti?*"

"That is a polite way of saying it," Caleb said. "Are you sure it wasn't more of *Kaust du daut Frintschoft hia rut rieme so daut wie auleen rede kjenne?*"

"That's maybe closer," John said. "I'm sorry I don't have one hundred percent recall."

"That's what I told you after that chemistry exam in 1957," Caleb said. "That's why I dropped your grade to an A–. That second version you're giving me would be more of an imperative: 'Can you clear those relatives out of here so that we can talk privately?'"

"That was the gist of it, yes. He was impatient. He wasn't playing nice."

Caleb fiddled with the joystick on his wheelchair. He moved the chair forward and backward, just slightly, and John realized this was one of his tics when he was thinking. Caleb continued, "What kind of medication?"

"Franz said a mood stabilizer. Thiessen mentioned Haldol."

"That's an antipsychotic," Caleb said.

"Yes," John said. "It's also used in treating bipolar disorder."

"Did they get out of the room?" Caleb asked. "He wanted everyone out?"

"Yes. Even Eva."

"What did he say to you then?"

"Two things that I found striking. First, he said, 'I know I'm not sick. I was in Mexico.' Then he said, 'Our people have a hard time there. I think somebody stole from us.'"

Caleb poured himself more iced tea. He looked at John. "Did Levi say why he went to Mexico?"

"He said it was to see our people in the colonies."

Caleb spoke rapidly now. There was no letup between his questions. "Did Levi say who the somebody was who was stealing from him?"

"He said stealing from *us*."

"In Levi's case, I would guess that was probably an example of the royal 'we,'" Caleb said. "Do you have any theories about the culprit?"

"I wonder if Levi's comments at the end were connected in any way with Campbell Ministries. They have a fairly pronounced footprint in the Mexico Mennonite colonies."

"Ah, Wyndham Campbell," Caleb said. "Our own local Billy Graham."

"That's a little disrespectful of Billy, don't you think?" John said.

Caleb laughed out loud and slapped his skinny thigh. He said, "I have studied the film clips of the early Graham crusades. I have studied the mannerisms. Campbell learned many lessons from watching his hero. The speaking cadences, the use of the gesture and the pause. The way he holds the open Bible when he talks. It's textbook Billy. Sometimes Campbell even slides into a fake Southern accent."

"Please tell me what else you know about Campbell."

"A few things. But you asked whether Levi Schlegel flew to Mexico? Come with me, while I run a little search." He turned the wheelchair and hummed out of the living room down a short hallway. He entered a room and flipped on a switch. John followed.

"Welcome to my inner sanctum. Pardon the clutter, and please don't trip over the cords. I've duct-taped most of them to the floor to avoid tangles. At my age you hate to see people fall. Here's a chair. Make yourself comfortable." Caleb leaned over and removed a stack of scientific journals from the chair's seat cushion. A silver pole lamp with three metal cans affixed to its length stood close by. Caleb dropped the journals on the floor to make way for his guest.

"Sit down, young man," he said, patting the chair. "I need you to talk to me."

John stood in the middle of the room and turned around in a full 360 underneath the slowly rotating ceiling fan. Industrial-style shelving lined the room and bore a daunting freight of hardware. John tried to make sense of it. There were at least four different screens, a fax machine, a laser printer, an international weather monitor, and reams of cable snaking everywhere, plugged into ports with blinking lights that played out in patterns like deep-sea anemones. John counted four separate power strips, all their outlets occupied. A bigger structure with grids of ports and lights occupied half of one wall. It seemed to be some sort of command structure for Caleb's setup. *What are these things called?* John searched for the word. *"Servers"?*

He had put off buying a computer so far in his life. He liked his Selectric in the second-floor parsonage office, the feel of real books. But he was staring down the necessity of change. The room mocked him and left his inner Luddite huddling naked and afraid. For here was Caleb Epp, a Prospero of the future, putting John to shame. One look at this room spun John's head completely around, and for him, it spelled the end of the old era, BC, Before Computers.

John wondered how the building could handle the electrical load and who paid the electric bills. He thought of a set in *Voyage to the Bottom of the Sea* or *Space Family Robinson*. The mad professor named Epp sat in front of John in his motorized chair and reached up to turn his cap around catcher-style on his aging cranium. Then he hunched over his keyboard and began to type. Electronic messages flashed across the screen. Caleb picked up his pace, looking at scribbles on a yellow pad. More messages flashed, then stopped. Some pulsed slowly, like deliberating lightning bugs. Caleb turned around and said, "Give me about five minutes."

John went into the living room to look at Caleb's family pictures. Then he heard Caleb's voice. He returned to the lair. "I see that Levi went to Mexico at least three times in the last couple of years," Caleb said, looking at the screen.

"How do you know?" John asked.

"I am a hacker," Epp said, with a savage grin. "I am looking at flight records and other databases."

"How far does the Campbell Ministries footprint extend?"

"Here is what I know," Epp said. "He owns a ranch in the Flint Hills that he bought two years ago. He flies frequently between his airstrip there and Kansas City. He claimed his airplane stowage fees were mounting at the Marion Hills airfield and he wanted investment property. I would guess the entire Schlegel clan and the in-laws see dollar signs flashing with all this talk of a national park."

"Does Campbell also fly to Mexico? I mean, commercial or private flying?"

"I think he has an associate he flies with. I can look into that for you."

"Thanks, that would be good," John said.

"You think I am a genie and all you have to do is rub a lamp?"

John was so surprised by this that he snorted. "Sort of like that, yes." He looked at Caleb with a kind of wonder. "You dazzle a country boy like me. I'm starting to get the idea. And I am also wondering about something else: Can you corroborate that Campbell's project in Mexico is legitimate, is it real? Is it an international development agency, another NGO?"

Epp curled his lip. "Now you are asking me to ascertain if these godly projects are all what they're cracked up to be. I'm no prophet, John. I read numbers and schedules. I mess around with data. I don't discern spiritual truth."

"But, Caleb—"

"I am a scientist, not a man of the cloth." Caleb's wrinkled mouth twisted into a grotesque, toothy mask. "I leave those questions to the theologians and ethicists. That is your bailiwick, is it not?"

"Should you be doing this?" As soon as the question spilled from his mouth, John felt like he was twelve.

"That depends on who you ask. My friends in the guild call me Little Hans. What else do you need to know? I might be able to help."

"Okay, let me revise that. You shouldn't be doing this. But would you do something for me?"

The bank of lights on the server flickered. Now it was Little Hans's turn to make John wait for an answer. His eyes showed a strange, uncanny light. "I am happy to observe that Reverend Reimer still has a sense of curiosity. That is the beginning of wisdom. You must have a desire to find out."

"I think I have that," John said. He felt like a boy receiving affirmation after stealing eggs from a bird's nest.

"Now you are talking my language," Epp said. "I noticed you were not too thrilled with my sun tea. May I brew you a pot of coffee?"

"Thank you, that would be nice."

Epp cruised down the hall and banged around in his kitchen. John gathered his thoughts and scribbled on a legal pad. Epp came back into the room. "Okay, what do you need to know?"

"Tell me if this is possible," John said. "Complete background check on Campbell Ministries, including financial transactions in the past three years. Business initiatives in Mexico, Denver, and Kansas City."

"You don't ask for much," Epp said.

John recognized the gift for brutal sarcasm. Strangely, he recalled Epp as a professor of rigorous standards but sweet disposition in the late 1950s. There was something much harder about him now. Maybe that is what the crusts of time did to a man.

Epp continued, "To obtain this information can be . . . delicate. They can trace you. They don't want people getting through the security checks or breaking passwords. And it takes longer when one doesn't want to leave tracks."

John said, "I'm sure you have that all figured out."

"Let me pour you that cup of coffee. Then I will get to work," Epp said. "You have made me *most* curious with all your questions. Come back here tomorrow night about this time. I might have something for you."

A half hour later, John left. Caleb was back in his lair, adjusting the backward cap on his head as he stared down the screen. He didn't look up. "Could you please see yourself to the front door? Pardon me, but I have to get started."

As he closed the porch door behind him and walked into the night, John wondered what he had set in motion.

⟶

On the following evening, Caleb wore a number 23 Bulls jersey over a T-shirt and a pair of cargo shorts. He leaned back in his Barcalounger. His pencil-thin legs were extended in luxurious comfort. He had on leather sandals over a pair of black socks.

"There's coffee in the kitchen. Would you mind bringing it out and pouring?" Caleb said.

"I can manage that." John fetched. He brought back two steaming mugs and handed one to Caleb.

"Sit down, John. Here is what I have for you."

"I am listening."

"I accessed their credit rating, which is shaky at best. I had to penetrate strange firewalls I have never encountered before."

"And—"

"Between the two of them, Wyndham and Carol Campbell have fourteen credit cards, most of which are stretched to the credit limit."

"Do you have information on Mexico?"

"I don't think he banks there. He's a loyal American citizen. Plus, if I have to dig into that I will ask Katie to give me a crash Berlitz course. My Spanish is not strong. How is your *español*, John?"

"Nada . . . y pues nada."

"That's what I thought. But here's the thing. Campbell's credit rating was even more tenuous a year ago when he and Carol had seventeen cards maxed out."

"That is a lot of plastic."

"Yes. I conjecture that Campbell has a new source of revenue. I don't think they're controlling their spending. Yankee thrift is not inscribed on the man's habits. Or hers."

"What do you mean?" John said.

"Have you seen the Victorian mansion that Mrs. Campbell is restoring in Marion Hills?"

"No."

Caleb clambered out of the Barcalounger and climbed onto his motorized chair. He pulled up his black socks on his ragged shins, then nudged the lever forward on the right armrest. The chair glided out of the room. "Follow me," he said. John trailed the humming wheelchair into the lair. When it stopped, he looked over Caleb's shoulder at a screen.

"Here we see an American Express monthly accounts payable record," said Little Hans. "Also Mastercard. I should mention they are renovating a house in Kansas City. It was originally listed as a 'distressed masterpiece.'" Caleb brought up a black-and-white photo. John squinted and looked closer.

"I'm surprised Franklin didn't design it for them."

"No. This was built by a name architect in the late 1940s."

"How big a name?"

"The biggest. Frank Lloyd Wright. The Campbells are chasing not only wealth but also status. For those habits one needs hefty revenue streams."

"How many houses does a man need?" John asked.

"Well, if I had the answer to that question," Caleb said, "they would call me Tolstoy, not Little Hans."

Chapter 36

Early one morning two weeks after Levi's death, a green Buick rolled into downtown Marion Hills and eased up behind a Harley-Davidson touring bike parked outside Little Pleasures. When John walked into the bakery with a *Wichita Eagle* under his arm, Rachel motioned him over. She leaned forward with her palms flat on the surface of the countertop and raised an eyebrow at the big shiny sedan outside. It was polished to a candy-apple finish. "I thought it was a four-ton bottle of olive oil when he drove up. Big guy came inside and chatted me up. I flashed back to an executive I met once at a conference in Oahu. One of my first gigs with a catering outfit."

John was feeling reckless so he said, "Did he hit on you?"

"The executive or this guy in the Buick?"

"The executive in Hawaii. You know I prefer backstory first."

"I was twenty-one years old, working behind the bar. I thought the executive was interested in me but, you know . . . youth. It took me a while to figure out he was gay as a goose. Expressive, low-key, a communicator, you know? And, this customer I just met, same thing. In another life he'd look good in a fedora. He said he was looking for you. Identified you by name. Casual but very inquisitive."

"What's his name, and where did he go?"

"Tom. Tom something, Brubaker? Hostetter? Dockheimer, maybe. Was on his way to the church to find you. Said he wanted to talk to the preacher who did Levi Schlegel's funeral. I told him you often stop by here for breakfast before you go to the office."

"You know my habits. I'll take a regular coffee and a cinnamon roll," John said.

"To go?" Rachel asked.

"No, for here. He'll be back." John was in no hurry. He paid and left a couple of dollars in the tip jar. Then he sat down at the back of the room facing the front door. He opened the paper. Rachel brought his food and coffee to him. He ignored the cutlery. He absentmindedly tore chunks of the roll off with his fingers as he turned the pages. Brubaker or Oppenheimer or what's-his-name was now probably chatting up Linda Ebel. After fifteen minutes, there were four other people in the shop but no sign of the stranger. A burly redhead wearing a bandanna and engineer boots stalked across the street and straddled the Harley out front. He kicked the starter with a flick of his leather heel and the engine roared to life. John watched the biker and decided it was time to move along. He finished his cinnamon roll and told Rachel thank you. When he exited, the door gave its little ring.

⟶

At the church, John did his stealth walk down the hallway. He imagined treading on rice paper. Linda's door was ajar. From inside came the murmur of a low voice and a delighted soprano peal of laughter. A scent of nicotine announced a stranger in the house. John pushed the door open and made a knocking motion. "I understand a search party is looking for me." He smiled broadly at his secretary, who was trying to suppress her laughter. Then she grew serious.

"John, I want to introduce you to Tom Dockhauser. Tom, this is Reverend Reimer."

"Call me John," the minister said. "You apparently already have many names in our little town."

"Pleased to meet you, John." The man unfolded his frame and stood. He was at least six five, and he grasped John's hand. Age was gradually grafting itself onto his youthful frame, and he had the scuffed, dry skin of a smoker. His head was close-cropped blond curls going gray, boyishly Tim Robbins minus the goofy. He still had the attitude of someone who could move fast if he cared to. He gave John his card. John looked at it. It said Centurion Insurance and underneath his name: Claims Investigator.

"Call me Tom." The man's voice rumbled like a Harley and his eyes flickered around the office. He was an individual who paid close attention. He swept up a pair of sunglasses on the desk in his big hand. He wore a blazer and a heavy white pinpoint shirt, open at the collar. *His slacks look tailored and the Italian loafers are probably hand-tooled,* John

264

thought. Tom reached across the desk for Linda's hand. "Thanks for indulging me, Ms. Ebel. Of all the church secretaries I have met—"

"I will listen to your stories, any time," Linda said. "It was a pleasure meeting you, Mr. Dockhauser." She dabbed at the corner of her eye with a handkerchief. Her face was still flushed with laughter.

"The pleasure is all mine," Dockhauser said. Then he turned toward John.

John led Dockhauser down the hall to his own office. He turned on the lights and closed the door behind them. He motioned to one of the wing chairs. "Make yourself comfortable. Cup of coffee?"

"Your secretary plied me with several rounds of your fair-trade brew, thanks," said Dockhauser. "It's nice to know that when I drink a cup of java, I'm not oppressing a campesino somewhere." He paused. "Interesting girl there, doing the work of the church. I come with questions about the death of a patriarch, and she gets me to produce funny stories. Brilliant evasive action. You must enjoy working with her." He put his Ray-Bans inside a leather case and then inside his jacket breast pocket. He looked around the study like a curator appraising new material. "And so I sit in the sanctum of the Mennonite high priest."

He got up and, with his hands in his front pockets, walked to the window and looked at the framed picture of the shepherd and the sheep next to the open curtains. John noticed it had been reframed in quality oak. Linda must have taken care of that. Dockhauser turned back to the desk and pondered the stack of books piled on it. He took in the stray, scribbled Post-it notes stuck to various portions of the desk and said, "A man of learning, am I right?"

"Don't get carried away," John said. "How can I be of service? I presume you're here because of Levi Schlegel's death?"

"Did you speak with the coffee shop lady?"

"Rachel," John finished. "She said you were looking for me."

"Let me be direct, John. I have more people to see today, and I might want to circle back again. I understand that you conducted the funeral and are also a friend of the Schlegel family. And that you were at Levi's bedside shortly before he expired."

"Yes," John said, "to all of the above."

"I'm a death claims investigator. There is a policy to pay out. Before that happens, my job for Centurion is to ask questions and confirm the pedestrian details that have already been reported. And—"

"Ask away, Mr. Dockhauser."

"You were in the room with him shortly before he died."

"Yes. I spoke with him a few minutes before his cardiac arrest. When I was called back in, they were working him over with the crash-cart paddles."

"And I have it confirmed by two individuals that the deceased requested his family leave so he could talk with you privately, just before he died. Could you tell me more about that?"

John met Dockhauser's gaze. "He did. He spoke in Low German to clear them out of the room. He wanted to talk to me alone."

"Did you often hear him speak Low German?"

"No."

Did it strike you as interesting that he wanted to ask you this out of earshot of his own family members?"

"It surprised me, yes. He said a couple of times, 'Don't let them do this to me.' I asked who they were. He didn't say. He asked for my help and said he was afraid someone was taking advantage of him. I wasn't sure what kind of help he meant. This was a paranoid habit of Levi's for many years. He was careful with money. Ruthless, even."

"Did he have enemies?"

"Rich men always do. A lot of folks at the funeral weren't sad to see him go."

"Can you be more specific?"

"For starters, there are people in Chase County that weren't fond of him. He's been an advocate for the tallgrass prairie park. The local chapter of the Republican Party doesn't look too kindly on friends of the feds. Franz can no doubt tell you more about that. But the main issue in communities like this is competition and resentment. Some of those at his funeral had been bought out by him so they didn't have good memories."

"Yes, that is a truth universal. But I'm interested in why Levi trusted you with his final thoughts. What did you learn?"

"My bonds with the Schlegels go back very far. His wife, Eva, the artist, was an acquaintance of my wife, Viola, when they were growing up in Oklahoma. Eva was several years older, but they were familiars. Vi died earlier this year."

"I am learning that certain Mennonite connections grow very close," Dockhauser said.

"I would also add thick and ingrown," John said. "And don't get me started on incest. But you asked what I learned in that final bedside conversation. The answer is, I didn't learn much. Levi was incoherent.

His heart monitor at that point wasn't encouraging. They had him in restraints because he had torn out his IV. He was on tranquilizers. His emotional outbursts were hard to control. Let me add that Levi was a big, imposing human. I saw him throw a food tray off his hospital bed a few days before that."

"How big a man was Levi?"

"About your size. In fact—and this will sound strange as I say it—he bore some resemblance to you. Even down to several of your gestures."

"Go figure," Dockhauser said. "I tell them I'm about to retire and they send me to bloody Kansas just to find I'm investigating my double."

"You must be important to Centurion. Where's home base?"

"Cincinnati," Dockhauser said. He laughed bronchially. "It's a sizable policy. Centurion brought me in. When the green eyeshades raise questions, I get assigned. One last gig for the company, they said, then you're free. I flew into Kansas City, took one of the company cars. This is a part of the country I've never seen. You from around here?"

"I grew up in western Kansas, farm near Meade, close to Dodge City. Moved away a long time ago. I was minister at another church in Marion County more than thirty years ago. My congregation in Chicago views this as a kind of rest sabbatical."

Dockhauser watched John's expression. He said, "I am guessing this was not entirely of your choosing and you have some ambivalence."

"You are a quick study, Mr. Dockhauser."

"That's Tom. So how is your sabbatical turning out?"

"Not sure it's a slowdown, to be honest. The first thing to greet me when I arrived in town was a young man, baptized in this church, arrested by the local sheriff for shooting his brother in the back of the head. During a card game. Then he shot his friend across the table in the face." John watched Tom's expression.

Tom said, "Yeah, I read about that. Double murder. You walked straight into bleeding Kansas."

John said, "Does that amuse you? The wild, wild West indeed. But tell me, are you really about to retire? I know several guys who've retired early and their lives fall to pieces. Other guys work till they drop so they don't have to think about what they're trying to forget. The options all seem bleak to me. How about to you?"

"I'm beginning to think I'm not the only investigator here," Tom said. "Reverend Reimer, where did you develop that edge you're showing?"

"That's John. I just think there are complicated reasons when men like us keep going to work this late in the game."

"Okay. Since you're curious. I lost someone." A swift shadow of misery crossed Dockhauser's face. He interlaced his fingers and enclosed a bony knee. He leaned back in his chair. "What is it that Conrad said about work? 'I don't like work—no man does—but I like what is in the work—the chance to find yourself.'"

"Good one," John said. "I lost someone too. Right before I started this interim assignment in Marion Hills. Scattered her ashes at Montrose Beach bird sanctuary in Chicago."

"Your wife?" Dockhauser said.

"My life partner, yes," John said. He looked at Dockhauser. "Do you know of what I speak?"

"I do, as a matter of fact," Dockhauser said. "Lost him four years ago on the West Coast, then spent a year wrapping up his estate. The man was the best in the business. A legend in his own time. Taught me pretty much everything I know. The clichés don't do him justice. Some of us think the people we love will live forever. But was it your intent to turn this into a pastoral counseling situation? If it was, you're damn good at it."

"No, I was trying to remember the other details of my conversation with Levi. He repeated himself very emphatically. He said, 'Something is not right.' He also said, 'Don't let them do this to me.'"

"He didn't explain who they were?"

"I asked. He didn't explain. It was as if he thought I already knew. He was probably delirious at that point. When I drove away, somebody chased me down in their pickup to return to the hospital. Levi had coded. It couldn't have been more than ten minutes after I left. I saw the last efforts to resuscitate him."

"Have you talked with any members of the family since?"

"I have. All of them, but mostly Franklin and Eva."

"I have to review the hospital charts and talk with the doctor later this morning. How do you pronounce his name?"

"Doctor Thiessen," John said. "As in 'tea.' He was Levi's attending physician at Marion Hills."

"Yes. That one. I'd like to talk with a few other individuals as well. How about we meet up tonight for dinner? Would your schedule allow that?"

"I'm open. Any place you had in mind?"

"I don't know the restaurants. It's sparse in these parts, isn't it? Aside from a drive to Wichita, you know anywhere I can get a decent martini? That might be nice for starters. And please tell me, why is it so difficult in the middle of this country to ice up a glass of gin and sprinkle it with a little vermouth? For crying out loud."

"I'm not a drinking man myself, but there's a place out at the reservoir called the Kingfisher Inn," John said. "Quiet. Meditative. It overlooks the water. Some of my more decadent parishioners have mentioned the nice bar. We can get a table, maybe outside. Reminisce about the people we've lost."

"Yes, and I will probably think of more questions to ask you."

"I would like that. Leave your car here in the church parking lot. We can take mine. Five o'clock too early?"

"That's perfect." Dockhauser rose creakily from his chair. He stopped by Linda's office on his way out. John heard the laughter erupt again. The guy seemed to have a lot of punch lines. John still didn't know what they had been joking about. But his mind was racing quickly ahead.

After Dockhauser left the building, John walked around the church a couple of times to get some fresh air and went back inside and picked up his office phone. He dialed John Schroeder.

The voice on the other end of the line said hello. John said, "Reimer here."

"Yeah," said Schroeder.

"You still interested in that excursion to the Flint Hills? Want to scope out some black semitrucks?"

"I'm all in, Reverend. Name your time. This dirt farmer was starting to wonder if you had chickened out."

"How about Friday night?"

"John, that sounds good. I would suggest eleven. Come over to my place and we'll take my truck. Wear your commando black."

"You've done reconnaissance."

"Yes. I also don't want you to muddy up your fancy four-wheel drive."

"I'll call to confirm," John said. He stood up and felt the thick-pile carpet underfoot. He took a few practice steps of moving soundlessly. *Like a ninja*, he imagined.

Chapter 37

That afternoon, Eva called and asked if he could come to the house.

When John arrived, it was Campbell who let him in the front door. "Good to see you, John. Be forewarned—Eva's in a bit of a state."

The family members were gathered in Levi's living room with the shades drawn and the lights turned low. Eva sat crumpled in Levi's favorite easy chair, sipping ice water from a glass. Franz stood at her elbow and asked if she wanted anything besides Tylenol. She shook her head slowly, as if too sudden a motion would set the gongs clanging within. Carol adorned the sofa beneath the Russell paintings. She was still dressed in her running clothes but looked fresh.

"Missed you this morning," she said. "I thought you would be out there for the usual four miles."

"Well, I wanted to, but I ended up fielding a call from Lakeview."

"Everything all right in Chicago?"

"Yes. Routine. Figuring out the date of my return to the big city. Alan Wiebe wanted to share his thoughts."

"Well, we need you here," Eva said, looking up. "Aren't you staying through the end of fall?" Her eyes pierced John. "Sit down. Here, close to me." She gestured to the end of the sofa near her chair and patted the armrest. Carol moved over to make room for John. Franz was in the kitchen rinsing dishes. John detected a trace of cigarettes in the room and surmised the tall man from Centurion had recently occupied this length of sofa.

Eva set down the glass of water on a side table and reached for John's hand. She looked at him and began. "Julia and Ken are tied up all day fixing a mechanical breakdown in the milking shed, and Franklin is likely shoving rocks to and fro with his beloved Bobcat. I told them I wanted to talk with you and they approved. I wanted them here but—" She moved her hands in front of her in a gesture of frustration.

"Tell me how I can help," John said. Had he said something off-key during the funeral, committed a faux pas in his inimitable classic style? If he had, Linda surely would have told him. Now his thoughts turned to the absent members of the Schlegel family. Maybe they had their reasons for avoiding an interview with the claims investigator.

"We have a problem, John," Eva said. "And I need to figure out how to handle it."

"Are you talking about Dockhauser?"

"He's the one," Eva said. "How did you know his name?"

"He came by the church this morning."

"He is everywhere, this man," Eva said. "He is making some trouble for me."

"What kind of trouble? What did he say?"

John watched Campbell out of the corner of his eye. The man was working to achieve a pose of studied neutrality.

Eva resumed. "He said the death certificate that Philip Thiessen signed at the hospital was sloppy. Those were his words." Carol and Franz nodded. "He said he was also going to need to investigate several additional circumstances. I think he used the phrase 'loose ends.'"

Franz interjected, "Are you sure you heard him say that, Mom?"

"I'm sure." Eva scowled at her oldest son. "You were maybe not in the room. I think you were running for coffee."

"I heard him say that, Mom," Carol said, conciliatory.

"Is this a surprise" John asked. "It sounds like standard operating procedure. That's how insurance companies do it."

"John, this is a stalling tactic," Campbell said. "'SOP' is only one term for it. Centurion doesn't want to pay out on Levi's life insurance policy, so they concoct 'loose ends.' Believe me, I've seen the way these guys operate. Endlessly inventive and slimy. They know how to stall. There's a reason these insurance guys step lightly in their fancy loafers. So now they're going to cast aspersions on the family physician."

John thought of telling Campbell his loafers weren't too shabby, either, but instead looked around the room. He wanted to guess the size of the life insurance policy. Maybe Dockhauser would tell him.

Franz interrupted his thoughts. He had pulled up a kitchen chair beside Eva's and was holding her other hand. "Mom, it's best to stay calm. John is right. These are routine questions when a policy is as substantial as Dad's. It's business. Dockhauser is just doing the standard procedure here. We stay calm, we answer the questions, we deal with the *Anglischer* in a reasonable manner. Let's be patient and let the bureaucratic wheels turn. Everything will be fine."

John looked at Eva. "Do you know where Dockhauser was going next, who he was planning to talk to?"

Eva started to answer but Franz interrupted her. "John, Mr. Dockhauser didn't share his game plan. I don't think we know what he has in mind. I'm sure he's talking with Thiessen, though. Maybe you could sound him out. Try to find out what kind of investigation this is. We're kind of curious."

"Yeah," Campbell added, emerging from his torpor. "I'd also be tempted to ask this Cincinnati river rat why they must dump their filthy questions on us."

"I'm not sure I understand," John said.

"Maybe you don't know the Ohio Valley like I do." Campbell smiled without mirth.

John patted Eva's hand. "I'll see what I can find out. But I have no special insight. You might get clearer answers from an attorney than from me."

Eva looked at him. There was steel in the glance.

John said, "I'm sure you're nodding because you already thought of that. Forgive me. Sometimes when I'm trying to be helpful, I state the obvious."

Chapter 38

The bartender at the Kingfisher Inn was none other than Rick—the intake specialist at Marion Hills Hospital. John looked again. The young man sported the same tortoiseshell glasses and his Woody Woodpecker shock of curly hair showed slightly more discipline. But here, wearing a collarless black cooking jacket and a towel slung over his shoulder, he didn't seem the same person at all that John had met only a few weeks ago. Then he had thought the kid was still in high school—obviously a wrong first impression. This adult version of Rick was stirring a silver spoon with rapid circular motion in a tumbler filled with ice and bourbon. Now he carried the drink to the end of the bar for a customer and placed it on top of a square napkin. Returning, he recognized John.

"Reverend Reimer, nice to see you. Welcome to the Kingfisher Inn!"

"You, too, Rick. And I hope under better circumstances. Is this your moonlighting job or the real thing?"

Rick was already looking past the preacher at the insurance investigator towering behind. "Tom Dockhauser," John said to the man trailing him. "This is Rick, the bartender."

"We've already met," Tom said, climbing atop a barstool.

"What's your poison?" Rick said.

"Tanqueray martini, very dry, up, lemon twist. Thanks," Dockhauser said. He reached down the length of the bar to retrieve an ashtray. "The Reverend tells me your establishment is the closest thing to cocktail royalty in this county."

"How would he know?" Rick winked and put a handful of ice into a shaker, turned a green bottle upside down over it, and counted off four shots. He shook in a splash of vermouth, closed the shaker, and gripped it with one hand. He rattled it around with a strong wrist and the necessary conviction.

"I am learning that it is for the Mennonite high priest to know many things," Dockhauser said, looking at John.

"What'll you have, Reverend?" Rick spoke as he smoothly poured the contents of the shaker into a chilled glass that he pulled from the fridge below the bar. With a knife he took a spiral of lemon peel off the fruit in his hand and twisted and then squeezed it before dropping it in the glass.

"Ginger ale. On ice."

"For you, I'll skip the umbrella. You gentlemen staying for dinner? I have the perfect table out back. Best view in the house of the reservoir."

"We'll take it," John said.

Dockhauser spoke, "Maybe in about a half hour or so? This is a cozy little bar, so please let me enjoy it for a bit. Don't take this the wrong way, but it almost doesn't feel like Kansas."

"In Marion Hills we take that as a compliment, sir," Rick said.

John watched the old man and the young man exchange signals. Dockhauser took a short pull on the martini and declared, "Ah, bliss in six ounces." He got Rick's attention and pointed at his drink: "Say, buddy, I know a bar in Cincinnati where you could make serious money with those mixing skills of yours."

"Thank you, sir. You flatter me."

Dockhauser took out a pack of Kools and put a cigarette between his lips and lit it with a steel lighter. He dropped the lighter back in his sport coat pocket. He inhaled with a sense of deep contentment and blew out a stream of smoke. Then he said to John, "It has been quite a day in your little hamlet of Marion Hills."

"Enlighten me."

"Your local doctor, Doctor Thiessen, is it? My, oh my . . . what a piece of work."

"How so?"

"John, please tell me, how does anyone in this town take such a man seriously?"

"What do you mean? Thiessen is the mainstay at Marion Hills Hospital."

"How on earth? Good God, man, I've seen a lot of Podunk medical incompetence in my time, but this is flagrant."

"You have to understand who came before him," John said.

"Tell me," Dockhauser said.

"Well, back in the old days, there was a local physician named Erb. He was famous for administering thorough breast exams upon admission to every woman who came through his office, regardless of her chief medical complaint. Eventually this came to light because women were talking."

"Women talking, huh?"

"Yes. Exactly."

"What happened to him?" Dockhauser asked.

"He went to Branson, Missouri, where he retired. Should have been stripped of his license. Preceding him was a guy named Ledbetter. I know what kind of doctor Ledbetter was because I saw him for a consultation once. I was a student at the college. How can I put this delicately?"

Dockhauser motioned Rick over to order a second martini. Then he said to John, "Amuse me."

"Ledbetter told me to take down my trousers, and he looked me over. I had pus coming out of my dick and I was pretty worried. He asked me how much promiscuous sex I was having. I was a freshman at the time. I said no promiscuous sex at all, so far as I knew. Now I'll confess I was a little fuzzy then about an exact working definition of 'promiscuous.' For the record, I hadn't had sex yet, not even with Vi. Ledbetter gave me a crooked smile. I didn't know how to tell him I was a virgin from Meade. He took a sample off the tip of my organ for the microscope, by way of a flat glass slide. That glass felt awfully cold, let me tell you. Then Ledbetter said, 'Looks like gonorrhea. We'll get the labs done and I'll update you as soon as I can. In the meantime, I would suggest you wear a rubber for all your future fishing expeditions.'"

"Was Ledbetter really his name?" Dockhauser started working on his second martini. Rick moved out of earshot. "I suppose you were lucky it wasn't syphilis."

"Yeah," John said. "I didn't hear from the guy so I finally called. His nurse told me I had a urinary tract infection. She phoned in a penicillin prescription. And Ledbetter continued his campaign for another twenty years of keeping the boys at the college morally pure."

Dockhauser was philosophical. "Well, you're taking some of the shine off this pretty cow town, aren't you? As far as I can tell, Thiessen seems to have emerged from a long, hallowed tradition of incompetence, moral turpitude, and outright dereliction of duty."

"I am guessing Thiessen didn't appreciate your questions today." John drank up the last of his ginger ale and motioned Rick over. "Please put the drinks on my tab," he said.

Dockhauser said, "No, the tab is mine. Shall we retire to the veranda?"

They sat in the breezeway at a table for two. Spread out before them was the reservoir, a bare ripple across its surface and a waddle of ducks cruising near the shore. In the far distance a motorboat throbbed with a skier in tow. Rick brought menus and told them the special was Atlantic cod with French fries and slaw. Both men said yes.

Dockhauser waited for Rick to go away and then he said, "I asked Thiessen very simple questions. To start with, how does a man who passed his physical exam six months earlier with flying colors suddenly turn into a doddering wreck with heart palpitations and need to be put in restraints to flatten out his temper tantrums? The physician who signed off on that exam in Kansas City said Levi Schlegel had the mind and body of a fifty-five-year-old. He was emphatic that Levi's condition was robust. Extraordinary, even, given his age."

"Excuse me," John said. "Why did Levi get a physical in Kansas City six months earlier?"

"It's standard practice when a client ups their life insurance policy the way Levi did. Centurion requires it, especially for someone his age and given the size of the policy. That physician went even further. He told me Levi insisted on a stress test, you know, walking and jogging on a machine while monitored."

"How did Levi do?"

"The doctor said Levi's fitness was off the charts."

"Why do you think he upped his policy?" John asked.

"It's not in the nature of the business to ask," Dockhauser said. "Lots of people do it, especially aging citizens who have the means. The boys in our back office told me the new policy Levi took out was quite a screamer."

"I suppose you're not at liberty to say how big a policy."

"No, I'm not. But one of the biggest the Kansas City office ever wrote."

"Or to discuss the beneficiaries."

"Changes to the beneficiaries raised red flags, too."

John noted that Dockhauser used the plural. "Did you see Thiessen's medical charts on Levi?"

"He was angry that I wanted to look them over. They were junk. Sketchy to the point of criminal neglect. They told me nothing. Look, physicians hate insurance companies and don't believe we know how to read. But I've read lots of charts. I've never seen anything this amateur."

"Did you sense he was withholding information?"

"Yes, I do. You can't simply record arrhythmia as the presenting condition without seeking the underlying causes or conditions. When I summarized the report of Levi's physical six months earlier, Thiessen said, 'Our bodies do crazy things at this late stage. There are mysteries we do not understand.' I rarely lose my temper, John, but this man made me want to haul him in cuffs before a medical review board."

The fish and chips arrived. John ordered a bottle of sparkling water and a couple of side salads. Dockhauser asked for malt vinegar and was delighted when Rick brought it out. They ate.

John wanted to ask how the conversation with the Schlegels had gone, but to do so would reveal he knew Dockhauser had been there. That didn't seem wise or appropriate. He wondered if Thiessen had told him what kind of tranquilizer he had used on Levi. Best to wait to talk about that, John thought. If Haldol was the issue, Dockhauser would almost certainly figure that out. At this point, John wasn't quite ready to spill the tangled family story about manic depression or reveal that he had developed a habit of going through other people's medicine cabinets.

Dockhauser was speaking. "Besides the death certificate, which appeared to have been done by a fourth grader, there was no autopsy."

"Thiessen didn't order one?"

"No. It didn't seem to have crossed his mind. Or the minds of any of the Schlegels, I might add. Maybe too many people presuming the old man simply aged out."

"So, what's your angle?" John asked. They were each putting away a slice of Key lime pie. More water skiers appeared, and the drone of outboard engines began to spoil the calm. Dockhauser finished his cup of coffee. He wiped his mouth with a napkin.

"I have more people to talk to," he said. "I might need directions out to this architect son's place in the Flint Hills."

"Franklin?"

"Yes, that one." Then, without warning, he added, almost as an afterthought, "Say, does the TV evangelist, what's his name, Campbell, strike you as a little jumpy?"

John said, "I've never been close to Campbell, if you want to know the truth. We have significant theological disagreements that usually chill discussion."

"He's someone I need to talk with again, I think," Dockhauser said. "But conversations can't always answer the hard scientific forensic questions."

"What do you mean?" John asked.

"I mean I'm thinking about a request to exhume the body. This would involve the Kansas Bureau of Investigation, a pathologist from a city larger than Emporia, and a backhoe."

"You can't be serious."

"Oh, I'm serious all right. Keep it under your hat for now, thanks. It may not come to that."

Leaving the Kingfisher Inn, Dockhauser made sure to tell Rick goodbye at the bar. He paid the bill and slipped his business card and a folded twenty-dollar bill across the counter to the young man. "Pleased to meet you, Rick. I think the Ohio Valley is calling. When you decide to come out, give me a ring."

"I will, Mr. Dockhauser," Rick said. He looked at the preacher and the investigator. "I hope you two had a pleasant evening."

"If you don't watch out," John said, "you'll start to pose a threat to the Copper Kettle."

"You can play in the big time, Rick," Dockhauser said.

Rick's countenance lit up. John thought the young man had just glimpsed the road out of Kansas.

Chapter 39

John picked up the phone. It was Schroeder. "You ready to go?"

John said, "I thought we were on for tomorrow."

"Nah, tonight's better." The bonsai cowboy was insistent.

"The Bulls play tonight," John said. "And the Sonics are making the series interesting."

Schroeder said, "Microwave a little hot dish and keep Michael Jordan company, huh? You plan to watch alone? That don't seem right."

"Come over and join me. I have a super taco kit. It heats up real nice."

"I don't know what the hell you are describing but everybody and their dog is watching that game tonight, Reverend. Which suits our purpose," Schroeder said. "One of those big, black semi-trucks is out there and we should take a look."

"Truck, schmuck," John said. "Let me tell you, if there's no fleet of UN helicopters with Russian pilots aboard named Vlad, I want a full refund."

Schroeder didn't laugh. "I have a strong intuition you will be richly rewarded by this outing. Bring a flashlight. Dark clothes. A cap. We don't want your white mad professor hair all lit up like *Back to the Future*. Wear a jacket. It's June, but nights can still be chilly."

Reimer felt a tiny creature of déjà vu climb the back of his neck. It perched there, rubbing its claws, waiting.

"What time?"

"Come by my place around eight. You'll be home in time for the evening news and all of Michael Jordan's game highlights."

John pulled up in the muddy yard of a battered prairie farm. A spattered pickup was parked beside a blue Olds Cutlass and a Honda dirt bike. A diminutive American flag was wired to the metal bar rising at the rear of the bike.

He knocked on the wood-framed screen door. A weather-beaten blonde with strands of gray hair pulled back in a ponytail came out to the porch. She wore old cowboy boots with decorative white stitching, and she was as tall as John. She had an expression like a sad roadhouse singer that seemed to ask the preacher what the hell are you doing here. She wiped her soapy hands on the back pockets of her jeans. Her eyes didn't miss a thing.

"Reverend Reimer, hi. I didn't recognize you in that black hoodie. I had no idea you had a Chicago street gang ministry. How are you doing?"

"Sally. I'm doing well. It is nice to see you." John put both palms on the front of his sweatshirt. This thing is something my daughter gave me at Christmas. I'll admit it feels nice on a night like this."

"You feeling a chill?" Sally said. She pointed across the yard. "John is giving a sick heifer medical attention. He said you could find him there if he wasn't ready yet." She turned on her heel and walked back inside.

Reimer crossed the yard. When he entered the barn, all the smells of his youth came back. Ripe hay and manure and bovine sweat. Decades—and on this farm, generations even—of man and beast cycling through the seasons. Schroeder hadn't used this as a milking facility in twenty years—he was strictly interested in beef production now and farmed a couple sections of wheat and barley—but the stalls, still intact, and the concrete floor ghosted the outline of yesterday's twin rows of Holsteins.

Schroeder stood in the far corner of the space. The white, untanned crown of his head shone under a single light. An Angus heifer occupied a metal chute that limited her movement, but she munched contentedly on some sort of mystery mash from a feeding trough. Schroeder readied a syringe.

"I see the doctor is in," John said. "Such a big needle you have."

Schroeder patted the flesh on the cow's shoulder and swabbed it with a clean rag dipped in alcohol. "Little case of pneumonia. Got to provide a boost so Lulu doesn't give up."

"What kind of boost?" John asked.

Schroeder said, "Antibiotic. In the old days we used to inject amphetamines, too. When they have pneumonia or, with the feedlot calves it's often the shipping fever, you have to keep them on their feet. Their inclination is to lie down and die."

"Somebody could drive cross-country on that dose," John said. Schroeder held the syringe up vertically to the dying shaft of sunlight entering the open window.

"You've got that right." Schroeder stuck the needle in and pressed the plunger. The heifer rocked the chute briefly. "A very simple antibiotic cocktail. Cow cocktail. I've saved a few animals with this stuff." He pulled out the syringe and detached the needle with a gloved hand. He threw the works in a tray of alcohol and covered it with a plastic lid. "You ready to go?"

"Ready for your rodeo," John said.

Schroeder gave John a stern look. "Hell, with that hood up, you look stupid as Tupac. And don't ask me how I know his name. Why don't you park your car in my shed? Door is open. Your vehicle is like the Annunciation, and I'm not sure we need that tonight."

"Very hush-hush?" John said.

"Well, yeah."

Schroeder walked to the head of the stall and looked into the heifer's eye and ran his hand down the side of her face. "I'll let you out in the morning, Lula." The heifer ignored him and chewed the mash. "Eat it all up, atta girl!"

On the ride to the Flint Hills, John noticed two rifles in the rack behind his head. Schroeder lit up a cigarette and dropped the half-empty pack of Marlboros into his pocket. He cracked his window a little. John wondered what the farmer had in mind. He imagined what Nancy would say were she sitting between them. The little creature of déjà vu danced on the back of his neck again, less playfully.

To get his mind off the rifles, he thought about the drugs pumping through the heifer's system, the way Schroeder handled that syringe. He was reminded of the glass-fronted fridge in the farmers' Co-op store, the rows of legal substances for proper livestock care. He thought of the lineup of giant field implements at Halston Industries on the edge of town, many with plastic tanks that could hold a thousand gallons of chemicals—fertilizers or pesticides or herbicides or some such cocktail— to make the crops grow. After DDT was banned, there was Roundup. Is your field Roundup ready? Breadbasket of the world. Better food through drugs and chemicals. We bring good things to life.

As they crossed into Chase County going east on 50, John was struck with a vision: a pharmaceutically and chemically drenched rural scene in a country still in love with the nation's War on Drugs. These country folks were all playing with lethal substances. He remembered how Julia's husband, Ken, had gone on a rant one afternoon as he described Paraquat. "They spray the shit out of these goddam planes onto their fields as if it's manna from heaven," he had told John. "A lot of this toxic crap can kill you on contact. It's insane." They had been in a little field watching the kid goats scamper around and headbutt each other.

"Do your neighbors agree with you?" John had asked.

"Hell, no," Ken had said. "I'm merely a hobbyist with unrealistic notions of organic farming and sucking up Levi's money to boot. In fact, when I use the word 'organic,' most of my neighbors wince or openly snicker. I don't manage enough acreage to be serious about food production. But, boy, does my photogenic wife make pretty pictures. And it they don't say it, they think it."

"She does make pretty pictures," John had said. "Consider yourself a lucky man."

Schroeder spoke now and pulled John out of his reverie as his imagination drifted into the land of Julia's face. "You're quiet tonight."

John said, "I'm thinking about the cocktail that will save your cow's life. Thinking about chemicals."

"Philosophical stuff," Schroeder said. "Thoughtful. All your book learning. Keep talking that way and you start to sound like Caleb Epp."

"I wish I were half as smart."

"Yep." Schroeder ground out his cigarette butt in the pickup's ashtray. The Flint Hills started to take contour. The fields disappeared and the vast spaces of the original grassland prairie grew dark and showed dots of cattle roaming the distance. The sun descending directly behind them cast fantastic shadows and the pickup sent out a long dark shape on the road ahead that trembled and darted, both chased and created by the F-150 itself.

Schroeder said, "This guy who popped up around town the last few days in his fancy clothes, what's that all about?" He glanced sideways at John. "Know anything about that?"

"Insurance executive," John said. "Guy from Cincinnati. The Schlegels are reviewing their policies with him. That's what Franz and Eva tell me."

Schroeder shook his head. "Yeah, he didn't look like he's from around here." He lit up another cigarette. He was smoking more than usual, and that was a lot. "Look, I've been a little mysterious about this excursion, I know."

"Yes, you have," John said. "You might just as well put another hood over my head and lead me into the dark shelterbelts of Cottonwood Falls. Or one of those very sketchy roadside stops in Strong City. But I thought we were visiting the Campbell airstrip."

"We are. And I know you have your own reasons for disliking the man. We're visiting the airstrip where Campbell started flying his plane out to Kansas City a couple years back." Schroeder continued, "But you know Kansas City is hardly his only destination, don't you? And there's more than one plane been spotted on that strip."

"Why don't you stop the tease and share all your suspicions?" John said.

"Some kind of contraband, if you want the honest truth," Schroeder said. "That's what I think. When they put up that bigger machine shed that doubles as an airplane hangar, I figured storage was important."

"What do you do, stake the place out with binoculars? You ever thought of bringing Sheriff Mingus in on this if you suspect something illegal? You plan to make a citizen's arrest?"

Schroeder got a disgusted look on his face. "Mingus is a wingnut. Impulsive and half-cocked. I don't trust that fucker and you shouldn't either. Besides, I have friends around here," Schroeder said. "Let's leave it at that. And let me say something about you, Reimer, if you don't mind. We go back far enough so I think you'll allow it. I've heard several things about your dustup in Chicago, and I was sort of surprised you would go along on this night ride without more information. But I'm glad you're along. They were right about you. You periodically go crazy, don't you? Like an unpredictable streak of badass. Somebody in Meade told me a few stories, too."

John listened serenely. He said, "Sounds like you've been talking with my older brother. I've had many of my best insights out walking at night."

"I'll bet you have," Schroeder said. "Hold that thought." He slowed and turned off the main highway onto I-177. They traveled that road awhile and then Schroeder wrenched the wheel. The rocks kicked up by their tires chunked the underside of the truck. John grabbed the armrest. Schroeder made several more turns.

John said, "I have no idea where we are. Maybe we're the ones who are impulsive and half-cocked."

"Could be," Schroeder said. He pulled over onto the shoulder and killed the headlights. A hill directly in front of them breasted the Milky Way; the waning crescent of the moon hung like a torn, dirty fingernail in front of a thin scraggle of clouds. Schroeder inched the pickup slowly up the hill. He was following an ancient and very obscure two-track.

"What are you doing?" John said.

"Letting my eyes adjust. We'll drive by natural light from this point on to our parking location. Then we'll walk, so you can have your moment of revelation." Schroeder drove the pickup at the slowest possible speed along a barbed wire fence. After a mile, the road dipped into a hollow. Schroeder nuzzled the pickup into the stand of trees and cut the engine. "Close the door softly, thanks. No noise is preferable."

John got out of the pickup. A bird of considerable wingspan swooped through the treetops.

"Owl," Schroeder said. "Great horned." He stood beside the open door of the pickup cab and took down the top rifle from the rack behind his seat. He checked his pockets and put a couple of bullets in the chamber. He cradled the weapon in the crook of his arm so it pointed downward. He reached under the driver's seat and brought out a ring of keys, which he pocketed.

"You sure you need that?" John asked.

"A man like me never knows," Schroeder said. "You can take the other rifle if you want."

John heard the buzz of his own thunderstruck silence. This was starting to feel like a mistake.

Schroeder said, "Don't worry. There aren't any people where we're going. Almost never on Thursdays. Especially not tonight. They're all watching Michael Jordan, remember?"

"Let me take a look at your toolbox," John said. "There might be something I can carry. And if anyone asks later, tell them I had no idea what I was talking about."

"Here," Schroeder said. With a turn of a key, he opened the side toolbox behind the cab. John rummaged around. His hand emerged with a cat's-paw crowbar about two feet long and Schroeder gave a low whistle. "Damn, son, you've got yourself a nasty lethal weapon there. You sure about that?"

John balanced the crowbar in the palm of his hand. "Did I ever tell you my grandfather was a water witch in the Ukraine back in olden times?"

"No, you didn't."

"Not on the Reimer side, but Mom's side of the family. He used a little crowbar just like this. He scoffed at the forked stick. He'd balance the bar in his hand, here at the fleshy part of his hand, right at the junction of his thumb and palm. Walk around with it, to and fro, till it fairly jumped off his hand and buried its pointed head in the ground. Found water every time. People hired him for his services."

"Where in the Ukraine?"

"Altonau. Now better known as Kherson. In the Krim." John flipped the "r" on the last word, so it sounded almost like two syllables.

"You are one fine bullshitter, Reverend. We're not water witching out here, at least I don't think we are tonight. But carry it if it makes you comfortable. Who told you that tale anyway?"

"My older brother. That's why you shouldn't believe his stories about me. For a stern Kleine Gemeinde elder, he is a gifted fabulist." John had a sudden urge to urinate. He slipped the curved end of the crowbar into his jacket pocket and walked over to the tree, unzipped, and watered its roots.

Schroeder waited. He said, "Up ahead. Let's go slow. I expect you will show me your powers of divination."

They walked a couple hundred yards, following the two-track along the fence. As they approached the crest of the rise, a short metal tower as if built from an Erector set came into view. It had a wind sock at the top, hanging at a forty-five-degree angle, catching a hint of a breeze. Further on stood a galvanized steel building. John turned and looked back at the hollow they had come from. Schroeder's pickup was now invisible. The wind sock straightened out parallel to the ground then, and a trace of ozone in the air promised a thunderstorm barreling across the land miles away. John scanned the horizon for lightning but didn't see any. A prairie dog skittered across the road.

They came to a cattle gate that interrupted the barbed wire fence. "Watch out, here. Let's not cross quite yet," Schroeder said. He took out a pair of field glasses and looked through them at what seemed inchoate darkness. "Hold on. There's somebody parked by the double-wide. Looks like we have a new guy. And the semi is there all right." A light went on inside the low double-wide trailer. Someone moved around the interior.

John said, "So we have company? Maybe Michael Jordan is losing his star power."

"Maybe somebody had the same idea we did," Schroeder said.

John stood with his hands in his pockets. He stared at the landscape that Schroeder was scoping. "You stake this place out very often?"

"At least a dozen times in the last few months," Schroeder said. "And I've compared notes with my buddies. Generally, there are only two guys that go in and out of this property besides the semi drivers."

"And who would those guys be?" John asked.

"Campbell and someone who, by all appearances, is his business partner. Often flies out with him. Mexican guy named Salazar. At times he is dressed like a ranch foreman, other times in a three-piece suit. But the guy inside there right now is not him. That's not Salazar. I've never seen this guy. A punk." Schroeder looked through the field glasses. "Good Lord, boy has a mullet big as a prairie dog. What is he doing? That can't be. He's putting something under the mat. What the hell? Are those keys?"

John heard from a distance the pickup truck door slam and an engine turn over. Schroeder turned abruptly and gave John a shove. "We have to hightail it back. Now!" They ran back on the two-track beside the fence. Then they flattened themselves down in some tallgrass.

John could smell the native vegetation that had grown in this place undisturbed for so many millennia. It provided momentary distraction from the drama unfolding. He thought about the bluestem and the switchgrass, plants all of six to seven feet tall, with root systems that went down just as deep or more, all that biomass locked in the dirt. Kansas stubborn. The scent of ozone drifted in again. They heard the pickup truck's engine burble and roar through a couple of overgrown dual exhausts, then the sound faded down the road.

"Dumb mullet in a big-ass pickup," Schroeder said.

"He's in a hurry," John said, as he picked his way across the cattle gate.

"Not only that," Schroeder said. "If he's working for Campbell, I wonder if he turned on the motion detector. Usually there's a yard light turned on close to the wind-sock tower."

"Are we trespassing here?"

"I don't see any signs, but yeah, probably. Maybe." Schroeder's voice sounded detached, as if the question held no interest.

"What were you planning to do about the motion detector and yard light, if I may ask?"

"Shoot them out," Schroeder said. "That's why I brought this along." He jiggled the rifle in the crook of his arm. "Come on, let's go. I think that kid actually left a set of keys under the mat. And I have no idea why."

John took a while to recover from his sense of moral vertigo. "Maybe the Lord is smiling upon your enterprise," he said.

"Sometimes he opens every door," Schroeder replied. "We won't even need your little crowbar."

Chapter 40

They entered the yard. The Volvo eighteen-wheeler was brand new, with shiny chrome exhausts thrusting into the sky behind the tractor's stretch cab. John entertained the uncomfortable thought that there were sleepers inside, but Schroeder sauntered around the ebony truck and wrote down the number on the Texas plates. Small gold script on the driver's door announced, W. Campbell, LLC. Schroeder put on gloves and stood on the running boards and tried the door handles. All locked up, like the back twin doors of the trailer.

"You said the kid left keys under the mat," John said. "I think you were serious. Maybe he left keys for the truck, too."

"Interesting possibility," Schroeder said. "Some of us think somebody's maybe doing an inside job on Campbell." John recalled Levi's deathbed rambling: "I think somebody stole from us."

They crossed the yard to the double-wide, about a hundred yards away. The structure had white plastic siding and featureless windows under a red metal roof, and it rested on a bed of roughly troweled cinder blocks. The ground smelled of spilled diesel. They climbed a set of wooden stairs to the front landing.

Schroeder lifted the welcome mat. "Bingo," he said. He held up a ring with one key. Then he used a flashlight to peer through the front door window. "Wow. Cathedral ceiling."

"Let's take a pause," John said. "You think somebody's doing an inside job on Campbell. I guess I'm imagining the guy with the mullet left the key for his contact, who is on the way to get inside. And it wasn't us. But now it is us."

"You're saying somebody else is on their way," Schroeder said.

"Yeah. I'm not saying we should get in a rush. But I won't be surprised if someone drives onto the yard with his lights on high beam. Don't know about you, but I'd rather avoid that."

"I hear you, John. Don't get all hot and bothered. They're watching basketball. Nobody's going to take away your ministerial credentials." Schroeder keyed the lock and swung the door open. He went inside. John followed and closed the door behind him. There were two rooms off the hallway, cubbyhole offices. Schroeder kept his rifle pointing to the floor, walked down the narrow hallway, poked his head into each little room, and returned to stand in the galley kitchen. "No one's here. Let's keep the lights off, though. Say, what's this?" He pointed his flashlight at the ceiling, the cathedral arch with the popcorn sparkle finish, then lowered the beam to the coffee table. On it sat a couple of cardboard containers.

John removed a folded piece of legal notepad taped to the top box. The outside showed two words printed in black ballpoint: Hey Bro. John unfolded the paper and read:

> Bill,
>
> Your cut from the last run. Take the key with you! It's a spare. I think we can make this a monthly. Will be in touch next week about the best time. Keep it loose if you want to keep it!
>
> Midas

He handed the note to Schroeder. Schroeder scanned it and said, "What the hell?"

"Please let me hang onto that note," John said, reaching for it. He put in in his front shirt pocket. "Now, with your consent, I'm going to open the box."

"You want my permission?" Schroeder said. "Did you think I would say no? I don't think there's a snake in there."

John peeled the tape and pulled back the cardboard tabs. He reached down through bubble wrap and removed an object wrapped in crumpled newsprint. He unwrapped the paper. Inside was a wooden tchotchke, a little carved antelope. It was painted in a nod to realism. He put it down on the coffee table, where it struck a cute pose. In went his hand again, and out came another carving, this one of a South American tapir. Hardwood. It had good heft. It was bigger, a perfect office paperweight, and it smelled of a new coat of shellac. He sniffed it. Then he pulled out a brochure stuck in the side of the box. "Fair Trade Koinonia Crafts / Economic Development in the Name of Jesus" headlined the top of the front page. The typeface seemed familiar. It reminded him of the brochures he had seen in the college's library.

"What is this shit?" Schroeder said.

"Wait," John said. His hand dug deeper into the box and closed on a cool plastic wrapper.

This was no tchotchke.

He lifted a rectangular object from the bottom of the box. He felt a thick, dense resistance that gave only a little under his fingers' indentations. The object felt cool and impervious. He lifted it out. It felt like he was taking precious cargo from a mother's arms at a church baby dedication ceremony or raising someone from the baptism pool. He lifted it out into the beam of Schroeder's flashlight. The package was pure white and seemed to glow.

"Good God," Schroeder said.

It felt purposeful and consequential. John's arm suddenly felt very heavy.

"We are in a world of trouble, my friend," John said to Schroeder. He looked at the brick in his hand. "Someone is going to be very, very angry."

"We're taking it," Schroeder said. "Both boxes."

"Whoever misses this will come for it. His name is Bill, and he'll make somebody pay."

Schroeder dug in. "We take it and deliver it to Veblen."

"At least we agree on something," John said. "But we're nuts to walk out of here with it." "Maybe it's cassava flour," Schroeder said. Then he laughed at John's expression. "Nah. You are holding in your hand the most valuable cash crop the Mennonites grow anywhere in the world. Forget your turkey red wheat and your barley. These folks Campbell is visiting understand exactly how the agricultural markets work. Like my daddy used to say, 'Never argue with the market.'"

"We are a resourceful, hardworking people," John said. "The quiet in the land." He put the brick back in the box. He rolled up the tchotchkes in their wrinkled newspaper and packed them on top. Then he retaped the box.

"Is there anything else here we want to look at or take along for the return trip?" Schroeder asked. He beamed his flashlight around the corners of the room. He picked up a glossy magazine at the far end of the kitchen counter and briefly flipped through it. "Huh."

"What do you have there?"

"Pretty girls. One of the parties out here likes himself some *Playboy*. Do you subscribe, John?"

"I read it only occasionally," John said. "And when I do, it's strictly for the interviews and short stories. Does that have a subscription label on it?"

"No."

John said, "How much time do we have?"

Schroeder said, "I think we should get out of here before we regret it."

John opened a cabinet door under the sink. He found the trash container and took it into the living room and told Schroeder, "Can you get the trash containers out of those offices and bring them here? From the bathroom, too. All of it." He began systematically to remove trash from the container, one piece at a time.

Schroeder peered raptly at the magazine centerfold. "Huh. I always thought Carol Schlegel would be enough for any man. Maybe I was wrong." He looked at John sifting through detritus that seemed composed mainly of food wrappers and dirty Q-tips. "What the fuck? You always go through people's trash?"

"Half the time that's what being a minister feels like. No, seriously, let me tell you a secret. You go through people's trash, you hold the key to their soul."

Schroeder said, "If I didn't know it was you, I'd say you're smoking crack."

"Never," John said. "The body is a temple."

John scooped the trash off the top of the coffee table back into the container. Then he started on one of the office receptacles and he found it: a brown wrapper with a Kansas City mailing label for W. Campbell, LLC. John asked Schroeder to bring the magazine over. He took it in his hand and slid it into the wrapper. It was a match. Then he slid it back out again and a brochure fell out of the magazine. Schroeder leaned over and picked it off the floor.

"Here," he said. "This should be of interest."

John read the document. It was proof copy for a W. Campbell Ministries mailer scored with red ink. John recognized the proofreader's marks. A couple of Post-it notes were affixed to the copy. "Thanks," John said. "This all has to be presented directly to Veblen. I'm sorry but you'll have to buy your own copy of Hugh Hefner's finest off a newsstand somewhere."

"You'd make a man drive all the way to the big city."

"Yes. Now we should go." John returned the trash containers to their proper places. When he was finished, the men looked around the room. Schroeder insisted on carrying both boxes and tucked the rifle into the crook of his other arm.

"That's all right," John said. "At least let me carry a box for you. Tend carefully to that rifle."

"I'm carrying the boxes. Let's not leave anything," Schroeder said. "You have your lucky crowbar? Your divining rod?"

"Yes. But you mean *your* lucky crowbar." John flashed his beam around the interior of the double-wide. "Give me that magazine. Let me carry something." Schroeder handed it to him and John put it into the kangaroo pouch of his hoodie. "Let's go."

They stepped onto the wooden porch. Schroeder locked the door and put the key in his pocket. Then they set off across the yard, not toward the cattle gate, but a shortcut on an angle to reach the pickup sooner. They killed their flashlight beams and moved quickly.

Perhaps if they had been younger men, they could have made it to the barbed wire and held the strands apart for each other to go through, in that practiced move that old ranchers teach the young ones. They could have gazed at the Milky Way and admired the cosmic glories.

They were fifteen feet from the fence when the assassin came out of the dark, almost noiseless. He emitted a low snarl only when he was nearly upon them. He did not bark, and he sounded like a lion clearing a nasty chunk of phlegm from its throat.

In the moment John tried to put a visual together with the sound. *What is this thing? Is there a kennel with a timer gate? Is the motion detector really turned off? Where was this creature when they arrived a half hour ago?* The questions rushed at him after the fact in a confused whirl. Now he reacted before he could think.

Schroeder was walking ahead of him when the first snarl came. John caught a flash of black superimposed on the black night, speeding toward them from the left. He started to yell, "John!" but the killer had already left the earth, launching itself, a projectile fronted by an open mouth full of teeth. The thing was enormous. John had seen pit bulls and Rottweilers in Chicago, but this was something else entirely, a sort of mastiff wolfhound mix the size of a Shetland pony, with no redeeming personality.

"To your left!" John shouted.

Schroeder must have heard the snarl, too. He tried to swing the rifle around. The dog knocked him flat, a hit with the malice and intelligence of a penitentiary linebacker. Schroeder scrabbled with his fists and arms to fend off the teeth driving toward his neck. The dog clamped its jaws to Schroeder's arm and started to make big gulping lunges as if it wanted to go deeper, for the throat, and Schroeder kicked the animal now, doing everything in his power to delay. Repeatedly came the guttural rumble of phlegm in the animal's throat, the sound of fighting and conditioning, the persistent effort by a certain kind of human being to breed an animal designed exclusively for the kill.

Schroeder was screaming. John walked in behind the dog and swung the crowbar with all his might at the animal's back. It connected with the animal's hind leg. John had hoped to hear a crunch. The vibration through the bar and into his hand from the impact snaked through his wrist and elbow all the way into his shoulder. It came as an electric bolt of pain. It was as if he had struck a car chassis. He remembered once a long time ago his brother had told him, "This is going to hurt me more than it hurts you." In this moment he wished he had taken the bigger crowbar from the toolbox.

Now Schroeder said something, still screaming. But what? John had no idea. He felt like a slow student in the second-tier reading group. He needed more time to understand. After the third long scream he heard, "Not the crowbar!" Maybe the animal had titanium legs. The dog's snarl turned into a low roar of rage, and John didn't know what he would do if it turned its attention on him. He gripped the crowbar harder and swung again and missed. He swung so hard that he thought he had hurt himself. The dog looked away from Schroeder and fixed its gaze on John as if to say, "You're next, little man." Then it swiveled its massive head back to its prey, spraying blood and saliva from its jaws, content to resume its relentless work.

"The rifle, John." Schroeder was pleading, whimpering. *Yes, the rifle. That makes sense, doesn't it? But where is the rifle?* John looked around in the dark and tried to find it. The dog's initial impact as it hit Schroeder had knocked the weapon into the grass. But now there was so much grass and so little time.

"By the fence! Pick up the damn—"

The dog clamped down on Schroeder's arm and made a tearing, ripping motion. Then it let go to actually howl in his face. The man screamed again.

"Rifle!" Schroeder sobbed. John waited for the dog to spring. Watching it, he moved his hands over the ground and found the weapon. His hands cradled it and relearned it. The dog had completely shredded Schroeder's jacket. The man had stopped screaming.

Old memories. John raised the barrel and grasped the stock and felt for the trigger. He released the safety.

"Hey, Fido. Over here," he said, not loudly, and gave a whistle.

The dog stood still and raised its head from feasting on Schroeder's arms, then decided to answer the call. There was blood on its face and smeared on the grass. Schroeder had his arms up around his head in a fetal crouch. John took a step toward the dog, two steps. He walked toward the dog and whistled again. The dog launched itself like a missile. The mouth came at him like an open jackknife. He pulled the trigger, once, twice. The shots rang out as the dog's mass met the pointed barrel of the gun and knocked him backward. John felt the rifle smash into his hands from the impact and then he was prone on the grass beneath an immense load of canine weight. He could smell its fetid breath. Its back legs scrabbled.

He waited for the teeth to find his neck but the mass shuddered to a stop. It was stinking fur, dying flesh on top of his, its mountainous weight crushing him on the bloody ground of the Flint Hills.

He couldn't breathe, but he could hear his thudding heart, which he took as a good sign. When the monster did not spring to life and swallow him whole, he climbed out from beneath its carcass and crawled toward Schroeder on all fours.

Schroeder put up his arms to protect himself. John grasped Schroeder's hand. Schroeder hung on without speaking. His hands were shredded and slick with blood.

"Hey, buddy, it's me, John. You're okay. I shot the dog."

Schroeder stared and shook his head, uncomprehending. Then he spoke through dry, cracked lips, his voice coming out in a whisper. "You shot the dog."

"I did."

"You shot the fucking dog." Schroeder coughed and then began to cry and laugh in a long spasm as if his lungs were coming up. He tried to talk. What came out sounded like a sob. "You did a good thing, John. You did."

"How bad are you?" John pulled Schroeder's hands away to inspect his neck. It was raw and bleeding, but at least there was no pumping carotid. "You're going to be okay. At least I think you are." John helped him take off the ruined jacket so he could inspect Schroeder's right arm. The limb resembled steak tartare. John took a bandanna out of his back pocket and wrapped it around Schroeder's arm, using the four corners to tie two knots.

"My hands are a mess," Schroeder said. "But they're still working."

"Hold your arm up in the air. It'll slow the bleeding. You're lucky he didn't snag an artery. I can tell you this. You're going to live."

Schroeder looked fearful. "Unless that son of a bitch who let this dog out is still on the property."

"I don't think anyone's out here. Dog had to be kenneled. Maybe behind the hangar. I'm guessing we set off a trigger that released him. But I don't want to stick around and find out how. Let's go."

John surveyed the area for the debris they had dropped. He scooped up the two cardboard boxes. He picked up the rifle and nudged the dog's head with the barrel just to make sure. Its left eye was gone. No movement. He flipped the dog over and found the other hole in its chest. He felt the kangaroo pouch of his hoodie for the *Playboy* magazine. The crowbar was in there, too. Safe and secure. "Do we have everything?" he said, talking to himself. The adrenaline euphoria fogged the edge of his thinking.

They climbed through the barbed-wire fence in a delicate set of maneuvers because of Schroeder's arm, and then hobbled into a broken run toward the pickup at the end of the two-track. At the cottonwood stand Schroeder handed the keys to John. "I can't drive. It's all yours. Say, there's a blanket behind this seat. Can you get it?"

John racked the rifle in the rear window of the cab and helped Schroeder into the passenger's seat. He wrapped the blanket around the man. "Give me directions on driving out of here. I don't have any idea."

"I'm going to pass out," Schroeder said.

"No, you're not. Buddy, please don't go into shock. At least not yet." John buckled him into the seat. "Lean your head back. Hold up this arm with your good hand like this." John felt like he was arranging a hodgepodge set of unruly limbs into semblance of a sentient passenger.

"I'll make it, John. Here are my keys." Schroeder rummaged in the front pocket of his Levi's. "Here. Hey, I've got a flask in the glove compartment. Could you?"

"I can." John popped the glove compartment and found the flask. He unscrewed it and handed it to Schroeder. The man chugged a couple of swallows of rye whiskey.

He handed the flask to John. "Medicine," he said.

John said, "Don't mind if I do." The whiskey burned all the way down. John asked, "You have a water jug in this rig? And maybe duct tape?"

"Beside the toolbox in the bed of the truck. It's the green Coleman jug. There's also a towel inside the toolbox. Bring that. I need to mop up some of this mess."

John found the jug and gave Schroeder water. He climbed into the driver's seat and turned the jug up in the air and pressed the spigot to his lips and drank too. He noticed fresh blood still coming from somewhere.

He wrapped the towel as tightly as possible around Schroeder's arm. Then he took off his belt and cinched it around the towel, and to make extra sure, secured the whole package with several loops of duct tape.

John put the hoodie up over his head and pulled a green John Deere cap down tight over the whole works. He turned the ignition.

"Guide me out of here," he said to Schroeder, slumped against the passenger door. He drove the two-track slowly, lights off. When they were back on the tarmac of I-177, he said, "And tell me, exactly what is our story when we get to the emergency room in Marion Hills?"

Schroeder began to laugh.

"My buddy's jumbo dog was running off leash outside of Strong City. I fought it with my bare hands and this thug shot it twice with a thirty-aught-six. Now am I gonna need rabies shots, or what?"

The night peeled away before the rushing headlights of the pickup. John thought about the boy with the mullet. He looked at the boxes labeled Koinonia Crafts that lay on the floor of the cab and began to think about the trouble ahead. Presenting the evidence to Gus Veblen. Questions that Dockhauser might have. John mentally compartmentalized. This probably had nothing to do with Levi's death. There was no reason to go into it with the insurance man. As for Veblen, those carefully wrapped bricks would speak for themselves. Explaining how he and Schroeder had entered private property and discovered them would be more complicated.

He thought about the dog growing cold now on the ground of Chase County. It had done what it was supposed to do. He looked at his hands on the steering wheel.

Schroeder said, "Drive faster, old man. This towel is almost soaked through."

John tromped the accelerator. He wanted more speed, but a ticket was the last thing they needed right now.

Chapter 41

The man in the white coat swabbed down with antiseptic the mess of Schroeder's arm after the nurse cut off his shirt. John saw that Schroeder's upper body was a latticework of raw scratches, cuts, and bloody scabs starting to harden. Schroeder began to smile as if comically amused.

The intern asked John, "What's with this guy?"

"Hey," Schroeder said. "Even in the pain, I bring the fun."

"There's your answer," John said.

It was the same doctor who had given Levi CPR. His nametag read, Luke Kyle, MD. Under the bright light, Kyle swabbed Schroeder's neck with disinfectant.

"Shit!" Schroeder said.

"You're lucky he didn't rip your throat out. Big dog?"

"You think?"

"You probably want to file a police report," Kyle said. "I mean, none of my business, but if you file an insurance claim—"

"We're going to see the sheriff about that as soon as you patch this man up," John said.

Kyle did a double take and looked at John. "Reverend Reimer, is that you? Call me Luke. Don't know that I recognized you in that getup. You been riding dirt bikes? Hunting coyote?"

"Entertainment takes many forms in this part of the country, doesn't it?" John said. He dropped the hoodie and put the John Deere cap back on, covering his white hair. Then Kyle started to irrigate Schroeder's slightly less damaged left arm. He looked at John and said, "Seems we meet again under strange circumstances. You sure it was a dog and not a cheetah? Or did you get ambushed at a pit bull ring?"

John ignored the comment. The less said the better. A nurse came by and with her eyes ordered John out of the room and into a waiting area. John was happy to cooperate and stop answering questions.

They wheeled Schroeder's gurney away. The man held his arms up in the air like pieces of flayed meat. Forty-five minutes later Kyle emerged from the intensive care unit. Stripping off his rubber gloves, he spoke to John. "You wrapped that towel around his arm pretty tight. Good use of duct tape. Almost a compression bandage. He's resting now."

"I hope you didn't give him a sedative," John said.

"No, he's wide awake," Kyle said. "Mostly adrenaline. He's all keyed up."

"I was afraid he would pass out in the pickup," John said.

"Can you tell me how it happened?" Luke asked. "Schroeder said it was a friend's dog."

"But definitely not a friendly one," John added. "You give him shots?"

"Yeah, standard procedure. You don't want rabies. I hope someone dispatched the animal. Your buddy will have to come in for more shots."

"Thanks, Doctor—"

"Luke Kyle, at your service."

A nurse pushed Schroeder in a wheelchair while the rancher bombarded her with monologue. The nurse seemed weary of listening. "Dog got out of the kennel. Wouldn't let go of my arm. Thanks, doc. You do good work." Schroeder's neck had a square gauze patch on it. He sounded delirious.

"You told me about the dog already," Luke said. "Somebody take care of that dog?"

"Indeed he did," Schroeder said, pointing to the preacher. "Put him down right in front of me. I got lucky."

"You're going to be all right," Luke said. "The rabies shots will make you right as rain. Sorry it took so long to patch you up. Very messy. A bit of rending and gnashing of teeth, if you know what I mean, and dirty. Just how long did you roll around on the ground?"

"We have another appointment to go to," John said.

"You two take care of yourselves," Luke said. Behind his smile was the demeanor of a high school principal. "I mean that, no cliché intended. Your paperwork is taken care of, Mr. Schroeder. Remember to drink your fluids. If you start to run a temperature, call us immediately, you hear?"

John assisted Schroeder out of the wheelchair. He helped him put on his jacket. His arms were bulked out with bandages. They walked to the pickup outside in the parking lot.

"You left the boxes on the floor of the front seat like this?" Schroeder asked.

"Where else would I leave them?" John asked.

"These motherfuckers are going to come looking for them. I'm surprised we don't have a tail on us yet," Schroeder said.

"Let's visit the sheriff," John said.

"I hope he's in the office. It's pretty late."

"Say a prayer, Schroeder."

"That's your line of work, John."

"Get in the pickup."

John looked at Schroeder and Schroeder returned the favor. A huge smile was pasted across his face and his expression conveyed borderline hysterical. "John, are we living the fucking adventure, or what?"

"In the pain, you bring the fun," John said. "Your words, not mine." John peeled rubber as he zigged out of the parking lot, and a half mile later he zagged onto Main Street in Marion Hills. The light was on in the sheriff's office.

"Let me do the talking," John said. "I think Doctor Kyle or maybe the good Nurse Ratchet with the unibrow jacked you up on a feel-good pain reliever. You'll crash when it wears off."

"I fear it's wearing off already," Schroeder said. "But just to keep your mind from worrying, you think you could carry these two boxes into Veblen's office? I'd sort of like to get them out of our possession."

"I'm on it," John said.

"Roger," Schroeder said. He lit a cigarette with the pickup's lighter from the dash and leaned back in his seat. "Give me a moment to gather my thoughts."

"I'm going in," John said. "Suit yourself."

Schroeder ground out the cigarette on the parking lot gravel with the heel of his boot and followed the preacher into the sheriff's office. Veblen looked up and tried to understand the apparitions appearing before him.

"It's fucking two in the morning, you guys. Who the hell are you and what are you doing here?"

"We come bearing gifts," John said to the sheriff.

Chapter 42

If Veblen was surprised by the appearance of the two men at this hour, his granite countenance didn't show it, at least after his initial outburst. He sat comfortably at his round oak table full of books in his stocking feet. He held a clothbound volume that he closed and set down. He scrutinized his visitors and stood up. Then he very deliberately poured Jack Daniels into a tumbler on the table and paused. "Care to share a glass with me? You both look like you could use a little." The men shook their heads. "Suit yourself," Veblen said.

On the table an art book lay open to a full-color reproduction of a painting that depicted an army general on horseback. The man had curling, lavish locks of blond hair. *The hair makes him look like a Vegas lion tamer*, John thought, but it also reminded him of Absalom, King David's son and seditious prima donna, whose demise came packaged in one of John's favorite Bible stories. The man's hirsute wealth proved his undoing when, riding his mount, he snagged his hair in some low-hanging tree branches and dangled helplessly before getting slaughtered by his dad's bodyguard Joab. Three spears through the chest. The hair also reminded John of Robert Plant's luxuriant tresses—he had glimpsed them on the back cover of a Led Zeppelin album during his daughter's high school years in Minneapolis. But General George Armstrong Custer rivaled all these icons in glory. Veblen appeared to be in the middle of a major research project He had spiral notebooks open and notes scattered across the table. There was a much dog-eared and coffee-stained paperback copy of *Son of the Morning Star* and a few old postcards scattered about that featured more glamour shots of Custer and a series of Native American chiefs in full war regalia. John identified Sitting Bull and Crazy Horse. And Red Cloud, the most photogenic of the bunch.

John was sorry to interrupt Veblen's scholarly meditations. The sheriff displayed poker face as he watched the two men enter his office's inner sanctum. Schroeder set down two cardboard boxes on the table. He looked like a car crash victim. The boxes were marked with wrapping tape that bore the running banner Koinonia Crafts. Veblen had never seen John look so gnarly. He considered the preacher's getup—a black hoodie and a John Deere cap. John looked unhappy but jumpy with adrenaline. He needed a shave. There was dirt on the knees of his jeans. For his part, Schroeder looked like he'd been in a gang fight. He moved slowly.

"Gentlemen," Veblen said. "Please sit down and give me a full report. What's that on your neck, Johnny Schroeder? Vampire bite you?"

Schroeder looked around the office and couldn't find words. John figured the adrenaline had worn off.

"Don't tell me all at once," Veblen deadpanned. He puffed on his bulldog pipe and drank some rye. "Come over here. What are you bringing for my inspection?" he said to Schroeder. "Some of that bric-a-brac they move over at the Etcetera Shop? I wasn't planning on doing any decorating. At least not with this shit."

Schroeder tried to separate a couple of blinds with his bandaged hand so he could look out the front window. "Sheriff, you might want to lock your front door," he said.

"You tease me," Veblen said. He put down the pipe. "Be my guest." He looked at John and nodded toward the front of the office. "Lock the door. Lower the blinds. And, Mr. Schroeder, please tell me who beat the living shit out of you. Did they use a Weedwacker or run you over with a riding mower? May I offer you a couple of Tylenol 600s?"

The rancher did not care for the jesting or the scrutiny. John walked to the front of the office, lowered the blinds, secured the door, and returned to the oak table where he sat down.

"Let me explain," John said. "We've just come from the hospital where Doctor Kyle treated Schroeder's wounds. Let me back up a little before that to a location in Chase County where we took a drive earlier this evening. That is where we discovered these." John stood up and put his hand on the boxes. "You need to see what we found. We decided these would be safer with you than with us."

Schroeder explained: "Sheriff, what John is trying to say is that we are scared as fuck."

John continued. "Schroeder is an old acquaintance of mine. We go way back. Lately he's been telling me about strange vehicles, semitrucks that are causing a stir among the ranching folk in the Flint Hills."

"Semis? Really?" Veblen said. "Cattle trucks? Sounds spooky. You guys auditioning for the Hardy Boys? Can you give me an exact location?"

"Black semis. Unmarked. Arrivals timed with nighttime flights in and out of an airstrip northwest of Strong City. Believe me, I've been skeptical, too. I have goaded Schroeder for more than a month now about his conspiracy theories. He doesn't like my questions."

Veblen looked at Schroeder but pointed at the preacher. "It saddens me to see tension between old friends."

Schroeder said, "He mocked me. Man comes from good country stock but has turned into another smug city liberal, I'm afraid. But he's not mocking me anymore."

"You should have taken this up with the sheriff in Chase County, guy by the name of Mingus," Veblen said.

Schroeder said, "Don't care for the man. Know him and know of him."

Veblen continued. "Knowing Mingus, I think he would have gladly looked into it, especially if the feds are involved. Whose airstrip?" Impatient for an answer, Veblen tamped out his pipe in a heaping ashtray and repacked it from a pouch of cherry tobacco.

"Wyndham Campbell," John said.

Veblen struck a match and held it to the bowl while he sucked on the mouthpiece. The burning tobacco released a fragrant cloud of smoke. "Part of your clergy prayer breakfast circle?"

"If there's a prayer breakfast circle with Campbell, I'm not in it," John said.

"Well, okay, some of us prefer to pray alone. I understand, given my limited agnostic perspective. Stop mystifying me already. What did you boys bring? And where exactly at the location did you get these?" Veblen began to open up one of the boxes.

"Permit me," John said, as he moved Veblen aside. He put on a pair of rubber gloves that he was carrying in his hoodie's kangaroo pouch. He reached into the first box and brought out a carved longhorn steer. He brought out a carved jaguar and then a tiny howler monkey, painted in vivid detail. He brought out a carved campesino hunched and bowed down under a heavy load on his back. The figure was skillfully made to evoke a viewer's sense of pity, and it would make a fine display on someone's fireplace mantel, a reminder of less fortunate souls in the hemisphere. John arranged these figures on the table in a small circle where they kept General Custer company.

"Like I said, bric-a-brac for the Etcetera Shop crowd. What's your point?" Veblen asked.

"The box is labeled Koinonia Crafts, and that is what we found. But we also found this. Like the prize inside a box of Cracker Jacks." John reached in again. The object he brought out loomed brilliant and white in his palm. It was majestic, the compact brick wrapped in plastic. He laid it gently on the table. "It's heavy," John said, "though we haven't put it on a scale."

"Okay," Veblen said. "The other box?" John watched his eyes, to see if they dilated.

"Same thing, except African wildlife. Tchotchkes wrapped in newspaper, and at the bottom, another brick," John said.

"Sentimental third-world themes for first-world consumption," Veblen said between puffs of his pipe. "I don't know what offends me more, the carvings or the dope." He motioned at the white package with his pipe stem. "Oh, hell, all this stuff needs to be fingerprinted. What else did you get your grubby hands on? Did this fall off one of those black trucks?"

"The truck was locked. Texas plates, by the way," Schroeder said. "It was parked on the property."

"Specifically, we found this stuff in a double-wide mobile home there," John added. "Somebody's office suite."

"You mean Campbell's. Just say it. You trespass other people's property on a regular basis, Reverend Reimer?" Veblen said.

"Didn't see any signs," John said.

"How'd you get into the trailer? You guys break and enter?"

"Didn't need to," Schroeder continued. He sounded slightly high. "Saw a punk in a pickup truck leave a key under the mat. It seemed, sort of like—"

"Serendipitous," John finished the sentence. "I will stop short of saying providential."

Schroeder brought out the key from his pocket and handed it to Veblen.

"But you haven't told me what tried to bite your head off," Veblen said.

"That's the dog part," John said. "That comes later in the story." He held out a note to Veblen and said, "This was taped to the top of the box."

Veblen read it. "Midas? Are you kidding me? Fast-forward to the dog part."

"The dog attacked when we were heading back to the pickup. We'd parked a half mile down the road." John took off his cap and pushed the hoodie back. It suddenly felt very hot in Veblen's office and the man's cherry tobacco wasn't making breathing any easier.

"I suppose you'll tell me next that dog was as big as Arnold Schwarzenegger." Veblen smiled.

"Yeah. Dog weighed probably a hundred eighty, two hundred pounds. I've never seen a canine that big in my life. Or felt one. It fell on me after I shot it." John didn't smile.

"You mean to tell me these fools dropped a couple of kilos of pure product inside a double-wide and left you guys the keys to the kingdom? And then someone springs the hound from hell on you while you're on the way out? You expect me to believe this story?"

"No," John said. "But it's completely true."

Veblen gave the men a disgusted look.

John said, "We're here because we're in over our heads. I know because I've been over my head before."

Schroeder changed the subject, eager to explain his own theory. "It looks to me like an inside job. Little thieves taking from the big kahuna. Somebody on the inside of the operation out there in Chase County is skimming and sharing the wealth. Whoever Midas is, I think he's ripping off his drug-lord bosses."

"You think Midas is the same guy who left the key under the mat?" Veblen looked at Schroeder with contempt. "This is one cockamamie story. And you strike me as unlikely boy scouts. Tell me what this Midas fellow looked like. You saw him, right?"

"Well, maybe this was just the messenger for Midas. Very young, very green. Big mullet, big, badass pickup truck." Schroeder hesitated. "So, to wrap up the story, there was a dog. I thought it was something else when it hit us as we walked off the property. It took a chunk out of me, maybe a few chunks."

"What'd you do?" Veblen said.

"It went for my neck. I threw John my gun. We're lucky we weren't both eviscerated. Thirty-aught-six. John shot the dog."

"You shot it," Veblen said, looking at John.

"Twice," John said. "It was one of those situations. It was either kill the dog or be dog food."

"But you entered the property unscathed and didn't see anything that might have you for supper. The dog only appeared when you were leaving?"

"Yeah," Schroeder said.

"Probably kenneled," Veblen said. "The question is how it got out. I can't believe there was no one on the property. Were there cameras?"

"Not that we could see," Schroeder said.

"To be honest, I don't know what to do with you or your story," Veblen said. "Or with what you have brought me. But it opens new and exciting vistas, doesn't it? I suppose I should thank you for your good citizenship, your crime-busting posse service." He went silent and seemed deep in thought. "Say," he said, "could you give me just a few moments? There's something I need to tend to. I'll be right back."

He exited out the back hallway and returned five minutes later. "Let me confess," he said, "my reading adventures with General Custer have been seriously interrupted tonight. Your find in the Flint Hills throws me off my game. So much so that I forgot to tell you, Reverend, I have news about that youngster you met here on your first visit. Remember Billy Ray? Speaking of young and dumb, that blond Mennonite kid Billy Ray Baumgartner who shot his half brother? And then his best friend?"

John looked down at his shoes. "Yes, what about him? Do you have news?"

"Extremely interesting news. Turns out he left a message for us on the wall of his cell when we held him here. Before he went up to the big house in Abilene. I don't know how he got hold of a pencil but he did, and he wrote what looks to be a twisted sonnet on the wall by the lower bunk. He's in the maximum-security wing at Leavenworth right now. I wondered if you could take a moment to look at the message and tell me what you think. I am guessing it means something but I don't have the proper biblical references to call up a lucid interpretation. I already snapped pictures of the writing, but you should see it for yourself. I am a simple historian. I know you are more of a literary man. Would you mind?"

"Not at all," John said. He was happy to be of service. He looked at the boxes on the table. Veblen got up and put the merchandise back in the boxes with the note from Midas. He asked Schroeder to carry them to the walk-in safe in the room behind the reading area. When they were deposited, Veblen closed the metal door and gave the combination knob several spins.

John said, "What are you going to do?"

"Well, first thing when morning light breaks is I call the Kansas Bureau of Investigation. They'll take this stuff off my hands and secure it as evidence before they begin a formal investigation. You don't know any of this, do you hear? Just shut the fuck up and don't talk about it. Second thing I'm going to do is make you guys sign an affidavit that what you have declared here to me is entirely true. You will sign under oath." He looked at John and made a weary expression. "Oh, right, you don't do oaths. I forgot. You will *affirm* that what you have told me is true. I will ask both of you to come in here tomorrow to write and sign reports. Then you pledge confidentiality about everything you have told me. I am sure I won't have any trouble asking you to keep this buttoned up, will I?"

"No, sir," Schroeder said.

"Good. Now follow me," Veblen said, "and I'll show you that writing on the wall. You need to see it. It's pretty cryptic, if I may say so myself. Boy's been reading too much biblical prophecy. Hell, Campbell could maybe provide a perspective with all his learning of that kind. But the poetry! My, oh my, I wonder if young Billy Ray was an idiot savant. Maybe harbored a secret wish to be John Keats. It might offer clues as to what went on between that young man and his older half brother. Who, by the way, likely communes with the devil."

Schroeder and John followed Veblen down the hallway into the empty chamber with its three sad cells, its vertical steel bars, the welded steel bed frames and the metal toilets, the gray concrete floor. The room smelled of moldy piss. "It's right in here."

They followed him into the third cell, the one Baumgartner had occupied. Veblen pointed at a smudged spot on the wall near the baseboard and gave them a flashlight. "It's by the foot of the lower bunk. You Bible readers will know what to make of it. I'll turn up the lights in here. I've got them on a dimmer switch."

John bent down. He looked for the writing scrawled in pencil. He bent down lower and scrutinized the wall. It was scratched and smudged, but he saw nothing. As he scoured the surface with the flashlight, he heard the slow creak of the cell door on its hinges and then the click of the latch. He spun around.

Veblen stood outside the cell, holding the keys.

"What?" Schroeder said, uncomprehending. "What the fuck?"

Veblen smiled at them. His silence was terrible, and he let it ride.

"There's no writing, boys. Please listen up real good now. Go ahead and get comfortable. Sit down and listen.

"First, don't you ever trespass on someone else's property again. I don't care if you find Midas's gold fucking toilet and the treasure of the Sierra Madre besides. You have complicated my life beyond measure. Even if there is something to what you found, the lawyers will have a field day with improper seizure of evidence. I should hand you over to Mingus because it happened in his jurisdiction.

"Second. Someone probably has you both on security camera tape. Two kilos of cocaine have gone missing. Do you know what you are dealing with? These are people who would throw you in a wood chipper without second thought after removing your fingers, one at a time, with pruning shears. If they figure out who took their tchotchke boxes, they will come for you and do unspeakable things."

John's voice left him. He stood up to grasp the bars of the cell. Schroeder sat on the lower bunk. He looked at the floor in a dull haze of shock and pain. He looked like he wanted those Tylenol 600s.

"Third. You might have stumbled onto something big. Congratulations, Schroeder, on fulfilling your dreams of a conspiracy come true. Not the feds, not the UN, but an entity far worse in terms of causing you immeasurable worry and grief. So, stifle your fantasy of hometown heroes. You went about this in the absolute wrong fucking way. Neither of you had any business doing what you did. You're stupid pikers, that's what you are, and if Marion Hills is turned into a Five Points bloodbath because of your shenanigans, I will personally hold the two of you responsible."

Veblen ended his lecture. He tapped out the spent ashes of his pipe on the bars of the cell. The ashes drifted to the floor and John could smell them. All the freshness gone, all the stale reeking scent mingled with the other myriad smells of fear and dirt inexorably accumulated in this sad space for the past seventy-five years.

Veblen looked at John through the bars. "I might have to call that hotshot lawyer girlfriend of yours from Chicago to come get your sorry ass out of jail. Let me noodle on that for a few minutes and decide if I want to cause the breakup of a beautiful friendship. The two of you might ponder the state of your personal relationship to your precious Lord and Savior and compose a few alone poems. I left pencils in the cell in case you want to write them on the wall."

Veblen turned on his heel and walked out of the room. The steel door clanged shut behind him. After a couple of minutes, Schroeder looked up. "The motherfucker. He can't possibly leave us in here, can he?"

John sat on the lower bunk beside Schroeder and said, "I don't know. Veblen might be a little overwhelmed himself."

The sheriff let them suffer for a full fifteen minutes before he returned. John wondered if the man was doing an experiment—trying to discover if either John or Schroeder would panic to the point of puking.

When the sheriff showed up, he had the appearance of someone who had spoken with angels. He was having a very good time. He turned the key in the lock to the cell door and swung it open. "I'm a patsy," he said. "Keeping you locked up here the rest of the night would be the best way to protect you numbskulls from the jackals. But I can tell you need your beauty sleep. So, get out. I expect you here tomorrow—excuse me, today—at three to write full statements. If you don't show up, you'll meet me in court.

"And, Reimer, I have to warn you. You are guilty of killing someone's animal, and people like that are usually more concerned about their pets than they are their relatives, friends, neighbors, or lovers. I give you fair warning. Now I have several important calls to make."

"Just one other thing before we go," John said. "I nearly forgot about this. It may provide more perspective about one of the prime subjects." He hauled a *Playboy* magazine out of his hoodie's front pouch pocket and handed it to the sheriff. It was still encased in its original brown wrapper. "There's a brochure for Koinonia Crafts next to the centerfold, where we found it in the double-wide. And please keep me posted on the investigation in Chase County. I have an interest in where that goes."

"I'll bet you do. Now go feed your sheep, John, or get your ducks in a row, or whatever animal metaphor works for you." Veblen patted John's arm. "Remember, three o'clock."

John drove Schroeder home to his farm. When they arrived, Schroeder opened the door to the machine shed. The men stood in the doorway of the steel building.

"See you in about twelve hours?" Schroeder said.

"I'll pick you up. Quarter to three. Sleep tight."

John backed the Range Rover onto the dried mud in the middle of the yard and headed into town to the parsonage. It was nearly four in the morning. He drove into the garage and hit the remote button attached to his visor flap to close the automatic door behind him. Once inside, he didn't bother listening to his phone messages. Moments later, he stumbled into bed.

John had no illusions about a thing called providence or any sort of God's-eye-is-on-the-sparrow theology. Vi's death had cured him of that kind of thinking. In fact, any more, the cloud of unknowing was just about the only theistic avenue that made sense to him. Now he thanked his maker that Veblen hadn't locked him and Schroeder in that dismal cell any longer. The weight of fifteen minutes had been crushing.

But maybe Veblen was right; holding them overnight in the cell would have been the safer bet for their own protection. That thought lodged in John's brain like a fishhook he was afraid to pull out. John tried to drift off. A childhood prayer crossed his lips. Now I lay me down to sleep . . .

Chapter 43

Another lesson awaited him in the morning. He awoke with a start at six. That was late for him but there were special circumstances.

He stood in his bathrobe and brought a carton of eggs and orange juice out of the fridge. He looked at his skillet on the stove. Had he forgotten something important in the car? He went to his bedroom and checked the pockets of his jeans and hoodie, then carried the clothes to the laundry room. Something seemed off. He looked at the connecting door to the garage. He was relieved to find it locked.

The hair rose on the back of his arms as he thought of entering the garage. He threw his filthy clothes into the washing machine, sniffed the hoodie, and turned his face away. He put a big load in the washer, including some of his running clothes. He dumped in laundry soap and turned the knob to the heavy cycle and punched the start button. With dread, he looked again at the door to the garage. Then he opened it and walked into the cool chamber.

There was a clue in the air, so he let his nose lead him. In the garage, over the smell of gasoline in its metal can next to the lawnmower, and the dank, sweating surface of the concrete floor, came something else entirely. It floated toward him like a bad dream.

There were a couple of spots of blood drying on the concrete next to the Land Rover's passenger door. He opened the door and jumped. The gamy bouquet turned into a wall of stench. An enormous severed head looked at him from the front seat. One eye was open and blank, the other destroyed, blown out of its socket. The dog appeared to ask a question and its clipped perky ears stood up as if to inquire. The head lolled sideways on the padded leather seat, almost tipping over, a big puppet with a blackened tongue swelling between massive jaws. The entire front seat was a mess of viscera and dried blood. Someone had used a bone saw or an ax to present this trophy.

The preacher checked the door leading to the outside of the garage and locked it. He wondered why the person who did this had not just firebombed the entire parsonage or put a bullet in John's skull. It wouldn't have been hard.

Maybe they just wanted to send a very private message. Maybe they didn't want to draw a fleet of FBI agents to Marion Hills. Or, if Schroeder's theory were correct, maybe they had to practice discretion to avoid blowing their own ongoing grift of the kingpins. John didn't know.

Maybe they were just biding their time and enjoyed inflicting paralyzing fear in their victims. If that was their intent, they were doing a good job of it.

John took an old towel from the rag box, spread it out on the edge of the seat, and rolled the head by one ear onto the terry-cloth surface. Then he wrapped the whole mess in a couple of plastic grocery bags. He went to work on the leather upholstery with soap and water and a bottle of glass cleaner. He used a sponge and a roll of paper towels.

His momentary impulse to take a picture of his car's interior surprised him, and he quickly swept that idea aside. Veblen would certainly categorize this as a crime scene. He wondered whether to include this incident in his written affidavit for the sheriff.

He paused and went back inside to the kitchen. He needed a coffee very badly.

In fact, he needed several cups to clear his mind. He opened a package of preground that Katie Nikkel had brought him the week before. He wondered what she would say if she could see him now. He inhaled the rich aroma of ground beans, poured the coffee into the rinsed gold filter, topped out the machine with water, and pressed the button. He read the package label: Koinonia Farms Fair Trade Brew. Belize-Mexico-Colombia. A picture of a smiling brown campesino adorned the front of the package. It could have been Jesus. In the background a setting sun lit up three photoshopped hills. Koinonia indeed. While the coffee brewed, he put on some pants and his slippers and a T-shirt. He came back to the kitchen and poured a blip of two-percent into the mug and watched it swirl through the rich black brew. He carried it out to the garage and set it down on the workbench.

What had Schroeder said out at the Flint Hills? Something about Mennonites recognizing a cash crop when they saw one? But Koinonia was Campbell's brand. John had Campbell very much on his mind.

As if to punctuate that thought, he heard his answering machine click in the living room. He drank coffee and listened. The person speaking in hesitant phrases was Carol Campbell. John imagined she was wondering whether she had a live audience. He let the machine do the talking. He took another sip and looked at his watch. Why was she leaving a message this early in the morning? Maybe Campbell had told her he had John Reimer on video footage.

John picked up the dog's head in the doubled plastic bags with their convenient handles. It was like a giant cabbage. He looked at its size and went to his basement and returned with Tschetter's empty bowling-ball case, which the welcoming committee had left in the storage room. *Now this is serendipity*, John said to himself. He dropped the head into the case and zipped it up. He put the case on the back seat of the car, on the floor.

He checked the front seat of the vehicle again. The damage wasn't terrible. The seat appeared to have Scotchgard on it. But he looked more closely. An outline of the dog's severed neck seemed permanently stamped on the seat. It looked like the state of Texas; the viscera had bled along the border of the Rio Grande, forming that little southernmost tail pointing to Mexico. He tried more paper towels with Murphy's Oil Soap but the towels started to pill up when he attempted to obliterate the outline. He applied distilled white vinegar and scrubbed.

The phone rang again. From a distance, this call he didn't recognize—a man's voice. He went back to the workbench and took another slug of coffee and wiped his mouth with the back of his forearm. He picked up a new Dobie pad. He didn't want to wreck the finish of the leather, but he didn't like that Texas outline much either.

Nor did he like that vinegar aroma. He thought about air fresheners, the kind cab drivers favored in Chicago, aroma wafers dangling from lighter knobs in a full array of options: evergreen, vanilla, lemon zest, oak, tobacco, jasmine, heaven forbid. He decided that wouldn't do. Nancy would extract the truth from him, and he tried not to think about that ugly scene. He rolled down all the windows of the Land Rover and let the vinegar do its work.

When he was finished, he did a walk-through of the house to make sure no one was lurking. Then he took a shower with the bathroom door open.

After he toweled off, he put on a pair of red Everlast boxer shorts. He pulled on a pair of khakis and a white pinpoint shirt. Then he sat down with a pen and legal pad beside the answering machine.

He listened twice to the first message from Carol. She wasn't completely intelligible. "John, I need to talk." Background noise, maybe a high-speed blender or hair dryer, garbled her voice. She continued, "It's urgent, Campbell is in trouble, and he's not telling me anything. I am in a state. Mom and Franz aren't talking either. I'm in Kansas City at the house. Please call me back." Then her contralto voice did an uncharacteristic dip, ending with what might have been a hiccup or a sob. John wrote down her number.

The second message, from Dockhauser, indicated that he, too, was in Kansas City, at his employer's regional headquarters, and he wondered if John could meet him at Watson Library at the University of Kansas in Lawrence. Noon, Saturday. John heard the sounds of violent coughing, and then Dockhauser managed to clear his throat of phlegm. He mentioned the Kansas Bureau of Investigation. There was a court order, he said, to obtain library borrowing records for several individuals, friends and acquaintances of Levi Schlegel. Dockhauser said John was familiar with several people on the list. "I thought you might provide us with thoughts about a few of the references." He asked for a callback within the hour.

The last message was from Nancy. John was surprised he had missed her call. He must have been in the shower. Her message began with the word "John." She let his name hang in the air. He focused on what she felt by the way she said his name. She drew it out, lengthened the single syllable into one of those Southern near-diptych formations. How did she do that? He picked up on the frustration. "This will sound crazy to you, and of course I expect you will tell me that. But I would really like to see you this weekend if that is possible. I have been thinking about our time in Door County. I need time with you, John. The distance relationship isn't working so well for me. I will also tell you it's not working out for the Lakeview congregation. But that's an aside. Forgive me. I am a woman with needs, I'll be the first to admit it, you know? Here's a proposition: I have a business appointment in Kansas City on Saturday morning. I could meet you for lunch in the Plaza. If I don't see you this weekend, I don't know what to do with myself. Please call me and let me know. I love you."

314

⊸

When he dialed Carol Campbell, she picked up on the second ring. "John?"

"Carol, I got your message, sorry I was occupied. You sound distressed."

"Very much so. It's about Campbell."

"Do you want to talk about it? Does he want to talk about it?"

"Campbell is not here. I can't go into it on the phone. It's a long shot but I wondered if you were up for a road trip. You could meet me at the house." She gave him the address.

"That might work," John said. "I have business in Lawrence tomorrow. What time? I was planning to drive up this afternoon."

"What kind of business?"

"Family business. There are details I'm still settling with Vi's estate. Lawyers, you know."

"Well, with those I am familiar," Carol said. "Why don't you come for dinner—if you don't mind a kale Caesar. Do you eat lamb chops? I'm on one of my crazy new diets, I'll warn you in advance."

"Did you say, 'Hail, Caesar'?" John asked.

"I said kale Caesar."

John found himself nodding in the face of too much detail. "How about six o'clock?"

"Drinks at five, dinner at six. I will see you then, John. I know it's a bit of a drive."

He called Dockhauser's number, but the man didn't answer, so John left a message that he would meet him at noon Saturday at Watson Library. He could pick up a Jayhawks cap for himself and a new one for Caleb Epp.

He saved his last call for Nancy. She picked up her phone immediately. He imagined the lovely Penelope sitting by her phone, waiting, longing, pining. He was right.

"I have been barraged with phone calls this morning. What is the meaning of this?" John said.

"I don't do meanings. I only listen carefully and then make a plan. You know how I work."

"I do," John said. "Lucky for you I have business in Lawrence and Kansas City. I'll be in your neck of the woods."

"What kind of business?"

"Family business."

"Can you be more specific?"

"Vi's estate. Closing out a few details."

"I thought you handled that in Chicago."

"There's some land stuff in Meade I'm wrapping up. Kansas lawyers."

"Legal stuff. The afterlife of the dead," Nancy said. "I know all about that."

"I'll bet you do," John said.

"And I want to provide you with new experiences in Kansas City, John. And I want to talk with you about your return date to Chicago. Details of the last church council meeting."

"Are we meeting on church business, then?"

"Well, I wouldn't go that far." Nancy's voice slowed when she wanted to play frisky.

"Okay. Listen—I have to manage my schedule before I hit the road this afternoon. Right now, I'm debating calling in the pulpit supply. I don't think I'll be able to get back to Marion Hills for Sunday service."

"Well, that is practical of you, Mr. Man. Why don't you pack a little suitcase, one of those cute carry-ons. I will meet you at the Embassy Suites Hotel in the Plaza. Maybe for dinner Saturday evening? That's the earliest I can arrive."

John thought, *This schedule is working itself out without any intervention from me.* Now and then he had a passing warm vibe about Calvinism. "I'll meet you in the hotel lobby at six."

"John. Is there any reason you are proving so amenable right now? So cooperative? Are you holding out on me?"

"No, Nancy. This is my natural disposition."

"Of course it is."

"Goodbye, Nancy. I'll see you Saturday."

"I love you, John."

⁂

He put a new coat of shine on his Oxfords before he laced them up. He packed his little suitcase because he listened to what the woman said and then he sat at the kitchen table and wrote out his statement for Veblen in eight pages of longhand. As documents go, it was nearly comprehensive. He began with an account of how long he had known Schroeder. He explained how he had mocked Schroeder's conspiracy theories about

Chase County earlier that spring, to the point of nearly destroying their friendship.

He wrote what he knew about Campbell's activity in Denver and Commerce City. He did not reveal what he had learned from the octogenarian genius Caleb Epp about Campbell's business operations and precarious finances based on hacked credit-card accounts. He thought Epp would appreciate it if John left him out of the story.

John described finding Jeffrey Arnheim dead in a sleeping bag in a split-level house just outside Denver. He mentioned meeting the fiancée Delores and her cliff-diving daughter, and her friend-maybe-cousin the bartender Celeste, who knew curious details about Campbell's unique brand of sadism. He explained that this man, a successful evangelical broadcaster and preacher, had sold Jeffrey Arnheim a house. Maybe not sold, but transacted in some mysterious way. All of this, John said, had heightened his interest about Campbell's operation in the Flint Hills. He admitted that his curiosity had gotten the better of him, and for that reason he had indulged Schroeder's desire to investigate the property.

He described the discovery of the cocaine amid the tchotchkes. He described how he shot the dog, and Schroeder's narrow escape. What he didn't talk about was that the dog's head had been dropped off in his garage a few hours later, so he secured it in a bowling-ball case on the floor of his vehicle for final disposal.

He described how it felt in the hospital room when Levi Schlegel coded. He mentioned Schlegel's plea for a private conference with John before he died and his repeated phrase, "Please help me."

John concluded with a statement, "I affirm that the above narrative is true," and signed and dated the bottom of page eight. He put the statement in a manila envelope and sealed it and wrote across the front: For Sheriff Vebler: Confidential.

He called his church secretary, Linda Ebel. He told her he had been called away on emergency family business, and she would need to contact pulpit supply for the Sunday service.

"Not to worry, John. You know we have a go-to list ready at all times."

John thought about how he had deployed the phrase "family business." The way he used it, it could mean almost anything. But no one questioned the sacrosanct value of "family." That he knew.

The family business, the business of family, the deaths of family members. The bonds that hold and break families apart. Family systems.

The dead and their assets. He went back to the parsonage and packed his suitcase and threw it in the back of the Land Rover next to the bowling bag.

As he drove away from the parsonage, he wondered if his unseen visitor would pay a return visit or maybe tail him to Kansas City. He dropped off the manila envelope at Veblen's office. Veblen wasn't in, so John gave the envelope to his deputy, Jerry Siebert. This, too, was fortuitous, John thought. He didn't want his statement to turn into four hours of interrogation.

Then he drove out to Schroeder's farm to deliver the bowling case. It felt heavy in his hand. Schroeder's wife said her husband was out in the barn, administering medicine. John walked across the yard.

"What's this?" Schroeder said. He moved stiffly and wore a sweatshirt to hide his bandages. His hands were gloved.

"Feel the weight," John said. Schroeder gripped the bowling case by the handles. "This was delivered to me early this morning. They left it on the front seat of my car. But it wasn't this nicely packaged. It was still baring its teeth."

"What the hell?" Schroeder said.

"They delivered the dog's head to me personally. Maybe they figured I was into taxidermy. Someone has watched too many mob films. I should be talking to you right now with cotton pads in my cheeks."

Schroeder's face was a different shade of pale. "What do you want me to do with it?"

"I don't know, but for your sake and mine, please make it go away—permanently. And don't tell me how or where. I'm getting out of town for the weekend," John said.

"I hope we don't find you filled with bullet holes and lying in a ditch. You write your statement for Veblen?"

"Yeah."

"You tell him about this?" Schroeder gestured at the bowling case.

"No. I didn't tell him about that."

"Where are you going?"

"I have family business to tend to in Lawrence and Kansas City. Details to settle from Vi's estate, some land in Meade."

Schroeder gave John a wary look. "The KBI is investigating Campbell's operation in Chase County," he said. "They were out there early this morning with three vehicles and a chopper."

John smiled. "So even the choppers have become real."

"I guess so," Schroeder said. "A tow truck. They were breaking down the truck trailer. I just heard from one of my rancher buddies south of Bazaar."

"They find anything?" John said.

"I don't know. They're also looking into his larger network. Apparently it ran through Junction City and Manhattan."

"Manhattan, Kansas?"

"Of course, but who knows what more they'll find if they keep digging?" Schroeder couldn't help but laugh. "Apparently also links in Denver and Las Vegas."

"Schroeder, if you want to get hold of me, I'll be at the Embassy Suites Hotel in the Plaza in Kansas City. You're the only person here who knows. Thanks for keeping it under your hat. But if you need to reach me, you know where to call."

"Okay, John."

"And be careful," John said to the bonsai cowboy, who picked up the bowling case and began walking it toward his pickup.

"Oh, don't you worry, John. I'm on my toes."

John climbed into the Land Rover. His gas tank was three-quarters full. He'd make it to Emporia before filling up and grabbing a sandwich. He drove the Thirteen Mile Road to 50 East and turned on his cruise control.

Chapter 44

The house in Kansas City had a horizontal roofline that hid its expanse, and it lay behind a six-foot-high brick wall extending the length of the block. John noticed the electric eye on top of the wall and rang a buzzer. The metal gate swung open with a low hum.

A stand of birch trees clustered at the modest entrance. The woman opening the door stepped back in a dramatic welcoming gesture. John took in the black tights and a loose gray basketball jersey. Her tan feet were caged in Roman-style sandals.

"I am thrilled to see you, John." Her voice was low, mellifluous. She extended a cool handshake and stepped in for an embrace.

He didn't recognize her. She had cut her hair short and painted it black, and the structure of her face had elongated to a degree just short of horsey. Her lips curved into a promising pout. Her eyes were magnified in twin pools of violet eyeshadow. John remembered her a couple months earlier at the high school track in Marion Hills. There she had projected attitude valiantly holding off the years. Now she embraced herself in a way reminiscent of mature Vegas stars: gelid, older, commanding. It was as if she had left Marion Hills far behind.

"Your phone message had me worried," John said. "But you look the picture of calm."

"I put up a good front, don't I?" she said. "Lots of practice. Truthfully, I've been a mess. I am so glad you're here. Let me hang up your jacket."

She gave John a tour. "Sorry it's in transition. My usual redecorating mania." She picked her way through the interior, letting John peek at a few rooms along the way. The house from the outside had seemed modest. Its small galley kitchen hailed from an earlier era when designers hadn't learned to biggie-size a room that served mostly as receptacle for a fridge, stove, and modest breakfast nook. The metal cabinets had been finished in pale lemon yellow. Work was underway on the countertops. A broken slab of granite leaned against a wall, awaiting removal. John had expected something grander. Walking through the hallway clutter, he saw that the relatively narrow width of the house from the street view hid its considerable depth.

"Double lot?" John said.

"Actually, a triple," Carol said. "I call it a shotgun ranch. Campbell brags that it's a modified Usonian. Nobody knows what he's talking about."

"Frank Lloyd Wright?" John said.

"Yeah. You're a smarty-pants. No wonder Franklin gets along with you so well. Let me tell you. This house is a maintenance nightmare, starting with a leaking roof. The man was seriously overrated. I'll be honest, I wanted something with more presentation possibility. But you know, at our age, stairs stop making sense."

They walked out of the kitchen and continued through a long hallway to the back. "The main den. Campbell is making it over as his study." Carol stepped around a pile of lath board, several pails of wall plaster, and a collection of trowels. A white canvas tarp covered the floor. Carol gestured toward the room that opened out dramatically from the doorway. John followed her. The room was big all right, a giant sunken chamber with a bank of Craftsman stained-glass windows lining the south wall. Opposite was an uninterrupted strip of clerestory glass that threw natural light into the hunter-green space. The smell of recently applied paint hung in the air. A gray metal desk that didn't quite work in these surroundings dominated one end of the room. It was piled high with manila folders and several pairs of bifocal glasses. John saw the top folder labeled Koinonia Enterprises. The view from the bank of windows showed a yard sloping down a hill adorned with scattered Japanese maples.

"Campbell is away on business?" John began.

Carol let his question hang. She led John out the back door of the den on a flagstone path angled down the hill to the yard's open space, protected from street view by the front brick fence. The flagstones took them to a long, low house that matched the midcentury lines of the bigger edifice but also mimicked something else, almost akin to a villa nestled in ancient Tuscan hills among vineyards. Carol let them in through a sliding door. Dark-red cherrywood of polished parquet rippled beneath John's feet. A gifted contractor had labored to make a floor this beautiful. The habitation had the snug feeling of a bungalow but the expansive flooring opened the space. A couple of end lamps were switched on, but the overall effect was dark luxury. Enough money had been spent to make the new space feel old.

The effort almost worked. Walnut veneer walls defined a living area with a hearth at the far end. A twenty-foot-wide abstract oil painting, shades of seaweed and gray, filled one wall. It looked like an upstart's interpretation of a Turner storm at sea. Or maybe just brushstrokes enjoying a self-referential moment. Beneath it a couple of bookcases fronted by barrister's glass carried a load of art books on medieval and Renaissance history. A bronze miniature of a Henry Moore piece rested at one end. John looked at it and tried to understand whether it was a womb or a skull. He had to admit to himself he wasn't very good at abstraction. The living area showed a black leather sectional with a couple of Chippendale wing chairs finished in gold-and-black tapestry. The Scandinavian coffee table was so understated it could have disappeared. It held a heavy crystal pitcher loaded with ice and beaded with condensation. Beside it on the copper serving tray a plate held strips of lemon peel, olives, and little silver spears. Carol brought out two stemmed glasses. She poured from the pitcher. She stuck an olive on a spear and dropped it into her glass.

"I made us a pitcher of martinis," she said. "I want to answer your question about Campbell's business trip, by the way. I just need help saying what I'm about to say."

"I've never had a martini before," John said.

"I can help you with that. Would you like a lemon peel?"

"Yes, thank you."

She twisted it above his glass and dropped it in. He raised the glass to his lips. He drank. "This is refreshing. Thank you. Might I also trouble you for a glass of water? I can get it if you direct me."

"No, let me," she said, heading to the kitchen that occupied a modest nook in the main living area. He stood up and walked in the opposite direction toward the fireplace mantel. Pictures were arranged on top of the marble slab. The biggest was an indoor family portrait of the Schlegel family, a black-and-white shot. The three oldest kids showed their young teen spirit and Franklin, the tiny cub, looked nine or so. Eva sat in the foreground with her arms around a collie's neck. Levi stood at the back of the group, with his arms crossed proudly. Another photo showed a late-teenage Carol Campbell sitting next to Betty Ford. They drank coffee out of crystal cups with their pinkies extended. Betty's lipstick was smudged, and she was hamming it up for the camera. A podium stood in the background with Fourth of July bunting.

Carol came back with two tall glasses of water. "There you go. Now where were we?"

"This is delicious. A hint medicinal, but I like it. How do you make it?"

"This is vodka. The purists swear by gin. But I've never been a purist." She pouted a little and then impishly met his gaze. "Hell, I'm not even that pure."

"Your call left me worried," John said. "You said you needed to talk. So, talk to me."

"I think Campbell is in a world of trouble. You asked if he's on a business trip. The fact is he is *always* on a business trip. Welcome to my life. The problem this time is he didn't tell me where he was going. In fact, he said he couldn't let me know. It's not like him. Just saying this now, I feel like I'm ratting him out."

"Please go on."

"I asked him if everything was all right, and he said yes. He said it was a meeting with one of his backers, though I didn't completely understand. There was a bad connection. He might have said bankers. Either way I can tell when he's holding out on me. Something else was eating him. After all these years, even silly me knows when someone close is laying down a line of bullshit."

"When did you last see him?"

"Eleven days ago. He flew in with one of his partners, Roberto, and stayed here the night and flew out the next morning. He told me he would call, but he waited a full three days to get in touch. When he did, he wouldn't tell me his location. I haven't heard from him since."

"Not even a postcard from Acapulco?"

"No. Are you trying to be funny?"

"Roberto? Roberto who?"

"Salazar. He supervises the coffee operation in Belize and Mexico. As far as I know, he also manages the Koinonia nonprofit."

"So not to change the subject," John said, "this little house you have built here shows the imprint of a master builder. Did you get your brother to design it?"

"Absolutely not. He wanted to, but surely you know anything Franklin designs and builds turns into a massive cost overrun. Campbell wouldn't allow it. Neither would I."

"I didn't know that about Franklin. Though he did tell me about one job on the East Coast where he got into financial difficulty. I think he said Connecticut."

Carol took a long pull on her martini. "Yeah, there was that. Was that the only one he talked about? Fortunately for him, Daddy bailed him out. As usual. Nobody in the family wanted to talk about it. A real sore point."

"Did Campbell and Franklin patch things up?"

"I think so. At least they resumed saying hello to each other. Look, don't get me wrong. I love my little brother. He is *so* talented. But he's also an irresponsible pain in the ass."

John mused on this. Carol refilled his glass from the martini pitcher. John stood up and was surprised what it did to his sense of balance. "You mind if I put a cube of ice in this?"

"No, go ahead, it's in the freezer."

John went to the kitchen and dropped two cubes from the ice tray into his glass. He looked at the fridge magnets while Carol kept talking. The one featuring a cliff diver got his attention. "Daddy always loved his little boy," he heard her say.

"You said nobody in the family wanted to talk about it. What about your mother? What about Franz?" John asked.

"My mother is a sphinx, John. She hides in her white house and paints her pictures that she sells to politicians and fancy professors. She doesn't talk much. She keeps all her kids at bay. Franz takes after her. He's a man of few words. He and Dad have managed the business together and prefer not to talk about anything of consequence. It drives Campbell crazy. I guess when you get right down to it, most of us prefer not to talk about it if we don't have to."

John stopped to reflect on what he knew about Carol and her husband, the things he knew because his source and buddy Caleb Epp had told him. How many credit cards were overextended? Fourteen? Fifteen? It seemed to John that on at least one level Campbell and Carol had their own problems talking about money. In John's experience, the affluent were the most practiced at pretending it didn't exist.

He thought about the two boxes of tchotchkes and cocaine he and Schroeder had hauled into Veblen's office. Of necessity, there was so much he couldn't say, so much he needed to withhold. And if Schroeder was right, the authorities were taking apart the double-wide office and airplane hangar in the Flint Hills even now, while he and Carol sipped this cold delicious beverage and she babbled on about her predilection for silence. He debated whether to ask Carol what she knew about Campbell's Denver activities.

Maybe tipping the rock ever so slightly upward at one corner would let in some light. Of course, it could also free up the bugs crawling underneath. Carol said, "I'm going to put the lamb chops in. You like to eat at six, don't you?"

"I'm old school that way," John said. "But whatever suits you. Please. I sometimes have to remind myself that eating at five is not appropriate."

"You're a runner," Carol said. "I know that ravenous feeling." She bounced off the sofa in her tights, and her feet moved gracefully across the parquet. John admired her lines in the gray basketball jersey. He looked at her tanned, naked feet in their Roman footwear.

He said, "So what makes you believe Campbell is in trouble? Surely you have more to go on than just a feeling."

She ground a pepper mill over the lamb chops and looked out the back window of her carriage house kitchen. She chopped fresh rosemary on the butcher board and sprinkled it over the meat. She brought a wooden salad bowl out of the fridge, heaped with torn kale, and shook up a jar of Caesar dressing. She poured it over the greens and mixed the works with a couple of wooden spoons. She carried a plate of croutons out from her butler's pantry and dropped them on top of the salad and mixed it some more. "Well, he did say one other thing that I remember. He said, 'I miss you, Carol, and I wish I could tell you where I am. But I'm not at liberty to do so at the moment. Be safe.'"

"Is someone threatening him?" John said. "I mean, tied to a chair or something?"

"It crossed my mind. I don't know what to think."

She forked the lamb chops from the roasting pan onto a serving platter. These were delectable morsels that could be handled like lollipops. She poured cold white wine from a carafe and plated John's portion.

"You like it?" Carol said, after the first few bites.

To answer, John forked a second helping of salad onto his plate next to three more chops. "Delicious. I've never figured out how to cook lamb. You have the secret."

"You're welcome." Carol ate and then suddenly said, "Oh, I'm sorry! Would you like bread? I didn't put any out—I'm trying to avoid carbs."

"Bread is good," John said. "But the croutons in your magnificent 'hail, Caesar' salad certainly count, don't they?"

She laughed and mocked him. "Hail, Caesar!" She bowed with both palms extended before her toward the floor. She returned from the kitchen with a warm baguette in a basket that she put on the table with pads of cold butter.

John tore off a piece with his hands and used it to sop up the lamb chop juices in the serving plate. "May I?" he said.

"Be my guest."

He chewed on the bread and washed it down with the cold white wine. Carol observed him with pleasure.

When he finished, he leaned back and said, "That was amazing."

She made espresso in a sleek Italian countertop machine and brought the brimming demitasse cups to the table. John noticed her steady hand. She put out a little dish with four brown sugar cubes and took a bottle of sambuca out of the freezer and brought it to the table. She poured a couple of shot glasses full of the clear fluid. The smell of licorice mingled with the coffee.

"You are probably wondering why you bothered to invite me over," John said. "I'm afraid I'm not of much help about your primary question. You want to find Campbell. I wish I knew how."

"I was hoping my modest feast would help jar loose some ideas," Carol said. "My family has always been impressed with your resourcefulness, you know. Resilience. We idolize you to a certain extent. Dad was especially taken with you. Franklin said he enjoyed entertaining you out in the Flint Hills. 'He's a man of ideas,' Franklin told me."

"That is a gross exaggeration," John said, deciding how much he could tell Carol. "I don't know where Campbell is. But I do have a story for you that has bothered me ever since I came to Kansas in April. Please forgive me if it offers only cold comfort."

"I'm all ears," Carol said. "Do you want to take a stroll around the grounds before you tell me?"

"Sure, show me around."

"You need to see the secret garden before it gets completely dark," Carol said.

She put her arm through John's, and he patted her hand. He hoped it came across as reassuring and clerical. She led him outside. They walked on the grass. The trees cast lengthening shadows in the evening sun, some of them knifing across the main structure of the house which seemed buried in the landscape like a long, drifting flatboat. At the base of the biggest tree toward the front of the yard a stand of ferns grew in profusion, some of them chest-high. John moved his hand through the fronds and felt their gossamer touch. A breeze blew through. He asked what kind of plants these were and Carol told him they were ostrich ferns. "I wanted to mix it up a little with the monotonous lawn, you know?"

She walked with a light step, brushing against him with an occasional accidental and not-unpleasant bump. He could feel a slight tightness behind his eyes, and he told himself there would be no nightcap.

She showed him her greenhouse full of flowers, a variety of daylilies and orchids. The smell of the orchids hit him wrong, and there was a gazebo at the very back of the property, about fifty feet away from the detached three-car garage with a second-floor studio. They visited a built-in barbecue station, and off the back of Campbell's den and study, a patio with an outdoor kitchen. More, more, there was always more, and then it became too much. John had a sensation of very light felt hammers starting to pummel the inside of his brain. A nascent migraine edged in behind his temples.

They returned to the carriage house. Carol told John, "You said it would be cold comfort. I want to hear it." She looked at him again and said, "May I get you a glass of ice water? You look a little tired."

"I came to Marion Hills by way of Denver in April," John said. He took the glass of water from Carol's hands and drank deeply, then leaned back in the wing chair. "I went through Denver because an old friend, Marvin Arnheim, told me his son had gone missing, and he was worried. Concerned. Not exactly panicking, but close."

"You're talking about Jeffrey," Carol said.

"Yes. You know this son—in fact, at one point you knew him pretty well. You and Jeffrey were king and queen at a homecoming event many years ago. I remember watching the two of you. You made a handsome couple. I should also say you were lucky not to have continued that relationship."

Carol sat up straight on her sectional sofa. Her voice conveyed a slight hesitation. "I know Jeffrey passed away in Denver, though there have been no details. The silence makes me think suicide. He had pursued a strange series of careers. A restaurateur? The owner of a chain of car washes? A street preacher? I lost track. But what does this have to do with Campbell?"

"Hear me out. I met Marvin in Denver and stayed there a couple of days. Alan Wiebe was there too. Marvin told me Jeffrey was engaged to a young woman named Delores and he introduced me to her. She was a restaurant manager wearing a huge diamond ring. Mind you, Marvin and I were both skeptical. Jeffrey had gone through four marriages after his first divorce in Marion County more than thirty years ago. Delores was slated to become number six, though she didn't know that until Marvin told her. Marvin did not hold back about his son's history. But Delores and a good friend named Celeste started to talk, so we listened. I was hopeful they would lead us to Jeff, but they were as worried about his location and status as you are now about Campbell.

"They put us in contact with a realtor named Fenimore. They said he had been close to Jeffrey and they often met for lunch. They were also involved in Bible studies and the Promise Keepers. They had what they called a 'street ministry' on Colfax Avenue. Jeffrey was known in the community of his followers as Doctor Jeffrey. And Delores and Celeste mentioned a third character often seen with these two guys. Can you guess who?"

"Campbell?" Carol's face showed fatigue.

"That's right."

"What restaurant did Delores work for?"

"Casa Bonita."

"Oh, for the love of God, you can't be serious."

"Oh, but I am. Delores had started as a cliff diver. Her daughter was diving off the rock into the pool when we were there. Smart kid about to start college on a scholarship."

"I hope you are not feeding me some tall tale. Are you saying Campbell was part of this ragtag band of brothers? And if so, why does it matter?"

"Not only was he part of it, it turns out he was the owner of the split-level that Fenimore sold to Jeff. Did you know anything about him buying and selling renovated housing in Denver? This was in a suburb, Commerce City. I couldn't get the details straight from Fenimore, who stopped talking with us after we discovered Jeff's body."

"You *what*?"

"Jeff was squatting inside a house he'd supposedly purchased. Or at least put down the earnest money. Fenimore showed us the house when we asked to see it. I have my doubts about a conventional purchase. It looked like squatting to me. For one thing, Jeffrey didn't believe in banks—he considered the banking system to be the work of the devil."

Carol guffawed and smiled. "He might just have been right about that." She grew serious. "How did he do a financial transaction then?"

"Cash only. He used payday loan outlets, if the paper trail in his car was any indication. You know, Western Union, pawnshops. Legalized loan sharking, you name it. He had access to some cash, even though he was living out of his car most of the time. His dad had settled a financial gift on each of his children shortly before the alleged house sale. And I learned from Fenimore that he made his earnest money payment on the house in cash. My guess is Fenimore and Campbell split it. A sizable amount. But tell me, did you know about their real estate business in Denver?"

"No," Carol said. "I had no idea."

You know, how do I say this? Jeffrey's theology over the years became quite vivid . . . and fantastical, even. Conspiratorial. Not all study of the Bible has benign effects. We found Jeffrey dead in his sleeping bag in the master suite. Parked beside him were his Bible and a copy of *Left Behind*, the end-times thriller everybody is raving about. All the signs suggested he had been living there for a while. He had a broken pelvis, probably from a fall off the back deck, and the autopsy showed high levels of amphetamine and opioids in his system. He'd been dead several days. Fenimore, the gonzo realtor, didn't seem to know that he had broken into the house and taken possession before the sale actually closed."

"And Campbell? Did you see him?"

"No. We learned some things, though, talking with Celeste. I have a feeling you and Celeste would get along. It turned out that Campbell was something of a regular at the establishment where she tends bar. He usually came in with Fenimore, sometimes with Jeff."

"And?"

"Carol, this part of the story is dark, at least it is for me. I've turned it over in my mind and the more I do the darker it becomes. It may seem like a small detail. But it begins to take on larger importance. This is the cold-comfort part."

"Stop with the teasing," Carol said. "Out with it!" She sat cross-legged on the sectional sofa. She had removed her sandals and held her naked feet in her hands as if shivering a little.

"Your evangelist husband who says he ministers to the 'whole man' is a sadist. The bar's owner proudly maintains an aquarium full of piranhas, and on designated nights he ran a betting pool for his customers. He would drop a white lab mouse into the water. Estimates and bets were placed beforehand as to how long it would take for the mouse to be consumed by a frenzied pack of fish. Campbell was an enthusiastic and repeat participant. He had wanted to drop the mouse in the tank but the owner told him to back off."

"High-stakes betting pool?" Carol asked.

"I don't know what that means," John said.

"I mean was it for a lot of money, like in the thousands, or five-dollar bets? Like, real damage or the stuff little boys do?" Carol's face was wan. "What did Celeste think of all this?"

"Celeste finds it beneath her contempt. But she had a job as bartender and couldn't afford to walk away."

"Sounds like a bar fronting for the bookie action and that's where the real money is being made. What else did she say about my husband?"

"Campbell was super excited about the game. He tried to pay the owner for the privilege of dropping the mouse into the tank. He was quite invested—I would guess both financially and emotionally. The deep personal involvement in the game is what I find disturbing."

"That's a doozy of a story," Carol said. "I would guess after hearing that you might not give a damn what happens to Campbell. I didn't realize you hated him so much."

"I don't hate him," John said. "I think, based on his behavior, that he is a sadist. He probably needs psychiatric help. The reveling in the mouse's dismemberment. The overt barbarism. I'm curious, has Campbell ever shown an interest in dogfighting or cockfighting, that sort of thing? I mean, perhaps during your mission trips to exotic places?"

Carol's eyes flickered with anger. Her hands gripped the edge of the seat cushion.

"You might be right that I don't care all that much what happens to him," John said. "I believe certain actions reveal character. And I am not saying clergy are not without their foibles, maybe even secret fears and pathologies. Lord knows I have my own. But this demonstrates a fundamental cruelty of spirit. It's hard to square with what Campbell calls his ministry of compassion." John thought about sharing the details of what he and Schroeder had found in the Flint Hills. It was a passing thought, and he snuffed it out almost as soon as it crossed his mind.

"What are you counseling me to do, John?" Carol said. "Why are you telling me this?"

"I am not counseling you to do anything. But maybe for starters, stop being so innocent. Ask a few questions. If you are worried about Campbell's whereabouts, contact law enforcement. Report him as a missing person. If I were you, I'd start with a call to Veblen in Marion Hills. He may have ideas."

"For not counseling me to do anything, that's quite a list," Carol said. "Why Veblen?"

"I trust him. He is also smarter than the average cop."

"Is Campbell in trouble?"

"The signs as you report them indicate trouble," John deflected. "If he's on the road and not telling you his whereabouts, it's possible he is running for whatever reason. But all kinds of things are possible. I can't lie to you. I have doubts about your husband's integrity. And it gives me no joy to say that."

I can't lie to you. I also can't tell you everything I know.

"I wanted to ask you something else," Carol said. "It's about the insurance guy that ordered Dad's exhumation. Dockleganger, what's his name?"

"Dockhauser. What about him?"

"It is awfully strange. Why would he order the body exhumed? Franz and Eva say that it's typical of the insurance industry. That they'll do anything to avoid a payout."

"I don't know. I would ask Dockhauser directly. He works for an outfit named Centurion. Dial them up and ask for his direct line. My understanding is that Franz is basically correct. The business has built-in hurdles that make a payout on a large policy a tedious, grinding affair. An insurance man would call it due diligence. So, in this case, an autopsy is an automatic part of the agreement. At least that's what I was given to understand. But again, I'm not privy to the legal contract. You'd have to ask Dockhauser. Or Franz."

"Franz is in communication with Dockhauser. The doctor and Franz are both on his shit list for not ordering an autopsy. But, do you think . . ."

"Do I think what?" John asked.

"An autopsy means they are looking at cause of death, right?" Carol said.

"I'm not a doctor or an insurance investigator. I would guess they want to know beyond a reasonable doubt what the cause of death was, to satisfy the insurance company's protocols."

"Do they doubt Doctor Thiessen's testimony or the coroner's death certificate? I mean, what are you suggesting?"

"You have me there. I think they seek scientific certainty. But this is only amateur speculation. I'm sure we will have an answer from Dockhauser soon enough."

"I'm thinking I need to drive back to Marion Hills," Carol said.

Before he left Carol's carriage house, John used the restroom. He wasn't sure the lamb was settling comfortably. He locked the door behind him and turned on the light and fan. He opened the medicine cabinet's double mirrored doors. This was becoming a habit of his, he realized. An old man scuttling around, sifting through other people's property, looking—for what, exactly? A dirty business, but he couldn't help himself. *Foibles. Of course. I have some of my own.* He surveyed a couple of tall glasses filled with makeup brushes, tweezers, various other tools for the everyday presentation of self. There were stray bits of hair and detritus on the glass shelf. A smear of lipstick on the inside mirror of one of the cabinet doors. Fancy brands of tooth whitener. He picked up a container and looked at the bottom of it, saw the price label, put it back. Jars of cosmetics and cold cream. Perfume. He looked at the labels. France. Italy. On the shelf above, a bottle of Pepto Bismol.

It reminded him of Franklin's medicine cabinet. There was once more the Depakote, the lithium, a prescription for Risperdal. Medication not to fool around with. He wondered what he'd find if he rummaged through Franz and Julia's bathrooms. Maybe he needed to invite himself over. Was the whole family manic depressive? He looked at a glass full of disposable razors and a can of men's shaving cream, a product called Denim Lather. A little juice glass overflowed with cotton swabs and several different models of fingernail and toenail clippers, emery boards. Gently, he closed the doors to the cabinet and let the water faucet run.

He wondered if Campbell was sharing this carriage house while the larger residence underwent its thorough do-over. He emptied his bladder for what seemed a very long time. While he washed his hands, he held the bar of soap up to his nose. It gave off that peppery guava tone he associated with Carol. He turned on the faucet again and reopened the cabinet. He hauled the Pepto Bismol bottle down, uncapped it, and took a healthy swig. He capped the bottle and returned it carefully to its place.

He finally emerged. Carol was on the phone in her kitchen, beginning to raise her voice. John didn't know how long she had been on the call. It was probably a strategic distraction from his inordinate amount of time in her bathroom.

"What do you mean you have to rewire the entire kitchen?" she said. "That was not in your original estimate! Okay, so you need to revise the estimate, do you?"

John watched her face contort in anger.

"You didn't know how serious the wiring issues were, is that it?" She was almost shouting now. He escaped to the living room and sat down in a wing chair and picked up a magazine. It was a travel brochure for Cozumel and Belize. When Carol returned, her smile was tense. If she had planned to seduce him, the talk about Dockhauser and Levi had taken all the love potion out of the atmosphere. John imagined that was a lucky break for him. If he had stared very much longer at Carol's lovely Roman-sandal-clad feet after dinner, who knows where that could have led?

He could almost hear her say: *Telling a woman she has made bad life choices will get you nowhere. Who do you think you are, anyway, John Reimer? And thank you for that wonderful foot rub! I'd be happy to return the favor in kind!*

Chapter 45

He awoke with a headache grazing his temples. Six o'clock. The inside of his system felt coated in grease and alcohol. He got out of bed and drank two glasses of water. He put on running clothes and took the elevator to the hotel's fitness room where he found a row of treadmills. He got on, and once relaxed into his gait, he looked around.

Three machines over, a guy was running as though his life depended on it. Clad in bright yellow marathon running gear, he was tall, hirsute, and sweaty. He nodded good morning in John's direction and then returned to watching the news entertainment on-screen. Three photogenic pundits shared a couch, with the perky blonde taking center. She sat at the edge of the sectional and talked in rapid pitter-patter while compulsively smoothing her red pencil skirt over her thighs. Bookending her were two young men about ready to rush their preferred fraternity. The threesome appeared to have grown up in the same neighborhood of Shawnee Mission.

John looked at the screen and listened. The line between news and commentary was unclear. The sandy-haired man spoke of Randy Weaver and the ongoing fallout from Ruby Ridge. The other male sidekick, with the mannerisms of a slightly oversized leprechaun, observed that the size of the government settlement for Weaver, whose wife and son had both been shot and killed by FBI agents, was more than three million dollars. He went on to say that although this would appear to be admission of guilt by the U.S. government, it was worth considering that an Idaho jury would have demanded a lot more. The blonde nodded vigorously, head going like a Sesame Street puppet. The sandy-haired guy chimed in about the tragedy of federal overreach. He recapped the Waco massacre at the Branch Davidian compound. Leprechaun man threw in more data buds on the bombing of the Alfred P. Murrah Federal Building in Oklahoma City a little more than a year before.

A photo of Weaver clad in an orange prison jumpsuit came up on the screen, then a headshot. John realized the hard, chiseled face reminded him of certain portraits of John Brown. The square jaw and heroic martyrdom. The shooting, despite the passing of time, was still picking up media traction, not losing it.

John cranked up the speed on his machine for a finishing kick. When he was finished, he worked on deep breathing, toweled off, and returned to his room. In the shower, he pivoted to the day ahead and wondered what his various appointments would bring.

Dockhauser called him and told him to walk over to the Centurion offices, a mere six blocks away. "We have a couple of things to review. I should let you know the people from KBI will meet us in Lawrence."

"They are?" John said.

"Yeah."

"Is this some kind of grilling?"

"Nah, nothing like that. I think it will be completely friendly."

John wondered what that meant as he walked into the Centurion office building. He signed for the doorman at the front desk and took the elevator to the fourth floor. He walked down a gray carpeted hallway and somebody behind frosted glass said his name.

"Come in." The hollow tone sounded sepulchral. John swung the door open. Dockhauser was stubbing out a cigarette in a crystal ashtray and looking at his notes through a pair of bifocals. His tie was loosened around his neck, and he had undone the top button of his striped blue-and-white pinpoint.

"Hello, John." He extended his hand. "I think you can be of help. I'm going to lock the front office door and be right back. Make yourself comfortable. I just brewed coffee. Want some?"

"Sure. With a touch of milk."

We have a few things to cover."

"The autopsy results came back a couple days ago," Dockhauser said. "I'm kicking myself we didn't get to this sooner. Exhuming a body late in the game always compromises an investigation. It should have been done right away. Especially before the embalming. This is the problem with exhuming a body. It makes for ill will all around. And it raises suspicion, both of the doctor and the family. Nobody seems to have read the company policy."

John put his coffee mug down. "Dumb consumers? There was a lot of fine print, am I right?"

"Yes. But my sense of the Schlegel clan is that 'dumb' doesn't explain it. Those with a policy of this size are generally aware of their responsibilities."

"Are you saying someone purposely avoided having the autopsy carried out?"

"I'm not quite there yet."

"So, negligence or premeditation. Why do you say the autopsy raises suspicion?"

"The pathologists found anomalies. More analysis is underway. Plus, we knew about Schlegel's preexisting condition from his medical records in the central office."

"He was bipolar. Manic depression."

"You know about that, too," Tom said. "My impression is the family kept that information pretty much under wraps in Marion Hills." He lit another cigarette and inhaled on it slowly. He brought the metal coffee carafe back from the front office lobby and topped out John's mug. "How did you learn about that, if I may ask. I'm not even sure Thiessen had a handle on Schlegel's psychiatric diagnosis. When I talked with him, he just chalked it up to angry old man syndrome. There's your dumb guy. A simpleton. Or else playing dumb."

"How could Doc Thiessen not know?" John said.

"For certain conditions the family saw outside physicians. Big-city physicians, I might add. They apparently knew how to operate with discreet and separate databases. But, John, how did you know that?"

"Franklin told me. And Eva recently confirmed it when we talked. Like the rest of the community, I had always assumed she was the fragile link. Franklin jokes about her playing her game of Emily Dickinson, the weird lady painter working in solitude. While all this time it was Levi with serious psychiatric issues. The community has a high tolerance for eccentric millionaires. Call the man 'a real character' or 'a stubborn old cuss.' Then call the woman 'crazy.' Painting her pictures in the big white shed on the prairie."

"Our lab guy mentioned several pharmaceuticals," Tom said. "Risperdal, lithium, Depakote. Haldol. Seemed like a lot of stuff, from his perspective. You'll recall I told you that six months ago, Levi was a picture of health. Very high functioning."

"I do recall, yes," John said. "Sometimes bipolars go through phases. Productivity broken by bouts of depression. Levi always had a great deal of energy. Overachievers can get a lot done. What most people in the community never suspected was that probably had to do with his manic condition." John remembered how Schroeder had talked about "cow cocktail" as he injected a heifer in his barn. The people and their animals and their crops on the plains seemed to all be swimming in chemicals, or at least that's how it was starting to look. "And your list is basically standard medications for bipolar disorder," John said. "Doctors are constantly experimenting, aren't they?"

"You've been brushing up on your medical lore," Tom said. "Maybe I can get you a job at our lab in Cleveland."

"Just a little reading," John said. "Don't flatter me. And a wife who was on psychotropic drugs for the better part of twenty years. I should tell you, the bipolar condition has probably been passed down in the Schlegels, based on what I've seen."

"What have you seen? Where have you been looking?"

"I don't know quite how to tell you this."

"Go on," Tom said.

"Based on the contents of their medicine cabinets, I would guess both Carol and Franklin take after their dad."

"Well, we should get you into Franz and Julia's places so you can complete your search. Maybe you need an invitation over to the show farm." Tom laughed. "How did you manage to conduct your sweep?"

"You see very far into my heart, Tom. These people trust me. I have been a friend of the family for many years. Vi's life intertwined with Eva's back in Oklahoma a long time ago. I get along famously with the Schlegels. I praise their fine culinary skills. Their love of nature. Their style. I enjoy their company. And I reward them by snooping. It makes me feel like a bit of a shit."

"If it's just a little bit of a shit, you haven't pushed yourself far enough," Tom advised.

"Here's one more piece of the puzzle I have questions about."

"Go ahead."

"I had dinner at Carol Campbell's last night. That's one reason I'm in Kansas City this weekend. She and Campbell are redoing a house on a sizable property here in town. A Frank Lloyd Wright Usonian. Naturally, they've altered and enlarged it because they need space to roam. She complained about the leaky roof. She has built herself a fancy carriage house, something that could be set down in the rolling hills of Italy. Nice wood paneling, little touches of Florence in the fifteenth century. But unlike her mother, she has a thing for abstract art."

Tom said, "I'll bet she made a lovely dinner for you. As far as Frank Lloyd goes, that man probably should have never been granted his engineer's license. What did Campbell say?"

"Campbell wasn't at home." At this, Dockhauser's eyes twinkled with pleasure and John noticed and tried to ignore it. He pushed on: "That was one of the reasons she had me over. She's worried about him. She said he's been away for several days and won't, or can't, reveal his whereabouts. She's afraid he's being followed, or blackmailed, or something."

"Okay. But what does this have to do with Levi's death? Or are you going to tell me how you rifled through her medicine cabinet, too?"

"I think I already did. It profiled a lot like Franklin's. And I don't know what it has to do with Levi's death. I'm not always the best at connecting the dots. I thought that was your job."

"Tell me something, John. Did Carol know anything about your recent adventures on the Campbell property in Chase County? Or did she let on that she knew?"

John looked down. He was momentarily speechless.

Tom continued, a little sternly now: "I would guess not, if she had you over for a nice, quiet dinner to ask for pastoral support in her time of need. Unless, of course, she is very skillful, conniving even."

John recovered his tongue. "What do you mean about my 'recent adventure' on the Campbell property?"

"Don't act so innocent. Veblen filled me in. Sometimes it pays to get to know the local sheriff. I can tell you with a fair degree of confidence that the situation doesn't look good for Campbell. The Kansas Bureau of Investigation people, about to meet us in Lawrence, have also opened up an investigation on him and his entire nonprofit social service operation. As he calls it, 'the Lord's work.' Or whatever you want to call it. I get confused by the terminology. Lately in Kansas I feel like I'm rolling downhill under a tidal wave of theological bullshit."

"John Schroeder told me the KBI was getting involved," John said.

"Did he tell you they have Campbell in custody?"

"No," John said.

"Wyndham Campbell is being questioned at a high-security federal facility outside Leavenworth. They've also brought in several associates, including a guy named Salazar. It seems the good evangelist has been moving expensive white product up from Mexico in semitrucks loaded with fair-trade coffee and peasant art. A classic bootleg operation. Networked all the way from Reno to Junction City to the Twin Cities."

John looked at his hands. He clasped them together and made a little church steeple with his index fingers.

Tom continued. "Veblen told me about you and Schroeder. He was livid that you would pull such a dumb stunt. Though in the same breath he admitted you two broke it wide open. He is in awe of your courage and thinks you have a death wish. You might want to tell Carol to put a hold on her high-end remodeling. I'm not sure how it's going to turn out for her and the television preacher."

The insurance investigator fastened his top shirt button and snugged the knot of his necktie. He bounced out of his office chair and put on a blue linen sport coat. "Tell you what, let's get lox and bagels around the corner and then drive to Lawrence. You haven't had breakfast, right? You will need the energy."

"Do you think Campbell has something to do with Levi's death?" John said.

"I don't know. The money trail suggests Levi was an investor in Campbell's operation. What he knew or didn't know, I have no idea. I'm quoting Veblen on that. But I don't know how we get from point A to point B. Right now, I want to see those library records. We obtained a court order. That means there's probably something, not nothing."

"What kinds of books?"

"Books borrowed by a number of friends, family, and acquaintances of Levi. A lot of the books seem to be about drugs, overdoses, toxicity, poisons, chemicals, and whatnot."

"A lot of overlap there," John said.

"Yes," Tom said.

"You're going on the assumption he was poisoned," John said.

"Without a hypothesis, it's hard to ask the right questions. Overmedicated perhaps. But we still have to move from the circumstantial to the empirical."

"I'm learning," John said.

Chapter 46

Tom let his big sedan drift down Massachusetts Street in Lawrence at a stately pace and braked at an intersection, waiting for the light to turn. John looked at the scenery, a profusion of halter tops and big, bold hair. A woman dressed in baggy, rust-colored linen shorts and a peasant shirt tossed her coppery tresses with a nod of her head as she crossed in front of their car. The look she turned on the two men in the car conveyed the simmering cool of a Pre-Raphaelite goddess.

Dockhauser spoke out of the side of his mouth. "PhD candidate in anthropology, or would you say gender studies? I've seen her twin at the University of Cincinnati. Does she want to ask you a question?"

"I hope so, but if she does, I'm too afraid to answer," John said.

"Yes, shaking in your boots, preacher man," Tom said. A scent of patchouli drifted out of a gift shop with windows filled with bleached skulls, batik skirts, beads, and jewelry. John smelled the weed, too. He wondered how long Lawrence's downtown would continue to resemble Haight-Ashbury. The thought took him back to the brief period he had spent in this town. In a way, he hoped that snapshot of serenity would be cast in amber, because the next summer in Lawrence, 1969, had erased all peace and harmony when a couple of Black students in two separate incidents were shot in the back of the head by police downtown. By then he and Vi had moved to Minneapolis, for a new church assignment, but every close relative in Kansas had asked them if they'd heard the news, and were they safe? Now he looked for the button in his armrest and rolled his window up.

They drove up Mount Oread. They stopped at a security kiosk and Tom showed the officer a document. The gate went up and Tom followed signs to a visitor parking lot. Further on, the limestone mass of Watson Library gleamed in sharp, Gothic outline.

John remembered sitting in its cold, drafty space hunched over books so many years ago. The memory gripped him. It had lasted all of two semesters. He did not think often of that rough interregnum, before he abandoned a graduate degree in comparative religion and decided instead, at Vi's urging, to accept the senior pastorate in Minneapolis and continue his education in pastoral counseling.

—⁂—

The librarian wore a pair of black slacks and a cream-colored top under a square-shouldered, red-plaid jacket. John thought she might be auditioning for a guard position at the Tower of London. She met the men at the reference desk in a main hall lined with the card catalog, row upon row of wooden drawers in row upon row of upright cabinets. The rows marched in straight lines like the tall, arched windows that ran the length of the hall. "Welcome to Watson Library," she said with a toothsome smile. "I'm Alison Ainslee." John noticed her fingernails were painted glossy black. "Call me Allie. I'm a reference librarian on duty today. If you have any questions while you're at work, just come here and ask for me."

She led them to a private seminar room. Inside, at a pocked and polished oak table sat a couple of men wearing blue suits and skinny ties. In the corner of the room, the top shelf of a parked black metal library cart was stuffed with books. One end of the table carried the freight of several desktop computers and a bulky dot-matrix printer.

"Pardon the mess, gentlemen. This is where we're starting the transition to the electronic card catalog," Allie said.

The two men could have been twins, although it was immediately clear that the senior of the partners was in charge. John noted that they didn't show the signs of wear and tear he associated with Chicago cops. They moved like small-town, semipro baseball athletes and had the clean-cut profiles of first-stringers. The suits seemed to cramp their style. The little gold pins on their lapels, KBI, announced their agency.

"Sorry if we kept you waiting," Tom said. "Tom Dockhauser." He shook hands with the older of the two men, Cafferty. The younger one, Foxx, said hello and waved from where he sat.

Cafferty said, "No, not at all, we just arrived." Tom introduced Reimer as the clergyman who had a long history in Marion Hills. The two men nodded.

Foxx said, "So you're the preacher. Also, a real, live Jayhawk. Your reputation precedes you. It's a pleasure." He stood up to shake John's hand.

"I don't know what reputation that would be," John said.

"We know your kind, with that special brand of humility," Foxx laughed. "A Jayhawk by way of Chicago, huh? A big-city boy. Tom has told us some of your secrets."

"Tom doesn't know the half of them," John said.

Cafferty showed a gold incisor when he smiled. He became serious. "Hey, I know you guys want to get to work. We'll stop horsing around and get out of your way. And one more thing, Reverend. Do you have a card? We might have further questions for you down the road."

"Sure." John handed Cafferty his card. "That's my Chicago address. If you need to reach me in the near future, try Marion Hills Mennonite Church." Then he turned his attention to Tom after the KBI men and Allie had left and quietly closed the door.

"Here's the deal . . ." Tom began.

"They want to talk with me about Campbell."

"In all likelihood, yes."

"It's all in the report I wrote for Veblen."

"Of course." Tom nodded his head and began to take books off the library cart and spread them out on the table before John in a rough semicircle. John wondered if he were treating them as building blocks in a sort of Stonehenge theme.

"These titles were all checked out in the last year by a select number of individuals who have borrowing privileges at the University of Kansas and a connection to Levi Schlegel. Consider it a fancy Venn diagram. I am not at liberty yet to share with you the names of the individuals on that list. What I can tell you is their connection was through family, professional acquaintance, or friendship. These names might include rivals and enemies."

"Well, that would mean a pretty broad swath of humanity. I think what you're pointing to is an inside job."

"A high percentage of the cases I work on point to an inside job. But not all of them. What I want you to do now is read at your leisure. And take notes. Share those with me at the end of the afternoon. It's basically a three-hour tour. I have calls to make."

"You just want me to read and take notes. You think if I read well enough, I'll eventually find the 'open sesame' code."

"This is an open-ended exercise," Tom said. "Indulge me. Keep an open mind. You're a scholar who believes in revelation through the written word. You remind me of this writer, J. Hillis Miller. I read some of his stuff when I was at John Jay. He famously said, 'The millennium would come if all men and women became good readers.' Maybe a bookmark will drop out of a volume with somebody's phone number. A scribbled annotation on the back of a Chinese fortune-cookie insert. A sheet of paper with invisible ink. You never know. And if you find interesting annotations, mark them so I can take pictures. By the way, Hillis Miller was a Southern Baptist preacher's kid."

John was not impressed. "Yes, the literary critic. And I believe I heard it first from a Southern Baptist who once said, 'The Bible has all the answers.' This seems like an unorthodox way to catch a killer."

"Again," Tom said carefully, "I sit here in the presence of a man with his own unorthodox ways of operation, am I right? Sorry we won't allow any crowbars." John saw that Tom was enjoying himself. The claims investigator paused.

"We had a case once in a cute college town in southeastern Ohio, upriver from Cincinnati. Smack-dab on the West Virginia border. Suspect chloroformed his ex-girlfriend before he stuffed her into a storm drain near the wastewater treatment plant. The guy looked like Opie. Always living on the sunny side of life and very popular, but his professors thought he was slightly weird. Some of the convicting evidence included his library records. He was majoring in chemistry. His study carrel was stuffed with books on toxicology." Tom stopped talking.

"Sometimes they can't help but announce their guilt," John said. "Say, you ever been to Fly, Ohio?"

"No, why?"

"It's out that way. I know someone in Fly who I met in Chicago once. I've started talking about her as little orphan Annie. I should tell you the story sometime. Not now, we have immediate business to get to." John looked at the books spread before him and selected one. It was bound in a fresh, updated set of boards meant to shore up the deteriorated binding of an anonymous tome nestled within. He didn't notice that Dockhauser had already left the room and quietly closed the door.

John opened the book to the title page: *Poisoners and slow poisoning: a narrative of the most remarkable cases of poisoning. London: J. Dicks,* [*1865?*].

He began reading a vivid account of Pope Alexander VI, also better known as Roderic Borgia, first a cardinal and then the pope at the end of the fifteenth century. According to tradition, his family became synonymous with the deployment of lethal potions. He had ascended the papal throne the same year that Columbus sailed for the New World, he was the first pope to openly proclaim the children he had fathered, and he would eventually be denounced by the Dominican firebrand priest, Savonarola, on account of his grifting, fornication, and bald-faced corruption.

John took a blank yellow legal pad from his briefcase, got out a ballpoint pen, and copied a passage verbatim. It spoke of this special pope:

> His reputation for sanctity outstripped that of all his competitors. The words of Scripture were constantly on his lips. The good of the Church and the welfare of the poor were the themes of his most frequent prayers and conversation. The world was deceived, the people were charmed. Cardinal Roderic, in wisdom, was compared to Solomon; in patience, to Job; in meekness and divine zeal, to Moses.

John worked through a stack of the other books, consulting indexes for words that he had scribbled in a list. The pharmaceutical terms were far more relevant to the case at hand than an ancient account of the papal family named Borgia. But the lists in the reference books made him tired, and he had never been very good at reading lists closely:

Poisoning and drug overdose

Driesbach's handbook of poisoning: prevention, diagnosis, and treatment

Handbook of Poisoning: diagnosis and treatment

Poisoning and toxicology compendium: with symptoms index

Clinical toxicology

Handbook of poisoning in dogs and cats

Handbook of emergency toxicology

Several older titles summarized case histories, and they compelled John's interest, for instance, *Reports of trials for murder by poisoning: by prussic acid, strychnia, antimony, arsenic, and acouitia: including the trials of Tawell, W. Palmer, Dove, Madeline Smith, Dr. Pritchard, Smethurst, and Dr. Lamson: with chemical introduction and notes on the poisons used.*

He got up to take a bathroom break and wandered out to the reference desk. Allie pondered a computer screen. "How's it going?" she asked.

"I could use a coffee," John said. "Would that be possible?"

"I'll get you one. Cream? Technically we're not supposed to allow beverages in the seminar room but I think I can make an exception."

"Thanks."

"I normally hate being someone's beverage service but you're different. Are you always this charming?"

"Thanks again. I don't want to be any trouble. I'd go get it myself," John said, "but I don't want to cross the legal authorities."

She gave him a warm smile. "Dockhauser told me you were a smooth operator. No, not like that. He meant it in the best possible way."

"I like to think of it as trying to meet expectations."

He returned to the seminar room. He rifled through the reference book indexes for key words. He looked for signs on the pages. Allie brought him a coffee.

"You're too kind," he said.

"I hope you find what you're looking for," she said.

He looked at the entries on Depakote and lithium and Risperdal and Haldol—the quartet of substances Tom had referenced in regard to the autopsy.

He wasn't sure, but he thought he saw a mark near the entry for "lithium" in a reference work. It was as if a pencil point had been used to apply pressure in the left margin. Just a single dot. A tiny divot. He wondered if a schmear of DNA lurked nearby. He looked at the page with the light from the window casting a kind of topographic relief on the paper. An indentation. Somebody had pressed that pencil point. He looked through the other reference works. The indentation appeared again, once more in proximity to "lithium." He looked for similar marks against the other terms. Somebody had scribbled "bipolar" on a yellow Post-it in blue ballpoint ink, but it looked like undergraduate cursive. John sighed and marked the page. He noted the titles where the dots had appeared, and these started to form a list. He pulled out another older title from the stack. *The great oyer of poisoning; the trial of the Earl of Somerset for the poisoning of Sir Thomas Overbury, in the Tower of London. And Various Matters Connected therewith from Contemporary Mss.* The very first page caught his attention: "The younger's career of guilty enjoyment,

PRODIGAL SONS

magnificence, crime, and degradation will appear in the transactions which are the subject of the following pages."

Toward five o'clock Dockhauser returned to the seminar room. He looked at John. "Anything?"

"An entertaining account of the Borgias, true aficionados of the poison arts. Other than that, I never want to look at another book index or reference work in my life."

"Anything at all?"

"Several indentations. Maybe I'm imagining. But somebody was especially interested in lithium. I'd like to know who checked out these particular books." John pushed his list in front of Dockhauser.

Tom said, "According to tradition, Pope Alexander VI was poisoned with a substance called *cantarella*. Other sources say malaria did him in. After he died, his swollen corpse had to be wedged into a coffin a couple of sizes too small. What he needed was a piano crate. He was big to start with. The thing was a mess. Like slapping a three-hundred-pound pizza dough into a minuscule bread pan."

"Well, aren't you full of lovely anecdotes," John said. He opened his notebook and showed Tom the list. "Even if lithium is what you're looking for, this still doesn't tell us whether it was an accidental overdose or intentional poisoning. And it tells us nothing about motive or the specific agent. I'm tired. I need rest. I have a date in Kansas City."

"Let's go," Tom said. "I don't want you to miss your date. Where are you taking her?"

"She's taking me. She understands food better than I do. I'm just a joyrider."

"I'll bet you are," Tom said.

John packed his briefcase. He handed Tom his notes. The librarian, Allie, poked her head in the room. "All done?"

"Yes," Tom said. "Thanks. Please hold the books a couple more days. I'll be back tomorrow."

"It was a pleasure to meet you, Reverend Reimer," the librarian said. "Come again. You do have an alumni guest card, no?"

"Allie, call me John. You are part of a wild Kansas adventure. Thank you. I won't forget the experience." Then he looked at her and Dockhauser. "Can you tell me who checked out the anonymous tome on the Borgias? Maybe just a last name? Several last names?"

Dockhauser shook his head. Allie said simply, "Oh, John, so many people do. I wouldn't know where to begin."

"Thanks a lot," John said.

When Tom dropped him off at the hotel, it was nearly six o'clock. He asked at the main desk if there was a message for him. The concierge handed him a sealed envelope. He opened it. Inside was Nancy's handwriting on a piece of hotel stationery. "My room or yours? I'm in 637."

John went to his room and threw off his jacket. He wanted to dial Nancy but needed to place another call first. He dialed. When he heard the voice, he said, "Caleb Epp?"

"Yes, John. I was expecting to hear from you."

John said, "So you already know that Campbell is in federal custody . . . About the Schlegels, I mean the whole family. All of them, but Levi's activity most of all. . . Yes. A deep dive. Yes. Yes. Can you do that?"

He listened and heard Epp say very distinctly, "You want to talk about the money. I understand that. You want to talk about off the books? I'll tell you about off the books." John could hear the hum of the wheelchair over the phone as Epp played with the joystick. Forward, reverse. Back and forth. Apparently Epp was keyed up.

"What do you mean, off the books?" John asked.

"Have you ever heard of a place called Las Vegas? Levi had more than a passing interest."

"I will be back in Marion Hills on Monday," John said. "I will stop by your house first thing in the morning." He paused. "Eight o'clock. And yes, I will bring an Entenmann's coffee cake. And a box of chocolate donuts." He listened to Epp ramble on and then asked, "Doctor Epp, what did you just say? I missed that."

Caleb Epp repeated himself. "I said you are doing very well, John. Don't let your attention wander. Keep your eye on the dead man."

Chapter 47

Nancy stood framed in the doorway to her hotel room. She wore a pair of jeans and one of his white V-neck t-shirts. He had to admit she looked better in his shirt than he did. She had her hands shoved down deep into her front pockets. She had painted her toenails fire-engine red, and she put one foot forward. "I had my nails done in honor of Chicago. Do you like them?"

"John?" Her voice was low. She stretched out the syllable, giving it an edge of warning. She stood with that particular tilt to her hips that agitated him. "Do I look all right?"

"Nancy, I told them I am here on family business."

She put out her arms so she could encircle his neck. Then she stood on tiptoe. "I want all the details," she said. "And, yes, absolutely, let's talk all about family business."

He buried his nose in the hollow of her shoulder where it met the collarbone, angling his head for a better approach. He inhaled and caught a hint of candy and suntan lotion. She had told him it carried traces of myrrh. He held her close until he could feel her heart beating in her ribcage.

"You," she said. She stood back and looked at his face. "I hope you understand that I am here with an ultimatum. Because I really can't go on like this."

"Meaning?"

"Being apart from you. Come in here," she said. She pulled him into the room and shut the door. She sat him down in one of the easy chairs by the window. "Don't panic. You looked suddenly afraid. I mean I need you back in Chicago." She sat on the edge of the bed and put earrings into her lobes. She pulled on a pair of sandals.

John watched her and let his imagination run away. "It might please you to know I plan to return to Chicago ahead of schedule," he said.

"Things are unraveling here, aren't they?" Nancy said. "There have been complications. I see it all over your face."

"Not unraveling. But the situation has taken a strange turn."

"I knew already during the MCC auction," Nancy said. "You were keyed up that day and I also know you were holding out on me."

"I took the storm that night as a sign. And a good one. I don't consider this a fling or an affair or a late-in-life romp in the hay. But at the present moment, I find myself in the role of a distracted preacher." John looked at his watch. "I would willingly explain myself over a modest bowl of chicken soup. I spent yesterday evening in this fair city with the wife of Reverend Campbell. Let's call it a bout of pastoral counseling."

Nancy's eyes flared. "How was she?"

"Well, her husband is being held in federal custody outside of Leavenworth. She didn't know that, but I told her to call the sheriff in Marion Hills for an update."

"Is this one of your parish's surgically altered Mennonite beauty queens?"

"I'm probably enmeshed with the entire Schlegel family," John said. "If I denied that, I'd be lying. But there's no need to get nasty. She didn't put any moves on me. She did pump me for information. I learned she is in the dark about how her husband runs his business. I suspect she knows even less about how her dead daddy ran his. I also found out she had a special affinity for Betty Ford."

"What did Campbell do?"

"It appears he has been funding his various ministries of compassion with cocaine funneled out of Mexico."

Nancy paused. "Well, that's not nothing."

"No, it's not," John said. "I doubt if Carol knows. But she will almost certainly know in a very short time."

"There has been no publicity yet?"

"No," John said. "Veblen is running this investigation on the downlow. It's likely they want to build an ironclad case before they let the media in."

"This sounds very far from the work of the church, John. For a nice preacher you certainly know a lot of the inside details. I thought you had cured yourself in Chicago of your need to play Batman."

"Some would also say that what is happening here between you and me," John said, pointing at Nancy's chest and then his own, "is also far afield from the Lord's work. And by the way, you look very fetching in that shirt of mine." She beamed. He continued. "I can't begin to tell you what all of this means, but I certainly plan to. I want things between us to be good."

Nancy walked to the easy chair and sat down on John's lap. She leaned back against him and brought his hands up around the front of her chest to cup her breasts.

"I do, too," she said. "I want things to be good . . . I want things to be . . . permanent." He started to speak but she turned and put a hand over his mouth to make him stop talking. She looked at his brow. She ran her thumb over it and said, "This looks a little bruised. Will you tell me how this happened? Did you run into a doorknob?"

He winced and pulled away as she fingered his brow. "All in good time." John wondered how he would broach the topic of night-time dog hunting. He continued, "Let me tell you about the rest of my weekend trip here to the eastern reaches of bloody Kansas. Earlier today I spent time at KU's Watson Library, reading books about pharmaceutical medications and toxicity."

"What on earth for?" Nancy asked.

"It has to do with Levi Schlegel's death. I told you about the insurance investigator, right?"

"You mentioned him—what's his name?"

"Tom Dockhauser. He wanted to talk with me about Levi's last minutes alive. One thing turned into another. There was no autopsy done despite the requirements of the insurance policy. So Dockhauser's people ordered the body exhumed. Everybody's in an uproar."

"What did the autopsy show?"

"At least the possibility of overmedication. So far, inconclusive, though they are running more analysis. It could have been accidental. Plus, the man was eighty. Though in this scenario anyone with intent and the right skills could make it appear accidental. Such a death draws attention when the deceased is patriarch of a wealthy family. The next thing I know I'm being asked a lot of questions and I start getting curious myself."

"I am so surprised."

"It turns out that the various persons of interest, many of them apparently nice Jayhawks fans or at least alumni, are well read on the subject of medications and toxicity. The list includes friends and enemies who knew Levi. I should add, also several family members. The library was made to release borrowing records to the Kansas Bureau of Investigation by court order."

"You think somebody in the family did it. Maybe Carol."

"And maybe Campbell. That man's heart is a nest of dirty weeds. But if they did, what could the motive be?"

"Easy. Cashing out that big insurance policy. That's kind of obvious, isn't it?" Nancy said.

"They didn't clear me for access to the list of names. But Dockhauser thought I might have insight because I'm close to the Schlegels, so he sat me down to read for four hours."

"It's gone to your head, John. It sounds like you've embraced a career change."

"Nancy, the ministerial calling can appear a bit random. I put this under the umbrella of pastoral care because Levi asked for my help just before he died."

"You work the creative Sophist angle when it suits you. Smart man."

Nancy went into the bathroom where she brushed her hair. She took off the T and put on a bra and a button-down shirt and came out to sit on the edge of the bed across from John. He watched her bend down to adjust the straps on her sandals, saw how her body achieved a perfect arrangement of grace and angles and curves. Something welled up in his chest. He saw the look of concentration on her face. He knew eventually he would tell her everything.

"Promise to explain that bump on your eyebrow," she said. "Now let's go have a nice dinner. Then I'll bring you back here for a little nocturnal entertainment."

"You are a woman who holds many promises," John said.

"Family business," she said. "I wouldn't miss it."

⁂

The air-conditioning system hummed quietly. At least there was no rattle. John lay in the dark and images of fleabag motels and ancient hotel lobbies came to mind. Was he asleep or awake? Or one of the waking dreams? Then something else, a hospital room. It had a rough, cracked linoleum floor like the front entrance of a diner restaurant in Dodge City when he was a boy. He saw flies on a windowpane. He thought about all the dives he had slept in across small towns in the Midwest. Where was he? He struggled to orient himself. He had briefly dozed off and heard the beeping of a hospital crash cart.

He turned his head and saw Nancy. The sheets were completely off him.

"You were dreaming," she said. "I've been watching you."

"What did I do?"

"You made whimpering noises. You struggled a little. I couldn't understand your words." She reached for his hand. "You were very nice tonight."

"I was?"

"Are you playing dumb?"

"I didn't know where I was when I woke up."

"You're with me," Nancy said. She lazily traced a line across John's thigh.

"I remember something . . . were you talking about permanence?"

"Yes."

"Do I talk too much?"

"No, John. You're a verbal person. I like that."

"Alan told me once he was with someone who gave him several commands when they were in bed."

"What were the commands? Oh, that's nice."

"She told him, 'Don't smile,' and 'Don't talk.'"

"You are kidding. Oh, I will give you commands, but that is not one of them. Did she talk like Cloris Leachman in *Young Frankenstein*?"

"'Ovaltine? Warm milk?' Yeah, something like that. Can you imagine?"

"I can. But I prefer talking to you. You're a verbal signifying human, John Reimer."

"Look who's talking. And you are a very supple one, too."

"The talking cure." Then, a little bit later, "Okay, you can stop talking now."

"Do I have permission to smile?" John asked.

"Yes, absolutely."

Later she moved skillfully with him and then he felt her gaze touch his skin like a rain of manna. He thought of Blake's saying that the one "whose face gives no light shall never become a star."

She said, "What are you thinking about?"

He said, "You're the brightest star. Your face gives so much light."

"Which one is that?"

"Venus," John said.

"That's not a star, silly, that's a planet."

"Renaissance confusion. Keep talking, the distraction is good for me."

"I know it is," Nancy said. "What's the brightest star?"

"Do I have to keep talking? It's Sirius. Canis Major."

"Yes. Go to sleep, big dog."

Chapter 48

Reverend John Reimer, "Brothers and Sons,"
Marion Hills Mennonite Church

Luke chapter 15, beginning with verse 11:

> Then Jesus said, "There was a man who had two sons. The younger of them said to his father, 'Father, give me the share of the property that will belong to me.' So he divided his property between them. A few days later the younger son gathered all he had and traveled to a distant country, and there he squandered his property in dissolute living. When he had spent everything, a severe famine took place throughout that country, and he began to be in need. So he went and hired himself out to one of the citizens of that country, who sent him to his fields to feed the pigs. He would gladly have filled himself with the pods that the pigs were eating; and no one gave him anything. But when he came to himself he said, 'How many of my father's hired hands have bread enough and to spare, but here I am dying of hunger! I will get up and go to my father, and I will say to him, "Father, I have sinned against heaven and before you; I am no longer worthy to be called your son; treat me like one of your hired hands."' So he set off and went to his father. But while he was still far off, his father saw him and was filled with compassion; he ran and put his arms around him and kissed him. Then the son said to him, 'Father, I have sinned against heaven and before you; I am no longer worthy to be called your son.' But the father said to his slaves, 'Quickly, bring out a robe—the best one—and put it on him; put a ring on his finger and sandals on his feet. And get the fatted calf and kill it, and let us eat and celebrate; for this son of mine was dead and is alive again; he was lost and is found!' And they began to celebrate.

When we read this story, we generally call it "The Prodigal Son." And for most listeners, the story ends here. For us, the verses we just heard convey the story. Indeed, calling it the prodigal son's story is one way to make us selectively remember.

Unfortunately, the result is a distortion. We read with blinders on. We want insight, but we choose partial blindness.

I was reminded of this last year when I bought a set of bookshelves from the IKEA furniture company. I muscled the box into the trunk of my car. At home, I took all the components and hardware out of the box and laid out the instructions. I found that little wrench that IKEA sends in a plastic bag and got out my screwdrivers. Then I began the process of assembly.

An hour later I ran into difficulty. I made a phone call and soon my doorbell rang. It was my daughter. "Dad, what's wrong?" she asked.

She surveyed the mess I was making in my study. She took the directions in hand and looked at what I had done. Then she shook her head and asked, "Dad, you don't read very well. The holes are not matching up because you used two incorrect spacers. You got it wrong in panel six. I think you need to undo this here, and here, and take these screws out because they're the wrong ones. You need the short ones here with the Phillips head. And the long bolts and nuts happen in panel eight. We should start again from panel five." She took over the project and within an hour we had completed the task.

I was floored. "Dad, you don't read very well," she had said. Perhaps some of you have offspring who are smarter than you. May we all be so blessed. I am lucky my daughter shows me now and then how things work. Distressingly, the frequency of this occurrence is on the increase. "Dad, you're slipping a notch. You can't read. What is going on? You have a study full of books and yet you seem to be plodding along in the slow group. What is happening here?"

What is happening is that I'm a man who has assembled many bookshelves and built a few projects in my time. I like to think I am intuitive. Give me a hammer and a power saw and drill and I will master the universe. But in this instance my attention to the directions drifted. I thought I could figure the whole thing out instinctively. I was wrong. My daughter was right to question my reading abilities.

What I want to suggest about the text of the sermon for today is that we tend to read the first part and gloss over the second. We don't read the text through to the end. Like me with an Ikea project, we think we already intuitively grasp the project, so we stop reading.

We think we already know the story. And certain assumptions have crept in to prevent us from reading it with fresh eyes. The prodigal son, as we call him, has wasted his fortune in a foreign land. He is a dissipated libertine with no discipline. He is all appetite and no program, a debauched narcissist riddled with bad habits. He moves away from home, happy to escape supervision. He will fritter away Dad's hard work. Verse 13 tells us he "squandered his property in dissolute living." Fast cars, expensive scotch, whoring around. Recreational snorting of cocaine. Fill in the blanks yourself. "Dissolute living" invites a rich tapestry of images. Surely the father knew the character of his boy when he came to ask for his share of the estate. Even in the way the boy asks, we glimpse his shameless character: "Father, give me the share of the property that will belong to me." He wants it all and he wants it early. He doesn't say please.

But the father's response when this bad son returns home like a beaten dog melts our hearts. It feels like Charles Dickens's *A Christmas Carol*. It reads as a parable of God's infinite love, his boundless forgiveness of sinners everywhere. When Dad says, "Let us eat and celebrate; for this son of mine was dead and is alive again; he was lost and is found!" who among us does not give thanks for the miracle of God's infinite grace? This is what we believe constitutes the heart of the gospel. Dad throws a party for his returned lost son. It forms a neat parallel to the parable of the lost sheep, which my predecessor in this pulpit, Reverend Tschetter, memorialized with a picture in his office. I look at that picture almost every day and thank our church secretary, Linda Ebel, for having it reframed.

But my friends, we cannot stop here. The story Jesus tells is about *two brothers*, not just the prodigal. In verses 25 through 30, we hear about the older son, and we learn what *he* thinks about dad's decision to reward the younger brother's bad behavior. Now I know there are many oldest sons in the audience here today. And regardless of your position in the birth order, I know many of you have considerable experience running a business. Continuing our story in the gospel of Luke, we read:

> "Now his elder son was in the field; and when he came and approached the house, he heard music and dancing. He called one of the slaves and asked what was going on. He replied, 'Your brother has come, and your father has killed the fatted calf, because he has got him back safe and sound.' Then he became

angry and refused to go in. His father came out and began to plead with him. But he answered his father, 'Listen! For all these years I have been working like a slave for you, and I have never disobeyed your command; yet you have never given me even a young goat so that I might celebrate with my friends. But when this son of yours came back, who has devoured your property with prostitutes, you killed the fatted calf for him!'

Let us ponder a simple, serious question. Consider it a thought experiment. What if the oldest son is right? What if he is thinking clearly and his father's judgment has been clouded by sentiment and nostalgia? What if Dad's thinking has become a little sloppy?

What if this older son has witnessed for years his dad's deteriorating mental condition? He has worked closely with him and had opportunities to watch Dad's performance. This kind of thing is not new under the sun, you know. It looks to the oldest son like a case of senioritis, or dementia, if you want to get clinical. Dad's decision to reward the youngster's boorish, destructive behavior confirms it. Dad's cognition has slipped a notch, and in the business, this means he can be trusted no longer. He is erratic. The responsible thing to do is call him into account, as my daughter did when she asked me, "Dad, do you still know how to read?"

There is a possibility that a time will come when I abandon any effort to assemble an IKEA project because of mental unfitness. And I hope by then I will have the sense to dial up my daughter to come over and do it for me. These are the practical concerns of aging. They are also the practical concerns of any family business going through a change of who sits in the executive chair.

The older son is sober and can be trusted. No roulette tables, painted ladies, or dive bars for him. He has served his father faithfully many years. He hasn't squandered his inheritance. In fact, he hasn't even asked for his inheritance yet. Unlike prodigal junior, he minds his manners. He keeps his nose to the grindstone. And he has good reason to worry if the younger son is allowed back into the fold. Given kid brother's track record, he may well continue his destructive ways. Given enough latitude, the youngster could take down the whole enterprise.

Even the father's reassurance at the end of the story rings hollow if considered in this light. Dad tells his oldest boy: 'Son, you are always with me, and all that is mine is yours. But we had to celebrate and rejoice, because this brother of yours was dead and has come to life, he was lost and has been found.' It's a fine sentiment, but not entirely true. 'All that is

mine is yours.' Is that accurate? Can the father really back up that promise? It's bullish and optimistic but hardly tempered with common sense
about how the youngster is likely to perform given his history. And the
talk about being dead and coming back to life is nobly expressed. A less
poetic way to describe it is junior committed an act of fiscal recklessness
and returned home destitute and humiliated. Then Dad showered him
with gifts.

I see some of you shaking your heads. You're thinking, scripture is
supposed to be about love and the dead returning to life. Isn't that the
central message? It's all about the loving father. That is the whole point
of our faith! And here goes John Reimer on one of his crazy tangents.
He wants to take away Jesus's words of comfort and turn the story on its
head. What has gotten into him?

*John paused and looked at his watch, which lay face up on the pulpit
next to his Bible and notes. He needed to wrap this up. He removed a white
handkerchief from his back pocket and patted his forehead with the folded
cotton square. He could imagine his hair standing up vertically like a flame
under the heat of his brain. He put the handkerchief down on the pulpit beside his notes and drank from a glass of water. These were old-school moves,
but what he was doing in the pulpit on this Sunday morning was about as
old school as it gets. He set down the water glass and paused for effect.*

If you have any experience living in a family or running a business,
or both, who would you trust more? The sentimental aging father, willing
to overlook junior's spectacular meltdown, or the oldest son, who has
worked responsibly as a good and faithful servant? I know who I would
choose. It's obvious: Dad should hang up his cleats and turn it over to his
oldest boy.

*In the pew four rows from the back on the right, several members of
the Schlegel family stirred in their pew. John watched. He was surprised
Franklin was here this morning. The architect seemed focused on John's
words although he kept changing positions. He crossed his legs, then un-
crossed them. Carol sat alone. There was an empty space between her and
Franklin, and she looked straight ahead, immobile, hands clasped in her
lap. John wondered what she knew about Campbell's status by now. Eva,
in between Franz and Susie, looked almost shrunken, like a wrinkled doll.
Franz sat next to the outside aisle. He appeared to be writing something
down on the back of his bulletin. At the other end of the Schlegel entourage,
toward the middle of the pew, sat Julia and Ken. They were following John's
message closely.*

In a strange way, the oldest son sounds a lot like Jesus in another parable that we find in Matthew 25. But this is a hard parable, not a parable of comfort. It is known as the parable of the talents. In the story, Jesus describes a man about to go on a long trip. He entrusts money to several of his servants: "To one he gave five talents, to another two, to another one; to each according to his ability. Then he went away," verse 15 says. The first two servants get busy wheeling and dealing, trading, while the master is on his road trip, and each of them doubles their money while he is away. Upon his return, he asks how each of them performed in the marketplace. And the first servant says, "Master, you handed over to me five talents; see, I have made five more talents." He has turned five into ten. And the second servant tells the master, you gave me two talents and I doubled my money, too. Here are four talents.

The master is impressed and he praises these first two servants for their diligence. In a few words he tells them, Nice work, you have demonstrated that you can be trusted with the company's resources. Therefore, I shall trust you with more responsibility in the future. Then he asks the third servant, who had been given one talent, what he has to show for his efforts. And the servant bows and scrapes and says, "Master, I knew that you were a harsh man . . . so I was afraid. And I went and hid your talent in the ground." The servant digs up the talent and drops it in the master's hand, saying, "Here you have what is yours."

How do you think the story should end? Do you remember how it ends?

The master said, "You wicked and lazy slave! You knew, did you, that I reap where I did not sow, and gather where I did not scatter? Then you ought to have invested my money with the bankers, and on my return I would have received what is my own with interest. So take the talent from him, and give it to the one with the ten talents. For to all those who have, more will be given, and they will have an abundance; but from those who have nothing, even what they have will be taken away. As for this worthless slave, throw him into the outer darkness, where there will be weeping and gnashing of teeth." So we read in verses 26 through 30.

Here Jesus sounds very *unlike* the prodigal's loving patriarch! In fact, he sounds like the elders of my Kleine Gemeinde youth. In the parable of the talents, Jesus is attuned to judgment, not mercy. I can imagine this latter parable getting a warm reception in the chamber of commerce or a bankers' convention. Jesus seems to sign on for a flinty lesson in free enterprise, fiscal responsibility, and motivation. Even Milton Friedman would approve.

If I read this story right, Jesus sounds almost akin to the prodigal son's older, wiser, responsible brother.

I stand before you today as a variety of prodigal son. A prodigal son who left the home community and has never quite succeeded in patching up all the broken relationships. And I have been working for more than forty years at the task of reading and interpreting the Bible, seeking the face of Jesus. But I will confess that the more I read Jesus's words, the less confident I am in my knowledge of him. He continually says things that don't make obvious sense. I am pondering a sermon at some point in my career about the Jesus of Difficult Sayings. Indeed, many biblical scholars spend their lives investigating a whole body of Jesus's words which are called "the difficult sayings of Jesus." These sayings have been pondered now for centuries.

The restlessness in the Schlegel pew seemed to be spreading to other parts of the sanctuary now. John looked at his watch on the podium.

Take, for instance, Jesus's strange obsession with salt. A simple element, and so many ways to read it! In Luke 17:32 Jesus alludes to Lot's wife, who was turned into a pillar of salt. He says, in one of his more apocalyptic moods, "Remember Lot's wife. Those who try to make their life secure will lose it, but those who lose their life will keep it." Elsewhere, in Matthew chapter 5, he says this shortly after exhorting his followers to nonviolent behavior: "You are the salt of the earth; but if salt has lost its taste, how can its saltiness be restored? It is no longer good for anything, but is thrown out and trampled underfoot." It is striking how often our gentle Jesus resorts to violent language, isn't it? In a slightly different spin on this passage, the Gospel of Mark 9:49, Jesus says, "For everyone will be salted with fire. Salt is good; but if salt has lost its saltiness, how can you season it? Have salt in yourselves, and be at peace with one another." Jesus seems to be mixing his metaphors, don't you think? Is salt a punishment, a bad thing, or is salt something that helps us live with one another in peace?

Is it just me, or does Jesus at times sound like Yoda after a very intense journey aided by mushrooms?

Several people in the congregation began looking down at their feet. There was uncomfortable shuffling in the back pew, and a high schooler snickered in the balcony. John wondered how much further he could push it. His meandering thread was beginning to escape even him. But he stuck to his notes.

Why is Jesus obsessed with salt? As you know, salt is necessary for our health, but too much of it can kill you. Its duality is made clear in the Bible. In Deuteronomy 29:23 Moses warned the Israelites that disobedience will result in land "burned out with brimstone and salt, nothing sown and nothing growing, where no plant can sprout." The image is reinforced in Psalms 107:34 where King David speaks of "a fruitful land" transformed "into a salty waste, because of the evil of its inhabitants."

Now salt is a common element and certain forms of it are a valuable medicine, including lithium carbonate, one of the most effective treatments for bipolar disorder and major depression. We are all familiar with the phrase, "too much of a good thing." Such is the case with lithium, and lithium toxicity is well known. The same can be said for most drugs.

Caleb Epp sat in the front row reserved for wheelchairs. A lively elderly woman in a motorized wheelchair not unlike his own sat beside him. She knit her brow as she attempted to follow Reimer's message. Caleb had his chin propped on his fist. He leaned sideways and looked at John when the preacher mentioned lithium carbonate. He was slowly nodding, and then he very deliberately closed one eye, so slowly that only John saw it.

Impatience buzzed through the rest of the congregation. Many had lost the point of John's sermon several minutes earlier. Linda Ebel sat in her customary third pew from the front. Her puzzled expression had turned into a frown. John looked once more at his watch and decided to wrap up.

Jesus would have been familiar with the Greek word *pharmakon*, which translates as "drug." But in Greek it has several contradictory meanings. It can be translated as "cure." And it can also be translated as "poison." Finally, it can be translated as "scapegoat." The cure can also kill. It was maybe not lost on Jesus that this meaning of pharmakon as scapegoat quite possibly pointed the way to his own future on the cross.

More commotion disturbed the Schlegel pew. A gap had opened up. John looked. A figure, not quite running, disappeared out one of the back doors of the sanctuary. Then John saw Susie follow. He thought he heard a sob. Eva sat like a stone, a little distance from Carol, who had scooted over to grip Franklin's arm.

Jesus was a man of parables, and sometimes parables that teach very different lessons. And he was a man of difficult sayings. We can be thankful that he spoke clearly on at least one thing: the central commandment to love God and to love one's neighbor. As one of my younger colleagues has said to me, "Perhaps many of the Lord's words, like the *pharmakos*, should come with a warning label." And as Paul humbly confesses elsewhere in the scriptures, "For we see as through a glass darkly."

Lord, give us the gift of sight. May we hear your teachings, even the hard ones, that give life and light. Let us bow our heads in silent prayer as the organist plays the postlude.

The organist seemed eager to comply. She muted the notes for a full two minutes before she cranked up the volume from a heavily harmonic cut of French composer Duruflé's "Fugue sur le theme du Carillon des Heures." The people had been craning their necks, looking toward the back of the church when confusion started to ripple through the Schlegel pew. The organist glanced once more at the written note she had received from John just before the service started, instructing her to execute a full two minutes of quiet play at the end of the service. The notes burbled meditatively through the organ pipes, giving John time to exit; then the organist let go. The sound blasted magisterially to the height of the church rafters.

John was in the outer foyer and running toward the main doors. He could hear a woman's piercing wail outside come from the vicinity of the parking lane under the church carport.

Chapter 49

Sheriff Veblen looked at his watch and drove slowly toward the church entrance. He angled the cruiser in, blocking both lanes, and came to a stop.

He turned off the engine and stepped onto the pavement. He didn't have long to wait. He opened the right rear door of the vehicle and left it open.

Franz Schlegel came out into the sunlight. He shaded his eyes with his hand and looked to see the car directly ahead. He stopped.

"Sheriff Veblen, nice to see you this fine morning."

"A fine day, indeed, Franz."

"Are you here to meet somebody?"

Veblen gave him a broad smile. "I am. Reverend Reimer told me to expect you outside. And here you are." He nodded toward the open rear door of the cruiser.

Susie stood beside her husband. Confusion passed across her face and her expression began to crumble. She looked at the sheriff. John appeared in the doorway of the church. Susie said to Veblen, "What on earth are you talking about?"

Veblen took his hands out of his pockets. "Morning, Mrs. Schlegel." His uniform was more crisp than usual on this Sunday morning and his cheeks ruddier. There was no sign of his pipe. Now he stopped smiling.

Looking at Franz, not blinking, he took several steps forward. He removed his badge from his jacket pocket and held it up. "Franz Schlegel, I am here as an officer of the peace to arrest you for the murder of Levi Schlegel. You have the right to remain silent. Anything you say can be used against you in a court of law. You have the right to an attorney." Veblen hesitated and seemed to invest his final sentence with a twinge of irony. "If you cannot afford an attorney, one will be appointed for you."

Franz looked at the ground. His lips were parted to say something.

"No! No!" Susie's scream shattered every Sunday piety. "What are you doing?"

Veblen looked at Franz and at his wife. He said quietly, "Mrs. Schlegel, I would respectfully ask you to lower your voice." And then he said. "Franz, we can do this the easy way or the hard way. I'm not going to cuff you. Now please get in the car."

"Much obliged, Sheriff." Franz managed a smile, the kind he often wore when he was about to tee off on the first hole at Marion Hills Country Club. He turned to Susie. "Don't worry about me, Suze. Everything will be all right." He sat in the back seat of the cruiser. His eyes met John's, and he looked into the distance. Veblen closed the door, climbed into the driver's seat, and exited the carport with his passenger.

"No! No!" shouted Susie. She slapped the trunk of the cruiser as it drove away, then she turned toward John. Her face was a mask of white-hot rage before she ran.

Parishioners had begun to stream out the main double doors of the church. John took his customary position just inside the doors to bid the people farewell. He looked for the rest of the Schlegel family members, but he guessed that they had left by another exit. Susie was running for her car in the main parking lot.

Caleb Epp motored through the foyer and stopped his mobile chair to shake the preacher's hand. "I will be thinking about that message for many days to come, Reverend Reimer. You were full of difficult sayings yourself. Did you really say, 'Yoda on mushrooms'?" He winked and glided toward the sidewalk, his white, wispy hair blowing around his ancient pate. Once he exited the carport area, he put on his Jayhawks cap. It was a sunny day.

John didn't remember what his other parishioners said to him during the next fifteen minutes. It was lost to memory. A kind of roar persisted in his ears and their words blended in a gauzy shade of beige. He noticed some take the subtle route of avoidance, stepping carefully to the outside of the stream of people leaving the church so they wouldn't have to make direct contact with him.

The crowd exit finally slowed to a trickle. Katie Nikkel and Ann Hiebert were among the last to leave. They scrutinized John carefully. The retired language professor squinted her eyes and adjusted her glasses only to say, "You were speaking in code this morning, Reverend Reimer. I will expect a full discussion of this pharmakon business."

Ann Hiebert, the wizened retired medical missionary, was more succinct. "The screams out here were hard to take. I hope you got what you were looking for."

Chapter 50

After the sanctuary and foyer were empty, he waited for Cliff Buller, the sexton, to secure the main door. Then he walked down the hallway to his office. He entered and didn't turn on the light. The curtains were almost fully drawn and the dark, cool comfort of the unlit space was strangely healing. He put the Bible and his notes on the desk. He removed his suitcoat and threw it on the sofa by the door. He loosened the knot of his necktie and undid the top button of his shirt. Then he stripped the tie away and hung it over the coat tree in the corner.

There was movement in the doorway; he turned around. The door was ajar and Linda Ebel pushed it all the way open.

"You hung up that necktie with a lot of concentration and purpose."

"Yes," he said. "I did."

"Are you okay, John?"

"Yes. Why do you ask?"

"That was the strangest sermon I've ever heard. I thought for a while you were having a neurological event."

John replied, "I'd stay to explain why I preached it that way, Linda. I know it sounded rough in places. But I have to go now. They've asked me to come in."

"They?"

"Veblen. Some others."

"Veblen picked up Franz in the parking lot," Linda said. "Cliff told me. It was Franz, wasn't it? Cliff said he was in handcuffs." Linda crossed her arms across her chest and looked at John. He noted the way she considered him, not giving leeway. It was a look he was accustomed to from women who didn't tolerate avoidance. It was a look he had seen in Sarah, in Nancy, the kind his wife Vi used to inflict on him when she wanted information.

John said, "The rumors are already starting. Veblen didn't cuff him. I was there and saw it. I don't know very much right now, but I promise to give you a full briefing by the end of today."

"Thanks for the consideration. Are you going to talk with him?"

"With Franz?"

"Yes, with Franz."

"I expect to talk with him, yes."

John put on his suitcoat and stepped out of the office. He locked his door and walked outside. He drove out of the back parking lot to the limestone building downtown across from the courthouse. He saw Dockhauser's sedan and a couple of KBI marked cars. Veblen had prepared the waiting committee.

John went in. Behind the counter, the men sat around Veblen's library table next to his desk. The room smelled like aftershave and cigarettes. A Mr. Coffee sat on the counter and popped its erratic, explosive way toward the climactic perk. A tattered paperback copy of *Peyton Place* lay face down, spine busted, on the table next to the ashtray, which Tom was filling up rapidly with butts from a pack of chain-smoked Kool 100s. John felt the last bits of Sunday morning church fall away from him like rotten plaster on a stone edifice.

He removed a clean mug from Veblen's cabinet and poured himself coffee. He sprinkled whitener powder into the mug and stirred it with a swizzle stick.

Dockhauser made glancing eye contact with John. He raised an index finger from the surface of the table that he was restlessly tapping. "They're already saying you preached the sermon of your life," he said.

"You're a joker," John said. "My secretary thought I had a neurological event."

"The prisoner is impressed. He was babbling about it when Veblen brought him in," Tom insisted.

The other two men at the table began to laugh. John recognized them as the KBI guys he had met in Lawrence, Cafferty and Foxx. The older one, Cafferty, drained a can of Dr Pepper before crumpling the can in his paw and arcing it with a perfect hook shot into the corner trash bin. Foxx placidly watched the proceedings.

Veblen's deputy, Siebert, stood up. "Reverend Reimer? Gustav is out back talking with Franz in his cell. I have orders to bring you there straightaway."

"Let's go, then," John said.

They traveled the dank green cinderblock hallway. John thought this journey was starting to feel familiar. A cockroach crunched underfoot. John instinctively wiped off the bottom of his Oxford shoe on the concrete floor's gray paint.

The door to the bullpen chamber opened. Veblen stepped out. "He wants to see you alone," he said. "Don't worry about the time. There's no rush."

"Whatever it takes," John said. "I'll ring you from the intercom phone when I'm done. Do you have a confession?"

"I think he wants you to hear it first."

"You're not answering my question," John said.

"Just talk with him, okay? I have everything I need but I'm sure you'll get more."

⁓⚬

The room smelled like piss and a recent bath of ammonia cleanser. *Not exactly yin and yang*, John thought. *More like a blend of harmonies.*

Franz occupied the last cell next to the bullpen, the one where John had met Billy Ray in April, the same one where he and Schroeder had been briefly housed not so long ago. It was a cozy, familiar space. John walked toward it. He grabbed a couple of the vertical bars and leaned forward until his forehead touched the metal. He looked at Franz on the lower bunk. He inhaled the sour tang of concrete and steel. He gripped the bars harder and his hands came away oily. Maybe it was just his sweat.

"Franz."

"John. I never imagined it going like this."

"Likewise."

"But I think this is all about me. Am I right?"

"I think you're right, yes," John said. "It's about you."

The man inside the cell lay silently for the space of ten seconds on the bottom metal bunk. John waited and didn't say anything. He watched Franz clasp his hands behind his head and look straight above at the steel latticework of the top bunk all of four feet from his face. He wore his Sunday best minus his jacket, tie, and belt. His shoes had been stripped of their laces and were neatly arranged at the foot of the bed.

Franz sat up. He ran his big fingers through his pelt of hair. He got off the bed and put his hands in his front pockets. He stood in his stocking feet, half a head taller than John. Then he walked toward the preacher. He looked into John's face.

"I'm not coming for you, John. Don't worry. You can shake my hand. I'm the good son, remember? The responsible son. You know this. You told me so this morning."

"Yes, I did," John said. "So why did you do it? I know you must have had very specific reasons."

"Let's go over a few things," Franz said. He pointed at a wooden chair in the furthest corner of the bullpen. "Bring that over here and get comfortable. Get yourself another cup of coffee if you want. Let me tell you a story."

Chapter 51

"First thing I want to tell you, John, is I love you like a brother. You've always been an anchor. I can say that for the entire Schlegel family, I think." Franz looked relaxed behind the bars, in the manner of a priest granting his audience a few indulgences for the forgiveness of sins.

John wasn't buying. He said, "That sounds pretty, Franz, and I appreciate it. But this isn't about me. It's about you."

"Okay, I've never walked out on a sermon before. I sincerely apologize."

"I told Veblen that whoever came out of the church early was likely the person to bring back here."

"You can't seriously think I'm responsible for my father's death," Franz said.

"You walked out of that pew," John said.

"You made me damned uncomfortable," Franz said.

"That was the point," John said. "But it's not what I think that matters," John said. "The KBI has evidence. The insurance company has a coroner's report. There's a pile of books at Watson library that laid down a pretty clear trail leading directly back to you. Given the extent of your reading, you could have earned a doctorate in toxicology on the side. Come on, Franz. Stop talking in circles."

"The coroner's report showed nothing."

"Oh, but it did when they ran more tests. Ask Dockhauser. I'm sure you were relieved when they gave you the initial report."

"Dockhauser is a water boy for the insurance people."

"Who you were counting on for the policy payout. It's not that hard, Franz, to see through it. You're quite the scholar. You probably shouldn't have left your notes lying around in your home office, either. Was Thiessen in on it?"

"You'll have to talk to Doc Thiessen directly."

"I don't think I'll bother."

"Okay, then. Suit yourself. Since you're a man with all the answers, I'm wondering why you're here bothering to talk with me."

John said, "I don't have all the answers. I'm still wondering why lithium."

"Look, John," Franz said patiently. "Lithium stabilized my dad for at least thirty years. It turned a manic-depressive eccentric into a high-functioning financial genius. I watched him do the deals. I witnessed all of it. I saw him build it. Hell, I helped him build it. But at the end he was all out of whack. It happens. In fact, it happens to all of us. The meds are unpredictable. He was more than eighty years old. What else can I say?"

"You can say you gave him a nudge, very gradually. He was old, he'd turned into a grumpy old man, and he was losing his touch. You helped him to an early retirement. But something must have really scared you to administer the pharmacon. That speaks of a certain . . . desperation."

"Have you ever had your home searched by men going through your stuff?" Franz said, changing the subject. "Susie was outraged."

"It can't be all that much fun," John said. "But answer me. What scared you?"

Franz showed nerves for the first time. He moistened his lips with his tongue and drank water from a paper cup. He looked at John. "I have to say you did get your portrait of Levi exactly right. You recognized my father in granular detail. The mogul who became a prodigal. I spent the last five years trying to stop him from destroying the family business."

John said, "You were trying to protect the perimeter and the problem was on the inside, right? His ridiculous generosity in doling out money to Campbell's ministry projects and Franklin's architectural hoo-ha? His bankrolling Carol's fleet of houses and interior design hobby? Julia's show farm? You admired the way he made money but not the way he started pissing it away. Was it that you weren't satisfied with owning the car dealership?"

"Who told you I owned it? I didn't own it, not one cent. I worked for my dad, on salary. I never owned it. That's not what I cared about."

"So, you tell me Dockhauser was the insurance company's water boy, but you're also admitting you were Levi's wage slave. That's cause for resentment, I would guess. Am I wrong?"

John waited for Franz to reply and when he didn't, continued. "And what's this business I hear about Nevada? Tell me, what on earth is that about? I'm tantalized, Franz. I had no idea Levi had interests in Las Vegas. It sounds like somebody is making up tall tales about a nice Mennonite pillar in the community."

"How many kinds of crazy do you want to hear?" Franz said. "Surely you remember the former president at the college, Loeppky. I hold him partly accountable. Dad liked to pal around with him back in the golden age. They played a lot of golf. And Dad became one of Loeppky's biggest donors.

"And here's the thing about Loeppky. I mention him because he is strictly a tale to illustrate my own father. Thinking about Dad, I've often wondered how a genius turns into a self-destructive crank. A crank who hardly resembles his earlier self. Loeppky was a prime example. Here was this college prof with not one but *two* PhDs. A philosopher *and* a licensed psychologist. Guy as smart as Mortimer Adler."

"But way more charming," John said.

"Yes," Franz said. "Certainly. What was not to like? They made him president, and fundraising success proved his destruction. He apparently lost his ability to think. Loeppky always leaned on my dad for money. And Dad was a soft touch. By then, under the fundraising pressure and all the building projects, Loeppky's brain had turned to oatmeal. Just before he died, he was investing in penny stocks and spinning delirious speeches about the miracle of synthetic oil. Some of Loeppky's wingnut visions rubbed off on Dad, I'm afraid."

"Didn't Levi endow the alumni reception center during Loeppky's tenure at the college?"

"Yes, he did."

"That didn't work out so well."

"No. It became something of a joke," Franz said. "The students re-named it 'the conception center,' and not without reason. The interior de-cor of the place looked like the set of a cheap California porn shoot. God only knows what Loeppky and his administrative team were thinking. My father was humiliated. I told Dad he needed to put distance between himself and this guy. All of this is a roundabout way of saying that Dad, like Loeppky, got obsessed in his old age with the idea of easy money. He got the itch. Talk about prodigal."

"And that's where Las Vegas comes in," John said.

"Well, you've always scored high on the intuition scale, haven't you, John? I'll get to that in a minute. Let me tell you a story about a man named Levi. There was once a man in Kansas by that name. He was called after the third son of Jacob and Leah and he became the head of one of the strong tribes. His descendants were known as Levites. They were of the priestly class.

"And he amassed tremendous wealth, and he was blessed. He was already prosperous when he married a woman named Eva, and she bore him four children. And they dwelt in the land.

"And Levi was not satisfied. He wanted his cash to go further, he wanted it to *multiply*, but it would not multiply *fast enough*. Levi was smart. He was *talented*. So he went out to a city on the plain where the wealthiest gathered, and he sought the games where money can be made and he played."

John interrupted. "I like the King James Version, which you do very well, but are you telling me your father had a gambling problem? Can you be serious?"

"He lost upward of fifteen million over the past five years. Poker. Blackjack. Five-card stud. He had a thing for the cards and once he was in, he couldn't get out. He had started fooling around a long time ago. It usually happened during his manic episodes. I talked with Thiessen about it. I have to tell you, I saw it as a medical problem. There had to be a way to modulate his meds. But I could see Thiessen was in over his head. I knew more than he did so I took charge of the dosage. I'd been doling out Dad's meds for years so this was not something new. I tried to dial him back but he kept doubling down at the card table after his losses. He was out of control."

John held up his hand to interrupt. "You are telling me Levi was heavily medicated and gambling periodically in Las Vegas. Losing a lot of money in the attempt to make a lot of it, fast. And you were by his side through it all."

"Most of the time. I saw some of the wreckage happen up close. But Dad was also skilled at getting out on his own once we were on the Strip. He didn't appreciate me monitoring him, and he was not without guile." Franz looked at John. "You look at me like I'm weaving a tall tale. This is unvarnished."

"Go on," John said.

"He thought he could play but he was getting fleeced. He got in deeper. He wanted quick cash with faster turnaround. He slipped out on me repeatedly during our Vegas excursions. I learned long after the fact that he'd started to play with the big boys. He thought he could stay in it with them. He couldn't. I found him in a blackjack parlor at the Wynn one night. He finished the hand he was playing and I said that's enough. He'd also started to nip on the good Scotch, which I understand, because who can say no to a really good single malt? I knew the drinking was going to mess with his brain cells given his medication regime.

"I talked with our accountant. He told me, 'Franz, you have to reel in your dad. This is unsustainable. At the rate he's going, at a certain point you will have to liquidate assets to pay the debts. The path to bankruptcy may come faster than you think.'"

John said, "Did Eva know about any of this?"

"Not when it started. She was serenely painting her pictures. I didn't want her to worry. I let her know about a year ago. She agreed with me that Dad needed help."

"What kind of help?"

"She wanted him to go back to Menninger's for a consult. He wasn't interested. He was a stubborn asshole, you know. Opaque. Didn't like to explain himself."

"I know about the opaque part," John said. "When he sent all of you out of his room at the hospital and wanted to talk with me alone, he said he was getting shafted by someone, but I couldn't get a name. I still think he might have been talking about Campbell. He had lost his love for that man, hadn't he?"

"John, he never trusted him. Neither did I. And what's this I hear about Campbell being in federal custody?"

"They're questioning him outside of Leavenworth," John said. "You know, for the longest time I thought it was Campbell who did your father in. But there was no motive. It didn't make sense. For Campbell, Levi was a valuable revenue stream, an important sugar daddy. And Campbell's need for cash was more insatiable than your father's. Campbell is in deep financial straits. He's been running cocaine out of Mexico to fund his various ministries. He's probably going to do time. You might possibly end up his cellmate in a luxury federal penitentiary somewhere in the Rockies."

"That's mean," Franz said. "I didn't know you had that kind of vinegar in you."

John answered. "Mean, and entirely plausible. A patricide and a drug kingpin. The two of you might sing "Kum Ba Yah" together. I can't believe I'm saying this."

Franz ran his hand through his hair and paced inside his cell. "I doubt Campbell will fall. Campbell will claim he knew nothing about any of the activity and say he was used. He will play the innocent and the victim. Did you ever meet his partner, the Mexican guy, name of Salazar?"

"No, he never introduced me. Why?"

"Campbell will fob all of it off on that poor sap. You know the sheriff in Chase County, Mingus?"

"I've met him once. People have strong opinions about him."

"The only thing Mingus hates more than the feds is Mexicans. If you speak Spanish, he grows devil's horns. Campbell will do all right. Mingus will get rid of Salazar and make more friends in the Flint Hills. His main mission in life is to keep the county nice and white."

"Did Carol lose her love for Campbell?"

"Well, that's an intimate question. I don't exactly know. Why don't you ask Carol?"

"Did she lose her love for Campbell?"

"Yes. As I said, Dad had been fooling around in Vegas for quite a long time. He liked to keep the secret in his back pocket, a kind of private hobby. But it all started way back when, partly on account of Carol, long before Campbell ever came into the picture."

"How so?"

"Look, this is backstory I am guessing you know nothing about. You've certainly got sources who are talking to you but this is in the deep vault, even deeper than the family's secret history of whether Mom or Dad was the bipolar problem."

"You want to tell me about it?"

"You don't stop." Franz pondered. "I can hide nothing from you." He walked back and forth, with his interlaced hands cushioning the back of his neck. He came toward the front of the cell. John had the feeling that Franz wanted to reach through the steel bars and give him a hug. "You asked why Levi would have gone to Vegas in the first place."

"Not in so many words, but yes, I'm curious," John said.

"Well, the ostensible reason was financing of a tract housing development for a gated community. One of Dad's associates at the Lancers Club in Wichita had tapped him for a meeting with a building contractor in Vegas."

"And the real reason?"

"Carol came along on that trip. She was pregnant by Jeffrey Arnheim, who she claimed forced her in the back seat of his Chevy. Under further interrogation by Dad, she admitted 'he had been very persuasive.' This was a few months after their high school homecoming triumph."

John gave a long pause before he spoke. "Levi was looking for a doctor."

"Yeah. He found one. They took care of it. My brother and I were pretty angry. I don't remember seeing Franklin any more pissed off than he was then. He said to Dad, 'What are we going to do with that piece of shit, Jeffrey Arnheim? Is he getting off scot-free? Are we going to let him treat our sister like a whore?'"

John smiled. "Amazing. Maybe you should finish your King James Version account of the family Schlegel."

"Why?"

"It sounds like the story of Dinah in Genesis 34, featuring a lovely woman and her vindictive brothers Judah and Levi. On the other hand, I could also get you a copy of *Peyton Place* from Veblen's front reading table. I'm sure he'd be happy to loan it to you during your stay."

Franz said, "Dad got a doctor. Everything was handled quietly and professionally. Vegas eventually wrecked him, but it was a place where one could do business."

"She was fortunate to avoid hitching it with Jeffrey," John said. "She could have headed a long line of very disappointed women."

"Yeah, Jeffrey deployed to Vietnam and left her alone. Good timing. Eventually she got Campbell instead. Didn't exactly trade up." Franz sat down on the lower bunk. Misery walked across his face.

John stood and stretched. "Want a cup of coffee? I'll order us some." He went to the intercom phone. When Jerry Siebert delivered the paper cups to the two men and left, John resumed. "I wanted to ask you about this morning. Thoughts?"

"You did it skillfully, John. Your take on the prodigal son was a perfect trap. I didn't see it coming until it was right in front of me. You painted a family portrait of the Schlegels. Then you twisted that parable of Jesus into a tight little glove that fit my hand. You are one sick bastard. I only wish you had warned me the inside of the glove was running with fire ants. But from a rhetorical standpoint, I thought your riff on salt and lithium kind of went off the rails."

"Well, Franz, that's a line you can pull out when you explain to the jury why you poisoned your dad with lithium carbonate. Excuse me, overdosed him."

"My lawyer is coming in later this afternoon. Flight from St. Louis. I'll make sure to go over it with him."

"When your father asked the family to get out of his hospital room so he could speak with me, I knew it was somebody in the family. It wasn't that hard. He didn't trust you," John said.

"He didn't trust anyone. That's one of the things he taught me," Franz said. "Who do you think I learned it from?" The jocularity of the conversation was starting to leak out of the room now, and John felt his time was about up.

"You thought of yourself as his protector," John said. "You saw yourself as protecting him from his worst self. And you assumed the mantle of protecting the family. That's what the good son will think."

"Yes. But more than that I really had no choice. He was pissing away *everything*. Hell, he was in the middle of losing everything and I was witness! The family couldn't afford that. You got me exactly right in the sermon, John. I am the good son, goddammit! I didn't even own the dealership. That was all his. I was hired help! I never asked for my share! Carrying the water! Safeguarding the family fortune! Patrolling the perimeter! Taking care of Mom, my brother and my sisters. Who else was going to do the right thing?"

"So you killed your father for the greater good of the community. Nudged him over the edge with the pharmacon. I understand. I understand completely."

"The lawyers will figure it out," Franz said.

"Yes, they will. At best, criminal negligence, at worst, murder," John said. "You have a challenging road ahead." His eyes started to swim. He stood up from his chair. He approached the cage. He put his hands through the bars and Franz stepped forward. John gripped Franz's shoulders.

"Look at me, Franz. You're my brother. I'm praying the lawyers get this right. But you need to look deep inside yourself."

"Will I see you again in the next few days?"

"I'm afraid not," John said. "I'm going back to Chicago. I'm finished in Marion Hills. Do you think anybody in your family will ever want to talk with me again?"

"Try Mom," Franz said. "She's full of surprises. And please visit me. You're the only person I can really talk to."

"Maybe next year. Hear me out. I'll come to see you, wherever you are."

John went to the office intercom phone beside the door and picked it up. He listened briefly to Veblen's voice on the other end, then he said, "Yeah, we're done, and I'm out." He tried to keep his voice from cracking.

Coda

Chapter 52

Early in September, John packed two suitcases and four boxes in the Marion Hills parsonage and stowed them in the back of the Land Rover. He did a final walk-through of the house, starting with the basement, where he took another look at the leather bowling ball case he had purchased to replace Tschetter's original. The last detail. He'd wrapped it up. The bowling ball was snug in the guest room closet.

John returned to Chicago solo. The trip was what he needed, though for roughly seven hundred miles, he could intermittently hear in his head Alan Wiebe's motel stories make the monotony disappear. And the many voices at the farewell supper in the church social hall. The many unfinished conversations had both elated and exhausted him. The embraces and searching looks from old friends beginning to wonder who this man actually was. Relationships renewed, and others sundered before they could fully form.

When he arrived home in Chicago, he waited a full week before notifying the church council at Lakeview Mennonite Church that he was resigning his position as minister, effective on the first day of the coming New Year.

Then he waited another week before taking Nancy out for dinner. They sat in their usual booth on Bryn Mawr. David the bartender walked over to deliver personally Nancy's negroni. He set it down on top of a napkin. When he left, John took a gift-wrapped box out of his breast pocket and deposited it beside Nancy's plate. There was no live music this evening, but John appreciated the quiet.

"That's for you," he said. "I blame it all on Kansas. Denver, too. I got some ideas."

She looked at the package.

"Please open it."

Her hand shook a little when she took the paper off. She lifted the lid of the box.

"You crazy man."

"Put it on. I hope it fits."

"John—here, you do it."

He waited for her to say something more. Then he said, "It's not as big as the Ritz, and it's no moonstone, but I mean it with all my heart."

She put her finger on his lips to silence him. Her eyes were swimming.

He slipped the ring onto her finger. She looked at it. There was nothing bashful about this stone. "Oh, John," she said. "Thank you, yes. Yes." Then she put her arms around his neck and pinned him back in the booth with her arms and lips. She whispered something in his ear. "I'm going to wrap myself around you like an anaconda," she growled. She got out a Kleenex to blow her nose. "I'm a mess."

The performance brought David back to their table. He inquired if everything was okay. Nancy's eyes were bright. She held out her hand for David to see.

David said, "May I?" and took her hand and nudged the flashing gemstone. "Pardon me for being forward, but I wanted to make sure it was real," he said. "And that," he said, pointing to her hand, "in my old neighborhood they would call that a very nice *rock*." David gave John a searching look, his eyes opened wide. Then he returned to the bar to wait on a couple of customers.

As if reading David's mind, Nancy said, "Yes, I agree—how could you possibly afford this. It's ridiculous. I'm—"

"I sold my last parcel of land in Meade," John said. "Remember when I told everyone in Marion Hills I had family business to take care of that weekend in Kansas City? Mind you, I wasn't blowing smoke."

"Have I ever accused you of such a thing?" Nancy laughed.

⁓⸙

Their planning in the next weeks and months before the spring date intermingled with somber news drifting back from the heartland, news that would continue to filter the present into the future.

Franz was found guilty of manslaughter in the death of Levi Schlegel and sentenced to eight years in prison—with the possibility of parole after six. Franz's attorney called the verdict overreach and a miscarriage of justice. Pundits reflected on the meaning of such a light sentence in view of the intent and criminal negligence that had killed the old man.

Schroeder telephoned John and said he thought Franz got off easy because so many people, including jurors, felt little sorrow for Levi. Some believed Franz had committed an act of mercy, especially after they learned about the old man's gambling habit. As for Schroeder's professional direction, he scaled back his cattle operation and went to work for Veblen as a deputy sheriff. Veblen told the bonsai cowboy he needed somebody smart and inventive, even if he was periodically touched in the head. He exhorted Schroeder to try and rein in the wild streak—just a little.

Doctor Thiessen underwent investigation by civil and medical review boards and was eventually stripped of his medical license by the state of Kansas. He moved to Dade County, Florida, where he grew a beard and prospered, refashioning himself as a New Age health consultant specializing in pain relief, dietary supplements, and an experimental cure for erectile dysfunction that utilized substances familiar to the veterinary profession.

Carol Campbell divorced her husband, who was sentenced to fifteen years in federal prison in Colorado for drug trafficking. She decided to keep the house in Kansas City when she joined the board of directors of the Nelson Art Gallery. She also took over representation of her mother's studio practice and placed Eva's work in galleries from Santa Fe and Taos to Charleston, South Carolina. Meanwhile, Campbell would work on his act as a model prisoner, establishing a Bible-study ministry that he parlayed into a new national organization. He was granted parole for exemplary behavior after only five years behind bars, pummeled his way through an ugly bankruptcy, and then went into a new real estate venture with his former associate Fenimore Ramekin. They built their Denver business on the motto "We Keep Our Promises."

Roberto Salazar, Campbell's partner, was extradited to Mexico, as Franz had predicted. He was not heard from again. Rumor had it he was garroted in his cell with a piece of copper wire by an assassin on the payroll of El Chapo. In Chase County, Sheriff Mingus was fond of saying he had played no small role in "bringing that dirty goddam Mexican to justice."

Julia Schlegel, "Barbie," and her husband, Ken, sold the show farm and moved away from Kansas, relocating their entire operation to Door County, Wisconsin. There they concentrated their efforts on goat dairy products and meat. They packed in the crowds at their deli outlet in Ephraim and a Birria Bodega on a very tony retail strip in Wicker Park, Chicago. They sold off the Charolais cattle and the Tennessee walking horses because, in Julia's words (as captured in a PBS special segment), "we discovered that you have to get focused on your true mission if you want to succeed." Their prize Nubian goat Brat proved the matriarch of descendants producing some of the finest milk and cream in the world, the foundation for a gelato empire with outlets in Rio de Janeiro, Florence, Milan, and Barcelona.

Linda Ebel, the Marion Hills church secretary, applied to the master's program at Vanderbilt University Divinity School. She finished her degree, earning high grades and plaudits for her exceptional speaking abilities, and eventually took a senior pastoral position at the Shafter Mennonite Church of California. Her urban cowboy partner went along for the ride and became an agricultural consultant in the Central Valley. She sent a card to John at the beginning of her academic program, thanking him for all he had done, though John couldn't quite figure out how exactly he had encouraged her new direction.

In Denver, Celeste and Delores found their path. Delores left her management job at Casa Bonita and Celeste quit Brody's Lounge. Together, they opened a high-end taqueria that boasted the best mezcal and tequila setup in greater Denver. It wasn't big enough for divers to leap off the cliff walls into deep pools below, but it would do. How they financed it was known only to a select inner circle, but finding the right buyer for Delores's magic wedding ring had proven strategic. "Jeffrey gave me the gift that keeps on giving, didn't he?" Delores liked to say to Celeste on warm summer nights on their terrace, where they pledged to each other their eternal troth.

Franklin Schlegel, after finishing a commission for a new folk arts museum in New Orleans, decided to stay there. He hired an assistant and project manager from Trinidad and Tobago who created plans and schedules and made Franklin stick to them. After two years he found himself negotiating another divorce in order to marry her and, just as important, discovered that under her tutelage he was actually running a new project within budget and without paralyzing bouts of attention deficit disorder. At times he felt nostalgic for his old prodigal style and then he would kick himself. He and his project manager talked in fragmentary ways about tying the knot and she produced a cost-benefit analysis spreadsheet that eventually persuaded him. Her presentation skills were impeccable.

He didn't return to the Flint Hills except on rare occasions, and he offered to rent his visionary house in the rock quarry to John and Nancy every September. They happily accepted his offer. In years to come Nancy would wander out to her favorite spot on the prairie, the buffalo wallow by a stand of cottonwoods. More than a few locals commented that this hardnosed attorney had taken a mystic turn.

Billy Ray Baumgartner, who murdered his half brother and his best friend in Marion Hills with a Glock, is serving a life sentence in Leavenworth Federal Penitentiary. His mother, who moved away from the town after the murder, is rumored to live in a small Missouri community, where she works as a nurse's aide in a retirement center with a full continuum of care. She put her Marion Hills residence up for sale when she moved. The property is still listed as available, at deep discount, with a local realty office. John Reimer's efforts to communicate with her were unsuccessful.

Tom Dockhauser, the insurance claims investigator from Cincinnati, sent John and Nancy a postcard several months after their wedding. He said he was thinking about retirement now, full stop, and would be honored to host them at his vacation home in Charleston if they ever decided to visit. It would be several years before they took him up on it.

Eva stayed on the Schlegel property. She enjoyed her children and grandchildren's occasional visits and didn't miss the perpetual hovering. Her solitude was her refuge. Against time, she made art.

When it became clear there would be no payout on Levi's life insurance policy, she sat with her accountant and reviewed the financial damage. Then she acted strategically. She began by leasing the car dealership to Marvin Arnheim's youngest son, the Wichita accountant. The agreement included an option to purchase at the end of five years.

She interviewed the accountant before deciding on the terms of the deal, and she liked how he came across. He looked a lot like his dead older brother Jeffrey. The ghost hovered in the air between them during the interview, and momentarily she remembered the shouting matches of years before when Carol and Jeffrey nearly blew up the county with their displays of youth and beauty. This conversation was far more pleasant, and it ended with a signed contract. The dealership was renamed Schlegel Arnheim Motors.

The town marveled that Eva negotiated with the son of her husband's old critic and rival. The new minister at Marion Hills Mennonite was overheard to muse over coffee one morning at Little Pleasures café, while gossiping about the transaction: "Without death there can be no resurrection."

Jeffrey Arnheim was laid to rest in Ebenholzer Church Cemetery in May of the year after John Reimer returned to Chicago. By then his parents, Marvin and Verla, had made their peace. John drove from Chicago to central Kansas to do the memorial service in the old wooden church on the Thirteen Mile Road. The church overflowed with family and friends. Each came with their private memories of the superstar who had outrun his promise.

The cemetery plot was located under a stand of cedar trees, with a view of fields stretching away east to the Flint Hills. Buried in the casket with the urn holding Jeffrey's ashes were the man's high school basketball jersey, his Criswell Study Bible, and a carefully folded army uniform.

And that same spring, shortly after the wedding, John fulfilled his promise to Caleb Epp. Through a strategic connection in her law firm, Nancy procured a block of six front seats at midcourt in the United Center for game six of the Bulls-Jazz championship. Caleb sat in his wheelchair, practically on top of the court. Flanking him on his left was his favorite nephew Carl, who had driven up from the University of Illinois, where he was studying physics, and on his right a striking brunette, Julie, who intrigued Caleb with her talk of doing a new translation of *Gilgamesh*. Caleb stayed mostly focused on the game, clad in his Bulls sweatsuit and cap, waving his arms throughout the spectacle of the home team's victory, but Julie commanded attention. John and Nancy, sitting with Alan Wiebe behind Caleb and his bodyguards, observed.

Caleb thought Michael Jordan was fine, but he was most enthused about Dennis Rodman's rebounding and tattoos, calling him a "modern-day Queequeg." Caleb said, "Like me, he is a man of science and vision. His basketball IQ matches Phil Jackson's. How does he know where the ball will go? He sees it spin like a slow top. Compared to him, no one else sees it."

After the final buzzer sounded, in a crushing triumph for the Bulls, Caleb wheeled his chair onto the court and procured Rodman's autograph. His friends waited for him. When he came back to the sideline, it appeared that he had spent quality time on the Mount of Transfiguration. He pulled John over and made him lean down to listen. Caleb whispered hoarsely in his ear: "Okay, now I can return to Kansas in peace."

Chapter 53

Returning Caleb Epp to Marion Hills was John's excuse to pay a visit to Eva. It wasn't clear to him whether he needed to rebuild the bridge, ask forgiveness, or pretend that none of what had happened with her family—or his role in its unraveling—actually mattered. He talked about it with Nancy and she said, "Go."

Eva called the next day, speaking as if she had overheard their conversation. She said, "I have your portrait ready and you had better pick it up. I am not getting any younger."

Nearly a year had passed since he had left his interim pastorate at Marion Hills. He drove onto the Schlegel place and parked. It was late in the day and swallows skittered across the sky. The house looked smaller than he remembered; the paint on the soffits was starting to peel. Only one car occupied the circular driveway, a mud-encrusted gray Subaru.

John's knees were creaky from the drive. He found the path to Eva's studio. It stood lit up in late afternoon sunshine, its sliding door slightly ajar. This was now her habitation. He knocked and waited.

Eva came to the door and slid it open further so John could enter the shadows inside. Then she opened her arms and embraced him. "John," she said.

He looked at her and said, "I am deeply sorry about Franz. I am sorry it turned out this way." He turned aside to gather his composure. He removed his glasses and wiped his eyes.

"Don't be sorry, John." She waited a couple of beats and said, "You acted from your deepest instincts. Franz is the one who is sorry now. But don't worry about him. He will be okay. I talk with him every week."

"Don't try to tell me incarceration agrees with him."

"I will do nothing of the kind. You have to understand. Like you, Franz felt compelled to carry out what he believed was right and necessary. I understood what he did."

John looked at Eva for further clues. Her voice carried a hard edge. "If I had known about Levi's inclinations earlier in my life, I probably would have done it myself. I was saved from committing a terrible crime."

She said the words flatly and without apology. John looked at the old woman and dragged the handkerchief across his face again. Her eyes were without remorse, pitiless. She had on a painting smock and her white hair hung straight down around her neck. Her hands and arms appeared ready for mortal combat, there was paint under her nicked, worn fingernails. John flashed back to an early childhood image of his mother coming in from the milking barn, and how utterly powerful her forearms and hands had appeared to him when he was five.

"Come with me," she said. In the vast vault of the white studio, in the center of the space, she led him to an easel. She removed a cloth that covered a painting.

"I promised to finish your portrait. It took me longer than I expected. After your departure, I decided it needed more work." She walked away to let John consider his likeness.

The peregrine falcon stood on the gray granite ledge of an urban high-rise. Relaxed, its head tilted slightly to one side, the bird offered a clinical gaze, flecked plumage puffed out on its chest and its wings folded back, at ease. It was an aging bird, and the feathers on the crown of its head were slightly, almost comically, askew. She had gotten his likeness but it was no cartoon. It looked down at what it had just accomplished. Or was it looking out at the viewer? In one of its talons the bird held a bloodied slate-gray pigeon whose head was thrown back as if its neck had broken. A stray feather from the pigeon's breast had separated from its body and lay on the ledge where the rest of its feathers would soon be scattered.

"I decided on the falcon after conversation with your new wife," Eva said.

"How very interesting. What did she tell you?"

"That is our secret," Eva said. "I tried to capture what I know about you. Sometimes you need your inner darkness. We all do, to function like the predators we are. I know a lot of people around here took you for the good shepherd. Of course, you know the joke about the shepherd and the wolf: who should the sheep be more afraid of? So much complexity.

Layers and layers that go down and down and down. You are not sure if you're the apostle of love or the Son of Thunder. You hold contraries."

"You've been talking with Franklin," John said, and smiled.

"Yes. Let me also point out it was the church that made John the apostle of love. Jesus called him one of the Sons of Thunder. This doesn't even begin to encompass what he would become at the end of his days."

"You mean the author of Revelation."

"John, you are a man who likes to have the last word. That is not always a positive. Please do not move to an island called Patmos. John is complicated."

"I see Horus here, too," John said, pointing again at the painting.

"Yes. Before the Bible, we had the Egyptians. Their holy family included a miracle baby and a resurrection. The first religion of Moses. He gave it up, but must have remembered it even in renouncing it. You must seek understanding of yourself if you want honesty. And I would also tell you this: You are as dear to me as one of my own children."

"It's because of Vi, isn't it? You give so much sympathy because of her. It's undeserved, I tell you. It's starting to feel like a cheap trick."

"No, no. You endured the terrors of her illness. You cared for her. She told me. I know what you are made of, John."

She put her hand up and lowered it slowly until her palm descended with a slight pressure on the crown of his head. His body gave an involuntary shudder as if a wave had gone through him. He tried to speak but was wordless. She said something then that John tried to remember and later attempted to explain.

⁓＊

He had one more stop to make. He swung his car into the parking lot beside the sheriff's office.

"You wanted to see me," he said. He stood by the door with his hands in his pockets and waited. Veblen and the new deputy, Schroeder, sat at the round table behind the counter. Veblen puffed on his bulldog pipe and Schroeder started to stub out a burning cigarette.

Veblen motioned John over with a wave of his hand. "Yep. How did you know?"

"Caleb Epp told me I owed you one."

"Epp is worth a listen. Sit down, John. You driving to Chicago tonight?"

"Yeah."

"Long trip. Seven hundred miles, I reckon."

"I'll find a motel in Kansas City. I know a place. Drive the rest tomorrow."

"There's something I want to show you," Veblen said. "Schroeder said it was only fair. It might give you peace of mind. Cup of coffee?"

John said, "Don't mind if I do." Schroeder was already pouring a mug full. He brought it over with a little carton of cream. John pulled a chair up to the table and sat down.

Veblen had a manila envelope in his hand. He removed a photograph and lay it face down on the table. It was an eight-by-ten on glossy stock.

John waited. Veblen flipped it over. There was the face of a very young man with a fresh crop of acne across his forehead and nose. He looked like a passenger on a Halloween hayride. He wore a tentative grin and a very bad haircut. His eyes were tightly shut. John looked again then said, "The Mullet."

"Yes," Veblen said. "The Mullet. I believe he called himself Midas in that note you brought me."

"Why are you showing me this?" John asked.

"His body was found near a loading dock outside of Junction City, behind a container truck facility. One bullet at the base of his skull and a second shot to the spinal cord. I have more pictures here in the envelope."

"Save them. I'd prefer not to—"

"Well," Veblen said, "it seems your buddy Schroeder's theory is correct."

"Refresh my memory," John said. "Meaning what, exactly?"

Schroeder lit a cigarette very deliberately and clicked his lighter shut. "They carved a couple of X's on his chest."

"Marked him with a double cross," Veblen said. "Signs and wonders."

"Literalists, these guys," Schroeder said.

"He was just a kid," John said. Then he saw the black depths inside his coffee mug. He poured in more cream. "Look. He took the fall because of what you and I did."

"What we did was a good thing," Schroeder said. "Don't go all weepy and soft on me now. I won't let you cradle that dirty drug runner in your everlasting arms."

"Schroeder has a point," Veblen said. He stood up and parted the metal blinds to gaze outside. "Of course it's a shame. A terrible waste. It's what a certain kind of life and activity generally lead to. The boy not only joined a gang of drug-runners, he also decided he could steal from the big boys. And that's what got him killed. The KBI says the Mullet died because Salazar's people eventually did an audit and figured out one of their own was taking product for himself. Look, I understand your feelings. But the feelings are beside the point. The Mullet made his choices a long time ago. I would also observe that he was likely the one who planted that monster dog's head on the front seat of your fancy car."

"You could exhume that head and check it for DNA traces to confirm your theory," John said. "Just don't mention it to Epp. He might get ideas."

Veblen began to laugh.

"Nobody's exhuming anything," the bonsai cowboy interrupted, with a casual wave of his hand. "That evidence no longer exists. All we have to worry about is what the Mullet said before they put the bullet in his brain. They got two other associates of his, by the way, over in Missouri. Sort of a thieving ring within the bigger ring. Plots within plots."

"One hopes he didn't mention you to anybody," Veblen said. "Though if he didn't, that would fall into the category of a miracle. Doesn't your religion have a category like that, John?"

"Listen," John said. "I believe in the grace of God, but fairytale miracles aren't part of it."

"Well, then," Veblen continued, "Had he been as wise or as ruthless as the people he ripped off, he would have done you when he brought his gift to your garage. Maybe you're just damn lucky. I think the Mullet lacked an adequate amount of bloodlust to stay in the big leagues."

John stood up. "I don't get it. How did he know it was me?"

"Did you talk to anybody when you brought Schroeder to the emergency room that night? I'll bet you did. The Mullet put two and two together."

John suddenly felt a need to get on the road. He didn't answer Veblen. He glanced at Schroeder and said, "You think we're out of the woods?"

"I certainly hope so," Schroeder said. Then he gave John a quick embrace and looked him in the eye. "You don't believe it now, my friend, but you will. You did a good thing. And everybody in this town knows it."

Veblen looked on dispassionately and said goodnight.

"John, stay safe now, you hear? Maybe I'll run into you in another life."

Chapter 54

John took the elevator to the loft. Nancy opened the door before he could put key to lock. He dropped his briefcase and leaned the parcel wrapped in brown paper against the doorframe.

"My love," Nancy said. "You're home." She held him. She scrutinized his face for a sign.

He looked around the kitchen and tried to comprehend what had happened to his life. Nancy ran her fingers down his cheekbones.

"You're different," she said. "What happened in Kansas?"

"Maybe everything?" he joked. "Maybe I'm road weary."

"I want to hear it all. But listen, John, I have news that won't wait."

"What?"

"I got a call earlier today."

"Who? What?"

"W. W. III is dead. Waldo Wedel. Heart attack. Infarction. Four members of the Faith and Life board have already called. Grunau and Hofer were the first."

"God bless Waldo. What did Grunau say?"

"He says it's unanimous. They want to discuss the district minister position with you. They insist that you come out of retirement. Grunau's words were, 'Without delay.' I told them not to call tonight because you were driving back from Kansas."

"I don't fully understand what you're saying. Did they share any more details?"

"Grunau was talking too fast. I told him I didn't want to get enmeshed in your decision and couldn't start acting like your secretary. And Hofer mentioned something about Montana that I didn't understand."

John tore the brown paper off Eva's painting. He leaned the canvas against the fridge, nearly covering it. "I suppose I need to plan a layout for my study. Sooner rather than later. And where am I going to put this?"

Nancy looked at the painting up close, then stepped back. "Boy, she got you good." Nancy appraised John after pondering the image, and said, "Did Eva tell you we discussed this?"

"Yes, she did. And you said?"

Nancy ignored the question. "Did she tell you she thought about painting you as a shaggy dog?"

"Yes, and that seemed to amuse her," John said. "But seriously, I need a private gallery to hang this thing. My killer bird is not exactly fit for public consumption."

"Actually, I have just the place," Nancy said. "So much news for you tonight, I almost forgot to tell you this. I put down earnest money on a house in Gils Rock. Don't worry, it's not a mouse hotel. I need to show it to you. It overlooks the water. I have your office all planned out." She looked at John's expression and said, "Don't look at me that way. And, no, I'm not kidding."

He started to laugh and walked toward her. He felt her substance, the bend of her ribs. His hands slid down around her waist. When she looked at him, she traced with her thumb the slight bump above his brow.

"We have a lot to talk about. I'm so excited I don't know how I'm going to sleep tonight. You'd better promise to be nice to me." She muffled her words against the side of his head. She put her lips on his, then pulled away. "Oh, and I remember one other thing Grunau said about Montana. Some place called Wolf Point. What do you know about that?"

John frowned.

"What?" Nancy said. "Tell me."

After a while John said, "Don't get too excited."

She stared him down.

"All right," he conceded. "We'll figure out a few adventures, if you want. We'll see. There's a lot to say about the Big Sky. You heard right? Wolf Point? I have a strange connection there I tend not to talk about. I guess now I'm going to have to."

"You're damn right. Will you call Grunau tomorrow?"

He nodded. "I'll contact Hofer first. I get the feeling I don't have much choice."

"That's the thing about these guys you hang out with," she said as she clasped her hands around the back of his neck. "They can be pretty persuasive."

"In fact, I was thinking about Eva."

"What would Eva say?"

"Probably something like, 'It's a brand-new day. Embrace it.'"

Night was starting to fall, and they walked toward the big window. The wedge of Lake Michigan visible from that part of the loft was turning deep blue, a blue so deep that it was almost terrifying in its beauty, and all laid out beneath a sky changing from cobalt to pitch. John considered Nancy's face as she turned toward him. She was luminous. She looked at him now as if she hoped he could order up a thunderstorm. He stood beside her as she pointed to the lights beginning to blink across the landscape of their vast city, and he watched her eyes glance upward as they searched for the brightest star.

Acknowledgments

My greatest debt is to Dale Suderman (1944–2020), coauthor of *Unpardonable Sins* (2021), a hard-boiled crime novel set in Chicago that we published under our shared pen name David Saul Bergman. *Prodigal Sons* is my sequel to *Unpardonable Sins*. Some of the ideas for it grew from conversations with Dale during the late 1990s in Chicago.

I must also thank George Classen (1917–1993), Vern Classen, Ben Ollenburger, and Wally Kroeker for pivotal conversations over the years that informed this narrative. Each of you knows how to tell stories. And I have tried to listen. Further insight, special turns of phrase, and overall good judgment were generously provided by Traci Dziatkowicz and Elizabeth Classen Born. You possess the strongest kind of inner light, not to mention uncanny ability to distill and summarize human experience in fresh ways.

For their reading of earlier versions of this manuscript and very useful suggestions, I am indebted to Al Gini, Edward Kibblewhite, Wally Kroeker, Peter Kuntz, Kenneth Ontjes, and Carol Zsolnay. For further editorial direction and valuable feedback, criticism, and encouragement, I thank Sean McCann and Patti White. Finally, to my editor, Katherine Faydash, I owe a great debt for her consummate skill and judgment.

William Least Heat-Moon's work of nonfiction, *PrairyErth: (a deep map)* (Houghton Mifflin, 1991), was indispensable for writing about Chase and Marion Counties.

Chapter 8 includes descriptions of Casa Bonita Restaurant in Lakewood, Colorado. Many thanks to Vern Classen for introducing me to that landmark of Americana in the early 1980s.

The show farm run by Julia Schlegel and Ken Dahlke (chapter 17) was partly inspired by my reading of Stephen Heyman's *The Planter of Modern Life: Louis Bromfield and the Seeds of a Food Revolution* (W. W.

Norton, 2020), as well as many visits with Traci Dziatkowicz to the Door County Creamery restaurant in Sister Bay, Wisconsin, and the restaurant's dairy goat farm nearby.

The description of Klaas Reimer, founder of the Kleine Gemeinde community in Russia, which John Reimer quotes directly in his sermon (chapter 18), comes from P. M. Friesen, *The Mennonite Brotherhood in Russia, 1789–1910*, trans. J. B. Toews, Abraham Friesen, Peter J. Klassen, and Harry Loewen (Board of Christian Literature, General Conference of Mennonite Brethren Churches, 1978), p. 93.

The poetry John Reimer quotes in chapter 22 is from John Donne's "To His Mistress Going to Bed." Donne, the greatest metaphysical poet in the English language, was also the most eloquent preacher in the history of the Anglican Church. He was dean of St. Paul's Cathedral in London from 1621 until his death in 1631.

Chapters 26 and 45 reference key conflicts in the 1990s that marked the rise of recent extremist right-wing political movements in the United States, including the Randy Weaver debacle at Ruby Ridge, Idaho, the storming by federal authorities of David Koresh's compound in Waco, Texas, and the truck bombing of the Alfred P. Murrah Federal Building in Oklahoma City by Timothy McVeigh and Terry Nichols in 1996. That attack killed 168 and injured 680 people. For the narrative account and analysis of these events, I relied principally on Jeffrey Toobin's *Homegrown: Timothy McVeigh and the Rise of Right-Wing Extremism* (Simon & Schuster, 2023).

Regarding resuscitation procedures and hospital protocols for patients suffering heart failure, as described in chapter 31, thanks to Michael J. Born, who has many years of experience as an emergency room doctor, chief medical officer, and hospital administrator.

In chapter 35, regarding the use of Plautdietsch (Low German) and discussion of variants in phrasing, I am indebted to the linguistic expertise of two close friends: editor, author, and journalist Wally Kroeker, and New Testament professor Harold Dyck.

In chapter 36, the quotation about work that Tom Dockhauser repeats comes from the narrator Marlow in the first chapter of Joseph Conrad's novel *Heart of Darkness*.

Chapter 45 contains discussion of bipolar disorder and pharmaceutical treatment, as well as issues surrounding forensic toxicology and exhumation. I am much indebted to Kathleen Shannon, professor and chair of neurology at the University of Wisconsin School of Medicine and Public Health in Madison, Wisconsin. She was helpful in explaining several medical issues and providing additional resources, among them R. E. Ferner, "Post-Mortem Clinical Pharmacology," *British Journal of Pharmacology* 66, no. 4 (2008), 430–443; Michael Kennedy, "Interpreting Postmortem Drug Analysis and Redistribution in Determining Cause of Death: A Review," *Pathology and Laboratory Medicine International*, August 3, 2015; T. Richardson, "Pitfalls in Forensic Toxicology," *Annals of Clinical Biochemistry* 37 (2000): 20–44; and Stephen C. Schoonover, MD, "Bipolar Affective Disorder and Recurrent Unipolar Depression," https:// link.springer.com/chapter/10.1007/978-1-4615-8049-2_3.

In chapter 46, Tom Dockhauser quotes the literary critic J. Hillis Miller on the importance of reading. See Miller's *The Ethics of Reading* (Columbia University Press, 1987), p. 58. Chapter 46 also alludes to a crime in Ohio where a college student's library use helped convict him of first-degree murder in a West Virginia court of law. That murder happened while I was an associate professor at Marietta College, and I am grateful for further recollection and illumination of the actual police investigation from former colleagues and friends in Marietta, Ohio, including Ed Osborne, Robert Walker, Bill Hohman, and Carole Hancock.

As part of his effort to solve the crime, in chapter 46 John Reimer reads for an afternoon in Watson Library of the University of Kansas in Lawrence, the place where I conducted most of my research toward a master's in English degree more than forty years ago. For the titles Reimer reads in the history of toxicology, my thanks to the University Library at Northwestern University in Evanston, Illinois.

In chapter 51, I make reference to the Lancers Club in Wichita, Kansas. Thanks to Bradley Born, professor of English at Bethel College in North Newton, Kansas, who suggested it might form part of the backstory for Levi Schlegel. See Denise Neil, "Space that Held '70s Lancers Club Ready for New Vision," *Wichita Eagle*, April 11, 2021, 1C.

All Scripture quotations used by John Reimer when he speaks from the pulpit are from New Revised Standard Version Bible, copyright © 1989 National Council of the Churches of Christ in the United States of America. Used by permission. All rights reserved worldwide.

www.ingramcontent.com/pod-product-compliance
Lightning Source LLC
Chambersburg PA
CBHW070803030726
47504CB00003B/678